ROAR

Volume 6
Scoundrels

Edited by Mary E. Lowd

Bad Dog Books

2015

ROAR Volume 6
First publication 2015
Second Edition 2018

Edited by Mary E. Lowd

Cover by Teagan Gavet
Copyright © 2015

Published by Bad Dog Books
www . baddogbooks . com

BAD DOG BOOKS

TABLE OF CONTENTS

For Buck C. Turner

Thank you for editing the last four issues.

FOREWORD

Welcome to the sixth volume of ROAR! The theme for this volume is scoundrel, and I've selected 28 tales that explore the theme from all different angles. There are light-hearted tales of lovable rogues. There are dark, dark stories of betrayal and worlds filled with shades of gray, where any choice at all might label you a scoundrel. There are good characters who make questionable choices, and there are villains to overcome.

When I was asked to take over editing ROAR, I knew I wanted to cast my net wide for submissions. There are many strong stories being told by writers in the furry fandom, but there is also fantastic furry fiction being written outside of the fandom. I wanted to pull all that fiction together and show the full range of what furry fiction can be. In this volume, you'll find stories written specifically for ROAR 6 by members of the Furry Writers' Guild, but you'll also find stories from sci-fi/fantasy authors who had never heard of furry fiction before I approached them.

There are so many kinds of furry fiction in this volume! Between these covers, you can read fantasy, science-fiction, cyberpunk, space opera, noir, slice of life, secret life of animals, fables, and literary fiction. And they're all furry! I was delighted by the range of styles that I saw among the submissions. It was a pleasure to read the submissions for ROAR 6, and I'm profoundly grateful to everyone who submitted, whether their stories were finally selected for inclusion or not. In the end, an anthology can only be as good as the submissions it receives, and I think this anthology speaks for itself.

Finally, thank you to FurPlanet for continuing to believe in the importance of a regular anthology of general audience furry fiction, and thank you to Teiran for giving me this opportunity to edit it.

I hope that you enjoy ROAR 6 as much as I have.

-Mary E. Lowd

There's nothing like a scoundrel to bring some excitement to a quiet life. When a good dragon faces off with a reclusive wizard, the wizard may be surprised to find that the dragon isn't the scoundrel.

SQUONK THE DRAGON

Pete Butler

S quonk the Dragon lived in the tallest tree in the world. He lived in the highest branches, in a nest made from "twigs" that, in truth, looked an awful lot like smaller trees.

The tree stretched thousands of feet into the air, so high that some of Squonk's bird friends liked to fly to the very topmost branches and make themselves dizzy by looking down. The tree was so big around that Squonk could tire himself out by flying down to the bottom and running all the way around its trunk—though it should be noted that dragons don't run much and tire rather easily that way. The tree was so strong that... Well, that a dragon could live rather comfortably in its branches.

Squonk lived with his mother, who was definitely not a dragon—she was a small blue bird named Mrs. Tweedle-Chirp. Now, it is true that birds generally cannot lay dragon eggs, and Mrs. Tweedle-Chirp was no exception. But, they can care for dragon eggs that they happen to find lying untended in the middle of the forest, assuming they are suitably ambitious. Of course, Mrs. Tweedle-Chirp couldn't raise Squonk all by herself; she enlisted the aid of every other bird in the forest at one time or another, and even a number of unfortunate flocks who just happened to be passing through. (Mrs. Tweedle-Chirp was not the sort of bird who tolerated the answer "No" from anybody.)

She needed the help. Feeding a dragon, even a small one, is quite an undertaking for a bird who can only provide one worm at a time. And the nest! Why, Squonk kept outgrowing nests as fast as his mother could get them built!

And grow he did, from a sickly, moss-colored little creature the size of a badger to a beautiful, emerald-green son the size of... Well, to be honest, Mrs. Tweedle-Chirp and her neighbors were at a loss for just what they ought to compare Squonk to. Dragons were quite rare in that part of the world, as were elephants, and whales, and anything else that wouldn't look tiny next to Mrs. Tweedle-Chirp's boy.

Life was very pleasant for Squonk and Mrs. Tweedle-Chirp and their neighbors, which is to say it was dull. Now, being a wise old bird, Mrs. Tweedle-Chirp was actually quite fond of "dull." But being younger and, well, much more dragon-y than his mother, Squonk was not so fond of "dull." In fact, he frequently wished that something, anything interesting would happen.

Squonk's wish came true when he met a wizard named Wendel.

Wendel was a successful wizard who had decided that it was time to stop fooling around with other peoples' castles and build himself a proper home. According to traditional wizard thinking, this meant building an enormous stone tower where you could perform magical experiments, or look across the land, or impress traveling sorceresses, or whatever else came to mind.

But Wendel knew that building an enormous stone tower would be like putting up a colossal sign reading "GREAT WIZARD LIVES HERE!" and that was the last thing he wanted, since that inevitably meant apprentices.

Oh, sure, you could try turning them away, but that never worked for long. The persistent little devils would just keep coming and coming and coming, and they'd start spreading rumors about how you wanted to keep all the magic to yourself and that you thought you were too good to teach anybody else, and that led to rumors you were an Evil Wizard bent on Taking Over The World. So unless you wanted to wind up with a horde of crusading knights and bad-tempered villagers making nuisances of themselves, you had to take the occasional apprentice or twelve from the nearby villages.

No matter how infuriating and useless they were.

Wendel had heard that some wizards liked teaching, but he had decided that either the rumors were lies or those wizards were hopelessly insane. (Which, contrary to popular belief, is not the least bit helpful when dealing with magic.) Apprentices were such incompetent morons! Spilling potions, getting into fights with each other, casting dangerous spells indoors, ruining experiments...

14

He remembered several years ago when one of his students was showing off his "mastery" of making things disappear and reappear with a very expensive item. While the "disappear" part had gone perfectly, nobody ever did figure out just where that dragon egg had reappeared.

So, as far as Wendel was concerned, apprentices were to be avoided at all costs.

But what to do about his home, then? He still wanted something very impressive and wizardly; what's the point of becoming a powerful wizard if you have to hide out in some disguised hovel, or build your stronghold out in the middle of a wasteland? No, he decided, what he needed was something big and non-stone-tower-y, which gave off an aura of "WARNING: IMPRESSIVE BUT CRACKED-AND-UTTERLY-UNSUITED-FOR-TEACHING WIZARD LIVES HERE!"

And in what he thought was a particularly brilliant moment of inspiration, he decided to make his home out of a giant tree.

He didn't want to chop down a tree and turn it into a house; any woodcutter could do that. No, he wanted to find a tree that he could carve his home into while it still lived and grew. Now that, he decided, would be roomy, impressive, and strike anyone who passed by as the work of a complete lunatic.

Of course, to pull it off, Wendel would have to find an uncommonly large tree—a tree that had already grown the size of a respectable wizard's tower.

For instance, like the tree in the heart of the old forest.

Which is how a wizard came to be puttering around the base of Squonk's tree one day.

Squonk noticed that the birds of the forest were all a-twitter.

"Oh, it's that wizard fellow, I'm sure," Mrs. Tweedle-Chirp said when he asked her about it.

"A wizard?" Squonk said, bouncing with excitement and making the entire nest sway. "Really?"

"Now don't you go getting any ideas, young man!" she said, fluttering about her son's head. "Wizards are trouble! You leave this one alone!"

But it was too late; Squonk was curious. As soon as his mother left, he hopped out of the nest and took flight. He wasn't about to pass up the chance to see a real, live wizard in the flesh!

Besides, he reasoned, I'm not going to hurt him or anything. I just want to look!

Now, you would think that a dragon flying amongst the treetops would be the sort of thing any fool would notice. But the treetops were so far above the ground and Squonk blended in so well with the leaves that Wendel had no idea that an extremely curious young dragon was circling him far overhead.

Wendel was far too captivated by Squonk's tree, staring up at what appeared to be a wall of solid wood. Why, a fellow could carve out a tower-sized nook in the center and the tree would scarcely even notice! Magnificent!

Of course, a wizard staring at a tree contemplating where he's going to put an entrance, where the master bedroom should go, whether the laboratory ought to be high up or maybe underground, etc., is not a particularly interesting sight. Squonk began to wonder if perhaps his mother had been making fun of him; how could this boring fellow be a wizard? So, he decided to swoop down for a closer look.

You might think that a dragon swooping down on you as you stared up a tree would be a very easy thing to notice. You would be absolutely right.

After a brief scream, Wendel did what any competent wizard would do when something enormous and dragon-shaped suddenly swooped down at him; he shot it with a lightning bolt.

Dragons are, as a rule, not much bothered by magic. Wendel's bolt of lightning didn't really hurt Squonk; it just scorched his nose and made him re-think the whole "swooping-down" idea. Which is what Wendel had been hoping for; it gave him enough time to get ready for whatever the dragon did next.

Nobody likes to pick a fight with a dragon; nature has given them a lot of weapons to choose from. They have flaming breath, fearsome claws, gigantic teeth... and Wendel knew how to protect himself from all of them.

But Squonk had been taught from a very early age to never, ever, ever, ever, ever breathe fire for any reason under any circumstances. After all, raising a dragon is enough trouble without the worry that he'll burn the entire forest down around you. As for his claws, well, most of the birds he'd grown up with used their claws less for "ripping things apart" and more for "sitting peacefully on the branch." And not owning any teeth, Squonk's bird friends weren't really inclined to bite anything that worried them.

In fact, it's entirely possible that Squonk would have grown up completely ignorant of ways to defend himself were it not for a mysterious crow who'd wandered through the forest several years back. This crow had taught the small birds of the forest—and one not-so-small dragon—a defense he'd learned in his many travels. He called it "Woodpecker Fu."

Wendel had never seen it before. Squonk demonstrated.

Squonk remembered the training. First: fly down to your enemy and flap like crazy so you hover in place.

Second: look for some part of your enemy that would hurt a lot if you poked it.

Third: peck vigorously, until your enemy runs away.

And that's what happened, more or less.

The windstorm Squonk kicked-up by all the flapping almost blew Wendel away all by itself. And the pecking wasn't quite "vigorous," nor did the wizard exactly run away; it was more like "peck once, blast your enemy about a hundred yards through the air, then watch him run off with a pronounced limp."

Just the same, Squonk felt very pleased with himself.

Squonk met his mother on the way back up to the nest—she'd been flying down to see what all the commotion was about. "You were right," he said. "Wizards are nothing but trouble."

"Well, I should say so, young man!" Mrs. Tweedle-Chirp said, fluttering around her son's head in a towering rage. "You could have been hurt! You could have been killed!"

"I'm sorry!" Squonk said, very much ashamed.

Mrs. Tweedle-Chirp berated her son all the way back to the nest and then sent him to his room... which, to be honest, pretty much consisted of the entire nest. But it was the principle of the thing that mattered.

And that was how Wendel felt about the whole situation, too. He hadn't been badly hurt; his backside had some thorns in it, his ankle was a bit twisted, and his stomach had a large bruise roughly the size and shape of a dragon's snout. But when you get ambushed by a dragon, that's getting off pretty light. And there were plenty of other enormous trees in the forest that, while smaller, were hopefully not quite so dragon-infested.

But Wendel had his heart set on this tree in particular. And he hadn't become a wizard just so he would give up at the first sign of trouble, had he?

So. There was a dragon in his tree. The question was, how to get rid of it? Blasting it away with magic was all wrong; it'd just annoy the dragon and burn the tree down. So... He'd have to trick it out! Yes! Now that was a good, wizardly notion; outwit the beast and then claim his new home.

Of course, that raised the question; how does one trick a dragon into leaving its tree?

Gold! Of course! Everybody knows dragons are greedy for gold!

So, Wendel spent the next week gathering up as much lead as he could and turning it into an enormous pile of gold.

"Now this," Wendel said to himself, "will get rid of him! Yes, seeing all this gold should trigger that dragon greed. He'll want more, and he'll go out looking for it. And even if he comes back, you can't have a hoard worth bragging about if it can fit in a nest!"

So, Wendel left the pile of gold where Squonk would see it. And, sure enough, one day while flying among the treetops, Squonk caught a glimpse of something yellow and glittery.

He swooped down to take a closer look and found a pile of something he'd never seen before. They were rocks, but they were yellow, and glittery, and... beautiful.

He spent hours sitting and staring at the rocks. What were they? They were the most wonderful thing he'd ever seen, even if they did smell sort of like that mean little wizard-person who'd singed his nose.

Finally, Squonk gathered up a pile of the strange rocks in his mouth—goodness they were heavy!—and flew home.

"Mrm!" he exclaimed. "Lrk whet uh fnd!"

"Don't talk with your mouth full, dear," Mrs. Tweedle-Chirp said, mending her corner of the nest with some fresh twigs.

"Mom!" Squonk said, spitting the mouthful of gold into the nest. "Look what I found!"

"Goodness!" Mrs. Tweedle-Chirp said, taking a look at whatever it was that had her son so enthused. "What on earth is it?"

"I don't know!" Squonk said. "But isn't it beautiful?"

"Why... yes, I suppose it is quite pretty, isn't it."

"Yeah!" Squonk said. "Wait here—I'll get the rest!"

"There's... more?"

"Yeah! A great, gorgeous pile of it!"

Mrs. Tweedle-Chirp cocked her head to the side. "Why on earth would we need more of it?"

Squonk stared at her. "Because... because it's so beautiful..."

"Yes, you've mentioned that. But what about the pile you have? I for one think it's already quite lovely. Would more really be that much prettier?"

"Well," Squonk said, shuffling on his four feet, "I suppose not..."

"And I really don't see how it has any other use. I mean, can you build a nest out of it?"

"No," Squonk said, frowning. Squonk knew a thing or two about nest-building; under his mother's supervision, he'd been building and re-building the family home for years. "Much too heavy for that."

"Don't suppose you can eat it, can you."

"No," Squonk said. "Definitely doesn't taste like food."

"Well, then," Mrs. Tweedle-Chirp said, turning back to her nest-tidying, "that settles it. If it's got no use except for you to look at, then we already have plenty."

"But Mom," Squonk said, "there's this great big pile of it still sitting in the forest! Just sitting there!"

"I've got an idea," Mrs. Tweedle-Chirp said. "Why don't you tell all our neighbors about it?"

Squonk perked his ears. He hadn't even considered that.

"Yes," Mrs. Tweedle-Chirp went on, "yes, I expect they'd like to have a little to look at, too."

"Yeah," Squonk said, warming to the idea. "Yeah! I'll go tell everybody!" Think of how pleased everybody would be when he told them about the pretty yellow rocks!

So off Squonk flew, telling every bird he could find—and he knew them all by name—about the pretty yellow rocks. Not everybody shared his enthusiasm; most of the sparrows weren't interested, and the orioles seemed downright bored. But many of the birds thanked him and, upon seeing the pile, agreed that a rock or two would look lovely in their own nests.

Mr. and Mrs. Caw-Caw, crows who were old friends with Mrs. Tweedle-Chirp, were particularly delighted.

"It's so shiny!" Mr. Caw-Caw said.

"And pretty!" Mrs. Caw-Caw said.

"And shiny and pretty!" Mr. Caw-Caw said.

"And pretty and shiny!" Mrs. Caw-Caw said.

"Yes!" Squonk said. "And glittery! Don't forget glittery!"

"Ooh!" Mr. and Mrs. Caw-Caw said, admiring Squonk's exquisite taste.

Birds flew to and from the pile of gold all day, some only visiting once, others visiting several times. Not all the birds were strong enough to carry even a single little rock back to their own nests, but Squonk was glad to help them out.

Disguised as a nearby shrub, Wendel watched in shock as the birds carried off the entire pile one piece at a time, aided by a dragon that should, by all rights, have been burning them to little feathered crisps for so much as looking at his gold.

Clearly, more planning was in order.

So, Wendel thought, and thought some more.

"It's unnatural!" he complained to nobody in particular. "A dragon shouldn't be living in a tree! Why, it's bad for the dragon!" he said, ignoring the fact that Squonk was obviously quite happy. "And the tree!" he went on, overlooking the point that Squonk's tree could probably hold quite a few more dragons.

"Maybe that's it," he muttered. "Maybe this fool monster just needs to be shown what a real dragon's home looks like, and he'll leave my tree for good!"

So, Wendel set to work finding himself a good, dragon-sized cave. Luckily for him, there were a few to be had in some mountains to the north of Squonk's tree. Next, he made another nice-sized pile of gold in it, since that's all a dragon really needs to get a good lair going—a nice cave, and some gold to hide within it.

Finally, he had to lure the dragon to it.

Wendel stood outside of the cave and disguised himself as a maiden—after all, everybody knows no dragon can resist a good maiden sacrifice—and started calling for help.

Wendel had to yell very loudly, since Squonk's tree was a long ways away, but after spending the better part of a day booming out enough "Oh, dear!"'s and "Goodness gracious!"'s and "Please, help me before the dragon eats me!"'s, Wendel finally enticed Squonk into coming over to see what all the fuss was about.

"Hello!" Squonk said. "Who are you?"

"Eek!" Wendel gave a scream that any dragon who'd met a real maiden would have found very suspicious. "The dragon has come to devour me!"

"Where?!" Squonk looked around in alarm.

Wendel gave another terrified-ish shriek and ran into the cave.

"Hey... where are you going?" Squonk said. "It's dark in there!" He followed the maiden into the cave. Poor thing, he thought to himself. She seems kind of stupid. Maybe she can live with me and mother until she gets a little smarter.

Once he was out of sight, Wendel disguised himself as a mouse and scuttled back out of the cave as Squonk lumbered deeper into it. And what a massive cave it was! Squonk had never been inside a cave before, and this one made a grand first impression. He forgot all about the poor girl he was following and curled up on the broad stone floor, his dragon instincts starting to take very firm hold. This, he decided, would be a lovely place for a nap.

When Squonk hadn't emerged from the cave by nightfall, Wendel gave a little cheer, congratulated himself on what a clever wizard he was, and got back to planning his dragon-free home.

So you can imagine Wendel's surprise when, three days later, he saw a very large green dragon flying around his tree.

Flummoxed, Wendel disguised himself as a small red bird and few up to talk to the dragon.

"Hello," Squonk said. "Have we met?"

"I don't think so," Wendel said. "Say, I don't mean to be rude, but what are you doing here? You're a dragon! Shouldn't you be in a cave?"

"Funny you should mention it," Squonk said, "but I found a really nice cave a few days ago. It was neat!"

"So why didn't you stay?" Wendel asked.

"Because it got so boring," Squonk said, rolling his eyes. "I mean, it's cold, the floor's all hard and not nice to nap on at all. I can't hear the other birds chirping and playing from way down in there ... it's a nice place to hide, but I wouldn't want to stay there!"

Wendel fluttered next to him, too stunned to speak.

"As a matter of fact," Squonk said, whispering (as much as a dragon can whisper), "I'm headed back there right now. I've been gone three whole days, and Mom's very angry with me!"

"Squonk!" a small, tweetering, and very angry voice said from someplace far above them. "Where have you gotten to this time, boy? Squonk!"

"I'd better go," Squonk whispered. "But if you find me later, I can get you some really pretty yellow rocks!" He then flapped off as fast as his enormous wings could carry him.

Moments later, Wendel saw a small, irate blue bird flying after the dragon.

"Well, no wonder he lives in a tree," Wendel said, fluttering back to the ground and casting off his disguise. "He thinks he's a bird! I've been going at this all wrong; he barely thinks like a dragon at all. Probably never met his real mother in his life..."

A very cunning idea started to take shape in Wendel's head.

Three days later, the forest was abuzz with excitement. There was a dragon flying around! One that wasn't Squonk! (Having heard tales of dragons not raised by Mrs. Tweedle-Chirp, the other birds kept well clear of this one.)

The dragon, enormous and green and bearing what one wizard hoped was a strong familial resemblance to Squonk, flew over to Squonk's nest. Squonk watched "her" intently as she swooped down to a large branch nearby.

"Why, hello!" Mrs. Tweedle-Chirp said politely, fluttering onto her son's nose. "I'm Mrs. Tweedle-Chirp, and this is my son, Squonk. Who might you be?"

"I," Wendel said from within his dragon disguise, "am his mother."

"Huh?" Squonk said.

"I beg your pardon?" said Mrs. Tweedle-Chirp.

"You heard me," the "dragon" said. "I'm his mother. Thank you for raising him for me, but I'm here to take him home."

"Mom?" Squonk asked anxiously, looking cross-eyed at his little blue mother.

"Hush, dear," she cooed from his nose. "I'm sorry," she said, turning back to the new dragon, "but there seems to be some mistake. You can't be his mother. I am."

"What?" Wendel asked, taken aback.

"I'm the one who's raised him," she said, sternly. "I'm the one who's taken care of him ever since he was tiny—well, tiny-ish, at least. I'm the one who's fed him, I'm the one who looks after him when he's ill. I'm the one teaching him how to build a nest, how to tell right from wrong, and how to get along with others. In short, madam, I'm the one who loves him, and I'm the one who has reason to be proud of what a fine young lad he is."

"Aw," Squonk said, blushing, "you're embarrassing me, Mom!" Mrs. Tweedle-chirp flew off her son's nose as he turned his head to hide his smile. She landed on a branch where she could look this other dragon in the eye.

"But... but you're a bird!" Wendel protested. "Birds lay bird eggs! Not dragon eggs!"

"Oh, maybe you did lay his egg," she said, "but that would mean you're the one who left it unattended in the middle of my forest. And, please excuse me madam, but I'm afraid I don't think very highly at all of you for that. If you were any kind of mother at all, you'd know there's a lot more to it than just laying an egg. In fact, I dare say that's the easy part."

"You... you silly little bird!" Wendel said, hoping to frighten Mrs. Tweedle-Chirp.

It didn't work.

Wendel tried baring his teeth at her.

That didn't work, either.

"Now, see here!" Wendel said. "I... misplaced that egg many years ago, and have been looking for it ever since! Now, you've done me a favor by tending to my son for me, but I'm back now, and mean to take him back to live among his own kind!" Which was exactly what Wendel intended, save that he didn't mean to stick around once Squonk was back among his own kind.

Mrs. Tweedle-Chirp scowled—which isn't easy for a bird, but Mrs. Tweedle-Chirp was up to it. "I'm sorry, madam, but I'm going to have to ask you to leave now. Good day."

"But..." Wendel sputtered. "Surely you want to be rid of him by now! Look at him! He's much too big for you to take care of!"

"Hey!" Squonk said.

Mrs. Tweedle-Chirp hopped off her branch and fluttered right in front of the older dragon's face. "You," she said in a voice of cold rage, "are without question the single rudest creature it has ever been my misfortune to encounter."

And she pecked him in the eye. Vigorously.

Wendel gave a yelp of surprise and lost his grip on the branch. He forgot he was disguised as a dragon and stopped being disguised as one. He fell quite a ways before landing on a branch that, while painful, at least kept him from falling any further.

"I'm sorry you had to see that, dear," Mrs. Tweedle-Chirp said, composing herself.

"Look, Mom, look!" a very enthused Squonk said, pointing with his nose towards a very confused man several branches below. "It wasn't a dragon at all! It was that wizard!"

"Well!" she huffed. "I never...!"

"He sure fooled us good, didn't he!" Squonk said, laughing.

"Well. I suppose he did at that, the rude little man."

"Hey," Squonk said as the wizard rubbed his injured eye, "I think you hurt him."

"Serves him right, didn't it. What did I tell you? Nothing but trouble, wizards."

"No, I think he's crying."

Indeed, Wendel was sobbing miserably.

"What's wrong?" Squonk asked, making his way down as his mother stayed by the nest.

"Why won't you go away?" Wendel cried.

"This is my home!" Squonk said, confused. "Where else would I go?"

"But... This is a tree! And you're a dragon! Dragons live in caves! With lots and lots of gold!"

"What's gold?"

"You know, that shiny yellow stuff you're so fond of."

"Wait a minute," Mrs. Tweedle-Chirp said, fluttering down. "You're the one who's been making so much trouble?"

Wendel nodded.

"And why," she went on, "should you care whether my son lives in a tree or a cave or anyplace else?"

"Because I want to live here," he said miserably.

"Ooh!" Squonk said, excited. "A wizard? Living in our tree? That would be so cool!"

"No it wouldn't," Mrs. Tweedle-Chirp said sharply. "Nothing. But. Trouble."

"Aww," Squonk said. "But he's been the most fun I've had in... Well, forever!"

"Doesn't matter," Wendel said. "I can't live in the same tree as a dragon."

"And," Mrs. Tweedle-Chirp said, "I suppose you'd try to evict me and all our neighbors next, hmm?"

"Of course not," Wendel said. "You're birds. You're small. You don't take up any space at all."

"Well," Mrs. Tweedle-Chirp said, "as you can see, my son and I aren't going anywhere. Squonk, kindly escort this gentleman back down. I bid you good day, Mr. Wizard." And with that, Mrs. Tweedle-Chirp flew off.

Dejected, Wendel wrapped his arms around Squonk's neck and let the dragon carry him to the ground. Wendel could have just disguised himself as something with wings, of course, but he was far too depressed to bother.

"Mr. Wizard?" Squonk said as he neared the ground.

"Yes?"

"Why can't you live here if I'm living here?" Squonk asked, landing.

"Because," Wendel said miserably as he slid off Squonk's back, "I can't have a dragon living on top of my home. They're dangerous!"

"Am not!" Squonk said, offended.

"Yes, but..." Well, the dragon had a point. His mother the bird was probably more ferocious than he was—which, in Wendel's opinion, said quite a lot about both the dragon and the bird.

Wendel shook his head. "Doesn't matter. There isn't enough room."

Squonk scowled and looked up at the massive tree. It stretched so far into the sky that it was going to take him a while to fly back home. Its trunk so thick that a hundred Squonks could have surrounded it with no trouble at all. "But there's plenty of room."

"No there isn't," Wendel said, waving his hand. "You're a dragon! You're huge, and you're going to get bigger yet!"

Squonk's eyes widened. "Really? When I grow up, I'm going to be as big as this tree?!"

"No," Wendel said, "of course not. But you'll get at least twice as large as you are now, and..."

Wait a minute. The tree was absolutely enormous. Even fully-grown, Squonk would be no larger to this tree than his mother would be to an ordinary tree. Could Wendel really live here without even noticing the dragon?

Then a thought made Wendel's face split in an enormous grin.

"Say," he said, "if I asked you nicely, would you be willing to occasionally swoop down and scare the shorts off of somebody? Like a would-be apprentice, for instance?"

Squonk thought about this for a moment, and then smiled. He wasn't sure what the wizard was talking about, but it sounded like it might be fun.

So, after profuse apologies to Mrs. Tweedle-Chirp and promises to stay on his best behavior, Wendel made his home in the tree. And Squonk had a fantastic new playmate who was a continual source of lots of interesting things.

And they all lived happily ever after.

At least, right up until the point where Wendel told Squonk just what an "apprentice" is.

But that's another story.

A wolf and a squirrel, living side by side, see their world very differently, their intrinsic natures leading to conflict. Can a wolf who doesn't mean to be cruel earn the trust of a squirrel? Can he keep it?

BRUSH AND SNIFF

mwalimu

The sun made Berek squint as he stepped out of the hut. "Thanks for letting me visit."

Detar stuck his head out, and they touched muzzles. "Thanks for stopping by."

Berek started toward his home. The village of Rundel-gadu was home to a couple hundred wolves, making it small enough that it was a short walk from anywhere to anywhere. The sights and scents along the way back to his parents' hut were all familiar to him, comforts he had known his whole life. Fires burned in open pits between the huts, tended by elder wolves as they talked and watched their cubs at play. A she-wolf beside one repaired a basket, while three males around another cleaned coneys from their traps. The meat would make fine meals, and the skins could be used for clothing or blankets.

There were no coneys today at his hut. Brak, his father, had a creel of fish he was cleaning while his mother Char and his little sister Shan prepared the herbs that would flavor it. "Did you have a good visit with Detar?" Char asked.

"I did," Berek replied, taking a seat beside his father. "He showed me some of the leather work he's been doing and shared some jerky."

"What else?" Brak handed him a scaling knife.

The younger wolf took the knife and reached for a fish. "We talked about pen-tura and moon of passage."

Berek recalled the conversation. He had asked to play with Detar's water wheel, and Detar had been reluctant because it was his pen-tura, which made it very special to him. "You never play with it anymore,"

Berek had said, but Detar was a couple of years his senior and Berek knew he mustn't disrespect a wolf who had completed his moon of passage.

"Pen-tura was a happy time, the happiest I thought I would be," Detar had said. "But moon of passage is something to be proud of."

Berek hadn't been too sure. Detar had his own hut now, but ever since going on his moon of passage, it seemed like Detar always had more important things to do. "Moon of passage sounds scary."

Detar had put his arm around the younger wolf. "Don't worry yourself over moon of passage. Your pen-tura is near, your last chance to enjoy being a kid. Rather than fretting over what's ahead, just have fun and enjoy it."

Berek held the fish against a flat rock and began cleaning scales off it. "He asked what I want for my pen-tura."

Brak looked up. "What did you tell him?"

"I said a water wheel like his would be okay, or maybe a mallet ball set," he murmured and scraped. "There's something I want more, but I was afraid he'd think was stupid."

Char perked her ears. "And what do you want most for your pen-tura?"

Berek shrugged, and turned the fish over to work on the other side. "I don't think it's something I can have."

His mother leaned over beside him. "Tell us, and let us decide."

Shan stopped chopping herbs and tried to listen. Berek glared at her. "You'll think it's silly," he said to his mother. "Can I whisper it?"

Char gave Shan a warning glance. Shan frowned but dipped her muzzle and went back to chopping. Char leaned closer, and Berek whispered his secret wish. Her eye ridges rose, and she turned to him. "That's different. I wouldn't say it's silly, but I don't know if it's something we can get you."

Brak finished filleting a fish, now obviously curious. "What does he want?"

Char stepped over and whispered to him. Brak's tail stopped, and then resumed a slow wag. "That's a tough one," he said as Char returned to her herbs.

Berek handed him the fish, scaled as cleanly and almost as quickly as if Brak had done it himself. Char smiled. "Do you remember what a mess he made of the fish the first time he tried to help?"

"He got better at it," Brak observed.

Berek let out an exasperated sigh as he reached for another fish.

Itchit and his best friend Chatta could not resist frolicking along their way as Tintch, Itchit's father, led them back toward Nesting Rock. "Watch this!" said Itchit, darting for a nearby tree. "See that branch? I bet I can leap up to it!"

"Stay close!" warned the elder squirrel. "The wargen have been setting traps. I barely escaped one this morning."

"We know," said Itchit. "The wargen traps are easy to spot once you know what to look for."

Chatta glanced around. "Just check for their scent, and don't go after nuts that look too easy," he said.

Tintch chattered and flicked his tail warningly. "Never think it's easy. The wargen are clever, and when you think you've outsmarted them, you might end up as a wargen meal."

"Wargen don't eat squirrels," said Chatta.

Itchit twitched his tail. "Yeah, they catch and eat rabbits, and there's always lotsa rabbits, so they leave us squirrels alone."

Tintch turned to them. "The wargen have left us alone before, but make no mistake. Wargen will eat squirrels if they get hungry enough." They continued forward.

Tintch froze, so Itchit and Chatta did too. "The path here is disturbed. Wargen have been here. They might be close."

"Then which way should we take?" asked Chatta.

"We can go around this way," said Itchit, starting down a side path through the undergrowth. "Let's go." He ran ahead of the others...

...and froze on the spot. "The ground here feels funny."

"Why is that tree bent way over?" Chatta asked, looking at a young tree beside the path.

"I'm scared," uttered Itchit, fighting the urge to twitch his tail.

"It's a trap!" Tintch chattered, spotting a taut rope attached to the tree. "Get out of there! Carefully!"

Itchit was still frozen in his tracks. "How do I..." He started to move one foot and felt something crackle beneath his feet. "I'll take a big leap away from this spot." He tensed his back leg muscles.

The instant he pushed off, something gave way beneath his feet. They heard several loud snaps, and the tree sprung upright, pulling up a bag that closed around Itchit much faster than he could have hoped to leap clear of it. "Dad! Chatta, help!" he cried as he flailed about inside the bag, clawing and struggling to find the opening, but the rope had pulled it closed like a noose. "It got me!"

Tintch scrabbled up a nearby tree. "Chew your way out," he said as he positioned himself to make the leap to the bag, which still swung from the tree. "I'll get you down." He was about to leap but didn't get the chance before he spied something that stopped his heart. "There's a warg coming fast. Keep trying to get out, son."

Tintch and Chatta had to retreat to a safe distance as the warg took hold of the bag, with Itchit inside. "Help, it's got me!" he continued to cry. "Dad! Chatta! Get me out of here!" But there was little they could do as the warg unfastened the rope from the tree while Itchit continued to struggle. It dashed off in the direction of the wargen village.

"Get back to Nesting Rock," Tintch told Chatta. "I'm going to follow!" He took off running as fast as he could behind the warg, traps be damned. "Itchit!"

Night had fallen on Nesting Rock, which was actually several boulders that lay among the grove of oak trees the squirrels called home. The squirrels were gathered around Tintch and his mate Pertat who were inconsolable. Getsh, an elder maiden, spoke. "The wargen have turned against us. For many seasons, they have let us forage in peace, giving us little reason to fear them. But now they have taken to setting traps, and yesterday, Itchit was caught."

Tintch's tail flopped listlessly behind him. "I followed the warg that trapped him as best I could, all the way to the wargen village," he said. "It was hard to keep up, and once it reached the village, I lost track of it. I came as close to the wargen village as I dared and could not hear Itchit or find his scent. It would have been too risky to enter the village without knowing where they took him."

Getsh continued. "The best we could hope for is for Itchit to escape on his own. A day has passed, and he has not returned, and wargen don't wait that long to..." She closed her eyes and couldn't finish the sentence. "As much as it pains me to say this, I fear Itchit is lost to us."

As Tintch and his mate wailed and sobbed, another spoke. "What are the rest of us to do now that the wargen are trying to trap us?"

With a sigh, Getsh responded. "We have two choices. We stay here and learn to avoid the wargen and their traps, or we leave and seek out a safer place."

The other spoke again. "We have already lost Itchit. The wargen are clever, and if we grow wise to their traps, they will try new ones until they catch us, one by one. If we are to survive, we must leave here."

There were murmurs of agreement as Tintch and Pertat continued to whimper. Getsh gave several flicks of her tail. "Then it is decided. We move on."

The mood was jubilant as the fire radiated warmth to the many friends and family who had come to share in the festivities. The pen-tura ceremony included many stories of Berek when he was younger, most told by his parents. Though their bellies were full, the smells of the wonderful stew prepared by Char and his aunt Morna still lingered in the air.

"We have heard many tales of young Berek, but he has many more yet to be lived," said Brak. He turned to his son. "This eve we celebrate your pen-tura, the last of your childhood. It is your time to treasure the joys of youth while you still can, for your moon of passage is but a few seasons away."

Berek beamed. "Thank you, Papa. Mama and Auntie too. Your meals are always the best."

Brak made a hand signal to Druk, the village woodcrafter, who stood opposite the fire. Berek noticed the gesture and watched in anticipation as Druk slipped away in the direction of his shop. Trying not to look too anxious, he looked around and smiled at the others around the fire circle. Moments later, Druk reappeared, carrying something large with a cloth draped over it, which he handed to Brak. "And now for the best part of all," said Brak, bringing the gift to place it before his son.

All eyes were on Berek as he studied the mysterious gift. Berek's ears perked, and his eyes went wide when he heard a scratching noise from beneath the cloth. With his heart beating faster, he reached out to lift the cloth away to reveal a cage. "A scurri!" he howled with delight. "You got one! Thank you, thank you!"

There were cheers and murmurs from others. Shan came forward, brow creased in confusion as she leaned in for a closer look at the cage. "You wanted a scurri for your pen-tura? You're weird."

Berek ignored his sister, eyes glowing as he studied the animal. "He's so cute! He's not even full grown." The scurri was shivering, huddled in the middle of the cage with his big bushy tail wrapped around him. "Look, he's scared of us. All us wolves around. No wonder he's afraid."

31

Detar stepped up behind Berek. "That's an unusual pen-tura, an animal. Do you know how to take care of him, what to feed him?"

Berek's eyes never left the creature. "I've watched them out in the trees. Scurries eat nuts and seeds and greens. And maybe other stuff. I'm gonna take good care of him!"

Brak reached in to rub his shoulder. "Whatever you do, be very careful that he does not escape. You have no idea how hard it was to catch one, and if he gets away, you might never catch him again."

Druk crouched beside him. "Scurries can chew through almost anything. I had to build that cage out of some of my hardest wood. It should hold him, but you can already see where he's tried to chew through."

"I'll be careful," said Berek.

"If you get tired of him, you can eat him," taunted Torka, his younger cousin.

Morna boxed Torka's ears. "That's not nice!"

Berek glanced up only briefly, and then spoke to the scurri in soothing tones. "Don't worry, I'll protect you. No wolf's gonna eat you!"

Itchit was certain he was going to die and become a wargen meal. He just wished it would hurry up and happen. All the scary sights and sounds just outside the cage, all the wargen looking in at him. Dying couldn't be as bad as living in constant fear. Oh, how he missed his family!

The unfamiliar started to become familiar when Itchit realized he'd been taken to a strange-smelling room where some of the wargen nested. Whenever any of them came close, he huddled to the back of the cage. He soon recognized one warg in particular was watching him the most. Sometimes, that one inserted its hand, and Itchit did his best to avoid the hand, but Itchit soon realized the hand wasn't trying to catch him. It was leaving acorns or other tasty seeds or greens, or cleaning his messes.

Char returned from the village herbalist to find Berek seated outside the family hut, looking fidgety and agitated. "What's the matter, son?"

"It's Brush," he replied. "It's been four days, and he still won't come near me or my hand." Berek was clawing lines in the dirt beside him. "I almost reached in the cage and grabbed him."

She sat beside him. "That only would have made him more afraid of you."

"I know," Berek replied. "So I came out here to sit for a while instead."

His mother gave a wag of the tail. "Getting an animal like that to trust you takes a lot of time and patience."

The young wolf sighed. "I know. But it's hard."

Char smiled at her son. Did Berek have any idea what he had gotten himself into when he asked for a scurri? If not, he was getting a lesson. Nevertheless, Berek soon resumed his vigil beside the scurri's cage. It wouldn't be the last such moment, though the struggle was not so much between wolf and scurri as between patience and impatience.

The first big victory came five days later. "He ate out of my hand!" Berek cried, smiling and literally jumping for joy.

The days that followed were punctuated by more small victories. "He let me touch his head!"

"I stroked his tail. It's so soft!"

"We touched noses!"

Berek sometimes returned from his chores to find Shan watching Brush closely. Berek knew he couldn't keep his sister away from the scurri, but he gave her plenty of warnings. "Not too close. Don't shout, don't growl, and don't show your teeth." Berek tried feeding different things to the scurri; Brush particularly liked sunflower seeds and, to his surprise, bits of dried meat. Berek also observed that Brush destroyed the husks of any acorns Berek fed him, much more than was necessary to get to the nut inside. When Druk came by to see how the cage was holding up, the woodcrafter explained to Berek that scurries need to chew on things to keep their teeth healthy, so Berek started giving him pieces of softer wood and cooked bones to chew.

More than half a moon had passed since his pen-tura, and Detar was over for a visit. "You're getting pretty attached to him."

Berek smiled at his friend, then looked back at Brush when he felt the scurri crawl over his hand. "He's funny to watch sometimes."

"When are you going to have him out of the cage?"

"I don't know," Berek replied. "I think Brush'll let me hold him, but I'm afraid he'd wiggle out of my hands and escape."

Detar studied the scurri. "I can make a harness for him. Then you could keep him on a leash."

Two days later, the harness was ready. Berek reached into the cage with it, and Brush nosed it. When Brush started to chew on it, Berek had to withdraw it. The next day the scurri was more cooperative, and Berek was able to slip it around Brush's body. With the leash attached, he coaxed the scurri out of the cage for the first time. Brush looked tentative as he took his first step out the door, then quickly jumped to the ground and darted for the exit, only making it the length of the leash. The scurri chattered and ran around, tugging often at the leash and looking exuberant to have some freedom to run. Berek smiled at the creature's antics and sat. Even within the leash's range, Brush had plenty to explore, and more than once, Berek had to give the leash a tug when Brush started to chew on something.

The following day, Berek brought Brush outside the hut. He wanted to hold the scurri while he walked around, but Brush acted jittery whenever held, preferring to be on his own feet. This too was a matter of patience and small victories in the days that followed. Berek picked up Brush from time to time, always being gentle and stroking him, sometimes giving him a treat. Brush eventually became more comfortable with being held, and Berek considered it a big victory the first time Brush crawled onto his arm on his own.

There were difficult moments too. Sometimes Brush fought against the harness and leash or got it wrapped around one thing or another. Brush liked to climb on things when he could and occasionally was difficult to coax down from the roof of the hut. One day, Berek made the mistake of putting Brush in his cage with the harness still on. The next morning, he found the chewed up remains of the harness scattered about the cage, so Brush was confined to his cage until Detar could make him another one.

They made steady progress. Brush began to trust Shan, Berek's parents, and close friends like Detar enough to let them stroke or feed him, but the scurri remained wary of other wolves. Sometimes Berek was able to have Brush along when engaging with friends or working on chores. The boy with the scurri became a familiar sight in the vicinity of the family hut and sometimes elsewhere in Rundel-gadu.

"Look, its scurri boy!" In front of Berek were Gomar and Hetch, who were a couple of years older than Detar and whom Berek usually avoided.

"Yeah, so what," said Berek, trying to walk around them, keeping his hands around Brush. "If you want one, go catch your own."

Gomar blocked him. "If I had one, I'd smell like a scurri too."

"Then don't catch one," said Berek. He felt Brush squirming in his hands, more agitated than usual. He stroked Brush to calm him, cradling his arms around him, and again tried walking past the two older boys. "I gotta get home."

Hetch and Gomar continued to block his way. "You gonna train him to hunt for nuts?"

The more Berek tensed up, the tighter he held Brush, which upset the scurri more. Unexpectedly, the leash came loose from the harness, and Brush leapt out of Berek's hands to the ground, bolting between the huts for the forest that lay beyond. Berek gave chase, but once Brush found his way into the underbrush, Berek couldn't keep track of him.

"Free! I'm free!" Itchit called out. "Mom? Dad? Chatta?"

Itchit's cries went unanswered, but he quickly realized he was on the wrong side of the warg village. He would have to explore further to find the way back to Nesting Rock. Night was falling when he found a grove of trees that he thought he recognized as one where he and Chatta used to play. After he nosed around in search of scents of his friends and family and didn't find any, he wasn't so sure.

Berek was in tears, holding the broken leash. "Brush escaped," he sobbed. "Gomar and Hetch were teasing me, and Brush was wiggling around, and next thing I know the leash broke and Brush was running for the trees."

Char hugged him. "I'm sorry, Berek. You were doing so well with him." She rubbed his back. "I saw how happy you were with him."

The young wolf continued to whimper while his mother stayed at his side. Then he stopped and sat up straighter with a determined look. "I gotta go find him. I gotta go catch him again."

Brak gazed at his son. "You can certainly try."

Berek looked up at him. "How'd you catch him before?"

"I tried a couple of different kinds of traps," his father said. "The one that finally worked was similar to the noose traps we use for coneys." Berek perked his ears. He had helped set those many times. Brak continued. "I had to modify it to close him inside a drawstring bag without hurting him."

"Can you show me?"

Itchit made himself a comfortable nest where he spent the night. He was safe enough from predators, but it was a lonely night, for he was used to being snuggled with his mother and father. The straps around his body were an annoyance and could get caught on something, so he chewed through them and slipped free.

Morning came, and he discovered acorns and greens were plentiful as he continued to explore. His teeth felt overgrown, so after several acorns, he chewed some bark to wear them down some more. Then he resumed his search for familiar territory.

At last he spied Nesting Rock. "Chatta! I'm back! Mom! Dad!" he called out as he sped toward the boulders he had climbed over so many times with Chatta and his other squirrel friends. But his elation soon turned to disappointment. None of his friends or family were anywhere to be seen. What scents he could find were old and faded, and the abundance of acorns and greens suggested there hadn't been any squirrels around for a while. He climbed the tallest boulder and looked around. "Anybody?" His tail drooped. "Is everyone gone?"

As Itchit continued exploring, he started crying, and then became afraid. If they were all gone, there might be dangers he didn't know about. He remembered what his parents taught him about hawks and owls—he should not sit still in the open for too long. Even so, the absence of any of his fellow squirrels whom he had so longed to see sapped him of his energy, and he soon just huddled crying. His family was gone. He didn't know what happened to them, but he was still alone.

Still alert for dangers, Itchit froze at the sound of something approaching. With a twitch, he looked around and saw a warg approaching. It was the one he called Sniff.

Berek kept his footfalls quiet as he approached the area where his father said he originally caught Brush. He knew the place well, a cluster of boulders where for many moons before his pen-tura he would sometimes come to watch the scurries frolic and play. He had toyed with the idea of bringing Brush here to play with the other scurries but had discovered that the scurries were gone when he last visited, much to his disappointment.

In his hands were ropes, a drawstring bag, and a few sticks and fasteners he would need to set the trap. He dreaded to think how long it would take to regain Brush's hard-won trust, but he had made the decision to reclaim his pet. First, though, he had to find him.

As Berek neared the boulders, he spotted Brush—at least he thought it was Brush; the harness he had been wearing when he escaped was gone. The scurri, crouched beside one of the boulders, appeared listless with his tail drooped behind him and occasionally made a bark-like noise.

"Brush?" Berek said.

To his surprise, the scurri didn't run away as he got closer. Berek set aside the trap gear and moved slowly to sit on a nearby boulder. Berek was certain by now it was Brush, for he doubted any other scurri would let him get this close. Brush moved from place to place, inspecting an acorn husk or climbing one of the rocks, so Berek decided to stay put and be patient. He understood well the importance of being patient.

When Brush came close enough, Berek held out a hand with a few sunflower seeds. Brush inched forward to nose them, then stuffed them into his cheeks. Berek smiled, and when his hand was empty, he curled his fingers to stroke Brush beneath the chin. Brush ate the sunflower seeds, then came up beside Berek's leg as if to ask for more. Berek placed a few on his leg, and Brush hopped up to eat. Berek rubbed him between the ears.

The dance continued, and eventually Berek was able to cup the scurri gently in his hands. With Brush nestled into place, Berek stood slowly and started back toward the hut. He glanced briefly at the trap accessories and decided to come back for them later. Brush was more important.

It wasn't the last time Brush escaped, but the next time it happened, Berek knew where to look for him. Berek decided to watch the scurri for a while to see what he liked to eat. It reminded him of watching scurries before he had Brush, and he wondered once again what had become of the other scurries.

Berek began sometimes allowing Brush to run free inside the family hut, a practice that arose when he decided against keeping Brush confined to the cage while waiting for Detar to make another harness. Brush had to be watched closely at these times due to his tendency to chew on things and to climb on everything. Outside the hut, Brush was kept on the harness and leash until Brush escaped again and returned to the hut on his own. Soon after that, Berek stopped using the harness and leash in the vicinity of the hut though he continued using it when he took Brush with him to more distant parts of the village.

Increasingly, Brush would crawl onto Berek's arm on his own and soon took a liking to perching on Berek's shoulder, where he rode sometimes when Berek was out and about on errands. The wolves of Rundel-gadu were often treated to the sight of Brush jumping off, checking out husks and other debris that lay on the ground, and climbing back to Berek's shoulder.

Pen-tura was as much a fun time as Berek had anticipated, even though he still had chores and duties. He enjoyed the time he spent with his father fishing or trapping coneys, much as he regretted having to leave Brush in his cage. The scurri had come to trust Berek's family and closest friends enough that Berek and Brak would sometimes return from an outing to find Brush outside the hut with Shan and Char. One of the few times Brush shied away from Berek was when the young wolf was gutting fish or coneys. Brak speculated that Brush might be bothered by the smell of blood.

As he enjoyed these times, Berek was learning skills that would help him to survive and to become a responsible and contributing member of the village.

Kamba, alpha of Rundel-gadu, wore his ceremonial headpiece and a colorful necklace befitting his status. "Berek, son of Brak and Char, you are growing stronger of body and mind."

"Thank you, Alpha," Berek replied, dipping his muzzle and squirming in his seat. Being seated between his parents was little comfort when he knew why he had been summoned. Seeing Dolan seated beside Kamba on their arrival had only confirmed his suspicions.

"Your childhood is drawing to its end," Kamba continued. "The time nears for your moon of passage. It is a test of survival. You will need to apply all you have learned, practice all of the skills you have acquired in your life, to demonstrate independence and resourcefulness, to persevere against hardship and adversity.

"For a full moon, you will live on your own at a place of your guide's choosing, up to half a day's hike from Rundel-gadu, surviving by your skills and your wits. You may take whatever you can carry with you, but no more than five days of food. Anything else you eat, you must hunt, trap, or gather on your own. Do you believe you are prepared for this challenge?"

The young wolf looked to his mother, then his father, then back at Kamba and Dolan. He didn't feel ready. He probably never would.

"I know how to catch fish and to set noose traps for coneys. I can start fire, and I know how to build a smoking cairn. I can set up my own tent or shelter without one if I have to. I am good with a knife, a hatchet, and other tools."

The alpha nodded slowly. "All this we have observed, Berek, and now it is for you to demonstrate that it is enough. Dolan has been selected to be your guide."

Dolan was Detar's father and had often been around when Berek visited, though less after Detar got his own hut. Dolan perked his ears and smiled. "Can you handle being alone for that many days?"

Berek's ears flicked. "Can I bring Brush with me?"

Kamba fixed his gaze on the young wolf. "There will be challenges and dangers you cannot guess. If your scurri is with you, there may be dangers to him. The decision is yours, but I suggest you leave him in the care of your family."

Char rubbed his shoulder. "We will take care of Brush while you are gone."

Berek whined. "No one knows Brush like me, and he trusts me more than any other."

The elder glanced between his parents, then back at Berek. "As I said, the decision is yours. Let us go over the rules. Your guide will lead you to the place where you will spend your moon. Everything you bring you must carry yourself. Dolan may only carry what he requires for himself. He will leave you in time to return here by sunset."

"Where will you take me?"

Dolan answered, "Your location will be secret, known only to me and a backup guide. If others knew, they might be tempted to come find you and render aid."

"Must I stay where you choose?"

"You need not remain in the exact spot, but you must be close enough for me or my backup to find you easily," said Dolan. "I will visit you every quarter to see how you fare. I can advise you and answer questions during those visits, but I cannot provide any food or supplies. If in my judgment you are faring poorly, I may declare a failed attempt and bring you home."

None of this was news to Berek who had known from a young age that all wolf boys must go through a moon of passage when they come of age, but to have it looming before him gave him chills. Some failed their first attempt. Some did not survive; he hadn't heard of that happening to anyone from Rundel-gadu, but he couldn't ignore the possibility. He took some comfort from knowing that Detar and many other friends had been through their moons of passage, as had his father and the elders back in their youth.

Only a few days remained before Berek's departure. He had to choose carefully what to bring with him—fishing and trapping supplies, a water skin, medicinal herbs, rope, the tent cover, his knife, and of course, the five days' supply of food. A cooking pot would be nice but was too heavy. He thought about whether it was worth bringing a bow and arrows or a sling, since he wasn't very good with either. The bow, he decided, was too bulky for as much use as he'd get out of it, but the sling was small, so in it went. There was much discussion over whether to bring Brush along; in the end, Berek could not be dissuaded from bringing the scurri, saying it would be an adventure for him too.

Early one morning as the full moon set and the sun rose, Berek ate a hearty meal with his parents and sister. He bid them goodbye as he shouldered his belongings. He was met by Dolan, and with Brush riding his shoulder, they set out.

The pack which had seemed light enough felt a lot heavier by the time the sun rose high in the morning sky. It didn't help that the hike was uphill, and though Dolan was patient, he offered no indication that they were getting close. They crested a hill and continued downhill into heavier forests. Arriving at a glade, they stopped to look around. Berek was expecting Dolan to say which way next when the guide turned to him. "We have arrived."

Berek shed his pack, being careful of Brush, and looked around the place where he would be spending the next moon. In one direction he spied signs of marshland through the trees, likely a good place to fish. There was no sign or scent of coneys in the immediate area but he knew they might be plentiful nearby. Plants with edible parts were in evidence, including mayapples and berry bushes, but there were also plants that were better avoided, such as nettles and honey locusts.

However, none of those things are what caught his attention the most. "There are other scurries about," Berek observed.

"Indeed there are," said Dolan.

"Is that why you chose this place for me?"

Dolan shrugged. "Truthfully, I don't remember any scurries last time I was here."

Berek stroked Brush between the ears. "You'll get to make some friends."

Dolan was impassive. "He might, but remember that you are here to survive."

Berek's hackles went up as he understood the guide's meaning. "I could never eat a scurri!"

"You say that now, but what if you had to choose between that and starving?"

Berek frowned but said nothing.

Dolan went on to point out a few things about the site before he departed for the village. The hike had left Berek as exhausted as after a long day working, and he still had to set up camp. As he took some time to rest, Brush was chattering with the other scurries and straining against the leash, so Berek removed the harness before setting to work.

The squirrels hunched in the undergrowth at the edge of the glade, watching the two wargen and wondering if they would stay or move on. Their past encounters with wargen had led them to fear the great canines. How much of a threat could just two of them be? What especially aroused their curiosity was that one of them had a squirrel at the end of a rope, and the squirrel didn't appear afraid.

They watched and waited. In time, one warg departed, but the other sat and rested as if intending to stay. After a moment, he freed the squirrel from the rope.

"Get away from him," one of the squirrels uttered under his breath. The new squirrel nosed about briefly, evidently unconcerned about the warg, then scampered closer to them and stopped.

Chatta emerged from the grass, and the two squirrels studied each other, whiskers and tails twitching. The newcomer spoke first. "Hi, I'm new here. Can you..."

"Itchit?"

Itchit's whole body twitched, and he darted forward. "Chatta?"

Chatta turned and bolted through the grass. "Itchit's back! He's alive!" he called out to the others.

"Don't be silly," said another squirrel. "Itchit's dead."

Chatta ignored her and circled back. "Come on, Itchit. I'll show you where to find the best nuts, and all the good hiding places..." He stopped. "Freeze! The warg is watching us."

"Oh, Sniff?" said Itchit. "Don't worry, he's okay. Are Mom and Dad here?"

Chatta's voice dropped. "Follow me." He led Itchit along barely-seen trails through the undergrowth, emerging moments later near a large fallen tree where they found Pertat and Getsh.

Itchit looked at Pertat. "Mom?"

"Itchit, is that you?" Pertat ran forward and sniffed her son, then circled him, her tail twitching with joy. "You're back! Oh, Itchit, look at you, all grown up. And we thought the wargen killed you. Your father tried to follow, but..."

"Where is Dad?"

They all went silent. Getsh finally spoke. "Your father is gone. The swamp beast got him last season."

"Dad... gone?" Itchit uttered. His tail drooped.

"I'm sorry," said Getsh. "Since our arrival here, we have lost three of our number to the swamp beast."

More squirrels gathered, and Itchit told his tale. "I don't remember much right after they caught me. I was inside a bag, then a cage. I tried and tried to escape because I thought they were going to eat me, but I couldn't get away. I was alone and afraid. The cage was really hard wood and tasted awful. But after the first couple days, it was always the same warg looking at me in the cage. His nose was close, and I could feel him breathing, so I called him Sniff. He put nuts and seeds and greens and water in the cage. He put his paw inside, and at first I was afraid, but after a while I wasn't anymore."

"But he's a warg," said one. "Wargen are dangerous."

"Not this one," said Itchit. "Come, I'll show you."

They returned to the edge of the glade where the warg was busy. Itchit and Chatta emerged while others remained hidden, some of them uttering warnings. "Stay back!" "Don't get near him!"

Itchit looked at them and flicked his tail. "It's just Sniff. He won't hurt me." Sniff was busy with some ropes and a big sheet of something as Itchit scampered over toward him. The warg looked at him and extended an arm. The squirrels let out a collective gasp as Itchit climbed onto the arm and up it to the warg's shoulder. Sniff's ears perked as he made some noises and touched noses with Itchit, who nosed him back and crawled to his other shoulder. When Sniff returned his attention to the big sheet and the ropes, Itchit climbed off and returned to the squirrels. "See? He's nice to me."

"I still think you're crazy!" said Chatta. "Come on, I'll show you some more."

Berek was hungry. He knew he should immediately start trying to catch his meals and make the food he had packed last as long as possible, but as worn out as he was, he decided to eat from his stash just this once. Some of the food he brought was only good for a few days, so he ate from that, saving the jerked meat that would keep longer for later.

Brush looked like he got along well with the other scurries. Berek was happy for him that he was having a good time, but the thought that Brush might rather stay with them when it came time to return home started to nag at him. Would it be fair to his pet to force him to come back?

There was enough daylight left to do some exploring. First he checked out the nearby river. Unlike the rivers and streams near Rundel-gadu that had well-defined banks, this one was bordered by a wide marsh. He might have to wade through an expanse of mud and shallow water to get to any fish. Tomorrow he would have to explore farther in search of a more suitable fishing spot.

He spotted some strange spoor in the mud and, moments later, saw what had produced it—an alligator. Berek thought of Wervin, an old wolf who sometimes visited Rundel-gadu to entertain with tales of his exploits hunting and killing alligators. Although Berek had been fascinated by the older wolf's stories, he wasn't about to argue with the village elders who said alligators were too dangerous and were better left alone. Unfortunately, that meant he would have to stay out of the mud. He would be safe enough on solid ground, but in the mud or the water, the alligator had the advantage. An unexpected encounter could end very badly.

Berek got out the noose trap. He looked at Brush and the scurries, and realized he didn't dare set it anywhere close by. Tomorrow he would seek out evidence of coneys a safe distance from camp.

The next morning, after reluctantly eating again from his food supply, Berek explored farther afield and found what looked to be a suitable place to set the noose trap. He returned and hiked along the edge of the marsh but couldn't find a good access point to the river beyond, or any pools likely to hold fish. An elder had once instructed that Rundel-gadu and its surrounding area offered options that might not be available in an unfamiliar place, but other places had options of their own that should be sought out.

He began to wonder if he should have brought the bow and arrows after all. Too late to think about that now. He had the sling, and though he wasn't the best shot with it, he would have time to practice.

Berek checked the noose trap and found it sprung with nothing in it. As he reset it, something landed on his arm, a grasshopper. Looking around, he saw that there were many of them about. They could provide nourishment, and if toasted over the fire, they were less likely to make him sick and could be quite tasty. For now, he would keep trying for fish or coneys. That evening, he foraged for mayapples, berries, and nuts. They would hold him over, but wolves were carnivores. Without meat in his diet, he might not last until the next moon.

Another day came. By afternoon, after resetting the noose trap for the umpteenth time, Berek hid close enough to watch it. It wasn't long before he saw a crow land on the bent-over tree, which triggered the trap and sent the crow flying and squawking. He thought the crow must be crazy if it thought that was fun, but with a sigh, he removed the trap and went in search of another place to set it.

Six days along, Berek was almost out of jerky despite his efforts to resist eating it too quickly. He'd had no luck finding a place to fish, no thanks to the alligator that was being quite territorial. At last, he caught a coney, which he gutted, cooked, and consumed ravenously, hoping it wouldn't be as long before he caught the next one.

The descending half moon brought his first visit from Dolan. "Kamba sends his blessing. Shan and your parents send their love," said the guide. "How do you fare?"

"I am worried I'll not have enough to eat," said Berek.

They walked around, and Berek showed him what he had found, talking about what he had tried. At the edge of the swamp, Dolan pointed to some small tracks in the mud. "Have you tried catching frogs?"

"I haven't seen any frogs."

"No, but they are here. You just have to know the signs to look for." Dolan went on to describe where he was most likely to find them and how to catch them.

At least Brush seemed to be doing fine food-wise.

"For a long time, I was stuck in that cage, inside this big den where Sniff and three other wargen nested," Itchit told his mother. "I call one of them Whimper. She is the smallest, and she looked in at me a lot when Sniff wasn't there. I think she's his sister, and the other two wargen are their parents."

"Four wargen. That's scary!" said Takkit, one of the young squirrels.

"I was scared at first, but they didn't hurt me. After a while I got used to it and wasn't afraid anymore. I still looked for a chance to escape, and then one day I got free and ran into the forest back to Nesting Rock. But when I got there, everyone was gone." Itchit started sniffing at the memory of that moment. "Why did you leave?"

"I'm sorry," said Pertat. "Many of us were nearly trapped. After you were caught, we feared the rest of us would get trapped too. We believed it was no longer safe to live near the wargen, so we left in search of a safer place, and we found here."

Itchit's tail bottled. "But you said the swamp beast here got Dad and a couple of others. That means it's not safe here either."

"The swamp beast came along after we were settled. We thought about moving again, but we decided against it," Getsh explained. "It is dangerous, yes, but it seldom comes out of the water and is easily avoided when it does. The wargen could come after us anywhere."

"I have not seen the wargen catch or kill any other squirrels. They get lots of rabbits and fish and fowl and sometimes deer but never squirrels."

Takkit twitched his ears. "Maybe the only reason they haven't is because we left."

Itchit sniffed again. "I searched all around Nesting Rock and couldn't find you. I was alone and scared. Then Sniff came to Nesting Rock, and with you gone, he was the only family I had."

After Dolan departed, Berek found a long sturdy stick and carved the tip to a point. That evening near dusk, he went in search of frogs. He didn't find any before it became too dark for him to monitor the alligator's whereabouts, of which he had to be constantly vigilant when he was in the water or the mud. The next day, Berek was more successful, bagging four of the amphibians and feasting on their legs. In the days that followed, Berek had to abandon most attempts to hunt frogs, because the alligator shadowed his movements too closely.

He practiced with the sling and quickly discovered it spooked the scurries—one more thing he could only do away from the campsite. His aim improved but his best aimed shots lacked force, while his hardest shots tended to be wildly inaccurate. The one time he hit a bird, it was only stunned and escaped easily. On occasion, he saw ducks fly overhead but never found evidence of them on the ground. He guessed they must be nesting on the far side of the marsh. The next coney to get caught in his noose trap was picked clean by scavenger birds before he discovered the catch. Most of his diet for the next quarter consisted of berries, roots, and grasshoppers. It was better than nothing, but without meat, he felt a big hole in his stomach.

His most enjoyable moments were when Brush came to his side. Anytime Brush climbed to his shoulder, it made him forget about his problems. None of the other scurries would get very close, but Berek learned to recognize some of them. One in particular who was often with Brush had a tendency to overreact when startled, so Berek named him Lurch.

New moon brought another visit from his guide. "Please, can you share some of your jerky?" Berek pleaded.

Dolan looked at him sadly. "You know I can't do that unless you want to concede."

Berek's stomach rumbled. Dolan hadn't even said whether he had any with him, but the younger wolf was sure he could smell it. Maybe it was his imagination. He hung his head. "Yes, I understand."

The guide studied Berek, glancing around. "Do you want to stay the full moon?"

He dreaded the thought of returning home a failure and having to start over later in another unfamiliar location. "I'm not ready to give up." Berek knew Dolan could overrule him if he thought he was at too much risk.

"If that is your choice," said Dolan. He looked around, his eyes stopping on the scurries. "You are not out of options yet."

Although he hadn't said it, Berek knew what he was getting at. "No, I still have options," he answered, telling himself he would never resort to that one.

Berek still had no success with the sling, the noose traps, or staying clear of the alligator, who evidently regarded the wolf as a threat to his territory. The craving for meat was getting worse, and somewhere inside, that primal instinct grew harder to ignore.

Brush was crawling on him and a couple of the others, including Lurch, were close by. As Lurch got closer, Berek's eyes were drawn to the scurri's back legs. He salivated, licking his lips. The next time Brush jumped off, Berek gave in to temptation and grabbed for Lurch, trapping his tail against the ground. He scooped up the struggling scurri and pinned it against a rock. Brush and Lurch both chattered loudly.

"I'm sorry for doing this," Berek said to the scurries, "but I have to survive". With tears in his eyes, he reached for his knife.

Berek knew Brush tended to back away when he used the knife, only this time he didn't. Lurch continued to struggle and scold as Berek brought the knife closer. Brush leapt onto the wolf's arm, making it harder to keep a steady hand. "No, Brush! Leave me alone!" he commanded, but Brush continued to his forearm and bit his hand hard enough to draw blood.

"Ow!" Berek howled as he flinched, dropping the knife and sending Brush flying. With his other hand still keeping hold of Lurch, he picked up the knife again and looked at the scurri through tearful eyes...

...and he put down the knife and released Lurch. "I'm sorry, little scurri. I'm sorry, Brush." He started crying.

Brush went for the knife and started to drag it away. It was too big and bulky for the scurri to get far, and Berek snatched it back, returning it to his belt. He watched Brush and Lurch bolt for cover. Berek licked the bite and wept bitterly, hating himself for what he had almost done. He heaved as his stomach tried to empty its contents, but there was nothing to come up save a little bile he felt in his throat.

"I'm sorry, Chatta, real sorry. I never thought he'd do that. He's never been like that with me."

Chatta was shaking. "I told you, wargen are dangerous. Wargen eat squirrels!"

Itchit had finally convinced Chatta that it was safe to get close to Sniff, and now this had happened. He felt mortified. "I don't get it."

When Pertat found out, she gave her son a good scolding. "Maybe you need to decide if you're with him, or with us."

Itchit would have plenty of time to think about where he had gone wrong. He had lost his fear of the wargen, especially Sniff, and maybe he shouldn't have. Had he been trying too hard to ignore that wargen are meat-eaters?

Due to the lack of proper meat, Berek felt sapped. He was lacking energy and getting weaker. The scurries who had kept him company were now staying well clear of him. Even Brush, the companion who had ridden his shoulder for many moons, kept his distance. After what he'd nearly done the day before, Berek could hardly blame the little scurri if he never wanted to be with him again. That felt a lot worse than being hungry. Don't get too close to the hungry wolf; he might eat you!

The noose trap yielded another coney, and this time he got to it first. Back at the camp, Berek restarted the fire and was preparing the coney when he noticed Brush watching and thought it odd. Gutting his kills normally repulsed the scurri. When Berek set the knife down to tend the fire, Brush scampered forward and tried to steal it. As before, Berek reclaimed the knife easily. He nearly shouted at the scurri for misbehaving, but he held his tongue. He had already betrayed the scurri's trust, and he couldn't be yelling if he hoped to regain it. Maybe Brush would be happier if he went wild, but Berek would miss him.

After two more days of grasshoppers and berries, Berek was getting ravenous for meat. Frogging stick in hand, he headed for the marsh. When he got close, he saw Lurch nosing around near the water's edge. Barely a stride away, low in the muddy water, was the telltale ridgeback of the alligator. The oblivious scurri crept forward to dip his muzzle for a drink.

"Lurch!" Berek shouted, hurrying forward. "Get back! Get away!" Lurch made a yip and leapt back and to one side. That same instant, the alligator lunged forward, snapping his jaws at the spot Lurch had barely vacated. Even more startled now, Lurch bolted for the underbrush. The alligator hissed. Berek took several steps back before glancing over to see Brush and Lurch.

"I almost died!" Chatta's heart raced. "First the warg scared me, then the swamp beast."

"Sniff wasn't very close," said Itchit. "I don't think he wanted to catch you. That sounded like a warning call."

"A warning?" Chatta's tail was still atwitch.

Itchit batted him with his tail. "Sniff can see higher up, and he saw the swamp beast. He just saved your life."

"He did? But why would he... after he..." Chatta's tail calmed. "Yeah, I guess you're right. If your warg hadn't come along, I'd be dead. But why would he save me after he almost killed me?"

Itchit nosed his friend, and they watched as Sniff turned away toward his camp. "I know his moods, and I've never seen Sniff like this before. He is very sad. Maybe it is because he is away from the other wargen, but since he caught you and let you go he has been sadder. He's hungry too."

Chatta's tail gave another twitch. "That's why I'm still afraid of him. How can you tell he is sad?"

"I spent many days in a cage watching him. If you pay attention to his face, his ears, his tail, and other parts of him, you can tell what mood he is in. And when I am close, he is happier."

"You're still not afraid of him after what he did?"

"What he almost did," Itchit corrected. "I tried to stop him, but I couldn't, not really. He let you go, but I still felt really terrible about it afterwards. I've been watching Sniff, and I think he feels terrible about it to."

Chatta cocked his head. "He's not one of us. How can you be sure?"

Itchit twitched his whiskers. "I don't think I am wrong. Come, watch."

After poking at the fire and adding some wood so it wouldn't go out, Berek lay nearby. With so little, even the most necessary tasks took a lot of willpower. He imagined what an easy time he would have catching frogs and fish if it wasn't for that damnable alligator. Why did his moon of passage have to be in such a difficult place?

From the underbrush, a scurri appeared with something stuffed in his cheeks. It was Brush. Berek watched as the scurri approached; Lurch and a couple of other scurries watched. When Brush got close, Berek perked his ears and extended an arm. Brush crawled on and climbed to his shoulder, then expelled an acorn from his cheeks.

Berek smiled and laughed, his tail wagging. "Good to see you, buddy. Are you trying to give me an acorn?"

He placed the acorn on a flat rock and pressed the flat of his knife against it until he heard it crack, then picked up the nut meat and chewed on it. "Ugh, this tastes awful! How can you guys eat these things?" Berek swallowed it anyway. So his hunger problem wasn't solved, but with Brush on his shoulder, the day had gotten a lot brighter.

He looked at the tent and his spare rope, and started to think.

"This might destroy the tent, but it'll be worth it if it works," Berek muttered as he finished rigging the improvised trap. It required a much larger tree with a branch hanging just so, and setting it was a lot of work. He prayed to the great ones that none of his ropes would break.

After a couple of trial runs, Berek brought the whole rig down to the swamp's edge. He knew the perfect tree and soon had a couple of loops of rope over the overhanging limb. He used his heaviest length of rope further along the limb to pull it downward, and rigged it to where he could spring it easily. He laid out the tent, scattered some camouflage over it, and attached the other loops of rope to the corners.

The alligator came close a few times, and when he did, Berek took a walk along the edge of the swamp to draw it away, then looped back to continue preparing the trap. The alligator was getting wise to his tricks by the time the trap neared completion, so Berek started taunting the alligator when he stepped away, throwing rocks at it and daring it to come after him, even drawing it out onto land once. Finally the trap was finished.

The next time the alligator came back, Berek held up his frog spear and taunted the reptile some more. "You want me? Come get me!" The alligator hissed and lurched. Berek hit his snout with the stick and danced away behind the trap. "Come on, just keep coming." The alligator continued forward, partially onto the disguised tent, bumping a rope attached to one corner. Berek crouched and poked the beast, holding the spear defensively. Half the alligator's body was on the tent. "That's it, just a little bit closer."

The alligator made another lurch, and Berek kicked the stake behind his foot, releasing the heavy rope. The overhead limb sprung up, pulling tent and alligator up off the ground. "Now I gotcha!" Berek called out.

Berek had been replaying in his mind all the things old Wervin had said. "If it can't see, its reactions will be slower." For the moment its head was wrapped inside the tent. "If its tail is loose, it will be harder to control." The tail was partially loose, so that might be a problem. "Their jaws are powerful, but you can hold them closed with one hand." Berek spun and from one side grabbed the snout with both hands. "Never forget that an alligator can kill you if you make a mistake." The beast thrashed about inside the tent as Berek made certain he had both upper and lower jaws in one hand before letting go with the other. He reached for his knife, only to discover it was missing from his belt.

Berek glanced over and saw it on the ground, where it must have fallen loose when he sprung the trap. He dared not let go with his other hand. He reached for it as hard as he could, but the knife was just out of reach. He strained harder, fearful that one of the ropes might give way. His hand and his shoulders were quickly tiring.

Brush appeared, scampering toward the knife, and Berek let out a gasp. "Brush, please don't take my knife!" he pleaded. But Brush continued forward and reached the knife, and Berek's heart stopped. Their eyes met, and the scurri's tail twitched. Then Brush nudged the knife forward.

Berek snatched it up and plunged it through the tent into the belly of the alligator. "Die!" he growled, withdrawing the knife and plunging it in again. The alligator thrashed harder, and its tail came free. "Hurry up and die, you filthy brute!" Again and again he stabbed into the soft underbelly of the creature. Blood spilled out through the wounds, soaking the tent, his fur, and the ground beneath. At last the alligator's thrashing became slower and weaker, and finally stopped.

Berek let go and jumped back a safe distance in case the alligator had one strike left in him. The wolf collapsed to the ground, panting, waiting for his nerves to calm. After a moment to collect himself, he picked up the spear and prodded the alligator with it a few times. Once he was certain it was really dead, he mixed the spilled blood with the dirt and used his fingers to paint his cheeks with it. He belted out a howl.

The howl made Chatta shudder. "Did you see that? Your warg just killed the swamp beast!"

Itchit leapt excitedly. "He did! He did! And now it'll never eat a squirrel again."

Chatta gazed at Sniff, who was still growling and showing his teeth, and gasped in disbelief. "Now do you see how dangerous he is?"

Itchit's glee was undiminished. "Sniff is a warg. Yes, he is dangerous, and he is fearsome. And he is my friend."

Chatta was horrified when Itchit scampered out toward the fearsome warg. The moment Sniff turned to look at him, the growling stopped, his lips relaxed over his teeth, and he reached out a hand. Itchit hopped onto his forearm. Sniff drew Itchit close to his muzzle, and they touched noses.

Berek had never had such a large animal to himself, and as he cooked and ate the alligator's heart and liver, he thought it a shame that none of his family or friends were here to share it with him. There was far more meat than he could eat, so after he had his fill, he cut as much as he could into strips to be dried and smoked, ending up with enough to last him the rest of the moon with plenty left over to bring home and share. He was careful not to damage the hide.

As he worked, more than a dozen scurries watched in fascination, and he spoke to them in gentle tones. Sometimes Brush approached him, and Berek enjoyed the chance to take a break and give the scurri some attention.

Ascending half moon was the next day, which brought another visit from Dolan. "I don't recall if I've ever had alligator before," said the guide when Berek shared some of the meat with him.

Berek smiled. "I can hardly wait to show the hide to Detar."

Dolan glanced at the stash of alligator jerky. "With that much meat, you should make it to full moon easily."

"Yeah," Berek replied. "I miss my family, but if I'm not hungry, I'll be able to enjoy the rest of the moon. I want to do some more frogging."

For his final quarter moon, Berek didn't bother with the noose trap. He ate coneys often enough at home and didn't know when he'd get to try frogs again, so he took advantage of the opportunity. He'd have to find out if there was a place to hunt them closer to Rundel-gadu.

Dolan returned at full moon, and much to Berek's delight, Detar was with him. Getting to show his friend around made for an enjoyable end to his moon of passage.

As they packed up his belongings, there was still one thing that worried Berek, and that was Brush.

"It looks like Sniff is leaving," said Itchit, as he watched Sniff and the other two wargen gathering up his camp.

Pertat was at his side. "Are you going with him or staying with us?"

Itchit's tail drooped as he pondered the question. "I don't know, Mom. I've gotten to like being with Sniff and the other wargen, but I don't want to leave you guys again." His tail gave a twitch up. "I wish you were still back at Nesting Rock. There haven't been any squirrels around since you left."

Pertat's tail jittered. "After what Sniff nearly did to Chatta, I am worried."

Chatta spoke up. "Itchit told me things and showed me things about Sniff. I'm still afraid, but not as much." He turned to Itchit. "If you go back, I'm coming with you."

There were squawks from some of the others. "I do miss Nesting Rock," Getsh said. "Can we be certain the wargen will leave us in peace?"

"They've been good to me," Itchit replied. "Some of the wargen scare me sometimes, but they never hurt me."

Pertat looked out over the glade. "Whatever we do, we better decide quickly. It looks like the wargen are leaving."

"Didn't realize the jerky was so heavy," Berek groaned as he hefted his pack.

"I can help with some of that," Detar offered.

Berek looked at Dolan. "When you saw me at new moon, were you thinking about failing me?"

"Only if you wanted to give up," Dolan replied, lifting the remains of the tent. He had declared Berek's moon of passage a success upon his arrival, so there were no longer any rules dictating what Berek had to carry himself. "I knew even if you ate nothing else, you wouldn't starve before my next visit."

Dolan didn't mention him begging for food, and for that, Berek was thankful. How many others in his position had done the same thing? He slung the alligator hide, which he insisted on carrying himself, over his shoulder. "Did I have a tougher moon of passage than others have had?"

"Tougher than some," Dolan replied. "Gomar killed a deer three days into his, so he had it easy. Turek had a rough time. He ate something—he thinks it was a turtle—that made him so sick he could barely move from his tent for days. Nanesh's supply of food was stolen by a raccoon the first night."

"I got heavy rains several days in a row," said Detar. "I was cold, and everything was so wet I couldn't start a fire for eight days."

While they had been gathering everything up, Berek glanced frequently at Brush and the other scurries. As they were about to embark, Brush ran toward him. Berek crouched, and Brush climbed to his shoulder. They began walking, and moments later he looked back and laughed. "I think the scurries are following us."

"Looks like it," Detar chuckled. "They must like you a lot."

"Probably because I killed the alligator."

Detar glanced over at him. "Don't you think that was taking a big risk, killing an alligator?"

Berek paused to glance back. "Maybe. I hope I never have to fight another alligator, but I'd do it again before I would ever hurt a scurri."

The return of a young man from his moon of passage was always cause for celebration in his village, and Berek's was no exception. He showed off the alligator's hide and skull and shared the jerky as he traded stories with others about their moons of passage. When the festivities died down and Berek was ready to relax away from the other wolves, he headed for the boulders. It pleased him to no end to see scurries about once again. Although Berek had more responsibilities, he often had Brush along for the ride, perched on his shoulder as the wolf went about matters in the village. Brush still slept in his cage sometimes, always with the door open.

Berek had his hut built on the edge of Rundel-gadu closest to the boulders. He would have to keep it presentable for visitors—not just friends and family, but she-wolves, including those on sun quest. It would likely be several years before he chose a mate, but as the elders liked to say, the first step in getting an oak tree is to plant a lot of acorns.

"This way," said Shan, leading the young she-wolf. "I won't be old enough for sun quest for three more years. What has yours been like so far?"

The she-wolf gave a swish of her tail. "This is the second village I've been to. I never realized how good my parents were at begging the hospitality of others until I had to do it myself. The wolves of Karbob-gadu weren't the easiest, but they treated me well, and I met some interesting folk."

Shan led her behind the family hut, between a few trees. "This is my brother's hut." They arrived, and she tapped the door. "Berek, you have visitors."

They stepped through the door and stopped. Two startled scurries darted around, collided, and chattered loudly at each other before bolting out a small opening. The two she-wolves looked up to see Berek seated on a log beside the bed. Another scurri was at Berek's side while a fourth huddled beneath the bed. "Welcome, I am Berek," he said.

"I am Olana, from Otten-gadu," she replied warmly and looked around the hut. Sitting on a shelf were several of his possessions, but the ones that caught her eye were an alligator skull and an empty cage. His chests and cabinets looked more securely latched than was typical; particularly the one that she guessed held foodstuffs. Her eyes returned to Berek. "You've got scurries in your hut."

"I do?" he answered and extended an arm toward the one beside him, who jumped on and climbed to his shoulder. Berek looked at the creature. "Did you hear that, Brush? She says I've got scurries in my hut. What do you think?" He tilted his head toward the creature, who nosed his ear.

"What did he say?" asked Shan.

"He says, I got wolves in my hut."

Olana laughed aloud. "You are crazy! Is this always what you say to sun questors?"

"I don't know. You are my first," he said. "Olana, this is Brush. That's Lurch under the bed. He won't climb on me yet, but he lets me pet his tail and his ears."

Olana's nose twitched. "How did you get to be so friendly with scurries?"

Berek sat up and wagged his tail. "It's a long story."

Loyalty and obedience are not the same; even a good dog can become a scoundrel when forced to choose between them.

FAITHFUL

Marshall L. Moseley

John Samclan, General of the Armed Forces of Seattle and Great Dane of the Sammamish Clan, was pulled from a deep slumber by the trill of a pre-uplift cell phone. He opened his eyes and tried to roll over, but Alyssa rested on his chest and their three four-month old pups lay across his lower body like furry brown belts pinning him to the mattress.

He extended a hand through the darkness and picked up the cell phone from the night stand; it was pod-shaped with a hinge at the top. He opened it gingerly, having never used it before—it was one of only three in the city. One for the Mayor, one for headquarters, and one for him.

"Who is there?" he asked.

"Major Kentpride, sir," came the feminine voice of his feline second in command. "Our scouts in Sequim report the enemy is on the move."

"In force?"

"Two thirds of their force, sir."

"And the rest?"

"Unknown," said the cat.

"Our people in Tacoma? And on the bay?"

"Ready, Sir."

"I'm on my way." He put the phone back on the night stand, then reached to turn on the lamp next to the bed—his thick fingers with their vestigial claws fumbling with the knob. He often envied humans—the only sentients other than the enemy with naturally evolved fingers. The light clicked on.

Alyssa raised her head from his chest, her brown and white fur pressed on one side where she'd been sleeping on it, her nose both dry and wet—John adored that. "What is it, John?" she asked sleepily.

"It's begun," he said. "The humans are in danger."

The ancient elevator creaked to a stop at the top of the Space Needle. John, all six feet four inches of him, walked upright into the Seattle City State's military headquarters, a giant, mostly dark circular room staffed with humans, cats, and dogs all in the same blue uniform as his. Some worked in pools of yellow light at small tables spread with maps, while others stood at brass telescopes around the dark perimeter and looked out of the curved glass walls toward Eliot Bay.

"General in the room!" shouted the first person to see him, a burly male private with clear bulldog ancestry. Everyone turned and snapped to attention.

"At ease," he said.

Kentpride walked up to him, her feline orange fur made more so by the artificial light. She handed him a pair of binoculars. "Bremerton reports the enemy main force is moving on the Hood Canal and proceeding southwest, towards them."

"Thank you, Major. Still no sign of the rest of their army?"

"No, Sir."

"Very well. Has the Council arrived?"

"Not yet," replied the cat. "But they've been notified. I'm sure they're on their way." Kentpride's triangular ears twitched in the involuntary cat expression of amusement.

John tilted his head to one side, acknowledging her unspoken comment on bureaucracy. "Well," he said. "Let's have a look at the bay before they get here."

John walked to the curved wall-high window and looked out at the city. It rolled away from him down to the water, a dark blanket sprinkled with dim and bright yellow lights—dim from the oil lamps, bright from incandescent bulbs. It had been one hundred and three years since Uplift and they'd only managed to get electric power five years ago.

Clearly a work of human design, the uplift virus had hit the world seemingly overnight. Only a select group of higher order mammals were affected: dogs, cats, squirrels, bears, rabbits, badgers, otters, sloths, kangaroos, a few others, and of course, apes.

All the damn apes.

The virus worked on the young in utero—non-sentient animals suddenly began giving birth to intelligent, changed offspring. The virus rewrote DNA, changing paws into hands, reconstructing hips, lengthening legs, and increasing body size and brain capacity.

"General Samclan?" came a soft voice behind him. He turned around to see Mayor Peters, a silver-maned, pink-skinned human woman in the latter part of life, dressed in a dark skirt and blouse. She wore the red sash of her office.

"The Council would like to see you," she said.

Beyond Mayor Peters John could see the Council standing around the largest circular table in the room, lit from above in yellow light. A gray-black tabby private was quickly spreading a map of Puget Sound across it. By the time John walked over to take his place beside it, the map was pinned to the table and each council member had been given a pair of binoculars.

He looked around at the Council of Seattle, all dressed as formally as the Mayor, all wearing their sashes—the Mayor; the Alderman of Cats, Krypton Camaspride, a tall male black-and-white Maine Coon whose bright green eyes conveyed a fierce intelligence; the Alderman of Dogs, Alice Bellclan, a tall brown and white Basset whose droopy long ears and thick eyebrows made her look sleepy and unfocused, although she was anything but that. And finally, the Council Chairman Andrew Pierce, a thirty year old human with blonde hair and a big voice. Pierce wore an ancient human white shirt with a blue tie.

"General," said Pierce. "Please report immediately.

No, thought John scornfully, I'll stand here silently but report later. "The apes are moving in force on Bremerton," he replied, and pointed at the map. "They are here, crossing the Hood Canal at Seabeck."

The damn apes. Within five years of uplift, human civilization convulsed and fell, falling into worldwide anarchy. After seventy years of small and large wars, the bears and rabbits came to rule the interior of North America. Humans and their former pets ruled the coasts in well-defended city-states. All the other species just tried to fit in.

But not the apes. The apes had taken all of Africa, India, and Malaysia, while committing horrific genocide. They had killed a billion humans in India alone and they would have taken the rest of Asia were it not for the tigers.

Still, it had been a faraway problem until twenty-five years ago, when a coalition of chimps, gorillas, and orangutangs put a colony-sized landing force on the Olympic Peninsula, the largest rainforest in North America. They drove out the bears in weeks and in the years since had been slowly moving east.

"Bremerton?" asked Mayor Peters. "So they are doing what you thought they would"

"Yes, Ma'am. But it's only two-thirds of their force. One third of their army is... missing."

"And you have no idea where they are?" asked Pierce evenly.

"Not specifically, no."

"But," said Mayor Peters, "You are implementing the counter-attack plan?"

"Yes," said John.

The council-approved plan called for the main force of the Seattle's army to be staged in Tacoma, just short of the Tacoma Narrows Bridge. A month earlier Pierce had proposed that the city's multi-species army counter-attack any ape incursion by crossing the bridge, overwhelming the small ape guard-force there, and flanking the apes as they moved west. The Council had approved it with the humans overruling the animals.

Mayor Peters glanced to her left, where Councilcat Camaspride remained silent. "You are not saying much," said the Mayor inquiringly.

"There is not much to say," replied Camaspride in his whispery deep voice. Mayor Peters' gaze fell on Councildog Bellclan, who met her gaze evenly.

John could see it in the mayor's eyes, see the thoughts connecting and unfolding. That uncanny human ability to integrate information and reach a conclusion not immediately apparent in the facts—it was what made them so good at science. And poker. She looked from the dog to the cat, sensing something incongruous.

Kentpride approached and handed John a slip of paper. He read it and looked up.

"The apes have taken Bremerton," he said. "And we've found the other third of their army," said John. "They are moving on the Tacoma Narrows Bridge."

"The bridge?" said Pierce. "But how did they know...?"

"It doesn't matter now," said Mayor Peters. "Our troops will be killed in their tents. Order them to withdraw."

"No, Ma'am," said John.

For a moment the table was stunned into silence. General John Samclan had never refused a direct order before.

"General," said Pierce, his voice remaining even, but with a touch of anger creeping in. "You report to this council."

"The council where every human gets two votes, but a cat or a dog gets one?" said John. "That council? Yes, indeed I do. With full faith and fealty. Come with me and bring your binoculars."

He turned and walked away from the table over to the wall-sized window that faced Eliot Bay. He gestured to the council members with his binoculars, indicating they should look out toward the bay. He raised his own, glad for the Dane ancestry that gave him a mostly flat upper snout. Water gleamed on the bay, and halfway across it the gleam became flat black.

John spoke while they all looked outward. "That black area is a flotilla of boats and rafts," he told them. "Filled with apes, coming from Bremerton to attack this city. Our city." He lowered his binoculars as did the council.

Mayor Peters turned toward him, her expression thoughtful. "You didn't—" she said.

"Tacoma reports apes on the bridge, sir! Their entire contingent!" called Kentpride from the center floor.

"Blow the bridge," ordered John, and looked out the window.

Due south, one point on the horizon of the Puget Sound flashed white, like a blue-white star twinkling brightly for a moment, then faded.

"What is going on?" asked Pierce.

John ignored him. "Tell the Labradors to blow the charges in the bay," he called over his shoulder.

"Yes, sir!" said Kentpride.

From a distance, due west, John heard a muffled 'BOOM', followed by another, and another. He raised his binoculars again, as did the council.

Out on the bay the flat black area rippled.

"Arbor Heights is ready, sir!" shouted Kentpride.

"Let them go," ordered John.

"General Samclan," said Pierce, angrily, "You will explain now." John ignored him and kept his eyes on the bay.

Out on the water the flat black of the ape fleet churned and boiled. John knew it wasn't possible, but he thought he heard screaming.

He lowered his binoculars and faced the council.

"Mayor Peters, I accept the authority of this council, but not against my better military judgement. And you, Mister Chairman," he said, turning towards Pierce. "You proposed and pushed through the most tactically unsound plan I've ever heard or read about. Walk over a bridge in the middle of a battle, the only bridge with access to the enemy and the enemy knows it? It would be, as the U.S. Army manual calls it, a killing chute.

"I ignored your plan. And I cannot order our Army to withdraw from Tacoma because it isn't there. It is indeed flanking what's left of the enemy, but by going further south through Olympia and marching north, overland."

"You had no right—" said Pierce loudly.

"I had every right," John interrupted forcefully. "I defend my humans, my city, my home."

"What is happening now?" asked Mayor Peters.

"I had Labrador water teams put depth charges in the bay," replied John. "And just now they blew them, when the apes were halfway across—apes don't like water like you do. Their boats are being swamped and they're drowning. We've also opened the shark pen at Arbor Heights. We have nets sealing off the north end of Eliot Bay. It's now a giant food bowl."

Mayor Peters eyes flared. "You could have told us. We would have approved a better plan."

"But then you'd know about it. Chairman Pierce would know about it, and you made a deal didn't you, Chairman? The King of Seattle or some such nonsense?"

"No, certainly not," said Pierce, beginning to bluster. "This is outrageous!"

"Then why did the apes think they could march across that bridge with impunity? Why did they think they were attacking a sleeping army? Why, Councilman?" John stepped toward Pierce, who stepped back, eyes wide.

John towered over the human. "I am John, General of Seattle, faithful Dane of the Sammamish Clan, and I will protect humans with my life. But the uplift virus made dogs intelligent and so it stole our innocence. For all that they are our enemy, apes and dogs know one thing about humans."

"What?" said the man, stepping back again.

"You can't be trusted."

Marshall L. Moseley

It's a big world, and it's hard for a little spy to know who to trust.

GERBIL 07

Huskyteer

"Good morning, James!"

That meant the Old Man had a mission for me. I sat up and ran a paw through my whiskers.

"Morning, Old Man. Gerbil-O-Seven reporting, ready once again to save the world and get the girl. What's the deal?"

"I do wish you wouldn't call me that."

"Why not? In gerbil years, you're eight hundred."

As he reached to open the cage door, I bounced out into his hand.

"Whatever it is, Old Man, I'm ready. I've fully recovered from my last mission, and I'm at my physical peak. I've been clocking two hundred RPM in the wheel, and my teeth can gnaw through a quarter-inch steel hawser. Psychologically, I'm up for any kind of physical or mental torture the bad guys can think of. Women want me. Men want to throw things at me." I drummed my hind feet. "Bring it on."

"I need you to plant a listening device in the gents' toilets at the Swedish Embassy."

"Oh." I tried to keep the disappointment out of my voice. "Wily old Swedes up to their tricks again, eh? I always say you can never trust a Swede. Never fear, they shan't take over the world as long as I'm around to stop them. And their women are gorgeous."

The Old Man's hand closed around me, and I found myself lifted until I was on a level with his eyes. I squeaked.

"James, listen carefully," he said. "You are not a Double O agent. You do not have a license to kill. You—are—a—gerbil. A genetically engineered surveillance tool. You carry tiny cameras. You plant tiny bugs.

65

The backchat is an unexpected—and unwanted—side effect." He tapped my nose gently with his finger. "You don't drink Martinis—you nearly drowned last time. Also, you're a girl."

"But my name's James!"

"Do you have any idea how hard it is to sex a two-day-old gerbil?"

"I'm Gerbil-O-Seven!"

"You're the seventh prototype in the series. Do I need to restrict your Netflix privileges again?"

"What happened to prototypes one through six?"

"You don't want to know."

I blinked one eye, then the other. "May I ask a question?"

"Sure."

"Why am I a gerbil?"

"Biologically, religiously, or philosophically speaking?"

"I mean, I'm kind of noticeable. Why not a rat, or a mouse?"

"Because their little naked feet freak me out, OK? Now get some sleep before your mission, and remember: you do not save the world. You do not stop and sit up in the middle of running for your life in order to make wisecracks. You just do the job you were created for."

As he placed me back in the cage, he added, more softly: "And stay safe. You silly little thing."

I curled my tail around my head and moodily examined my hindpaws, with their dark nails and delicate fuzz of fine hair—the cause, apparently, of my existence as me. Thanks, feet. Thanks a whole bunch.

The Old Man helped me into my webbing harness, loaded up with a selection of miniature survival tools.

"Now, because this is a delicate mission, you're going to be briefed by a specialist first," he told me. "Want me to carry you, or would you rather go in your little ball?"

"I'll drive, thanks."

The ball gave me time to think. Well, I was pedaling frantically to keep up with the Old Man, but the translucent red plastic kept me isolated with my thoughts. I took a corner at speed, doing a little jump and leaning hard right, and absent-mindedly ground my teeth. A delicate mission. Something only I could handle. My chance to redeem myself in the Old Man's eyes after the Mornington Crescent mix-up and what had become known as the Senior Officers' Biscuit Tin Snafu. But what was it?

I rolled out of the lift and followed the Old Man down a corridor. He stopped, knocked, and held the door open for me. I like to make an impressive entrance, so I drove full pelt into a filing-cabinet. The ball separated into its two halves on impact, and I hopped out at a pair of feet. Female, from the nail polish.

"Oh my God, look at his little harness! He's adorable!"

I flashed the Old Man a look. It said: See? Women want me.

He flashed me one back. It said: Please don't say that out loud.

"He's a she, actually. James, this is Marta Harris."

"Hi." I stretched a little taller and allowed my whiskers to tremble in that irresistible way of mine. Marta crouched down and laid her hand flat on the carpet, palm up. When I jumped on, she curled her other hand over me as she slowly raised me to her desk.

I like a woman who knows how to handle a gerbil.

"Can I, er, give you a pencil to chew, or anything?"

"No thanks, I'm on duty."

"All right." She released me, and lowered her chair so I was level with her face. "Now, listen carefully. We have reason to believe that there's a mole in the Belgian embassy, feeding sensitive information to hostile powers."

"Swedish embassy," I corrected, to show I was on the ball.

"The Belgians are working out of the Swedish embassy at the moment while they have some repairs done to theirs."

Swedes and Belgians! The plot thickened.

"You'll plant your bug, and if our Belgian tries to pass information to his contact, we'll have him. Let's attach this to your harness."

She clipped the listening device to the strap over my chest, where I could remove it easily. It was about the size of a sunflower seed and painted in black and white stripes to match. If anyone saw me, I'd just be a gerbil holding a treat. While wearing a harness. In the middle of the Swedish Embassy.

"That should be all the equipment you need," she said.

"What about a suicide pill? In case I get captured?"

"Don't tempt me," said the Old Man. "You're not going to get captured. If you are, all you have to do is keep your mouth shut so they don't know you can talk. Can you manage that?"

"I suppose so." I shuffled my hind paws.

"I can find you some rat poison if it would make you feel better. Now, anything else before we take you over there?"

I twitched my whiskers. "Just one thing. You say there's a mole in the Swedish Embassy? Well, soon there's going to be a..."

My quip was stifled by his hand as he scooped me off Marta's desk.

So far, it had been a run-of-the-mill mission. I scampered through the embassy door using a crisp packet as cover, hitched a ride on a briefcase to the third floor, then followed my nose to the gents', using the pattern on the carpet as camouflage. It was pretty nice, as washrooms go. Light poured through a floor-to-ceiling window of what I hoped was one-way glass. Soap and moisturizer in glass bottles. A pile of soft, white towels. I had a quick bounce before getting down to business.

Absolutely textbook infiltration, I told myself, running a paw through the fur between my ears. Now, where to plant my device? The embassy was swept for bugs regularly, but until that happened I had to conceal it from casual inspection. Fortunately, gerbils can get places larger secret agents can't. I swarmed up the pedestal of one of the basins and fixed the device among the downflow pipes under the curve of the sink. There! No other field operative could have done that. Not even one with really tiny fingers.

I was pretty dusty and cobwebby by this time. Fortunately, I was in the perfect place to clean up. I hopped over to the mirror. I could only see the tops of my ears, but they were looking good. I was pretty sure I was raffish. And rakish. Roguish, even. A loveable scoundrel breaking hearts in the name of my country. I allowed myself to drift into a daydream.

"For your courage and intelligence in the field, and for saving the world, I name thee Dame James of the British Empire," said the Queen, and she lowered the ceremonial sword.

The creak of the door opening snapped me out of it. I barely had time to squeeze myself behind the soap bottle before two men entered. My heart was going at double its usual speed; I calculated it at approximately 800 beats per minute. Could this be my mole and his contact?

To my excitement, they began to exchange coded signals. They leaned in close to each other, and one of them slipped his hand into the other one's trousers. Obviously passing information.

And then...

They made contact. The two of them spent a good five minutes passing information to each other, while I watched, fascinated. It must have taken a great deal of work to come up with a code as fiendishly complicated as this one. And my listening device would be sending it all straight back to the Old Man. Too bad they weren't actually talking. Just…sort of grunting and moaning. Good job I'd stuck around to provide an eyewitness account. As they separated and began to tidy their clothes, I leaned forward, trying to focus on their faces.

The bottle of soap toppled forward into the sink, and smashed.

I froze.

"Hell! A little rat! Or a big mouse!" Did I mention that fluent Swedish is among the many talents at my disposal?

No time to congratulate myself on my linguistic prowess. I made a flying leap from the sink, spreading my limbs for distance and twirling my tail for control. (All standard gerbil equipment, by the way.) I wasn't prepared for one of the Swedes to make a flying leap of his own and grab me out of the air. I tried to sink my teeth into his thumb, but he had me round the middle and I couldn't reach. He brought me level with his face.

"I think this is a gerbil, Lars."

"I don't care if it's a lemming, Jens! Kill the tiny pervert!"

"How dare you!" I struggled. "I'm in service to Her Majesty the Queen!"

Oops. I wasn't supposed to let on that I could talk. Especially in Swedish.

They stared at me.

I stared at them.

I remembered that if one of them was my mole, he'd be Belgian, not Swedish.

I realized this was the least of my problems.

"If Her Majesty the Queen saw you she'd jump on a chair and scream," said the first Swede, eventually.

"I very much doubt that," said the second. "The Queen looks like a pretty tough old lady to me."

"OK, talking gerbil," said the Swede with his hand round me. "I'm going to open my hand. Don't jump, please. Or bite."

"Give me one good reason why I shouldn't."

"Because you're interesting, and I want to look at you. Besides, you'll break a leg or something."

"Fair enough."

He opened his hand and I stood on the palm.

"Hey, you have a little harness! And tiny small miniature tools! Look, Lars, he's got a whole spy kit here!"

I tensed. If he carried on exposing my secrets like this, I was going to have to kill them both. Somehow.

"Everything you say to me is going straight to my headquarters," I told him. "They'll come after you if you hurt me. I'm very valuable."

"I just bet you are."

He cupped his other hand behind me on his palm. "And what is a little small valuable spy guy like you doing in here?"

I considered my options. If he knew I was onto him, he might get desperate. Or I might be able to blackmail him in return for my life.

"I'm here to catch a mole. I saw you make contact and pass information to each other, and my boss heard the whole thing through the bug I planted. Kill me and there's nowhere you can hide. Be reasonable, and you'll be out in a couple of years."

I was prepared for whatever reaction came—except, as it turned out, both Swedes roaring with hysterical laughter.

"Nobody here is a mole, little spy gerbil," said Jens. He'd held me securely as he shook with mirth, and I was grateful, if a little nauseous. "We were just...oh my Lord God, how old are you actually?"

"Eight months. And a week." I didn't mention the girl thing. Some people are weird about that, as if my being an entire different species was somehow less relevant.

"Let's just leave it as passing information, then." Jens decided. "But not to any enemies. OK? Would you like a biscuit? I have one in my pocket from the World Hunger summit this morning."

A biscuit? I stiffened. Was he telling me he knew about the Snafu, and my disgrace? Was this blackmail? On the other hand—I sniffed—he did have a biscuit on him.

Suddenly the door burst open, and a man with dark hair and wild eyes ran through. When he saw us, he pulled out a Walther P99; compact anti stress version, with the suppressor kit.

"Hands up!" he snarled. Both Jens and Lars obeyed, and I found myself raised into the air and held high above the hard, tiled floor.

This mission was putting whole weeks on my life. Months, even.

The gunman kicked the door shut behind him.

"You two are my hostages," he informed us as he kicked the door shut.

"We three," I squeaked. He didn't seem to hear.

"Hey, spy gerbil," Jens said out of the corner of his mouth. "Run down my sleeve."

"What?"

"Maybe you can save yourself."

I nodded, though he was carefully looking straight ahead, and dived down the sleeve of his jacket. He had nice cufflinks, I noticed. And hairy wrists. I passed the armpit and carefully scrabbled down inside his shirt.

"It's not funny!" snapped the gunman, just as I squeezed past the waistband of Jens's trousers. I must have been tickling him, but there was nothing I could do about it. I shinned down his shin and poked my head out of his trouser cuff.

Jens wanted me to get away, but I wasn't leaving my Swedish mole and his companion to die. They'd been pretty nice to me, and besides, I wanted the glory of their capture for myself. Using Jens's shoe as a mirror, I worked out the lie of the land. The gunman had edged my Swedish companions over to the sink and was standing with his back to the cubicles, where he could cover both the door and the window.

"So," Jens said carefully. "What, exactly, is going on here?"

Now was my chance! If our gunman was a proper criminal mastermind, he'd be explaining for ages. I zipped off in a zigzag pattern across the tile.

"I have planted a bomb in the conference room!" he crowed.

"Sounds like a good plan." Jens kept his voice calm. "Why are you holding us hostage in the gents'?"

"Because I thought it was the fire exit. But this ties in perfectly with my plans! When the bomb goes off, I escape in the confusion, and you two take the blame—after I kill you both so it looks like a lovers' suicide pact!"

A whose what now?

But I couldn't pause my scurrying to wonder about that. I finished exactly where I'd wanted to be: between the gunman's feet. A few quick movements, and his shoelaces were tied together.

"And why do you want to blow up the Swedish Embassy?" Lars put in. I wasn't sure if he was buying me time, or genuinely curious.

"I wanted to blow up the Belgian Embassy!" snarled the gunman. "But it was closed for repairs!"

I'd heard enough. It was time for action. He had a nice crease ironed into the leg of his trousers, which I used to help me scramble up. When the curve of his buttock prevented me from climbing any higher, I followed gerbil agent operating procedure C90 and bit him in it.

I was gambling all of our lives on something I've learned over a long career of popping up unexpectedly: humans, when startled, tend to throw their arms upwards. Sure enough, my target jerked and shot a hole in the ceiling. This was the moment when Jens, or of course Lars, should have rushed him while he was distracted. But neither of them moved. Do they not show Bond movies in Sweden?

I jumped, but the gunman's hand was too quick, and I found myself squeezed in his fist. My eyes bulged and my feet kicked uselessly.

"Interesting," he said, covering the Swedes with his gun while he stared down at me. "One of the surveillance gerbil prototypes. I thought they were an internet hoax."

At last! Someone had heard of me! With the aid of my reputation, I'd soon have this terrorist quaking with terror. And afterwards, I'd work on that line until it sounded a bit better.

"How utterly laughable," the gunman continued. His grip tightened.

"Go pass information to yourself!" I snarled, and I bit down on his finger.

He shrieked and shook his hand. I held on, though the world went blurred. The gunman moved forward, probably to dash me against a basin, but thanks to my cunning work with his laces he tripped and stumbled.

The gun went off again.

The window shattered.

The gunman put out his hand to save himself, but met only air.

I dangled from his finger. Everything was suddenly very loud, cold, and windy.

I wrenched my teeth free, and I fell forever.

"Are you sure about this?" the Old Man asked. Marta carried on adjusting my harness.

"She'll need it now she's been promoted to Surveillance Officer level, and it'll come in useful next time she throws herself off a building."

"I still don't understand how she survived." He rubbed me under the ear.

"Neither do I," I admitted. "Am I a cyborg? Why did nobody tell me?"

"You're small enough to have a non-fatal terminal velocity," Marta explained. "That means you fall more slowly than a human. Your weight's spread out over a wide area when you land, too."

I scratched my ear with a hind leg. Science was less exciting than a hitherto unsuspected superpower, but at least it had saved my life.

"You'll be pleased to know your Swedish friends got the building cleared, and the army disposed of the bomb." Marta cleared her throat. "James, we've got something to tell you. Haven't we?"

She glared at the Old Man, who stared at the floor. "That listening device, the one that looked like a sunflower seed..." he mumbled.

"Yes?"

"It was a sunflower seed."

For the first time in my life, I didn't know what to say.

"I'm sorry, James," the Old Man said. "You were so bored and restless, but my Chief told me my job was on the line if I ever let you anywhere near the field again. You know, after the biscuit tin thing. So we made up a mission for you."

"You utter, utter..." I ran out of words again.

"It was unforgivable. You almost died." Marta stroked my back.

"But I didn't! I proved myself and my license to kill has been, um, unrevoked."

"For the last time, James!" said the Old Man. "You do not have a license to kill!"

"But your active status has been fully restored, if you're quite sure you want to go back out in the field," said Marta, glaring at him again.

"Or you could retire," the Old Man put in hopefully. "With a medal. And a pension."

"Of course I'm sure!" I drummed my hind feet. "Is it on yet?"

She fastened the last buckle on the harness, tightened the straps, and made a couple of adjustments with a small spanner. "There. Try that out, the way I showed you—carefully."

My paw on the red button at my chest, I gave my whiskers a satisfied flick at the thought of the successful missions behind me, and the many yet to come.

I am James, Secret Agent Gerbil 07, serving Queen and country. And now, I'm a gerbil with a *jet pack*.

*At the intersection between forensics and fairy
tales, a cop must choose how far to follow the clues
and how much to believe.*

CSI: Transylvania

Kevin M. Glover

It was a crisp autumn evening in Brick Haven, a normally quiet, rural suburb of Seattle. The air was clean, the sky clear, the moon full and bright. It was the perfect night for a triple homicide.

The police had cordoned off the sprawling crime scene the best they could, their bright yellow tape eerily reflecting the flashing red lights of their haphazardly parked squad cars. They'd need a helluva lot more tape to hide all the blood and carnage though, what with the murders happening on top of a hill and all. And the stench... well Christ, there was nothing the cops could do about that.

Even though it was a half-past supper time and a mile or so off the main highway, a growing crowd of gawkers and lookie-loos had gathered; locals mostly, but some curious commuters too, drawn by the steady stream of news vans pulling in and the police copter circling overhead. There was even a catering truck there selling mocha lattes and hot fresh cups of Joe. A half-dozen nervous looking uniformed cops tried to keep the crowds and the news cameras at bay, but folks just loved a good bloodbath. They all pressed in tighter and tighter to get a better view.

When Granger, the CSI forensics specialist arrived in his beat-up Peugeot, wearing his trademark rumpled trench coat and dark glasses even at night, he expected a freak show, and he wasn't disappointed. He eyed the crowd and clicked his tongue when he spotted a redheaded little girl left sitting alone on her biker dad's chopper with a clear view of the slaughter. *And people think watching TV is bad for kids,* he thought as he worked his way through the crowd. One of the uniforms quickly escorted him through the throng and up the hill where he was met by the lead detective, Collins. Collins, a slight man in the best of circumstances, looked sickly and pale. He covered his mouth with a handkerchief.

"It's pretty gruesome," Collins warned as he held up the crime tape for Granger to walk under. "Like someone came through and chopped them up with a chain saw."

Granger grunted, non-committal like, then he glanced around at the bloodied body parts being tagged and photographed, mentally recreating the assault. "What do we know so far?"

"Just a couple of things; all kind of weird." Collins fidgeted. "We thought we were missing some chunks of limbs, but turns out all the vics were little people. Got enough bits and pieces for three of them."

"Little people? You mean like midgets?" Granger bent down to look at a small man's shoe with a piece of foot still attached.

"Midgets. Dwarves. Not sure I know the difference. Their IDs say they're from Eastern Europe. And get this: they're all with Interpol."

"Midget cops?"

"Seems like," Collins offered. "Supposed to be here on holiday."

"Some holiday," Granger snarked. CSI guys liked to snark, made them seem cooler in case the shades didn't work. Then Granger was drawn to something in the bush. "So, they weren't here working a case?"

"Not officially, but who knows? Could be they tracked some perps here. We think it may be someone wanting to send a message. Russian mafia maybe."

"Don't think so." Granger reached out with a disposable glove to grab a clump of bloodied reddish-brown fur from a dismembered hand. He shined a penlight at it. "I think our three little piggies got eaten by a big, bad wolf."

Collins wasn't laughing. He knew the CSI guys all had a morbid sense of humor, but he wasn't up for any shenanigans. Granger didn't care. He looked around the grass, drawn to several more dismembered limbs. The slice and dicing must'a happened pretty quick. There was a hand still holding a grocery bag here, another holding a sandwich over there. And a bit further down from that was a hand holding a French beret.

"And I'll tell you another thing—" Granger was examining the sandwich now with the tip of a pencil. He could barely suppress a smile. "Looks like one little piggy went to the market, one had roast-beef, and this little piggy—" Granger paused, pointing to the hand with the French beret. "I'm betting this one's the one that went 'oui, oui' all the way home."

"Jesus, Granger. Show some respect. These are fellow officers, man." Collins then looked closer at the fur and over at the claw marks scraped across the shocked face on a decapitated head. "What kind of a wolf could do this much damage? Must have been a whole pack of 'em."

"Wasn't no ordinary wolf at all, Collins," Granger said, removing his dark glasses for the first time. "This wolf was a werewolf."

"A werewolf?" The police chief could barely contain his disbelief, his voice booming as he lambasted Granger and Collins in his not-so private glass office. Everyone in the precinct only pretended to be doing their work as they strained to hear the juicy exchange. "Are you off your meds again, Granger?"

"I'm not crazy chief, just hear me out." Granger's voice was calm. His eyes flashed a bit of their old spark behind his shades. He'd had a bout of depression over the summer, became desensitized to all the day-to-day death he investigated. The bizarre facts of this case invigorated him in a way he hadn't felt in years.

"Hear you out?" The chief huffed and puffed and pounded his desk. "I'm supposed to call Interpol and tell them their three fine officers got shredded to bits by a goddamn werewolf with a hard-on for little people? What do you think this is? CSI: Transylvania?"

Running a close second to snarking, CSI guys were irrepressible know-it-alls. It took every ounce of restraint Granger could muster not to remind his boss that Transylvania was for vampires, not werewolves. *Werewolves, well, everyone knew werewolves hung out in... where did they hang out anyway? London maybe? At least the American ones did...*

"Don't zone out on me, Granger," the chief said, yanking Granger back to the here and now. "I want your full attention when I'm drilling you a new asshole."

"Uh, sorry, sir. I think if you just examine the evidence bag..."

"This evidence bag?" the chief taunted, holding up a small plastic bag smattered with a reddish powdery residue. "Your little wolf hair sample, was it?"

"It was there, sir," Granger said, surprised himself the fur had practically disappeared. He turned to Collins. "Tell him, detective."

"It did look like animal hair, sir. Can't say for sure it was a wolf's."

"Well, it's just a bag of dust now, boys." The chief shook the bag again for effect. "Maybe wolfie had a bad case of dandruff?"

"Could be the fur dissolves after the wolf morphs back into a man," Granger thought aloud, though he had no scientific explanation why it would.

"In a pig's eye," the chief snorted. "You based your whole theory on a clump of goddamn disappearing fur?"

"Well, there's the lacerations, and there's still the vics' guns, sir. We found two of them on the scene. Both unfired and both loaded with silver bullets. If our pint-sized policemen weren't hunting werewolves, why the silver bullets?"

"Yeah, the shells were coated in silver," Collins chimed in.

"But that don't mean these midgets were hunting werewolves," the chief challenged. "Was the fucking Lone Ranger a werewolf hunter too?"

"Sometimes, you just gotta trust your gut, sir."

"Every time I listen to my gut, all I get is heartburn." The chief took a deep breath and made a decision. "You know, Granger? You've taken some pretty wild leaps of logic in your career, but this one stinks like shit. You take a little 'me time' and pull yourself together. I'm putting you on mandatory leave. Go fishing or play sudoku or whatever you eggheads do for kicks on your days off. I'm assigning this case to Peterson."

"But, sir..."

"No buts! Get out of here."

Granger realized he'd hit the point of no return. He rose, started to leave, and the police captain stopped him with a look. "Forgetting something?"

"My badge, sir?"

The chief nodded his head and Granger unclipped his badge from his belt.

"Gun?"

The chief gave another nod, and Granger turned that in too. Then the chief cleared his throat. Granger swallowed hard and surrendered his sunglasses. The captain unceremoniously dropped everything in a desk drawer and slammed it shut. As Granger solemnly walked away, Collins turned to the chief.

"And me, sir?"

"I'd expect some bullshit theory from Granger, but you, detective? I thought you were smarter than that. I'm busting you back to meter maid."

"Good thing I kept the uniform," Collins said, and he slinked deeper into his chair.

Granger sat in his Peugeot contemplating his situation. He turned to the little stack of dog-eared soduku puzzle books scattered on the passenger seat and noticed an evidence bag he'd missed when he'd logged the other bags. He picked it up and started to go back into the station when he had a second thought. He bit his lip and then opened the bag. It was the personal effects of one of the triple homicide vics. He thumbed though the few odds and ends: an Interpol ID, a couple of photographs, a ticket stub, a hand gun, five or six silver bullets, and a business card from a local florist. Something about the card resonated with Granger. Maybe there was a way to salvage his career after all. He looked at the address on the card, grateful he knew the street. His Peugeot squealed out of the parking lot.

The It's Always Spring flower shop was an unpretentious sort of mom and pop store that Seattle was noted for. As Granger waited for the too cheerful owner to finish up with her customer, he was drawn to a display of wolfsbane—"Now in Bloom"—attractively arranged in the front of the store along with some other autumn decor. He'd never seen the lavender buds in person, always assumed they were a fictional plant invented for the movies. *Learn something new every day.* His mind went back to a poem he remembered from an old horror movie, something about autumn moons, blooming wolfsbane, and a curse. *For a few nights a month, a few months a year, even a good man, a man pure at heart, could turn into a vicious monster that killed with reckless abandon.*

Alicia Spring sashayed down the aisle to greet Granger with a big smile and a pierced tongue that made her talk kind of funny. "Interested in the wolfsbane, are you, sir? They are such pretty little flowers this time of year. I can fix you up a nice little bouquet. Would you like that?"

Granger instinctively reached up to remove his sunglasses and then painfully remembered he wasn't wearing any. "I'm a police officer, ma'am, running down a lead in a murder investigation."

"My, my. Murder by wolfsbane. They really are such misunderstood plants, aren't they?" As Granger pondered that, Mrs. Spring put two and two together. Or was it three and three? "Are you by any chance working with those nice little men that came in the other day?"

"The midgets?"

The shopkeeper nodded, a finger to her lips like maybe Granger had said a naughty word. "They say they preferred 'vertically challenged.'"

"Yeah, whatever. Actually, I'm following up on some of their leads."

"Well, I don't think I was able to be of much help, but they did seem interested in any places where I'd made wolfsbane deliveries this month." She scooted back to the counter and flipped through a rolodex, writing an address on a pad of lilac scented paper. "Turned out there was only one."

"The House of Sticks?"

"Yes, a little Chinese takeout restaurant over near the wharf. They get a delivery of wolfsbane every year when it's in bloom. Nothing else any other time, not even on Valentine's Day."

"Do tell, ma'am," Granger said, taking the slip of lilac scented paper in a disposable plastic glove. "Thank you very much." He left, his face stoic as always, but, internally, Granger could barely control his glee. *So, his three little piggies had gone to a house of sticks! But was it to flee from or find the big bad wolf?* Only a trip to the take-out joint would shed some light. Besides, Granger had skipped breakfast, and he was hungry.

Granger was trying to decide if he'd go for the chow mien or the steamed rice with his combination plate when he pulled into a little strip mall and gave the House of Sticks restaurant a quick once-over. It was nestled between a couple of sea food joints and a massage parlor. He spotted a discrete sign in the window of the restaurant that read "Lollipop Guild Friendly."

Granger wasn't sure what that meant until he went inside and realized the restaurant must cater exclusively to midg—er—the "vertically challenged." All the other customers and staff were little people. Even the tables and chairs were dwarf-sized, too. He got some curious looks instantly and definitely felt like he'd stepped into a child's playhouse decked out in Shanghai feng shiu. He asked for the manager as the waitress, a little blond number chewing bubble gum, tried to decide where to seat him.

"This one is fine," Granger said, and he sat down at one of the empty tables near the back. His knees came up near his chin. He felt just like Goldilocks sitting in baby bear's chair. He was nibbling on some crispy fried noodles when the manager, a little man wearing a wild bow-tie, came over and grabbed the chair opposite Granger.

"You're the CSI guy from the TV news report," he said. "The one investigating the triple homicide the other night?"

"Yep," he lied. No point telling the world he was technically off the case.

"You thinking this was some kind of hate crime against little people?"

"I'm not ruling anything out yet," he lied again. "But I am curious why someone here has ordered a wolfsbane delivery once a year for the past eight years."

"Ahh, those little blue flowers," the manager said. "They're for one of our regulars. Funny, she hasn't been in in a few days."

"She?" Granger hadn't considered that his wolf-man might really be a wolf-girl.

"Yeah, Rusty likes them at her table the first full moon of autumn. Says they remind her of the old country."

"Rusty?"

The manager nodded. "Yes, Rusty Pureheart."

Granger practically salivated. "Any idea where I could find her?"

"Don't know how she could be mixed up in any killing nonsense, but Rusty does like to hang out at this biker bar."

Granger was already taking out his pocket note-book. "This bar got a name?"

"Granny's Place," the manager said, then lowered his voice. "Not in a very good part of town if you ask me."

Granger nodded, his mind processing the clues. He flashed back to the redhead he'd seen at the crime scene, the one he'd thought was just a little girl. "Rusty likes motor cycles, and she's got red hair, right?"

"Yep, some of the boys call her Li'l Red." The manager smiled. "Li'l Red Bike Riding Hood." Granger liked the man's sense of humor. The manager leaned forward, a little conspiratorially. "I'm pretty sure you'll find her at Granny's Place." Granger was pretty sure he would too. But he'd need to make a pit stop first.

Granger wasn't much for GPS navigation systems, and he didn't know this part of town very well. The manager of House of Sticks had said the bar was up the interstate, near the Lumber Jack lumber mill, a few miles north of Brick Haven. "You can't miss the lumber yard's giant statue of this big Paul Bunyan-like dude slinging his axe. You can see it clear off the freeway," the manager had said. And he was right.

It was nearly night again, another full-moon inching its way overhead as Granger passed the lumber yard and pulled into the gravel covered parking lot of Granny's Place; a rough and tumble looking wood frame beer and dance bar on the outskirts of nowhere. Granger thought about calling for back-up, but he wasn't even supposed to be on this case. And what did he really have to report anyway? Just a lot of crazy hunches with some vague connections to fairy tales and ambiguous werewolf lore.

Granger took another look at the evidence envelope he'd opened earlier. This time he noticed one of the photos was of a pretty, thirty-something redheaded women, with large, bright eyes. *That must be her*, he thought. *My what big eyes you have, Little Red.* He put a few silver bullets in the gun, stuck the gun in his waist, and then double checked his pocket to make sure his secret weapon was still there. He'd picked it up along the way and thought it was perfect. He knew the three Interpol agents had been chopped to bits before they got a single shot off; so he needed something to buy him time if he needed it. He was pretty sure he would.

There were a lot of motorcycles parked in the lot, a few pick-up trucks too. Granger wondered if he'd be able to recognize the big chopper he'd seen at the crime scene, but all the bikes looked alike to him. Several had wolf emblems and accessories. *Was this a werewolf hangout, maybe?* But then there was also "Hello Kitty" paraphernalia on some of the other bikes. *Did cats and dogs mix it up?*

The telltale twang of country music drifted out of the bar as Granger neared the front porch and adjusted his tie. Damn how he missed his sunglasses. He grit his teeth and put on his best cop swagger as he went through the swinging doors, feeling a little like Gary Cooper in *High Noon*.

He was instantly assaulted with an odor he hadn't smelled so distinctly since childhood. Someone was baking honest to goodness, made from scratch, chocolate chip cookies, just like Granger's granny used to make. He swallowed hard, sauntered over to the bar, and ordered a tall glass of cold milk. He eyed the plate of fresh baked cookies on the counter in front of him. He eagerly reached for one when an elderly hand slapped his wrist hard. Startled, he looked up to see a sweet old lady bartender shaking her head in disapproval.

"You wash your hands, young man?" She spit into a glass and wiped it clean with a rag as she waited for his answer.

"No, ma'am," Granger said, shuffling his feet a bit. "You must be Granny?"

"What makes you say that, sonny?" Not a trace of irony in her voice.

"Just a hunch," he muttered. Then several other barmaids turned around, and they all looked like they could be someone's grandmother too. Granger showed the bartender the picture of the redheaded woman. "I'm a cop, trying to locate this woman. Maybe goes by Rusty."

Granger tried again to sneak a cookie as the bartender reached for the picture. But her other hand flew out of nowhere and slapped his wrist again. Harder than the first time. Granger flinched and sheepishly withdrew his hand. The bartender didn't bat an eye, just adjusted her bifocals a bit. "She's here all the time. Check over by the pool table," she said and pointed to the back. "She'll be easy to spot."

Granger's mind raced forward. *Why? Because of her red hair? Her diminutive stature? Her flea collar?*

"She's always wearing this cute little French beret."

Not tonight she's not! He flashed back to the beret left at the crime scene. As he started to leave, the old woman managed a smile.

"Come back for a cookie once you wash your hands."

Granger nodded, put a five spot on the counter, and gulped down the rest of his milk so fast it left a little white milk mustache. He slapped the glass down on the bar and headed for the pool tables. He eyed the crowd as he walked, wondering why everyone he spotted made a motion like a cat wiping its mouth. Granger never would understand Seattle's curious rituals.

There were two pool tables in the back, near a broken pinball machine. A couple of burly biker types were playing a game of 8-ball on the closer table. A third appeared to be playing a solo game at the other table until Granger noticed the top of a red head move around the far end of the table. Rusty! Her cue stick was taller than her by half, and when she came closer, he saw she was wearing a pink leather jacket that had "Bad Moon Arising" embroidered on the back. She didn't spot Granger right away. She was immersed in her game, eying her next shot. Then she felt it, sensed someone watching her, so she turned to see Granger. They stared at each other a full moment before she decided to speak.

"You? You're the CSI guy from that massacre in Brick Haven," she said, her voice silky smooth with a trace of a French accent. "Heard you had a pretty far fetched idea about what went down there."

"Did you? Your hearing must be pretty acute. Nothing's been in the news."

"My teeth are pretty sharp too. Want to check them out?"

"Not by the hair of my chinny chin chin," Granger said, unable to resist.

"Like I haven't heard that before." She rolled her eyes, and then her ears became more pointed.

"Can we take this outside? I'd kind of like to avoid collateral damage."

"I kind of like an audience." Now her nose started extending, turning more into a snout.

"I really think we should go outside," Granger insisted, revealing a hint of his secret weapon he'd cupped in his hands.

Despite herself, Rusty's mouth watered, her eyes widened in excitement. Her back arched as she sprouted a tail, and it ripped right out of the seat of her jeans. It started to wag a little as the werewolf transformation intensified; there was no holding it back now. The other pool players and bystanders stared in awe, too stunned to move or even utter a word.

"Come on, girl. Follow me." Granger didn't wait for a response, just turned his back to her and headed for the rear exit, making sure she could see his secret weapon at all times.

"Mon dieu! This isn't fair!" she shrieked as her body continued to contort and change, becoming more and more wolf-like every moment. And still she followed, jumping up on the pool table, her razor sharp front claws scratching the green felt covering. She rolled on her back, and her hind claws ripped through her cowboy boots. She rolled back onto all fours and pounced after Granger. More than a few spectators followed.

The back of the bar butted up to the back of the lumber yard. There were a few scattered cars parked here and there, but otherwise it was a pretty open area. *Good place to make a stand*, Granger thought as he stood under the only overhead light, bouncing his secret weapon in his hand. It was a worn and weathered tennis ball. He knew no canine could resist a game of fetch. He just hadn't been sure about werewolves. Now he was.

Little Red had completely transformed into the Big Bad Wolf when she exited the bar, her body covered in a reddish gray fur. A patron got in her way, and she slashed off his head with a single swipe of a clawed paw. The rest of the crowd eased back further as the werewolf pounced on the decapitated head and howled at the moon.

Granger had nerves of steel. He bounced the ball on the ground once, twice, then threw it as hard and far as he could towards the lumber yard. "Fetch!" he shouted, taunting Rusty.

The wolf growled, frustrated beyond belief that she could not resist the compulsive urge to play the childish game. She dropped the bloody head and bounded after the tennis ball with incredible speed. The ball hit the pole that held the giant lumber jack statue and bounced back the other way. The wolf jumped incredibly high and caught the ball in mid-air, her doggy drool-dripping fangs clamping down on it tight.

When she landed, she landed on all fours and stared directly at Granger, venom in her jaundiced eyes. With a few shakes of her powerful jaws, she shredded the tennis ball to smithereens and cast it to the side. *No more games*, she thought. Then she slowly rose back onto her haunches, now three times the height she'd been as a human. She howled once more at the moon. When she turned to face Granger again, he had his gun out and aimed. The wolf didn't rush. She knew the end was near for this meddlesome cop, and she wanted to savor every bite of his demise.

Granger fired six shots back to back. Rusty didn't even flinch. She snarled, her lips curling up like some wicked little dog smile. She flicked her long tongue across her jagged teeth. *Lousy shot*, she thought as the bullets whizzed past way too high. And then, she heard it. The sickly groan of old rusted metal and the tremble of something very big, falling very fast. She turned just as the metal pole holding the giant lumber jack snapped from where Granger's bullets had hit. Six shots, all in a tight line, had serrated the pole. The giant teetered for a second and fell towards the bar. Rusty the werewolf tried to outrace it, but the towering giant was gaining momentum. She risked a look back just as Paul Bunyan's axe went right through her, hitting her with such force it split her in half. Both blood, guts, and gore oozing halves convulsed for a moment and then went still.

Just like in the fable, Granger thought, *the wolf was done in by a wood cutter*. The crowd of bystanders gradually emerged from the shadows and trash dumpsters where they'd been hiding and slowly advanced to get a better look at the dead, bisected werewolf, who was even now starting to morph back into human form. Clumps of red fur dissolved in the wind. There was a smattering of claps that quickly rippled into a loud roar of applause. People patted Granger on the back and gave him the thumbs up. "Way to go, sonny," one old lady said, giving a fist pump. "That bitch deserved what she got."

Yup, the chief had to put him back on active duty now, Granger thought, just as his cell phone chirped. He looked down at the caller ID. *Speak of the devil. Had word of his success spread already?* He flipped open the phone quickly. "Granger," he said matter-of-factly.

"Hate to interrupt your R and R," the chief's staticky voice echoed from the receiver. "But I might have been a bit hasty in giving you some time off."

You think? Granger thought, but he said, "Oh?"

"Yeah. We've just found another goddamn weird John Doe. This vic is burnt to such a crisp. We can only ID him by his shoes. He's wearing some exotic glass slipper. The neighbors all think he was some kind of a goddamn drag-queen vampire."

A cinder-fella and a glass slipper, Granger thought. *Things were really getting interesting.*

The world in this story wasn't ready for uplifted cats, and the felians are still finding their place in a society that doesn't fit them. Kittytown is full of recent change, moral turmoil, and uncertainty about the future. It's the kind of place where scoundrels feel right at home.

HARD SCRATCHING IN KITTYTOWN

Blake Hutchins

I was holding the regular Friday meeting with my buddy José when I first laid eyes on Ming Talbot.

It had been a slow morning. José Cuervo and I were throwing darts. José was winning like always, and it was only my second shot of the day. I'd just missed the eleven for the third time and was considering throwing the rest of the darts at the floor, which I was reasonably sure I could still hit.

Then the door opened and this queen waltzed in. She was svelte and graceful, her seal point coat soft as velvet where it showed through her outfit. Her eyes had that intense China blue that makes Siamese look so arrogant and my blood burn hot.

My whiskers twitched at something else about her: trouble.

Trouble was an old friend from the days before the Change when I ran on four paws. My cannon was in a holster slung behind my chair, and I had a couple of steel balls in the drawer along with my second bottle of José. My spare pair, as I was fond of saying. This wasn't that kind of trouble, though.

I'd spent years of my life as a regular cat before the Change, so there's always a part of me that sees the cat first and has to adjust to the Changed version. This queen's ears sprouted from the sides of her head rather than the top, long and elfin. She was about three feet tall, twenty pounds, all muscle and curve. If Kitties still had tails, hers would have floated behind her.

Mrow, Shady, I told myself. Play it cool. I resisted the urge to lick my palm and slick back my headfur.

She smiled and closed the door behind her with one silky black handpaw. She wore a tight-fitting blue sari pinned at the shoulder with a pearl pin, over a tight-fitting sleeveless gold silk blouse, all set off with a matching embroidered headband. Like most felians, she didn't wear shoes, but she did have a silver and lapis ankle bracelet. It was hard to tell with my tequila-numbed palate, but I caught a whiff of perfume. She was not regular Kittytown, which made me wonder how she'd gotten to my office without getting scratched and sniffed.

"Shadowpaw Jones?" she purred.

"That's what the door says, kitten." I took my footpaws off the table and reached over to hook a suspender trying to sneak off my shoulder. Another couple of years, felian tailors ought to be offering bespoke outfits for toms like me. In the meantime, my clothes fit like a Bast-pissed shopping bag. The bomber jacket hanging by the door, made for a human kid, was the exception. It was real leather. I'd scored it at Goodwill, and it was my pride and joy.

I scowled into my shotglass as the queen took in the Cats in Heat calendar over the couch, the empty hooch bottles, the dog-eared Chandler paperbacks and raggedy catnip toy strewn across my coffee table with a scatter of old sandwich wrappers and grimy popsicle sticks. Some Kitties are naturally tidy. I'm not one of them.

"It's dark in here," she said at last, eyeing the closed blinds.

"I like it that way. It's easier on hangovers."

"Very logical, Mr. Jones." She said with a dazzling smile. "I had a harder time finding you than I expected. Quite a maze you have. Are you the only one here?"

"Yep. It used to be a school. City made it a Felian Entrepreneurial Zone. So far I'm the only taker."

"How lucky for you. May I take a seat?"

"Be my guest." I waved at the two felian-sized chairs in front of my desk. Made of bright yellow and red plastic, and originally for human toddlers, they were an afterthought to the big human-sized couch that dominated the room. Most of my clients were Apes with an interest in finding something or someone in Portland's Kitty community.

After she seated herself, we sniffed the air and did a little ritual grooming. Her elegant silvery fur was luminous compared to my black-on-gray tiger coat. She daubed at her forearm with a delicate pink tongue. Once we'd both sufficiently chilled, I drained my shotglass and poured another. I held up José in invitation, but she declined with a dainty twitch of her ears. I took a restrained sip.

"What do you want?" I said. The liquor sent a wash of comfort across my scalp and down my back. "Miss...?"

"My name is Ming Talbot. You're a private investigator, Mr. Jones."

"That's what the stencil on the door says, kitten. I didn't figure you were here for yowling."

Her bonhomie vanished. "Are you always this rude?"

I showed a little fang. "Yeah."

Siamese blue eyes flashed. "Since you don't appear to get much business, I should think you'd try to be civil."

"You aren't the first one, kitten. Someone referred you to me, or you wouldn't be slumming it in Kittytown. Why not cut to the chase?" I swirled the tequila around a little, took a sloppy lap.

Her whiskers quivered in irritation, but she got down to business. "It's my sister. She's missing. I'm worried."

"You have a ransom note?"

"Not yet. I'm expecting one."

"I've heard of the Talbots. Your humans have a lot of money."

"My family," she corrected me. "I'm—that is, we—are legally adopted."

"So call the cops."

"They said they don't deal with 'stray cases.'"

"Yep. Too busy busting ferals. Did you buzz the SPCA or the Humanes?"

She flattened her ears. "They're overwhelmed. Federal funds for felian assistance haven't been released, they said, so they're way behind."

I nodded, nodding being one of the many Ape habits we'd picked up after realizing humans were basically blind to our body language.

"Okay," I said, "tell me about your sister. She a littermate?"

"No. And we're technically half-sisters. Chen-Yi is from a younger litter with a different father. She's been gone two days."

I grabbed a pen and started scribbling some notes on a raggedy yellow note pad. "Maybe she's on a jaunt? Doin' some yowling?"

Ming sniffed. "Absolutely not. We're not outdoor felians, Mr. Jones. She left the house on Tuesday to go to the groomer, and never returned."

"Did she have an escort?"

"Our driver. His name is Robert Metz."

"Human."

"Yes."

I looked at the ceiling and scratched the back of my neck. "You trust him?"

"He's been with the family for years."

"Great. Where'd he last see her?"

She twitched an ear. "She had him drop her in Kittytown."

Ah, that explained my involvement. "Whereabouts?"

She took a smartphone from her purse and passed a handpaw over the screen several times. "Corner of Fiftieth and Sandy. That's Kittytown, isn't it?"

"Yeah. A rough part. Did he make a stink? The driver, I mean."

"Robert didn't want to leave her there, if that's what you mean, but she was... insistent. You see—"

"I got it," I cut in. "How old is Chen-Yi?"

"Four."

Born after the Change. OK, I marked that little detail. Felians matured fast and learned at a phenomenal rate compared to humans. We didn't know for sure whether our lifespan had increased too, but it was starting to look like we weren't on the old cat scale anymore. I was over twelve and not missing a beat.

"She's plenty old enough to be out and about on her own, I'd say."

Ming looked away, her whiskers quivering with suppressed anger. "Mr. Jones, you don't know my sister. She's young and headstrong."

My prospective client didn't approve of little sister. Interesting. On the other paw, the protective sibling thing was a point in her favor. One place where the Apes had us beat was in social cooperation. Challenge and rivalry came a lot more naturally to felians. On top of that, most Kitties who'd been actual cats for awhile scored even worse on that front. Me, for example.

I made a few notes. "You guys have a cattery pedigree, right?"

"Yes." One of her delicate little ears twitched. "How did you know?"

"The clothes. You had them made special. And Chinese names are typical for the breed. Bet you've got a lot more than Ming and Talbot on your scorecard, kitten. You got purebred written all over you." I cleared my throat and made a half-hearted swipe at tact. "Not that that's a bad thing."

She folded up her phone and put it back in the purse. "Thank you."

"No prob. So you have a pedigree. Those still count in some circles."

"Really, I'd have no idea."

I snorted. "Give me a break, kitten." Felians with pedigrees got first crack at university slots and other bennies. Me? I was alley trash to the Cat Fancy crowd. So was everyone else in America's Kittytowns.

"Just for the record," I said, "let's have your sister's full handle."

She sighed. "If we must."

I tapped my pen against the edge of the desk. After a moment, her eyes dropped. "Alright. Her name is Chen-Yi Bright Silver Huntress Talbot."

"Ain't that a mouthful. OK, kitten—"

Her ears flattened, and those blue eyes turned frosty. "I'm not a kitten, Mr. Jones! I am Ming Starry Queen of Heaven Talbot, if you insist on the whole pedigree business. You can call me Ms. Talbot."

"Whatever you say, Your Highness." I flicked one of my eyebrow whiskers.

She stood, gold-painted claws extended around her purse. "Don't bother, Mr. Jones. I'll go somewhere else."

I waved her back to her seat. "Look, I'm rough around the edges. Comes of being half-feral when the Change hit. But I'm the best. And I know the streets like—"

"Like a junkyard dog, eh?" Her eyes gleamed, and I caught a flare of sexual interest in her scent. Our species was what the Apes called "mercurial" and "promiscuous." And since the Change, we were like the Apes in not being confined to an estrus cycle, but felians just plain didn't have moral hang-ups about mating. Plus, whatever Changed us undid all the previous fixing at one fell swoop. Overnight, humanity found itself sharing the planet with several hundred million new sapients who started breeding like... Well, like cats.

So I stood, handpaws on desk, and gave her a level, no monkey-scat stare that made no secret of my own interest in her. "I'd shred a junk dog's bony ass any night of the week... kitten."

She responded with a throaty purr, and the rest was, as they say, the cat's pajamas. Except without the pajamas.

An hour or so later, after Ming had gone, I slammed down some kibble and coffee and hit the streets. Despite those starry blue eyes of

hers kicking my testosterone into orbit, something about the queen set off warning bells. She was unhappy with little sister, but scared of something, too. I wasn't getting the vibe that her reason for hiring me was entirely motivated by familial loyalty. But she'd left me with a whole raft of people to talk to as well as a happy limbic system, so it was time to go to work.

I wore my bomber jacket, my sling tucked in one of the pockets along with some ammo, the string ends dangling out so they'd be close to paw. I left the cannon—a Glock nine millimeter—in my desk drawer back at the office next to José, where they'd keep each other company.

One of the first things felians glommed onto fast after the Change was the story of David and Goliath. When the dominant species averages about five times your body mass, you look for equalizers. Hence the sling and half-dozen steel balls in the pocket of my bomber jacket. Not as good as a Glock, but less likely to get the cops on your tail. Almost every cat in K-town had fast paws with a sling, though a lot of alley bangers carried throwing stars 'cause they were "cool."

Stupid kittens.

I walked up Sandy between Fiftieth and Fifty-Fifth, which was currently in the claws of the Midnight Tricks, a pretty nasty felian gang. Last month it'd been the Krispy Kats, a.k.a. the Krisps. Before that, the Bitey Boyz. Most felian dominance spats added up to little more than fur loss, but these gangs were plugged into Ape money, so they were tough customers.

The minute I crossed Fiftieth into the hardcore block of K-town, eyes started tracking me. I pretended not to notice.

The street was busy, mostly Kitties but with Apes minding a lot of the shops. A stew of felian musk and piss-markings mixed with the odors of smog and oil and asphalt, and the occasional welcome sting of coffee. On the way I passed a Plaid Pantry convenience store, a beat-up Sequential ethanol station, a boarded up hardware store, a few graffiti-scruffed buildings with broken windows that stood out like missing teeth, and the usual scatter of bars and sex shops. An SPCA-AA flyer stapled to a phone pole competed with a lime-colored ad for a Kitty punk band called the Dead Pelicans. I'd heard 'em before. Catfights had better harmony.

Stray as it was, K-town wasn't all bad. Mamas pushed their litters along in toy strollers. Toms and queens in a variety of fur patterns and secondhand clothes cluttered windowsills and sidewalks to catch some sun and a smoke. Under an overpass, a group of young toughs busted moves to a yowly-hop tune that sounded like a half-dozen felians getting murdered to a jungle-speed beat.

A few blocks later I was out of K-town, and in Portland proper, where the Apes play and a Kitty does not go—unless you're a smart ass like me. It took me ten minutes to get a cab that would take me, but soon I was headed uptown.

The groomer's was a modest-looking place in the ground floor of a brick building on a shady, tree-lined street in northwest Portland. The awning over the door read Oasis of Bast, bounded with little cat-cartouches at each end.

Wind chimes sounded a mellow chord as I entered; the place smelled of catmint, sage, and lemon. Soft jazz played in the background, accompanied by occasional bird chirps. I felt instantly out of place. I was a walking advertisement for secondhand alley cat cool in K-town, but here I stuck out like a dead rat on a banana split.

In front of me was a glass counter flanked by giant ferns, the front section low enough to accommodate felians. Behind the glass were bottles of various fur care products and perfumes, along with tchotchkes like jade obelisks and Egyptian cat statues. I resisted the urge to puke a hairball. The back wall sported several large mirrors.

"May I help you?" the receptionist asked. She was human, young, with a tanned hide, tight coils of reddish headfur, big dark eyes, perky posture. She reminded me of a squirrel. My Ape buddy Flanagan would have liked her.

I smiled. "Yes, ma'am. My name is Jones. I'm a private investigator hired by one of your clients, Ming Talbot."

"Oh," she said, clearly recognizing Ming's name. "Yes."

"I'd just like to ask a few questions about her sister Chen-Yi." Her eyes widened, and I added, "Don't worry, I've had all my shots."

She managed a weak smile. "Let me get my manager."

"Thanks." I stayed standing rather than sit in one of the felian-sized lounge chairs. Best not to intrude on their turf more than necessary.

They took long enough to account for a phone call checking on me with Ming. The manager was a heavier, shorter human with bleached headfur, caked on makeup, lots of gold rings on her fingers and ears. She wobbled toward me on gold high-heeled sandals I'm told Ape males find attractive.

I introduced myself with a little bow and offered my card. "I won't take much of your time, ma'am." I looked around. "Nice place. I can see why Miss Talbot thinks so highly of you."

She looked at me like I was a pee stain on the carpet. "Thank you, Mister..." she glanced at my card, "...Jones. We do our best. I'm Sandra Schwartz, the owner. Would you please come to my office?"

"Sure thing." I followed her out of fern land into a short hallway lit by a couple of Egyptian art deco sconce lamps. We stopped in a small room with felian chairs and a desk against one wall. A few family photos sat on the desk, all featured a couple of dark-headed kits. Papers were neat and in their trays. A painting of the Nile featuring happy Egyptians and plenty of cats occupied the wall behind me. Ever since the change, Egyptian cat stuff was the bomb. The canopic jars gave me the creeps, personally.

"So," I began after we took our seats. "I'm here about Chen-Yi Talbot—"

"Whatever is going on with her, we don't know about it," Schwartz said. "It's not our business once a client leaves our doors."

"Fine. Just let me ask my questions, and I'll be out of your fur. I believe she was here for a grooming appointment?"

"Yes."

"And she comes here Tuesdays, right?"

She sighed and tapped a long gilded nail on the desk. "Yes. Massage and combing, nail trimming, aromatherapy session."

"Sounds nice."

"You should try it sometime, Mr. Jones." But not here, alley trash, her cold tone said.

"Thanks. Maybe I will." I produced my notepad. "What time does Ms. Talbot usually leave?"

"I wouldn't have any idea. I'm not on the floor much."

"Is she alone?"

"Oh, yes. Her car drops her at the door."

"She's a regular, right?"

"Yes. Every Tuesday at two. It's a routine booking."

"She gets the same treatment?"

She gave me a smug look. "That's what our regulars do, Mr. Jones. That's why it's routine."

"She always leave at three?"

"Of course not. Her driver comes at four...." she trailed off.

Gotcha, mouseygirl, I thought. Little kitty ain't so dumb after all.

"So, Sandy," I said, putting my pad down. "Did Chen-Yi leave at four this time or earlier?"

"I don't think I want to continue this," she said, her face red.

"OK by me. I'll tell Ms. Talbot how well you cooperated. I'll be sure to mention that to the cops too, and the newspapers, and I'll make sure to mention she disappeared from here. Oh, I mean leaving here. Honestly, who knows what I'll say?"

She chewed on that for a few seconds.

"Look," I continued. "Chen-Yi's apparently a sweet kitten. I don't know why you're being such a bitch. She's missing, I'm trying to find her. It's that simple. Every day she's gone makes the odds worse."

She looked stricken, and I decided she might not be so bad under all that paint and reflexive bitchiness. A lot of humans loved cats but resented felians. Especially pushy ones like me.

"What time did she leave?" I asked again.

"I—I don't know. The usual time."

"Four?"

She nodded, lips tight.

"Her driver says she wasn't here when he came to pick her up." According to Ming, that is. The driver was next on my list of stops.

"Really." She was trying, but couldn't quite manage warmth.

"We'd better ask her beautician, huh?"

"I guess so."

"You keep a guest log?" I asked.

"We have a sign-in sheet for walk-ins, but not for regulars like Ms. Talbot. I'm sorry."

"Don't be," I said, dialing down to a more diplomatic tone now that I was getting what I wanted. "You're being very helpful. Who's the beautician?"

"That would be Mindy. She helps Ms. Talbot with her nails and aromatherapy. There would also be Amber, the masseuse. I'll go get them." She started for the door, but I held up a handpaw.

"Hold it a sec. Before you grab Mindy and Amber, I have a couple more questions." Curiosity and the cat, I figured, and plunged on. "Does Ms. Ming Talbot come here?"

"On occasion, yes." Schwartz seemed a whisker frostier on this subject.

"She's not a regular?"

She shook her head. "Hmhn-nnh. Quite generous when she's here, though. I understand she's a trendsetter in her circles."

"Of course, you roll out the red carpet for her."

"We treat her like all our other clientele..." She stopped herself. "Perhaps with a bit more care."

"She has a temper," I ventured, following the spoor of a theory.

"I didn't say that." She glanced away. "She has high standards, so I make a point of checking in with her personally."

Great. My latest fling was looking like less and less of a nice kitty. I pushed aside the memory of her ruff in my teeth and concentrated on the job.

"OK, let's talk to your girls. Then I'm out of your fur."

Amber wasn't much help, but Mindy turned out to be one of those observant folks who really liked felians. Maybe too much. Not in a kinky way, though. She was just a cat person who wasn't bothered that we looked like little fuzzy elfs these days. She had short bleached blond headfur and little enameled cat earrings. Before the Change, she probably put out food for strays like me. I could tell she was itching to stroke my head and offer me treats.

Those days are long gone, kiddo, I thought, addressing myself as much as her. We're out of Eden now, such as it was. I remembered when scoring a saucer of milk was the dietary highlight of my week. Eat, sex, fight, sleep, repeat. I still dreamed about it.

"Miss Talbot's such a sweetie," she said in response to my first question about Chen-Yi. "I really enjoy working with her. She's totally open about everything. You can just talk and talk with her. She has such soft fur—"

I took a hard grip on the scruff of my patience. "Yup, she's a sweetheart. Did you see anything unusual the last time she was here?"

She chewed on that. "Yup, OK. I sure did. She cut her appointment short by maybe... mmm... a half-hour? That would have been about, mmm... three thirty. She hadn't finished her manicure. I was massaging her distal phalanx to loosen up the claw joint—"

I leaned forward. "How'd she look when she left? Upset? Sad?"

"Oh, just the opposite. She was glowing because of her tomcat friend."

"Tomcat friend? You mean a boyfriend?"

"Oh, yes! At least it looked that way. He was handsome, sleek, black, quite a charmer."

"You're sure it was a tom?"

"Definitely. He was wearing a suit."

"What kind of suit?"

She frowned. "I don't remember. White shirt, or maybe gray. Tie, but I don't remember the color. His clothes were baggy, like they didn't fit right. But not as much as yours. Oops. Sorry."

More stray than purebred, I thought. "No, that's great. Where'd they go?"

"Across the street, arm in arm. That's all I remember." Mindy sat back and put her hands on her thighs. "So romantic."

"Think," I prompted. "Anything else?"

"Maybe they got into a car. I wasn't really paying attention very long."

Ming hadn't mentioned Chen-Yi's boyfriend. It seemed unlikely she wouldn't know about him. From what I'd heard about Chen-Yi's open personality, she'd have dropped some clues.

"Mindy," I asked, "did Chen-Yi happen to mention anything about her guy?"

"Oh yeah, that's the funny part I remember now. She mentioned she loved smoke, right?" She giggled. "I thought at first she'd started smoking—cigarettes, you know? And I told her that wasn't good for her health. But it turned out she meant this boyfriend. It was his name. Isn't that cute?"

"Cute. Sure. Does he smoke?"

She shrugged.

"Smoke. OK," I said. "Any idea where he lives? What he does?"

Mindy shrugged again. "I don't know. She said he didn't care about her money, and that meant a lot to her. She wanted to travel, you know? See the world with the right guy, that kind of thing."

"Thanks," I said, closing my little book. "You've been really helpful."

She beamed and nodded, sending her earrings swinging.

I waved goodbye to her and her boss, who'd been hovering in the scenery trying not to glower, and let the door tinkle shut behind me.

Back in K-town I went to my regular watering hole, named Ms. Kitty's, appropriately enough, a felian tavern owned by an enormous calico named Winchee. At over forty-five pounds, Winchee wasn't a queen to mess with. I was a beefy thirty-three myself, mostly muscle, and I wouldn't want to throw down with her. But we got along fine. She had my usual poison lined up and waiting by the time I reached the bar and hopped up on the human-sized barstool.

"Shadowpaw," she greeted me with a blink and an ear twitch. Behind the bar she'd rigged a sort of catwalk setup so she could reach the drinks and serve her customers.

"Winchee. How's things?" I took a couple of laps of tequila. The place was quiet enough, it being early afternoon in the wake of the lunch rush. A few strays slumped at felian-low tables. The air tasted of smoke and tom musk.

She looked around and then leaned in. "Rumor is, Night Market is comin' to town."

"Damn." That was news. The Night Market was a shadier-than-dark mobile bazaar rumored to move all sorts of nasty illegal stuff. It moved up and down the West Coast. No one knew for sure who the backers were—it could be anyone from the Mafia to the Jamaican cartels to Elvis. When the Night Market was in town, Kittytown went from dark to cut-your-throat-in-a-second dark. And I was trying to find a lost kitten in it. Great.

I tipped my hat back. "I sure would like to finish my current job before it gets here. Maybe you can help. I'm looking for an uptown queen, kitten. Siamese. Dropped off in K-town four days ago and—" I waved a handpaw. "Poof. *Desaparecido.* Any nip on that? Lord T's boys haven't seen or heard a whisker."

She shook her head. "Ain't sniffed nothin' on that. But if I hear anything on it, I'll buzz you."

She nodded. I took my glass to a corner table and used my cell to call Flanagan.

It took a few seconds for him to answer, but he picked up just before it went to the cop shop voice mail.

"Hey," he answered.

"Hey," I said. "Got a sec?"

"Hold on." I heard Ape chatter in the background, a burst of laughter, and he was back. "What up, dog?" he said. That was Kenny Flanagan. Bizarre sense of humor, even for a dog lover. But he was a good guy, a friend, so I didn't hold his slobbery companions against him.

"I need a background check."

"Maybe. If it's quick. Department frowns on strays using the database."

"C'mon. I don't ask that much."

He sighed, and I heard the characteristic inhalation that signaled a pull on a cigarette. "Okay, buddy, okay. What's the name?"

"Three names. First, Yi Shen Talbot. Missing cat case. Princess from a fat cat family."

"Ah." Flanagan was silent for a few moments. "Got anything yet?"

"I'm just getting started. The second one is Robert Metz, works for the Talbots as a driver."

"And the third?"

"That's more complicated. Can you run a string search on 'smoke' with a K-town address?"

"Portland or Vancouver?" he asked. Vancouver was on the other side of the Willamette River, across the state line in Washington. Its Kittytown only took up a couple of blocks.

"Start with Stumptown." I lapped my drink and thought about Siamese eyes.

"Feral or poster?"

"Hell if I know. Probably feral."

"I'll do what I can, but Christ, Shady, you know how many feral and stray cats were prowling the Metro before the Change?"

"Thousands. Litters of thousands."

"Right, so the Kitty Census is hit or miss on registering ferals."

"But only for old furballs like me," I reminded him. "If 'Smoke' was born post-Change, you ought to have a trace on him."

"Yeah, maybe. Like I said, I'll do what I can. Let me call you back."

"Deal. And thanks." I closed my cell and nursed my drink.

About twenty minutes later, Flanagan called with the goods. Nothing on Yi Shen. He had twenty-six possible leads on Smoke. Eighteen had addresses, all in K-town, so I started there. I went back to my office, grabbed my electric Kitty scooter, and hummed off to do the legwork. Not as boring as you'd think, since it was a lot like hunting.

Three hours later, I'd crossed nine off my list and was on name number ten: one Smoke Skimble, a six-year old according to his date of birth, residing in Northeast smack in the heart of K-Town. His den turned out to be in a weathered two-story, stucco-faced apartment building surrounded by a narrow lawn of yellowing grass. My boy was in Number Sixteen, assuming Flanagan's list was accurate.

I tramped up a flight of concrete steps onto a breezeway carpeted with rubber shag, made my way past flaking siding and the smell of stale piss until I got to Sixteen. The smell of felian musk was strong, with practically every intersection, turnabout, and doorway sporting a jumble of marker scents from the local toughs.

I couldn't reach the knocker without jumping, typical of Ape-built housing, so I tried the doorbell. Nothing. Then my nose caught a whiff of something disturbing. The Kitty sense of smell lost a step with the

Change, but it was still yards and furlongs better than Ape noses. I leaned against the door and caught the tell, despite the floral blanket of air freshener.

It was the smell of death.

Loosened bowels and an undercurrent of blood, to be precise. I could tell the corpse had been a meat eater, but not if it was Kitty or human. I suspected human on the basis of sheer volume overcoming the air freshener.

I cocked an ear and looked around. It was just after four on a warm summer Friday. People were getting started with the weekend. Nobody was around, meaning I didn't see anyone. I ought to have called the cops, but I slipped out my lockpicks instead. Luckily, this door didn't have a deadbolt, or I'd have had to bust a window.

Moments later, I stood in a closet-sized living room decked out with dark brown shag carpet and matching fake wood paneled walls. A couple of felian-sized chairs and a couch and coffee table sized for Apes filled the space. I didn't hear anyone breathing, and my whiskers weren't picking up air movement. I followed my nose to the kitchen.

The body lay on the linoleum on its belly, blood oozing from the back of the head. Human, male, black head fur with a scruff of beard around the mouth and chin. Overweight, reasonably well-dressed, meaning clean (except for the blood, of course) dress shirt, slacks, loafers. Cause of death was obvious: the back of the vic's skull sported a dent you could have poured a shot into.

The killer had to be human. Kitty muscle density was a lot better pound for pound, but the height of the fatal blow was a giveaway, and for something like this, humans had way better leverage.

How'd the killer surprise the vic? I didn't find anything interesting on the counter, no papers, no coffee machine, nothing to hold anyone's attention. Someone had to distract the guy long enough for the partner to sneak up. Either that, or the vic had been dealing with people he trusted.

I put on my rubber gloves, keeping my claws well-sheathed, and went through his pockets, careful not to leave any of my own hairs. No wallet, no ID, no keys, and oddly enough, no scent aside from human-normal. The bottom of one pocket yielded a crumpled scrap of paper with a phone number and an extension. That stiffened my whiskers. Couldn't put my claw on why. I tucked the paper into my jacket pocket.

When I shifted him to get into the front pocket, I noticed two things. First, he'd been dead long enough for rigor mortis to set, and since his body was room temperature, I guessed he hadn't been kicking for at least a couple of hours. Second, he was still wearing a ring, the fat kind some humans kept from their high school days. Flanagan still wore his. I had to use soap to work the ring off, but it was worth it.

The inside read *RWM* in loopy italic capitals.

Robert Metz. The Talbots' driver. I wasn't a big believer in coincidence.

Curiouser and curiouser, but I'd found the right Kitty to lead me to Chen-Yi. I slipped the ring back where it belonged, put the hand back where I'd found it. No sense tainting the crime scene any more than I already had.

I checked out the back rooms. The place was furnished like an empty box. The bedroom held a mattress on the floor and a cardboard dresser under the window, but that was it. Under the mattress, I found a couple of magazines. Nasty stuff with titles like *Furgash* or *Shaved Pussy*. Kitty porn, marketed to humans. One of the darker parts of the post-Change era was the sex market. I put the mags back with distaste, wanting to go home and give myself a full-body bath.

The bathroom wasn't much better. A dispenser of liquid soap sat on the counter. The lemon scent of cleanser drowned out everything, so I opened the window. Someone had wiped down the counters to eliminate telltale scent. The absence of hair indicated that same someone had vacuumed as well.

This was a lot of trouble to cover a Kitty's tracks. Unless the Kitty was rich enough to hold for ransom.

I knew some tricks of my own, though. We still shed a lot, just like pre-Change. Lots of little fine hairs like a vapor trail. We do it when we're nervous, and they get everywhere. Sure enough, a few strands of Kitty hair clung to the bottom edge of the cupboard. Some were silvery felian hairs, just like ones I'd scraped off my tongue that morning. My bet was they were from Ming's sister. Their scent reminded me of Ming, but different.

The others were odd. Mostly white, but black like they'd been dipped in ink for a third of their length. Natural color, but nothing I'd ever seen before.

Enough. Time to call the cops. I stepped into the hallway and took out my smartphone to call Flanagan when I heard a shoe scrape outside the front door. Several shoes, in fact, and human breathing along with it. A human wouldn't have heard a thing.

I bolted back to the bathroom. If these were cops, I had a tough explanation ahead of me. If they were thugs, I wanted to meet them even less. The window was open, and as luck had it, there wasn't a screen. I sprang onto the sill. Behind me, the apartment door crashed open.

"Police!" a human shouted.

They didn't have a line of sight to the bathroom, and I didn't hang round long enough for them to get one.

At least, that was the plan. I didn't count on a bullet punching through the glass next to me, followed by the crack of the report coming from outside. If it had hit me, it'd have been the equivalent of a human shot by an tank shell. I jumped, fighting not to go into full-blown panic mode.

For a Kitty, a two-story drop is nothing. Our skeletons are way more shock-absorbent than those of Apes. I hit the ground running. Another shot clipped the junipers behind me as I whipped around the corner. I had to get somewhere safe fast, while my stamina held out. Felians were a lot faster over short distances, but humans had the edge on endurance. If I didn't get clear pronto, there was no question in my mind who would catch whom.

I hadn't spotted the shooter. From the caliber indicated by the sound of the report, it had to be an Ape. But who was dumb enough to open fire with cops around?

I paused in the shadow of a rhododendron hedge to catch my breath and think. Best not to head back to my scooter right away. I crossed the street and slipped behind a rack of beat up scooters and partly dismantled Ape kid-sized bikes with chains trailing limp on the concrete. A couple of strays sprawled on a Shady stretch of sidewalk, their mangy coats and filthy clothes a sign of dismal health. I stopped to lay a couple of bucks on these guys. Number one rule when you're being hunted in the city is not look like you're on the lam.

"Thanks, tom," one of them croaked.

"'S'alright," I said. "Get yourself a decent place, huh?"

More likely he'd hunt up some crank—the drug problem was just as bad for us as for Apes.

I left them and went a little farther before ducking into the next dive I came across, a windowless shack called The Ninth Life. It had a Kitty-size door built into the regular one, like most places in K-town. Lights were dim, even for a Kitty bar, but not so much that I couldn't see how the scantily clad queen at the bar gave me the eye. I went to the bar and ordered a bowl of water, tequila back.

"Hot day, huh?" said the bartender, a ginger tom with one eye blinded by cataracts. He pushed the water in front of me.

"Uh-huh," I replied, grateful for the drink. "Make that the good stuff, OK?"

"You got it."

I looked down at my jacket's sleeve. I'd scraped it along the bathroom windowsill during my escape, marring the leather. Caught between the creases of the scraped leather was a single red hair. I picked it up and smelled it. Familiar.

Hoo boy.

The tequila came. I took a lap without tasting it and tried to organize my thoughts while the liquor burned my tongue.

The way I lined things up, Ming was playing games in an effort to take her little sister out of the picture. Why, I didn't know. It could be precedence in a will, sheer jealousy, a stolen mate. Occam's razor said money. Ming was working with this Smoke tom to yank Chen-Yi's chain, seduce her and get her off the radar. For that matter, Ming had probably been pulling Smoke's tail as much or more than she'd pulled mine, if she was talking marriage. Poor sap.

Chen-Yi had never been dropped off to wander in Kittytown; she'd never stumbled into gang trouble. Chen-Yi had been taken somewhere else instead, like Smoke's place. The driver knew about it or was a part of the plan. Maybe he had second thoughts or tried blackmail, but he was killed to cover the tracks. When I arrived at Smoke's little den, someone knew I was there and called the cops. That meant someone was waiting for me, probably the same person who shot at me. Maybe the shooter wanted me to panic and get picked up by the cops.

Possibly Chen-Yi was dead, but I didn't think so. She was too valuable. The Night Market was happening, and a pretty, elegant Kitty could command a high price to the right pervert, and that was one industry that saw Kitties as a huge opportunity right from the first days of the Change. Sadly enough, of the Apes out there who got off on that stuff, some had plenty in the financial department and nothing on the moral compass side.

What really bothered me was that the red hair I'd found on my jacket smelled of Flanagan. Of course, I'd been around him before, a bunch of times, and could have missed the hair on my jacket. But it'd been stuck on that scraped spot.

Damn it.

Was he the one who'd killed Metz? And shot at me? I got a sick feeling thinking about it. If he was headed for divorce, he might need the money, but I never figured him for the type to cross the line.

Or shank a buddy. I took another lap of the tequila. It wasn't top shelf, but it was decent.

The story was getting uglier all the time. One thing I couldn't put a claw on was my involvement. Why did Ming hire me? Second thoughts? To make herself look good to the police?

Any way you bit it, I wasn't happy about being a pawn in someone else's game. So I was about to rearrange the pieces.

The question I needed to answer was where the Night Market was going to happen. The street had plenty of rumors, but one thing seemed certain: it never cropped up in the same place twice.

I pulled out the piece of paper I'd gotten from Metz's body. The phone number had looked familiar, so I pulled my cell and checked the numbers there. Nothing. Hell with it. With a nod to the bartender, I hopped off my seat and wandered toward the back of the place, pretending to need the bathroom. But like most bars, there was an office in the back. Like most offices, there was a phone on the desk. I punched in the number and waited.

The phone rang once on the other side, then picked up. "Narcotics," a gruff Ape voice said. "Karpinski."

"Officer Karpinski," I said. "I'm calling for Flanagan."

"He ain't here."

"Has everything been resolved?"

"Who is this?"

I decided to take a gamble. "I'm working for you-know-who, Officer. Things are a little tense right now. She wants to know the status of things, you understand."

"You shouldn't call me here. I'm on the clock."

"Just doing my job. The boss wants to know if she's clear for the meet."

A pause. "No patrols around Foley's at all tonight. And she won't have to worry about the other guy, neither."

"The driver?"

"Nah, the P.I. He oughta be taken care of by now. Flanagan doesn't know, so don't tip him, 'K?"

"Got it. I'll pass the news on to the lady." I hung up.

Ming's motivation had just come clear. And I had a sinking feeling I knew why she was doing it.

I went back to my office and strapped on the cannon, a nine-mil Glock 26 semiautomatic with reduced trigger pressure, ten-round magazine. It was good for small felian hands, though I still had to use a two-handed grip to protect my wrists. Other felians used custom-crafted, kitty-sized guns, but these were typically .22 calibers with limited stopping power. In my view, the capability to drop a full-grown Ape in one shot was handy. I tucked an extra magazine in my jacket pocket, just in case.

Almost ready. I racked the slide to chamber a round before returning the pistol to the holster. I'd have put the safety on if this model had one, but Glock used something they called "safe action." Hopefully I didn't blow a hole in my ass by accident.

My options were limited. The cops were in on a crooked deal. My client was tail-deep in it. My best friend appeared to be part of it as well, which made my chest hurt. The smart thing would be to get lost for a week, then come out to collect my fee and watch Ming shed a few crocodile tears.

Chen-Yi wouldn't let me. I knew what it was like to be by myself, but there was a difference between being solitary and being alone. Chen-Yi was alone. Her lover had betrayed her. Her sister sold her out. Someone had to keep faith, even if it was a scarred up, alcoholic, middle-aged tom with a smart mouth.

The Foley Building was an old city-block-sized indoor mall that the city had stopped tearing down and then rebuilt, hoping to attract commercial renters, but it had sat empty for two years. An ideal spot for a clandestine market. An economic rave.

There was an airshaft grate at ground level and I went in through it. An Ape would have made a tight fit, but for someone my size, it wasn't difficult. I made my way nice and slow toward the interior, toward the distant sounds and smells that came down the shaft. Some human was playing country radio on crappy speakers. Felians couldn't stand that music. Too many years of cats being killed by hicks with shotguns.

When I stopped crawling, I was peering out of a screen into the main room of the old indoor mall. It wasn't much more than a mildewed box with a concrete floor. I figured the mildew covered my scent as much as it made my nose run. The air vent was at ground level, but my dark striped fur pattern offered decent camouflage unless someone shone a flashlight into the shaft and reflected the beam off my eyes.

The place crawled with Apes, attended by a few Kitties who mostly looked like they were fetching beers and hooking up electronics. At one end stood a stage with a couple of small speakers and a mike. A spotlight sat on a poker table set up in the midst of several rows of chairs. I estimated seating for about fifty altogether; this would be an exclusive auction.

I was no dumb cat. No way was I going to try to play hero to break up this love fest. I had to find Chen-Yi now, if they had her on-site. From what I'd heard of the Night Market, the hosts threw it together at the last minute, then paged the "guests." My bet was they brought everything in ahead of time to check it and keep an eye on it. The more variables to juggle, the more complex the task. I backed down the shaft and checked out the adjoining rooms, taking as much time as I could bear to move quietly and listen carefully. Fortunately, that was something we felians were made for, even with this monkey-aping body.

Bingo. I followed the smell of smoke to a room that appeared to be an old office. It was twelve foot square and mostly empty, except for scattered construction leavings and... damn it.

A human with a down coat and a knit cap sat and smoked. The door was closed, and a cigarette butt still smouldered on the floor next to the threshold. Behind him was a standing metal locker bank painted bright blue and sporting padlocks on the doors. Looked new, like it'd been hauled in for the occasion.

The smell of smoke made it hard, but my nose didn't pick up anyone else. I didn't hear any other breathing. But I was willing to bet Chen-Yi was in one of the lockers.

I had to get this burly Ape out of the way, and I figured I could take him if I moved fast. A gentle testing push told me the air vent cover here wasn't screwed in. I pulled out my sling and slipped a steel ball into the pouch, then looped one end of the thong around my forefinger and took a solid grip on the other end, pouch in my palm.

With a deep breath, I kicked out the grate cover and sprang onto the floor, releasing the sling pouch. The cover clattered on the floor, and the guy started halfway to his feet, twisting in the direction of the noise. I whipped the sling in a tight overhand arc like a flail. The ball connected with a solid thunk right on his forehead. He slid off the bench like his bones had turned to water, and lay unmoving. I gathered up the sling and ball and tried not to feel bad. Heart beating fast, I stepped over a broken plank and a couple of rebar rods and checked the lockers.

All of them were occupied, which made me furious. I found the right one by scent. The padlock was a cheap one, not the kind designed to survive a nuke. I could have shot it off, but that would bring the thugs that much faster. I fetched one of the rebar pieces and jammed it through the arc of the lock, braced myself against the locker door, and pushed. Pound for pound, felians are a lot stronger than humans. Not enough to match the overall muscle mass of an adult human, but we could exert a helluva lot more force than a thirty-pound child. The lock snapped with a sharp ping.

I flung the locker open and pulled out the kitten. She'd been tied up with nylon straps and a ball gag to keep her from chewing her bonds off. There wasn't any time to do more than sling her over my shoulder in a fireman's carry and beat paws back for the air vent. The felians I left behind haunted me. Someone was going to pay for this.

As I trotted down a grimy back alley through the chill Portland night, Chen-Yi's weight over my shoulder, I started to feel confident.

Until I heard the dogs.

No mistaking the skritch-skritch-skritch of their claws on concrete. The lack of barking meant they were trained guard mutts, which meant a fluff-and-scream routine wouldn't spook them. I caught their whiff a heartbeat later. They'd be following my tracks rather than pulling my scent out of the breeze. Small consolation as I got ripped into kitty sushi.

"Sorry, kitten," I told Chen-Yi. "We're dog chow. Me, anyway." I laid her down at the base of a dumpster and pulled the Glock. Holding it in a two-handed grip, I faced the dogs charging up the alley.

Rottweilers. Great.

I felt bad about plugging mutts, to be honest. They were poor domesticated dumbasses who didn't know any better. It wasn't their fault they worked for the Man. The bad Man, anyway. But if it was me or them, I'd take as many with me as I could.

They were quiet, at least by human standards, but they growled as they came. Felian night vision and superior motion sensitivity let me pick off the lead one right away. Kitties turned out to be natural shooters. The white coats blamed it on predator instincts when this detail came out, and the Pentagon types got giddy. Probably the only place a Kitty found a red carpet waiting was in recruiting stations. Downside was, when our blood was up, we didn't stay patient long, which included little things like following orders, staying put, and so forth.

The second mutt I pegged at point-blank range as he sprang from about eight feet away. I sidestepped his falling body and tried to reacquire the other targets. The muzzle flashes dazzled me, plus the gunshots were deafening to my sensitive Kitty ears. If my whiskers hadn't picked up the air currents of mutt number three, I'd have been a chew toy. I leaped straight up and fired wildly at the ground as he passed under me. I landed just in time for him to turn on his tail and slam into me. The Glock dropped away while we went into a rolling tumble. The world turned into a wall of clashing teeth and dog breath. My leather jacket kept him from getting a grip right away, and that was the break I needed.

I sank my claws into each side of the son of a bitch's muzzle, bit his nose and hung on for all I was worth. He tried like hell to shake me off, growling and crying as he banged me into the turf and pawed at me. Meanwhile, I jammed my size threes into the soft part of his throat and kicked for all I was worth, ripping my toeclaws through the loose skin. I got decent traction. A few seconds later, doggy wasn't trying to bite me anymore; he was trying to get away. I hissed and gave him a few extra kicks, then turned him loose. He fled, yelping piteously, leaving the hot scent of blood in his wake.

I coughed and spat to clear the taste of dog snot from my palate, then patted myself to make sure Lassie hadn't run off with part of me trailing from his gumline. I seemed to be intact, always a plus in any tom's book.

After retrieving the Glock, I gathered up Chen-Yi and staggered on down the alley. The adrenaline surge was ditching me with a huge payback of fatigue. We felians didn't get it as bad as Apes, but I wasn't going to get very far very fast. I thought about the cop I'd talked to on the phone. If the crooked cops were paid to stay clear, they could be paid to set up a dragnet for a rogue Kitty. I needed something to get their attention, buy me a window to get Chen-Yi to safety. I crouched behind a van while a black and white cruised by a block ahead. For a second, I imagined I caught a whiff of smoke again from the thug I'd dropped at the Foley.

"Great," I muttered. "The Marlboro Ape back there ruined my nose—"

Wait. That gave me an idea.

Handpaws shaky, I pulled my phone and made a 911 call. Where there was smoke...

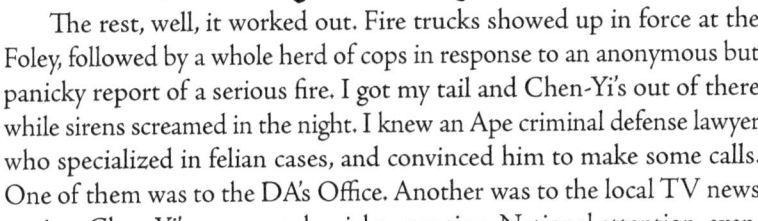

The rest, well, it worked out. Fire trucks showed up in force at the Foley, followed by a whole herd of cops in response to an anonymous but panicky report of a serious fire. I got my tail and Chen-Yi's out of there while sirens screamed in the night. I knew an Ape criminal defense lawyer who specialized in felian cases, and convinced him to make some calls. One of them was to the DA's Office. Another was to the local TV news station. Chen-Yi's story got the right attention. National attention, even.

Turned out a couple of the Night Market guys got picked up after all, and a firefighter had discovered a room with a dead man and lockers holding a bunch of felian kidnap victims. I kept my name out of things, for the most part. The public part, anyway. The official story was that Chen-Yi had escaped on her own and called 911. I had my fee from Ming, which I figured I'd earned.

Ming? She just vanished. We Kitties have a finely tuned sense on when to take a powder. Turned out the Talbots had put Chen-Yi first in their will, which pretty much explained everything about her motives. My guess was I'd been hired to throw suspicion off her by convincing people she was really worried about her poor sister. In the end, it seemed a really human thing to do, which didn't surprise me. After all, we felians hadn't had time to figure out how not to get sucked into the corrupt world of the Apes. But it meant I needed a meeting with José or maybe Jamison to kill the memory of her scent from my brain.

One loose end was all mine to tie up.

I came into the cop shop a few days after Chen-Yi's escape and looked up Flanagan. His desk was occupied by stacks of case reports and a monitor with a peeling Seahawks sticker plastered on the rim. He finished a phone call, replaced the receiver on its cradle, and managed a weak smile as he rotated his chair toward me. He looked like he hadn't slept in days.

"Hey Shady, that case of yours turned out pretty hot."

"Yeah," I said. "Thanks for the help." I paused and laid a handpaw on the back of a chair, flexed my claws so he could see. "No one else knew the addresses I was checking out the other day."

He blinked and cleared his throat before answering. "I didn't know what was going down with you, dude. I swear."

I didn't say anything. After a long moment, he rubbed his temple with a beefy hand, then let out a sigh. "Divorce lawyers are expensive.

Figured I'd send you on a goose chase, keep you busy. I heard about the shots fired. I didn't think... Jesus. Why couldn't you just lie low?"

"I got a little integrity problem, I guess. It's called doing my job." I raised my voice to emphasize the last three words.

"Jesus, keep it down, would you? Those were my dogs you killed." His voice was low, his tone plaintive. "I trained 'em."

"Cry me a river." I showed some fang. "There were four young queens being sold into the worst kind of slavery, and you and I know you were part of it. The technical term is 'accessory,' but let's just call it 'dirty.'"

He jerked his gaze away, the scent of fear coming off him hard and ripe, like a rat that suddenly realizes it's about to be dinner. Pushing himself to his feet, he went to confer with another Ape at another desk. When he came back, he sat down slowly, like an old man. "You didn't give up my name." There was a question in his eyes.

"Karpinski said you didn't know," I said. "Call it a last favor for someone I used to know."

He nodded, and there was nothing else left to say. I turned and walked out on the only real friend I'd made among the Apes.

Once a stray, always a stray. That's how it is in Kittytown.

Where would a scoundrel be—especially a feline one—without the moon to illuminate midnight hunts, trysts, and dances in the grass? The moon is a scoundrel herself, and only the twelve moon cats can keep her here.

Hold the Moon

Eric M. Witchey

There are twelve moon cats. There have always been twelve. There will always be twelve. I am Celeste, and I am eldest. I hold for the west of America. Youngest is Ionna, who holds in the Ukraine. Each holds alone for two hours a night. Each must choose another before she dies.

"Come and dance, Celeste." Andrea, a great great granddaughter, dances in the cool silver light of my last full moon night. She is a tawny, striped dancer. The toms stalk her heat. "Come dance!"

How can I not smile? I danced just so, long ago, but not tonight. My soul cries out to climb the moon trail and dance in the sky with old friends. I know in my ancient bones that I will leave my bed of dune grass and pad upward along the silver trail before dawn.

"Grandma Celeste." It is Victor, a gray barn cat, my eldest grandson. "I've brought you meat." He lays a rat by my head and backs away. He fears my dying. "You must eat," he says. "Your silver fur has lost its shine."

I smell the fresh blood. It is a good kill, a fat offering. I am not hungry. He sits and licks the gore from his six-clawed mouser's paw.

Andrea dashes between tufts of grass and into the shadows of bushes beyond the dunes. A yellow tom follows. A black tom heads him off.

Andrea laughs while they fight. She is too young, too full of the dance of blood.

Victor is too afraid of death.

The moonlight pulls at me. I look up into the face of our ancient prisoner. I roll my great, aching bulk, holding the moon's tail in place, keeping the trail into the night sky anchored to the earth. We moon cats hold thus to keep moonlight near for all who walk the night and hunt and fight and dance. And more, we hold for those like me who need a path into the sky.

It is near midnight, the alone time, the time when the moon's full strength is mine alone to fight, passed to me by Hela in the land of corn and flat fields, mine to pass to Lanni on the islands in the great western sea.

I stretch and flex my claws. I dig them into silver light and trap the moon's tail against the ground.

"Why won't you hunt, old mother?" Morgan asks me. "It is the best time of night. The moon is high and bright." Silver and black, lean and sleek, she came to our dunes and grass after her humans made children to tease her and take her place.

Always, since her first night with us, she has hunted beside me. Always, when I lay down to my nightly task, she asks me why. Always, I am silent while I work.

"You will die if you lie there forever like a great mound of coughed up fur," she says.

Tonight, I look to her with hope. I can no longer wait. I must choose. She is near. She is best. Not too old, not too young, not skittish. She is not one to chase sand in the wind. "Lie with me in the grass, and I shall show you the why," I say.

"Don't do it," Victor says. "The moon is full, and there is magic about her. It is always thus in the deep night."

"Shoo, Victor," Morgan says. "Can't you see that pain stalks her, that she does not eat, that she is weak?" Morgan comes to me and presses her face to mine.

"Lie with me in the moonlight, child. I have much to tell you."

She licks my cheek. "You taste like death, old mother. You taste as though you'll soon hunt the silver light trail."

"I soon will," I whisper.

"Bats!" Victor curses. He paces, tail lashing, too afraid to come near. "Leave her Morgan. She's fine. She'll outlive us all if you leave her be."

From the shadows of bushes beyond the dunes, Andrea and a tom whose voice I do not know scream their passions.

"For Andrea's kittens," I say.

Morgan lies near me, licking behind my ears. "What is for the kittens?"

"Morgan." Victor overcomes his fear. He bats at her. "Come away from her. Please."

116

I feel silly and old. I did not see that he is mated to her beyond one or two litters; they have the spirit bond. When they walk the silver path to the sky, they will walk together. "You love her?" I ask.

He stiffens. His tail fur stands out. His tom's pride will not let him speak of his loyalty to only one. Morgan's purr brings their bond to my heart as true.

"Then I must tell you both."

He pushes at Morgan with his head. "She is old and senile. Come. We will catch her mice. The rat is too large."

Morgan rises.

I drive the claws of one paw deep into the moonbeam to hold it. The other lashes out. Victor is younger, stronger, but not so long with the hunt and the fight as I. He bleeds. He backs away.

"Old Mother!" Morgan cries. She follows him.

"Attend me, Morgan!" I command. "For his sake. For the kittens you will have by him!"

She stops. She stares from wide, golden eyes. "You know."

"I know. I see the litter in your eyes."

"It is magic. They were made this very night."

"I will leave before this night passes. I must give you a great burden before I die. Attend me."

Reluctantly, she returns to my side. Victor watches from shadows that could not be without my diligence.

"You see me as fat and lazy and old."

"No, old mother—"

"I haven't strength to play games with you. You must become what I am, a moon cat. You must lie here in the grass for two hours each night when the moon is high."

"I have often lain with you, old—"

"Put out your claws, child."

"Against you? Never."

"For me, for your kittens that will be, for Victor."

She obeys.

"Next to mine, in the silver light, press your claws into the moon's tail. Pin it to the ground the way you might a rat's tail. Hold the moon the way you would hold a rat so a kitten can learn to hunt."

Again, she obeys.

"There are twelve moon cats. There have always been twelve. There will always be twelve. I am Celeste, and I am eldest. I hold for the west

117

of America. Youngest is Ionna, who holds in the Ukraine. Each holds alone for two hours a night. Each must choose another before she dies. I have chosen you, Morgan."

"You make no sense," she says.

I pull in my claws. The moon knows. It feels freedom at hand. It jumps.

Her instincts are good. She drives her claws deeper. Her second paw comes to play. Her eyes narrow and her teeth gleam.

"Good, child," I say. "Hold it."

"Old Mother! It's alive!"

"Of course it is alive. Can any cat doubt it? The trick is to keep it near so others may hunt and mate and play. The trick is to hold it until Lanni of the islands takes the burden from you."

"If I let go..." She inches forward. Silver-black shoulders ripple.

"No more shadows. No more flashes of tail and fur to chase. The blood dance of moonlight will be gone, and no cat will climb the silver trail into the sky."

She gasps. "It is strong."

"You will grow larger. It will become easier."

Victor slinks out of the shadows. "She can never let go?"

"One night a month, the moon sleeps." I say. "She must never let go while the moon is high."

He comes nearer. He lays himself next to her. He sinks his claws into the moonbeam.

I sigh. I wish I had known one such as he. So long, I held alone in the grass. My choice is good. I watch them for a while before I close my eyes and slip from my earth skin of fur and pain. I lick them each softly on the ear and pad along the silver trail into the sky to play and dance with long ago friends.

Leshi and her grandfather had fallen on hard times, and they needed a miracle—a miracle with feathers.

ERNEST

Lyn McConchie

Between certain worlds on a long spiral in time and space, portals open and close. Usually they are static, but, now and then, they move a few yards between being there and not-there. People go through them, sometimes willingly, sometimes by accident, sometimes by another's design. But, now and again, the traveler isn't willing and isn't human—although they too can have an effect where they arrive just the same.

Ernest was twenty feet up a tree when it happened. He reeled, crowed angrily, and considered his options as there was a feeling of spatial dislocation. It was as if the compass whirled about him, and he didn't like it. In fact, he disliked it so much that he spent the remainder of the night only half asleep, and, at first light, he headed home again. *Home was where*, he thought to himself, *when you had to go there, they had to take you in.* Unfortunately, home was no longer where it had been.

Ernest could fly well. It was moderately unusual for a domestic fowl, but he wasn't purely the Grey Barred Plymouth Rock he appeared to the untutored eye. He'd been bred on a small farm where they advertised that their chickens were excellent layers, sensible, mild-tempered, and mostly capable of surviving as free-range birds.

To this end, Ernest, like the rest of his kin, was only three-quarters Grey Barred Plymouth Rock; the other quarter was gamecock. It gave the huge rooster his fountain of bronze tail-feathers and collar of red-gold feathers around his neck. It had also given him the ability to fly quite well. Left out at night, his kind roosted high up in a tree out of predator reach. It also gave him a passionate sense of territory, and the aggression

121

to defend it at need. As a final gesture, the mix had endowed him with hybrid vigor and a size larger even than his main breed. The rest was as advertised down to the usually mild temper—with humans whom he liked.

Except that the previous day, even a mild-tempered bird might have revolted against events. At six months of age, Ernest had been sold to a small hill farm. There, for a year and a half, he'd ruled the roost, produced a positive fountain of magnificent pullets and young roosters, and been gentle as advertised.

I rule! I rule. This place, this land, my wives, and these humans are mine!

He was right, until someone came to visit for the weekend with a very small yapping dog that persistently chased the hens, culminating, one afternoon when everyone was away for a couple of hours, with a dastardly attack on a pullet.

Ernest, help, save me! She had squawked, and Ernest had provided assistance.

Dog, enemy. My land, my wife. Run or die.

The dog, an idiot, had not run, and—Ernest's gamecock ancestry well to the fore for once—he'd attacked. The yapping bundle of fur—only half the size of the big rooster who was well armed with a formidable beak and razor-like fighting spurs—had succumbed while Ernest stood on the dog's body announcing victory.

I won; I vanquished the enemy; I am Ernest, Lord, King!

The owners of the dog hadn't seen the outcome as amusing or even justified. They'd threatened, and Ernest's owners had pronounced sentence—to be carried out in the morning. That would have been that, except their daughter—nine, blonde, and the one who mainly cared for their poultry—had been devoted to Ernest. While accepting that her parents would not alter their decision, she reasoned that if her friend weren't around, it would be hard to do anything to him. At dusk she'd sneaked out and released him.

Where are we going? Oh, yes, all right, I'll allow it, but I hope there's food at the end of this?

She'd carried him half a mile down an old deer track, waited until he'd flapped his way up a tree, put a handful of wheat in a hollow where one branch met another, and gone home. She would never know what happened to him, but that half-mile had been crucial.

The random portal had opened right across the tree in which Ernest spent that night. And, at first light, he ate his wheat and began to make his way home. Except that home was no longer there, and his sense of direction was confused.

That tree faced the sun; if I go this way, home should only be... But, but, where is home?

He flew from tree to tree, pausing now and then to descend warily and eat from the banquet of bugs and greenery. There was something wrong about this whole scenario, but, precisely what, Ernest was unable to determine. He could only keep heading for home and hope all would be well once he reached it.

Towards evening he roosted in another tree, weary but well-fed. He must surely be close to home by now. Just a little further in the morning, and he'd be there. At first light he roused, dropped to the ground, and began to eat bugs in a small clearing where the earth was turned in a short narrow strip. He heard the sow coming first and ignored her. He was familiar with pigs. Behind her came a small, blonde girl, and Ernest halted his scratching. He stood in the shaft of sunlight that lit the clearing, clapped his wings, rose to his full height, and posed at the head of the turned earth. Sun struck bronze-green and brown-gold lights from his tail-feathers and a red-gold from the circle of feathers around his neck.

To Leshi he was a creature from myth—almost half her size, dominant, proud, and lit to glory by sunlight. He stood poised at the head of her brother's grave, the brother she had idolized, who had adored and protected his baby sister, the brother she missed with all her five-year-old heart. It was Year's End Day when presents were given to mark the coming of a new year, and her brother would never have forgotten her. There had been little of fairy-tales in her life and less of beauty, but in one flashing moment she believed that somehow, someway, he had sent this wondrous gift, this miracle of beauty to her.

"Vernest?" she asked in her tongue. It meant miracle, but the big rooster didn't know that.

She knows me; I must be near my home, and, see, how like my own little human she is.

He relaxed at his familiar name. The child's posture shouted admiration, awe, and respect. He pranced up making the small sound in his throat that was his greeting to that other child—now far away in a more civilized parallel world.

Leshi considered. The sow would stay where she was for a while even if untended. This miracle must be led home for the scrutiny of her grandfather. She found a few crumbs in her pocket from the single thick slice of dry bread that had been her breakfast, offered them to Ernest, and was delighted by the gentle way he accepted her tribute.

"Vernest, comdi."

She feeds me, she speaks my name, she treats me with respect, all is as it should be.

The rooster followed obediently until they reached the tiny forest hut that Leshi shared with her grandfather and, at nights, with the sow and five small scruffy hens. It was the hens on which Ernest immediately focused. He clapped his wings, stretched his neck, and crowed as Leshi scurried in to fetch her grandfather. The hens gaped and clustered about him. Never in all their lives had they seen anything so magnificent, so stunningly awesomely virile.

I am Ernest, your new Lord, let all know that I am here now, master of this place.

"Leshi, Is da?" Jahon was surprised to see his granddaughter back so soon and babbling about a miracle? He stepped outside and in turn became transfixed. A farmer all his life, he was under no apprehension that Ernest was a miracle, or not exactly, but the size, the quality, and the sheer majesty of the rooster stunned him. The bird must have escaped from some lord's flock. Never in all his life had Johan seen a bird so fine—or one so swift to take charge. A small grin curved his lips. If someone came looking in a couple of days it would be too late. The bird would have fertilized every egg laid, and—Jahon's eyes narrowed—if the creature bred true?

He turned back and scrabbled in a bag. There was a meager amount of grain there intended to help the hens survive winter. If it would bind this bird to the place it would be better spent now. In a series of jumps his mind leapt ahead. Chicks sired by this rooster would be finer than anything he'd ever seen, even chicks from his own poor hens. Before winter they would be old enough to sell, and they would fetch—by his standards—a very fair price indeed.

Ernest had temporarily finished with the hens and was approaching Leshi hopefully again.

Jahon thrust a half-handful of grain at her. "Give him this, just a pinch at a time."

He watched as the huge bird took the food carefully from the child's palm. Gentle too, but those spurs were not for show, Jahon suspected. A bird that size, if he became enraged, would not be a pushover. Leshi laughed as Ernest's beak explored her hand.

124

A good little human, yes, and the man too gave him respect; he might stay here for a while, just until his own humans found him. Besides, new wives were not to be overlooked.

"Vernest, mi Vernest." Ernest settled down beside her, enjoying the small stroking hand.

Involuntarily, Jahon smiled. Pasht Goddess knew there'd been nothing to smile about this past year in Mirray Lhandes. His son and his son's wife had been murdered by Shairne raiders from out of the desert, their home looted then burned, his grandchildren left with almost nothing. Jahon had managed to get the children away before they were found, and, thanks be to a merciful Goddess, he'd managed to snatch food, a few small items, and their tiny hoard of coins as he went. His son had died fighting; Mhari his wife—the daughter-in-law old Jahon had never much liked—had died too, but in silence. He'd give her that. She had to have, since no one had come after them seeking Jahon, the children, or the family's handful of coppers and the solitary silver ina.

Jahon sighed as he watched Ernest and Leshi.

After his son and daughter-in-law had died, Jahon and the two children had made for the seven-house village where his wife's youngest sister still lived. There was no room in her home for three more. She had sold him an elderly sow in pig for half the coins, the rest to be paid when the piglets could be brought to the monthly market attended by many from scattered farms about. The other half of the coins had gone to essentials.

His sister-in-law had, looking about her to make sure no one overheard, told him of the old hut up here, the owner dead almost two years. If no one knew where he, her grandniece, and nephew were, no one could protest their use of it.

Ten-year-old Malgan had taken a fever and died only a month ago before they could ask for help from a shrine of Pasht, now it was one old man and a small girl—and he feared desperately for Leshi and her future.

But from the Goddess had come a chance, a hope. If only all went well for a while it might yet be that Leshi could have a future. It seemed to Jahon as the months passed that Pasht was indeed good.

My land, my wives, my humans, I am Lord, Master, let no enemy come against me! Ernest was assiduous in his duties. His wives hatched chicks of marvelous size and looks, and most survived. Twice Ernest attacked a marauding kio—the rat-like scavengers of Aradia—that, faced with a bird of such size and temper, fled with a spur-gashed face.

Before the start of winter, Jahon left on an all day walk to the village market. With him went the carcasses of a dozen fat capons, all killed, plucked, and gutted only the night before. By village quality, they were magnificent birds. They sold for a price surprising even to Jahon so that he was able to buy supplies for the winter that were generous by his standards. He and Leshi ate better that year. Three times more in the next moon, he walked down to the market, the second time to sell piglets as well as chickens and to pay off his debt to his sister-in-law. The third time to breed the elderly sow to a boar, paying with two fine capons.

He returned to settle in for winter. No one knew they were there. They should be safe, and who traveled when the snows began? The answer to that was: no one except those who must.

It was a traveling mercenary heading from Surah to Mirray City on a promised contract who came upon Leshi before the snow was too deep, as she watched the foraging sow. Jahon had gone the other way to gather kindling and cut wood for their fire.

No brat would be far from home at this time of year, the mercenary thought, dismounting silently from his mule and dropping his pack. Her home would mean women, food and drink, perhaps something of value—if there were no men to drive him off. He stalked her with care on foot. The mule was trained to stand and would wait until he could return.

When Leshi returned to her home, he was behind her, silent and cautious. It had snowed lightly, soon after dawn, he studied the doorway and saw no tracks. The brat was alone, her kin probably at market or visiting friends while she was left to tend the pig. He could wring from her the hiding place of any coins, wait for those who would return, and ambush them.

He waited until she passed near him, stepped out, and seized her by one wrist. Leshi shrieked. It was foolish, futile, but in her terror she called for her miracle, the one sent by her brother.

"Vernest, Vernest!"

The big rooster had been scratching under a tree, unseen by the fighter. He knew that note of terror, his hens called like that when a predator threatened them. And this was his territory.

Mine, my little human, my land; you show yourself as an enemy, and I am Ernest; I fight as I stand, release my human.

Outraged, without hesitation, he attacked. So great was his momentum, aided by flapping wings, that when he reached the mercenary, he literally ran up the man's body and clung, claws fastened in the open top of the leather jerkin, wings beating the man about the ears, beak striking savagely at the startled eyes. In the following melee, Leshi wrenched free and fled screaming.

Ernest hung on grimly. *You do not run? I shall show you why you should, human intruder. I shall show you until your blood runs.*

The mercenary knew chickens, but those he knew were the small scrawny birds of the backwoods Lhandes. Ernest was four times that size, and, to the confused man, it was more like being attacked by an eagle. He was blinded by the savagely beating wings, and his grabs at the bird missed. Nor did they go unpunished, as Ernest lifted each foot in turn, striking viciously with his spurs at the man's face and clutching fingers.

In those moments, he was all gamecock—the small English bird bred for a thousand generations for one thing, to fight to the death, never backing down, never surrendering. This predator had invaded Ernest's territory, and it should die. The fight could end only way, of course, and would have, except for another who entered the scene. A dull thump resounded in the clear crisp air. Ernest rode his enemy down to the ground, standing, claws sunk into the invader's neck as he clapped his wings and screamed his triumph.

I am Ernest, my enemy is dead, I killed him, let my enemies beware! Then he stepped down and went to check over his territory, crooning reassuringly to Leshi as she reached out to stroke him in passing.

Jahon buried the intruder, after stripping him of everything useable. He hauled him far into the forest—finding the mule and pack when he did so. He sought out a small deep depression between two slabs of rock and entombed the mercenary there. But the booty the man provided would be valuable. A fine bow and a quiver of hunting and war arrows, a good knife, a sword and many other things he could use or sell, including a purse of the copper itari and silver ina coins. He would buy a generous bag of good grain for the bird with some of it, Jahon resolved. As a farmer he'd known that roosters could be belligerent, but who could have known a bird would fight like that—and for a child?

At the first spring market, he sold his booty cautiously, an item here, another there, spending coppers to buy the promised grain. He also visited his sister-in-law to assure her that he and Leshi had survived the winter. As a gift he brought for her a live daughter of Ernest. The pullet was half Ernest's size but she was still far larger and of much greater quality than any other hen in the village or surrounding area. Alvia was delighted with her gift.

127

"I won't ask questions about her. But there are those who'd value such a fine bird. If you have others to bring to market next time, could some be alive like this one?"

Old Jahon smiled. "Perhaps I might bring one or two."

Flooding the market would bring prices down, but if he brought only hens to sell, their offspring would be one quarter of Ernst's blood. He alone would retain the best of the line. It worked as he'd hoped. In two years, Ernest's daughters were known for their quality. In four years, there was enough money saved to buy yearly tenancy in a house in the village, a woodcutting license, and official pannage for his two sows. Moved to a small house on the edge of the village Ernest throve.

Ah, yes, admire me, I hear the words my small human uses: my name, and such sounds as 'bad man' and 'many chicks'; yes, respect me, I am Ernest, warrior and lover, and I hold my territory against all.

In six years, Ernest was an admired and established part of the village, and Johan with his flock and his relationship to Alvia had status amongst them—sufficient status that no one ever asked where he had obtained his magnificent flock leader. Why should they? Ernest's offspring, in a quiet, modest way, were providing a higher level of prosperity for them all.

Over those years, Jahon bred his chickens with great care. He might know little about genetics, but he knew farming practice. Breed the best to the best, and hope for the best. His flock was the finest in the area, and local farmers bought from him in preference to any other. Over those years too, Jahan had never heard of even a lord with a rooster that matched Ernest's description, and he wondered. What he wondered, however, he kept to himself in true peasant fashion. Ernest died quietly in Leshi's arms one fine cool day in early summer.

I am weary, let me sleep a while and then I'll get up and call my wives again. I am Ernest, warrior, lover, Lord of my territory, always your friend, but for now, let me sleep a while...

Leshi wept, and Jahon comforted her.

"He lived long, very long for a chicken, we had him for almost nine years and he was an adult when he came—and he knew you loved him."

"You won't...?"

Jahon covered his brief hesitation. No, it would not be seemly since the bird had saved the life of Jahon's granddaughter. Customs against waste or not, it would be akin to cannibalism.

"Of course not. He'll be buried as he should be. We'll take him up and bury him by Malgan."

Leshi nodded. "Yes, my brother sent him, it's right he should go back."

They went alone, carrying the body of the bird unobtrusively. It wouldn't do for the village to gossip. They buried Ernest at the foot of the grave, and Leshi patted the earth down very gently. She tossed leaves over it until no one would know that the grave had been disturbed.

"He saved me."

"Yes."

"I'm sure Malgan sent him to me."

"Perhaps so."

"I loved him."

"Yes, and he loved you." And involuntarily: "What a fighter he was. I'll never forget that man waving his arms all over the place, scratched and bleeding, trying to get Vernest off his face. An experienced mercenary beaten by a rooster."

Jahon laughed, Leshi's giggle harmonizing. There'd never be another bird like Vernest. Leshi would miss him, and, oddly enough, thought the unsentimental old farmer, so would he. He didn't know if Pasht had sent the bird to them or not, but next time he was near a shrine, he'd give thanks anyway. Thanks for a feathered, fighting, Year's End miracle that had given Leshi a future.

What tall tales do crows tell, sitting on their wires
in the sky? Do they believe each other?

Two Crows, Two Wires, and the Moon

Andrew S. Taylor

Two crows were hunched on two black telephone wires, and the moon hovered in the sky between them.

"I've been there," said the old crow to the young crow, who was then gazing at the moon. "I've been to the Sky-Stone. It was many years ago, and I barely escaped with my life."

The young crow cocked his head and batted his black tongue against the inside of his beak. He cast his sharp and beady eye upon the old crow. At times, the young crow felt a certain contempt for his elder's scars and mange.

"You went to the Sky-Stone?" The young crow clucked with incredulity. The two had just eaten a possum together, a flat one that tasted of rubber tires but a fine and fleshy possum just the same. It was always after meals that the old crow told fantastic stories.

"Indeed," said the old crow. "I did."

This did not seem plausible to the young crow, who knew full well that the Sky-Stone crawled with strange and dangerous creatures that hated crows and birds of all kinds, and that the Sky-Stone could fly faster than any crow and could never be caught up with.

He egged the old crow on. "How did you get there, gramps? Every crow as soon as he can fly tries to fly to the Sky-Stone and flaps till his wings are burning. But he never gets any closer. It flies too fast for any crow to catch it."

The old crow was not really the young crow's grandfather. The young crow only called him that sometimes to remind the old crow that he was old. This time, the young crow wondered if the old crow even heard him say it, as the old crow's head was then tucked under his wing nibbling at a gnat that had been pestering him thereabouts since Tuesday.

In fact, the old crow had heard him perfectly well but was pretending to ignore him. Sometimes, the old crow thought the young crow was extremely obnoxious. He was always boasting to other crows and, in fact, birds in general about all the shiny hidden treasures he'd found in the woods or the lunches he'd stolen from picnic tables. In fact, it was often the deft old crow who'd done these things, since the young crow was something of a klutz, but the old crow did not like to boast about his accomplishments to everyone like the young crow did. He only told the young crow stories sometimes, because the young crow always followed him around. He usually let the young crow get away with his stealing his stories, even as his anger slowly grew.

The old crow drew his head out suddenly. His black eyes burned bright orange because the Fire-Dog, which is what crows called the sun, was setting. The reflection shimmered in his eyes. At the tip of his beak, something wriggled, its little legs scrambling, and then suddenly disappeared. The old crow closed his beak and swallowed.

"That is the trick of it, you see," said the old crow. "You can't get there that way at all. You have to fly through the world to the other end and catch the Sky-Stone when it's sleeping."

The young crow tilted his head back and cawed. "That," he said, "is absurd."

"Find any empty well," continued the old crow, unruffled, "that is deep and dry and bottomless, and you can do it. You stupid young things are always after glimmers and sparks. But fly down into a forgotten old well that is deep and dark—any old well will do—and you can go through the center of the world to the other side and catch the Sky-Stone while it sleeps."

The young crow was suddenly very quiet. The things the old crow said made a certain sense. After all, he was always flying after things that sparkled, and, if there weren't any sparkles, he just wasn't interested. As a result, he had probably forgotten to notice important things like old wells that nobody drew water from any more.

"Okay, gramps," said the young crow, still trying to seem unimpressed. "I'm game. How do I do it?"

The old crow paused a moment, working at the bug that had momentarily lodged in his throat. He bobbed his head and continued. "The journey is long and difficult. You must fly down a narrow tunnel through the world, and, for a long time, the only light you can see is a little blue dime in front of you and another one behind. All else is blacker than the darkest feather. When you finally come out at the other side of the world, there is another well, but the bucket is hanging upside-down on a very long rope that goes right up into the stars—or down into the stars as the case may be. When you first get there, you almost can't see the end of it. It just goes straight into the sky, on and on until it looks like a little black string with a black dot right on the far end of it. So you have to grasp the well-handle in your beak and wheel the bucket all the way in."

"Why?" the young crow said snidely. "Are you gonna drink the milk from the night sky too?"

The old crow was unflappable. "No, silly bat. You need to get into the bucket to lower yourself to the Sky-Stone. As you said yourself, you can't fly there."

Again, the young crow realized that this made rather a lot of sense. You really couldn't fly faster than the Sky-Stone.

The old crow resumed. "The trick of it is, you see, that you get the rope with the bucket all reeled up until you can almost step into the bucket. By that point, the pulley is covered with so much rope that it rolls bigger and wider than the biggest bale of hay you've ever seen."

By now the young crow was becoming convinced that this was a true story. A rope that long would have to make a roll that big.

"So then you get into the bucket?" said the young crow.

"Naw, you don't," said the old crow. "Hold your harpies, already! You've got to wait for the right moment."

The young crow waited.

"When's zat?" he said after a few moments. The sky was turning purple as the Fire-Dog disappeared into the desert, dripping and melting like an egg over the world's edge.

"You've got to wait until the Sky-Stone is almost underneath you— or above you, as the case may be," said the old crow.

"Ah," cawed the young crow.

"Ah," cawed the old crow. He continued, "Once the moment is right, you let the well-handle out of your beak and hop into the bucket. Be quick! Once you let go, that bucket starts to drop into the sky, and, if you're slow, you miss the bucket and get hit in the head by the handle coming 'round the other way."

The young crow grew impatient. "I know that," he said, fidgeting back and forth so much that his wire was starting to wobble. "What happens next?"

The old crow continued, "Well, assuming you've timed the whole operation right, you'll be inside the bucket, falling towards the Sky-Stone, going very fast. It gets bigger and bigger as you get closer. First, you see the mountains, and then you see the valleys, and then when you're really close..."

"Yes?"

"...then you see the flying disk monsters."

"Holy Moses!"

"Yes," said the old crow. "Silver like the fastest river-fish and wider than a wayward umbrella, the disk monsters go whirling about, their beady green eyes a-spinning at the edges of their slippery bodies. They go whizzing and zooming in flocks of twenty or more, casting their round shadows over the dusty surface of the Sky-Stone. Their mouths are located in the direct center of their heads, on the bottom. Fierce and toothsome, they go hunting through the night for sparrows and gypsy moths, and anything else that flies."

The young crow was incredulous. "There are gypsy moths on the Sky-Stone?"

The old crow seemed to grow impatient. "Of course there are. That's where gypsy moths come from. Can't you see their deathly gray color? Can't you taste the dust on their wings? That's the dust of the Sky-Stone you taste."

"Ah," cawed the young crow.

"Anyway," said the old crow. "As I was saying, once you get close to the Sky-Stone you need to get out of the bucket, because otherwise you'll fall against the ground and get eaten by a disk monster. So you jump out before you hit. And make sure to fly above them! Any crow can fly higher than a disk monster, but long gone is the crow that flies beneath them.

"So, once you get flying, you keep going until you find a mountain-top, of which the Sky-Stone has many. Find a mountain-top, preferably one with a cave, and preferably a cave with a Mica Frost Dragon."

The young crow nearly fell off the wire and had to flap his wings several times to regain balance. In his excitement, he had been fidgeting back and forth on his wire so much that he had lost control of himself. The mention of a Mica Frost Dragon had simply been too much.

"Silly bat," said the old crow.

"Hey, stop calling me that!" said the young crow.

"No, there was actually a silly bat flying around behind you. It just ate a gypsy moth."

"Oh."

"So anyway, as I was saying. The Mica Frost Dragon is a special beast that inhabits the Sky-Stone at its highest reaches. It's a long snaky serpent with six clawed hands and eight legs and twelve wings, and each wing has two more hands on the end of them for a total of thirty hands. Also, there are two more hands on the end of its tail."

The young crow was impressed that the old crow could count so well. It definitely lent his story an air of credibility.

"The Mica Frost Dragon has skin as smooth as the freshly fallen snow, white and shiny, and it shimmers and blinks with rainbows full of all the colors a crow can see—light blue and light green and all the different kinds of purple come sparkling from its skin." (And that is, in fact, every color a crow can see.) "It flies about the mountaintops, smoking a long pipe filled with oak leaves and dried mosses. It sings between puffs of smoke. It is a most beautiful singer, this dragon! Far more beautiful than any bird in the blue world! It can sing in three voices at once, and they harmonize, these sad and wonderful voices singing like the milky stars themselves, the high and the low and everything in the wonderful middle all at once! It flies between the stony mountaintops, puffing and singing and moving like a flying silver lantern."

"What a wonderful beast!" The young crow was starry-eyed.

The old crow drew in close, making it clear that he was about to disclose the most important detail of all. "You can tell if a cave in the mountains of the Sky-Stone is home to a Mica Frost Dragon by the sound of its sneezing. Frost Dragons sneeze a lot."

"Ah," cawed the young crow.

"Ah," cawed the old crow.

"But why," said the young crow, "why would I want to do that?"

"So that you can hear its secret, of course!" said the old crow.

"It has a secret?" said the young crow. Already, he had forgotten himself and was starting to wobble on the wire again.

The old crow waited for a moment, letting the question hang in the air. He closed his eyes and opened his beak a little, as crows do when trying to catch a distant scent on the breeze.

Finally, the old crow spoke. "The Mica Frost Dragons are an ancient breed, and they have many secrets. Most you can never learn. They know how to fly to the stars and drink the sweet elixir of the Star-Spouts." That is what crows called comets, for they believed that stars were droplets left by flying jets of luminous, milky wine. "But," said the old crow, "most of these things they will not and cannot tell you, for they are impossible to speak of in the language of crows."

"Oh, well then," said the young crow in a huff. "So much for your story!" The young crow had lost his balance again but rather deftly tried to hide the fact by stretching out his leg and scratching his neck. "Darn these gnats!" he said.

The old crow knew that the young crow did not have a gnat. He continued.

"But what any Mica Frost Dragon can tell any crow is what any crow most wants to know—how to get to the Tinsel Castle!"

"What!?" The young crow squawked. There was a thunderous flapping noise, and, where the young crow once stood, a small cloud of black feathers slowly drifted. The flapping noise continued for several second far below the old crow and then moved in circles around him.

After a moment, the young crow landed again on the wire across from the old crow. "Dammit!" He shrieked and tried to regain his composure. "The Tinsel Castle? But, how can it be?"

The young crow was understandably flummoxed. The Tinsel Castle was the mythological abode of the Crow Gods, known also as the Clever Jesters or the Fire Thieves. They stole the light from the Fire-Dog, light which made the animals of the world learn to think, and the crows to think the brightest of all animals. They used their bright thoughts to build the castle. It was large, luminous, and extremely sparkly, but once the Fire-Dog saw what the crows had done—stealing its light and its brightness to build a castle—it punished the crows by putting a curse on the castle. Now, the castle moved around the world and could hardly ever be found, because it flashed and flitted to and fro, and could appear in different shapes, sometimes like a mountain and sometimes a tower the color of ice. It would disappear as soon as you looked at it. Crows were always dreaming of catching up with the Tinsel Castle, and they believed that all sparkly things everywhere were tiny parts of the castle that had been left behind when it passed them by, which is why they collected them.

The old crow continued, "The Mica Frost Dragons watch the surface of the earth and can see how the Castle moves. They can tell you where it is going to be tomorrow and the next day. Then you can go there before the Castle appears and be waiting for it." The old crow paused and then continued, "Of course, the Castle still disappears and changes very quickly, so even if you find it, you must move quickly enough to get inside and see the wonders of the Crow Gods. Alas, I was too old, my wings could not carry me fast enough! Perhaps if I was younger..." The old crow drifted off, seeming to reflect on a bittersweet memory.

The young crow leaned in close to his elder, his thin legs trembling. "And the Mica Frost Dragon will just tell me where to go?"

The old crow eyed the young crow with a secretive gaze. "To get the Dragon to speak to you, you must bring it a mushroom from the Valley of the Inverse Serpent, just south of the Blue Pool." The Blue Pool was a spot on the Sky-Stone that crows could see only when it was full. "Bring it the biggest mushroom you can find. Hold it in your beak and bring it to the cavern as an offering to the Dragon."

"What's that for?"

"It helps cure the sneezing."

"Oh."

"It's a narrow valley, and the dragons have a hard time getting to the bottom crevice where the mushrooms breed. Very frustrating for them."

"Ah," cawed the young crow, finally agreeing that everything was starting to make sense.

"Ah," cawed the old crow.

The old crow continued, "After smoking the mushroom and telling you where the Castle will be, the Mica Frost Dragon can be persuaded, if asked nicely, to fling you back towards the Earth with its tail. You ride on its back as it gains speed, swooping with a swiftness beyond what any crow can muster. When it's flying as fast as it can go, it whips around in a fast circle and shoots you from the tip of its tail like a slingshot."

"I bet those hands on its tail are very helpful for that."

"Indeed. Once you're shooting along through the stars, you must flap as hard as possible to keep the speed up. If you're too slow, the Sky-Stone awakens because it knows when a crow is flying fast around it, and it tries to swallow you whole."

"What? Why 'zat?" The young crow clutched at the wire, terrified, and then began shuffling slightly side to side.

"Because the Sky-Stone has ears better than any creature in the world. It can hear an acorn sip the morning dew. It can hear a cloud changing its shape. It can hear butterflies have doubts. So believe me, young carrion-feeder, that creature can hear a crow flapping its wings in a circle around its head. And if there's one thing the Sky-Stone hates, it's crows. That's why it always flies away from them."

The young crow ceased its anxious shuffling on the wire for a moment and peered skeptically at its elder.

"Hey, waydamminit!" said the young crow. "If the Sky-Stone can hear alla that, how come it sleeps through the disk monsters and the singing dragons?"

The old crow was undaunted. "That's obvious," he said. "It's used to hearing those things, just like you're used to hearing the squirrels natter. You sleep through that, don't you?"

"Well, yes," said the young crow. After all, you had to sleep through the squirrels or you'd never sleep at all!

"When you fly amongst the dragons and the disks, the flapping sounds of a little crow hardly stand out from all the other noises. But when you're just a little bit farther away, you stand out."

"But," the young crow was nervously shuffling again. "How can the Sky-Stone eat without a mouth? It's just a stone and it has no mouth!"

"Oh, it has a mouth alright—the Sky-Stone has a mouth as wide as its entire head. And, in case you hadn't noticed, the whole thing is just a gigantic head! That mouth of the Sky-Stone comes apart like a thick black crescent, wider and wider until the beast is all mouth and nothing but, and you can see into its dusky gray gullet, a cavern so vast that Star-Spouts and Glimmeroids and other sparkly things pass right through it like little fireflies. It's got teeth like giant slabs of granite, their many rings forming canyons and gorges the likes of which you've never seen, and between those teeth you can see the black and broken bodies of all the crows who did not make it."

The young crow was frozen in place. He glanced up at the Sky-Stone, which peacefully drifted through the dusky sky above them, and then back at the old crow. "But you made it!" he said, in awe.

"Indeed," said the old crow, watching the horizon. "And here I am to tell the tale."

The young crow was silent for several long moments.

"Gramps," he finally said. "I must find such a well and make the journey so that I can know how to find the Castle. Unlike you, I am young and swift! I'm sure I can catch the castle and get inside! I promise, when I do, I'll tell you all about the secrets of the Jesters! I must find a well this very night, once the Sky-Stone is down underground. Is there such a well nearby?"

The old crow had now buried his head under his other wing, in search of the long-sought Monday gnat. When he finally pulled his head free, his beak empty, he did not look at the young crow but watched the horizon again as if reading its secrets, the tales of its shifting and fading lights.

"There is one, young crow," he finally said, "behind Earl's Diner, off I-80. That's just two miles west of here as the crow flies." He paused again. "Shall we go there together?"

The young crow fell off the wire again, but this time did not circle back around. Instead, he kept flitting about the darkness above the old crow's head. "Yeah!" he cawed. "Yaw! Yaw! Yaw!"

The young crow flew about anxiously for many hours, waiting for the Sky-Stone to dip past the horizon, at which point the old crow—in no particular rush, to be sure—lead him to the well behind Earl's Diner. The well was, indeed, the most profound well for many miles, seemingly endless in its depth and darkness.

"Here we are, young one," said the old crow. "Your moment of truth is at hand."

The young crow flew up into the night air, his black wings spread against the blue-black of the sky. The crows have a name for themselves that humans do not know. It is a special crow-word which means "the shadows which pass over stars." From this lofty height, the young crow dove like a dark bullet, straight down into the well, shrieking with joyous abandon. From within the well came a soft thud. Field mice twittered and scattered into the tall grass.

The old crow dipped his head and managed, at last, to nab the Monday gnat. It had been there for three Mondays, which is irritating to say the least. Old crow was happy now, relaxed, as if everything in the world was in order once again. He perched himself on the tailgate of an abandoned pick-up truck, tucked his head in and slept soundly.

A battle of wits on a snowy cliffside could lead to a horrible price... or a wonderful new power.

INTO THE WIND

Rechan

Reach out, grab the stone. Breathe. Wipe the snow off. Almost there. Put weight on i—

The rock gave way. With a gasp he rocked back to the other hand-hold and hugged the frozen mountainside, listening to the stone's bouncing descent until the wind's howls swallowed it. The stoat huddled against the frigid rocks, his winter's white pelt taking some of the sting. He'd been so numb he hadn't noticed the wobble of the stone. Careless.

He did not look down. Instead Dagger stared at the ledge just two stepping stones from his destination.

A crack let him rise to catch the ledge's lip. There he hung. A rock jutted a few feet to the side at his hip level, the only good step in sight. Hand over hand Dagger nudged to the side, close to the stone, and brought his leg up.

Dagger's weight held, but when he started to lift, the boot slid off the slick rock and he swayed. A second attempt met the same fate. His limbs shook at the effort of holding him up this long, fingers screaming. One more try before scooting back to the last secure spot.

Again he caught the rock. Dagger curled up his torso and hips as he lifted. The boot slid and he swung with the motion. At the height of his pendulum's arc, he uncoiled his midsection's taut muscles, snapping like completing a flip. The motion carried him enough to roll over the cliff's edge.

For several moments, Dagger lay on his back, gasping the frigid air, not daring to look back the way he'd come. Now he accepted the pain, every inch a fire that gave no warmth. When Dagger was sure the mountain would not crumble away beneath him, he stood and searched for the path.

Once above the cruel climb the mountainside became a friendly stroll, leading up switchbacks and broad ledges along the southern face.

Soon he spotted the end of his journey.

A broad shelf hung out into the void, cast in murk by an arching overhang in spite of the high sun. Petrified trees, long since stripped of their leaves, and slender columns of stone assembled like soldiers guarding the ledge's center. Tight-packed snow coated every surface.

Dagger tensed his wits before striding onto the shelf.

Five paces in, the wind howled across the mountainside before gathering in a wall behind him. The barrier continued past a count of ten, strong enough he could have propped up against it. No retreating, then.

More wind scored the columns and trees, knocking loose snow to expose holes and grooves. Rushing air through these birthed a discordant song that lifted the fur along Dagger's back. The jagged melody rose before it scraped into words.

"Who dares intrude upon my domain?"

"I do." Despite straining in a shout, his voice barely reached his ears. "I come before you to give challenge, spirit."

"Challenge?" Insult, or perhaps amusement, curdled the disharmonic voice before the wind stopped as sudden as a slap. Silence sang in the absence of such a rending sound. Snow devils, picked up by a twirling gust, coalesced to craft the outline of a figure in snowflakes and the distortion of air. A gaze of ice, leering in menace, made the only distinct feature. "Tell me of this challenge," crooned the voice.

"It is said that spirits of Air are quite clever, and I am sure you are no weakling of wit. I propose to you a duel of minds."

The figure altered. Where once it stood, now floated a long and sinuous ribbon. The serpent eeled in lazy circles around him. "First you step upon my home unannounced, then before introducing yourself, offer poisonous flattery like I am an easily-won fool. Your insults are plentiful, traveler-yet-named."

Dagger winced on the inside, yet kept his face pleasant. A snake—how fitting a reminder to what he dealt with. Do not show weakness or hesitation. Normally they drank compliments like wine, but this one must be wary of them. "My apologies, my lenient host. I am Dagger. I ask your name in return."

"I am Bitter Tempest," hissed the column of cold. "It has been some time since entertainment has come to me, so I may yet accept this challenge. What boon do you seek, if by some miracle you are victorious?"

The stoat breathed in. Vapor off the spirit burned his lungs. "Teach me to become air."

For the span of a held breath, Bitter Tempest grew so still Dagger could not see it. The voice came from many corners at once. "What do you offer in failure?"

"Because my price is high, I offer you freedom to match it." Dread tickled up his guts like centipedes. The spirit could ask for anything.

At once the misty serpent was there, coiled around his legs tight enough he felt frost's claws through his trousers. "The challenges, I will choose."

Dagger bared his teeth. "Not until you've named a price."

The spirit's spade head rose and swayed before him, fangs bared, eyes boring into him as sharp as the cold leeching into his bones. Bitter Tempest's voice rose like before, a gale shearing through the trees and rocks. "You shall bring to me a child, a woman, and an old man. From them you will milk their screams, that I may harvest and weave into my own voice."

First bile, then resolve, seeped into Dagger's throat. "Agreed."

"I shall give you five challenges, which you must best all—"

"Three of five."

A sharp gust yanked at Dagger's whiskers. "If you wish to best three, then three tasks you will receive."

"Agreed. We barter how much time I have before each task begins."

"Agreed," cooed Bitter Tempest. "Shall we begin?"

As soon as Dagger nodded, a vicious blast tore him off the side of the mountain. Biting drafts swirled around him, burrowed through his clothes and beneath his pelt. He didn't see the ground before he dropped into the snow amid the trees.

Sitting up and shaking loose the cold from his face, Dagger found Bitter Tempest hovering above a barrel-sized boulder. "Look above." A fierce twister shook a single branch high on a tree, the force stripping snow and nettles. The now naked branch curved so severely it formed a great loop, the end of the branch actually wrapping around itself. "Behold this circle."

"I see it."

"Good. Regard me once more." The spirit swirled around the boulder. "Put this rock through that hoop."

Dagger's whiskers scrunched up. "This rock inside that branch? Will it even fit?"

"Yes, and yes," the spirit hissed, amusement sap-like on each word. "Unless you bow to my cunning and forfeit?"

The stoat scoffed. "How long will I have?"

"You are granted a week and a day, for you will need all the time for it," Bitter Tempest chirped.

While he did not let the spirit out of his sight, Dagger turned his focus inwards and perched atop the rock. For some time he sat. Not only was the boulder heavy but by merely pushing against it with his feet and rump, he found it rooted deep.

The rock's cold wormed through his trousers. He shifted in discomfort, the stone soon making his rear ache.

His rear on the rock.

Like a loosened arrow the stoat bolted across the snow and climbed the tree, the pain of his earlier climb drowned out by the idea. Perching on a limb beneath his target, Dagger took out his namesake and began hacking the looped branch's base.

Bitter Tempest hovered close at his back, accusation sharpening the spirit's words. "What are you doing?"

"Winning," he said.

When a gash sunk halfway through the limb, Dagger put the knife away, gripped the branch with his fingers and dangled. Hooking the tops of his boots under a lower limb, he flexed, the muscles of his spine and belly curling like the branch he held. Relax, clench. The tear widened, widened, and broke.

In a scramble he nearly crashed to the ground, but coiled himself around a branch and clung as the tumbling limb raked downwards. With more care he picked his way to the forest floor.

The loop waited for him. Lifting it, he strutted to the rock and threaded the stone through the loop before dropping the branch.

"No," said the spirit, "that's not right."

"Did you not say the rock had to go through the loop?"

The reply came as snow, rock, pine cones, and other forest leavings flew about like slingshots, air shrieking and wood splintering. Cold, hateful eyes cut through the tantrum to pierce Dagger.

Finally Bitter Tempest asked in a warbling wail, "Are you ready for your second task?"

"Yes, spirit. Please let us contin—"

A fierce burst of air swept Dagger up like a leaf caught in a storm. The cold tore into him snow stung his eyes and raked his whiskers, all while an undercurrent of a chuckle hissed at the edges of his ears.

His boots touched the ground but, going too fast, he slapped into a rocky cliff. Even while catching himself on the stones, he now hurt from the wrist up.

"Behold this stream," hissed Bitter Tempest.

Water gushed from a seam in the mountainside. It burbled and lapped across stones, filling a gap carved from flowing over centuries, before disappearing into a yawning crack at the base. The stream's song melded with birds merrily talking on vibrantly green pines nearby.

Bitter Tempest, in the guise of a predatory bird, leered at Dagger from an overhead stone. "You must create a twin of this stream beside it. And no, you may not split the spring down the center."

"How long do I have, spirit?" Dagger asked, flexing his fingers.

"Until the sun sets."

The bright star hung well off its zenith. Dagger wagered three, perhaps four hours remained. "I don't know if that can even be done."

A malicious snicker soaked through the spirit's answer. "That is my challenge."

Once more the stoat sat and considered the stream. No manner of chipping would let him mirror it, not with no tools and so little time. Nor was he such an artist. He rose and took a closer look. Too bad there was no pool, that he might regard his reflection.

Dagger's tail twitched. That might work. But where?

He stood and looked about at the trees and their contented birds. The climb had been sheer and barren. Yet past that cruel trek, life sprang in pockets. The mountain did not spurn life, only kept a high fence around it.

From his pack he removed a wedge of cheese and broke free a chunk the size of his curled thumb. Dagger crouched and rolled the cheese in the dirt, making sure it picked up tiny stones and grit. Pocketing the cheese, he searched and found a path leading up. Bitter Tempest remained behind, either keeping watch for trickery at the stream, or confident in its ability to find Dagger anywhere on the mountainside.

Perhaps an hour passed before Dagger found a suitably sheer vertical wall of stone. Fishing a piece of chalk from his pack, he drew an immense door upon the wall.

Dagger knocked upon the door thrice and said, "Brother spirit, Master of the Mountain, I visit you as family, come forth and greet your humble guest." This he repeated twice more.

When no response came on the third recitation, he worried it would go unanswered. Was this mountain barren of a spirit? Or did something other than stone claim it as home? How else would he manage to defeat Bitt—

A low rumble forced a flick to his ears. It began at his boots but eventually built with enough noise and quaking that the stoat gazed up to see if an avalanche might come crashing upon his head.

Cracks tore along the chalk outline and the cliff opened with a great creaking shudder. Out shuffled a giant stone figure, so huge it had to crouch and scuttle through the door like a crab before standing. Rocky flesh darker than the surrounding slate creaked with its movements. Much like Bitter Tempest, the mountain's master lacked many features, none to suggest a species or gender so much as an outline baring two arms and legs. It regarded him with a face eroded by time to nothing more than ancient crags to suggest eyes. Dagger stepped back and craned his neck to match gazes.

It spoke, and Dagger heard it less in his ears than in the thrum of his bones and gut. "You are no brother, no spirit. Certainly no kindred of that beneath the dirt."

Holding back the quiver of his spine and hiding his swallow, Dagger squared his shoulders and declared, "But I am! You doubt? Let me show you my strength." He crouched and mimed picking up a rock, while his free hand claimed the pocketed cheese. This he held up. "Any spirit might crush this with their fingers—'twould prove nothing. I am so small, yet even the tiniest, weakest part of me has granite bones."

Dagger put the cheese in his muzzle and chewed open-mouthed. Bits of gravel tumbled free, and he spat pebbles to the ground."

The spirit showed no reaction, but the weight of its gaze lifted off Dagger.

"I am known as Boulder's Son, spirit of a hill far yonder." The stoat pointed off into the distance. "Do you see the hill beyond the trees standing together as joined lovers?"

The mountain's keeper turned its head, the motion emitting a sound like iron giving birth, and stared off into the distance. The crags around its face crinkled as though squinting. "… yes," it said without conviction.

A knot in Dagger's stomach relaxed. So it was true entities of Earth hadn't the best of sight. "Forgive me, Master of the Mountain, for not asking sooner. What is your name?"

"Edifice," it said, turning to regard Dagger. "I am not yet convinced, Boulder's Son. You bear the fur of a mortal, like those that run about making war and other pettiness."

"This?" the stoat said, plucking at his fur. "It's merely a pelt. When I walk among the mortals, I find it best to hide what I am. Otherwise a crafty sorcerer or rival spirit might trap me or steal my power."

"Hmm. For that born of Earth, you are very small."

Here the stoat flared his whiskers, back bristling, and narrowed his gaze. "Do you remember being young, Edifice? Were you always so great and powerful, or did it take time for your home to grow so majestic? I am young, but one day my hill will kiss the sky, hopefully with the strength and beauty yours does."

"Spoken fairly," Edifice rumbled. With some grudging acceptance in the scrape of its voice, it said, "Welcome then, brother-spirit. You are my guest. Let us retire inside."

Before the giant could fully turn towards the door, Dagger shouted, "I cannot. Apologies my kin, but I did not disturb you for a welcoming visit."

Now Edifice's shoulders rose and great powerful arms groaned. "Company is not accepted easily or welcomed often, Boulder's Son. Privacy and quiet is precious, even from kin. Why do you come?" Each word came slower and more precise, the danger of a thousand avalanches teetering upon a ledge.

"Again I seek forgiveness, my kindred. I would not have bothered you, yet I have a humble request." Dagger leaned forward as a conspirator, glancing about with sharpened eyes and voice. "I was traveling along when surprised by this wicked Bitter Tempest. Do you know this foul name?"

"Yes," growled Edifice with the depth to loosen continents. "I know the fiend."

Dagger nodded. "I tried to end our conversation as swift as I could, but before I knew it, words were woven into a net that snared me. Bitter Tempest's cunning was too much for me, so I hope to find help in breaking the debt now owed."

"A fate many have fallen to. Air spirits, such vile thieves. Forgive me brother-spirit, I cannot help you; the spawn of Air lives upon my back for favors rendered. I cannot make war so simply."

"But I do not ask much of you, Edifice." Dagger afforded a slim, hopeful smile. "All I ask is that you might lend me your weapon for but a moment."

A chuckle like a rockslide tumbled forth. "That can be done, twice even if it troubles Bitter Tempest."

"Oh, it will."

Edifice turned and disappeared inside the door. At first Dagger grinned for his victory, but as time wore on, his mirth melted. He watched the sun dip lower. Entities of stone were slow. Would he have time to reach the stream? "Dust and ash!"

Finally, the giant emerged baring an axe the length of a tree, gleaming like liquid moonlight. Those born and living in the earth could harvest any of its veiny metals and gems, and spirits of stone held pride in their treasures, all master crafters. Dagger relaxed at the sight, and his fingers ached to hold the ocean of gold such a weapon could earn him.

"Here, brother-spirit," Edifice said and held the axe forth.

"Would you carry it for me? I have the strength for it, do not doubt, but the weapon is so long I would be overbalanced. Would be a crime were I to stumble and drop a masterpiece such as this."

"Very well." Edifice followed him to the stream, the stoat trying as politely as possible to hurry the spirit along, always strangled by the descent of the sun. They arrived as the glowing ember caressed the horizon.

Upon seeing Edifice, Bitter Tempest nearly boiled with a frenzy of wind. "What brings you to this contest, great Edifice?" The tone held back knives with deference.

"To see it won," said the mountain's keeper in good mirth.

The air frothed around Bitter Tempest. "You would aid some mortal for a chance to give insult?"

"Mortal?" Dagger's eyes widened and he turned to Edifice. "Weep over insults and give them in the same breath. The setting sun limits my task, and this is but a stalling gambit."

Edifice said, "I am deaf to venomous words. Unless a rule set in making of this debt is broken, let it be finished."

The only reply came as seething currents scouring the rock Bitter Tempest perched atop.

Dagger slashed a vertical chalk line beside the stream. "Plant the axe's blade here. Not too deep though."

A great shudder shook the cliff beneath the bite of Edifice's axe. In the scarlet glow of the sunset, the stream's reflection showed in its blade, an image clean and clear as a mountain pool.

Dagger grinned at the shuddering air spirit. "An exact likeness, wouldn't you say?"

A savage gust yanked Dagger and spun him with the ferocity of a thrown knife. Curling into a ball to protect his face from the cold, he rode out the tumbling wind until he met snow in a teeth-rattling crash. Regret for putting something in his stomach bubbled up along with the cheese. When stars finally lifted from his eyes, Dagger uncoiled to find himself back on the shelf where the challenge had begun.

"You think yourself amusing? Well then take my final challenge. I grant you no allowance of time, no quarter, attempt it now. Make. Me. Laugh." Each of those final words a blistering rend that tore at Dagger's pelt.

"Grant me more time," pleaded the stoat, "Your task is too harsh."

Malice boiled with barbed mirth. "You thought yourself sharp? For so much cunning you only now stumble over the truth?

Dagger panted, "But you ask too much, your price too steep! You are the cruelest and coldest being I have met."

"Oh ho, when cornered he balks. Will you cry or merely thrash like prey in the talons? Has your cleverness run and hid?"

After a moment's pause, Dagger heaved a great sigh and hung his head. "You have not a speck of humor inside you. I cannot make you laugh."

Bitter Tempest cackled, the sound of wind stripping bark. "Hahaha, pathetic creature. You have not seen the depths of my..." Words cracked like soured ice.

Dagger grinned as realization sank into the spirit.

The air went still and took on a graveyard's silence. Bitter Tempest regarded the stoat with naked hatred. Finally it spoke, the voice a gust's hollow susurrus through a cabin's uneven wall. "Very well."

For a moment the spirit broke apart and disappeared, becoming a light breeze caressing Dagger's face. A surge rushed down his throat, filling his lungs and for a moment he feared that he might burst, the spirit intending to kill him.

All at once he broke apart, the sensation of being everywhere and nowhere as the drifting currents tugged him about. A great pressure ached at his center and at once he gasped, back in his body, now teetering close to the rock shelf's edge.

"All you must do is take a deep breath and push," Bitter Tempest said, "but only as long as your breath can hold. May you gasp for air and find yourself too far above the ground," spat Bitter Tempest.

With a smirking salute, the stoat broke into air and whisked down the side of the mountain, thankful he needn't climb again.

A knight would sacrifice his life for his king, but what would make him sacrifice his honor? And who does he become when he's no longer a knight, just another dog in prison?

AT WHAT COST

Jeeves the Roo

The noble court stood in silence. Grim, piercing silence; almost as intense as the feeling of the court's combined gaze upon Delainy's kneeling form.

A cold hand on Delainy's shoulder made the dog's body tense instinctively. It gripped him tight, but not with the reassuring pressure of a friend or comrade in arms—with the weight and fervour of righteous indignation and judgement.

"Sir Delainy Marrall. You kneel before me, a once honoured member of my royal vanguard. But when next you rise, you will leave that honour on the ground upon which you rest. To be trodden into the stone by the boots of those you once called kin."

The King's voice rang out across the chamber, unfaltering and measured. Nevertheless, Delainy could feel the monarch's hand shaking upon his shoulder; betraying his anger, his sorrow, his disbelief at the very words now escaping his lips.

"I hereby strip you of your Knighthood. I revoke your titles and all their associated lands, possessions, and incomes. I cast doubt upon all oaths sworn by you, and free those in my service from any oath sworn to you. I brand you a traitor to your Kingdom and your King. I name you Scoundrel. I name you Darkheart. Hear this, and know that never again shall your presence be honoured, nor your past achievements lauded and praised. You are lowest of the low, and as you stand, know that never again shall you look upon the face of your King. Just as he shall never again look upon, or presume to even recall, your own countenance."

The hand left Delainy's shoulder. The King took a step back, and for a moment, just a moment, his eyes fell upon the defrocked Knight's own. Within the panther's pale blue eyes, like opals amidst the inky darkness of his face, Delainy saw such pain. Such frustration and sorrow. He didn't want to do this. Of course he didn't. He and Delainy, they were brothers. Not by blood, nor marriage. But by oath and by heart. By the way they knew and felt for one another, they were kin. But just as Delainy hadn't had a choice; just as there was no way he could have done anything differently in order to avoid ending up in this situation, neither did his King.

"Your Majesty..."

No sooner had Delainy spoke, he knew he was in error. Already he could feel arms beneath his shoulders. Pulling him upright, tearing him away from the world of nobility and Knighthood that was all he had known since his teenage years. He could see the King's face twisting with dark, terrible anger as it turned away from him, and the flick of the panther's hand. Bidding his remaining knights do what must be done with this traitor who dared to utter a single unbidden word in the King's presence.

A hand, gloved thankfully in leather rather than chainmail, slapped Delainy roughly across the muzzle for his insolence. The dog did not cry out. Did not yelp in pain, though he could feel his nose had been bloodied by the force of the strike. He knew that would only make it worse. Hands grappled at his bare arms and chest, pulling and pushing him, dragging him from the throne. Away from the King. Without dignity. Without honour.

Was this the life which now awaited him?

Delainy could hear the assembled nobles muttering and murmuring as he was dragged past them. He caught a few hissed, distasteful words passing through the tense, chilled air. Not directed at him, but certainly about him. The voices sounded so familiar; belonging to people with whom he had conversed at feasts and tournaments. Yet now, they possessed none of the joy and admiration to which he was accustomed. Instead, they were filled with vitriol. Not sorrow or resignation, but pure, fevered hate.

Thankfully, a door soon swung closed between the former knight and his former companions. The King's robed back, still stiffly poised away from Delainy's retreating figure, vanished from view, and a gruff voice grunted off to the dog's left hand side.

"Alright. Let's get this mutt into the dungeon, before I lose my cool and he loses an eye."

Delainy's head turned, looking to the source of the voice not with malice, simply curious as to which of his fellow knights was most eager to do him harm. Before he could turn his gaze upon the figure's face, however, with his eyes still travelling upward over the proud, snarling feline skull emblazoned upon the proud knight's chestplate, Delainy heard a strange whistling noise.

The cudgel swept through the air with such speed, Delainy felt the impact before he heard it. A thick, sickeningly dull thud. His vision exploded; dazzlingly bright and unbearable for a single instant, before rapidly fading to black. The snarling cat, his King's sigil, swam formlessly in the forefront of his mind for a second or two longer; his eyes open, but receiving only a sketchy memory of their last input. Delainy felt his body sagging within the arms of his captors, and suddenly he saw, and felt, and thought absolutely nothing.

"Hey."

When Delainy awoke, he started violently. Not due to the voice that had roused him back to consciousness, but because it was dark. So dark, he was afraid that the blow to his head had rendered him blind. It didn't take long for him to spot shapes in the infinite gloom around him, though. Dark stone walls. Dark chains. Strong, darkened wooden doors with metal panels which could be slid open or closed for the provision of food, or simply to gaze within at the wretched inhabitants.

"Hey, you're moving. I see you there. Don't try and play the innocent, sleeping victim with me, boy."

Delainy opened his muzzle, ready to tell the unseen speaker that he was no boy, but a Sir. A Knight. The words turned to ash on his lips, however, as he recalled the truth. He was no Knight. He wasn't anything, any more. Thus, if the owner of that harsh, throaty whisper was older than him, he might as well be 'boy'.

"I assure you, I am neither asleep, nor innocent. I trust we have that in common, friend?"

A softer, but still rather guttural burst of laughter escaped the blackness; echoing around the large, doubtlessly communal cell.

"Aye. No innocence here. Even those who didn't commit the crimes they're accused of, they're just as guilty as the rest of us. We're all guilty in the eyes of Gods and Kings. Guilty of being less wealthy. Less powerful. Less able to weasel and squirm and buy our way out of trouble."

The former knight could feel the hairs on the back of his neck prickling. He did not care for the way that this man was speaking. Yes, he knew that this was a prison. That he had no right to complain about his circumstances, or those with whom he was expected to share his new accommodation. Regardless of what Delainy knew, however, he still felt his senses sharpening. His body tensing, ready, if necessary, to defend himself against any manner of villainy which might fall upon him in this place.

"On that point, I'm afraid I must disagree. You speak to a former Knight of the realm. Few but the King wielded as much power, political or physical, as I. Yet still, I am denounced and judged guilty by the masses every bit as much as the Lords and the King and the Gods themselves."

Silence. Delainy smiled in spite of the situation. Even the echo of his former rank still gave even the most hardened criminal reason to pause. No man, not even the king, could strip him of that truth.

"Oh? Knight of the realm, is it? Well... it just so happens I'm the King, and as King I royally decree that you've got to be one hell of an idiot to try and convince me of something that ridiculous."

The dog's ears flicked in annoyance as the voice piped up again. He knew the speaker was almost certainly bluffing about not believing him. But just as he was capable of reading into the tone of his fellow inmate, Delainy had little doubt that he was laying himself bare to the owner of that voice with every word.

"Knight or not, though, you still want something from me. Right?"

Again, Delainy's cellmate delayed his response for a short while; either in an attempt to further unnerve the dog, or perhaps unnerved himself.

"Aye."

A simple answer. Delainy followed it up with an equally simple question.

"How long have you been down here, friend? Quite some time, I'll bet. Your confidence tells me this is far from the first time you've been faced with a new cellmate, and that you know these surroundings well enough for the darkness not to hold you back, were I to become violent."

From within the darkness, shadows stirred. A stone pillar, merely six or seven feet from where Delainy was resting, his back against one of the cold, grey walls of the cell, began to shift and move. A figure peeled himself away from the dark column, and stepped towards the fallen knight.

"Three years. Three years I've been down here. And a dozen weeks since I last shared this cell, or a conversation, with anyone but the guards at feeding time. And yeah, they're exactly as talkative as you're probably imagining."

Delainy nodded, though without once letting his gaze slip from the figure's now visible form; analysing every notable detail of the still shadow-clad shape to try and size up his cellmate.

"So, you're wanting to hear the news, I'd wager. Tales from the outside. The latest comings and goings in the Great City. The power plays, the..."

A deep, rumbling snarl; clearly canid in origin, escaped the convict's lips.

"I don't want to know about any of that pisswater. Tell me about the war. If you're a great and powerful Knight, tell me... are you here because your King is dead, and the new King doesn't take too kindly to his Knights having fought against him on the field of battle? Or are you some sort of coward. A deserter, or a turncoat, perhaps?"

This time, the silence belonged to Delainy, and he to it. He wanted to cry out, to tell his cellmate that he was no turncoat. No traitor. That he loved his King and the realm to which he had been bound with all his heart. For he did. But, as an honest man, Delainy could not make that claim. He could not say that he wasn't a traitor, because his King's judgement was accurate. He had betrayed the King's trust. He had betrayed all of his Countrymen. He was a traitor. And so, as the former knight's eyes began to grow ever more accustomed to the gloom, he sat there in dumb silence, and watched his cellmate's yellowed teeth twinkling in the dim light shining in from under the doorway; beaming at the knowledge of his discomfort.

Eventually, after several minutes of that same wordless stalemate; stubborn pride against manic, grinning mirth, Delainy could hold his tongue no longer. He had to say something, if only to distract himself from his cellmate's smile. A smile that betrayed how far he had fallen, to give this common criminal the moral upper hand.

"I am a traitor. But my treason did not cause the fall of this great Kingdom. We fought our final battle, just a week past. We sacked the

Oaken halls, and with the rebel Lords at sword-point, their armies fled or yielded to our forces. I myself put the High Lord Talleth to the sword at my King's command. I barred the door as his co-conspirators tried to escape, and watched my men slay each and every one of them. I could have been the hero of this tale. I was the hero of this tale."

The shadowy figure chuckled dryly.

"And yet, you are here."

Delainy growled under his breath. He nodded, running a hand through the shaggy, unkempt crop of hair which his mixed breed parentage had made impossible to tame.

"And yet, I'm here. All because my King would not see sense. All because he would not show a little mercy. Not mercy to a grown man. I would not have asked such a thing. Not even to a grown woman. But to greyhound pups. Babies. I asked mercy for babies, and for that, I am as you greet me now. Traitor, and scoundrel."

For the first time since regaining consciousness, Delainy allowed his eyes to fall closed. He bowed his head, shaking it shamefully.

"High Lord Talleth's children were in a private chamber with their mother and a nurse. We killed the guards. We killed the mother. And when I saw the nurse moving towards the children with that bottle... that black bottle. I cut off her arm before it could even begin to approach the little mouth of one of the two youngest, and slit the heartless cow's throat a moment later."

No longer was Delainy's cellmate laughing. Indeed, he seemed to have sobered up considerably during the course of the former knight's tale.

"She was going to kill the Lord's children? Starting with the twins? Poison the newest little Lord and Lady, rather than see them captured by their parents' killers?"

Delainy nodded, head still bowed, eyes still closed. He paused, recalling his actions on that day; every movement, every word. Every little detail.

"She was going to kill them. And when I stopped her, and told my fellow Knights what I had witnessed, do you know what they said? Do you know what the King himself said, when I told him the monstrous act that I had almost born witness to?"

Silence. Delainy's fists clenched at his sides.

"He asked me a question. He asked me... Did I know what happens to little boys and girls who grow up, seeing or hearing of how their parents were slaughtered?"

From the darkness, that throaty voice answered once more.

"They grow up into little killers. Little King Killers. They grow up into Rebels, like their martyred parents."

Delainy smiled.

"Yes. Yes, that's what he said. And then he told us to finish what the nurse had started. To kill them all, and end the next rebellion before it had even started. That was my King's judgement. His high and honourable wisdom. Madness."

That final word, that continued declaration of his supposed treachery, was all it took. Out of the darkness, a metal blade glinted as it was thrust forward. Delainy jerked sharply to the left, and he heard the blade scrape the wall where his gut had been mere moments before. The shaggy haired dog kicked out with his right foot, swinging it around to try and trip his assailant. At the same time, his right arm lunged for the blade still clutched in his cellmate's hand. The former knight's adversary was fast though. Too fast, given how awkwardly and stiffly the dog had been sitting. He jerked backwards, away into the black of the cell's depths, and laughed as Delainy leapt to his feet; trembling from head to toe with a surge of adrenaline.

"How long have you known, Traitor?"

Delainy snarled, hearing the word used against him as a curse far more piercing than any foul word he could conceive.

"Known? That you were one of the King's men, sent to see if I was fit for his mercy? If I was truly worthy of life in chains, rather than a quick death by the blade? Ever since you told me as much."

From somewhere to the dog's left, a quick rumble of anger echoed through the air.

"So... I let something slip? What was it. My common accent not convincing enough? Please, do tell. I'd love to know, so I can work on it for next time."

Again, a dry smile crossed Delainy's lips.

"So, you're one of the King's jailers. Perhaps even one of his interrogators. I guess that makes sense. I always steered well clear of you. Psychopaths on a leash. Murderers and rapists with immunity from the law, so long as they ply their craft only on those the King deems worthy. Well, my twisted friend, it wasn't your accent. That was impeccable. It was your facts. You knew them too well. Twelve weeks, you said. Over three months since you last learned anything of the outside world. So how is it, I ask myself, that a prisoner who hasn't spoken to a soul for three months, knows that Lord Talleth's two month old babies were twins?"

Though muffled, a failed attempt to keep it under his breath, Delainy could still hear the interrogator's curse as he realised his error.

"Don't worry, though. By the time we're through, a lot more than your professional pride will be wounded. I had to kill nine of my closest comrades to keep them away from those children. Seven more to get them and the servants who would lead them away to safety out of the hall's rear gate. Do you really think I can't handle one interrogator, even without my sword and my armour?"

The sound of spitting, of the interrogator hurling his hatred to the ground, brought a fresh snarl to Delainy's lips.

"Scoundrel, they call me. Darkheart. Saviour of the Talleth family and harbinger of a new rebellion. People spit on my name. You spit on the thought of such a loathed figure defeating you, though just a few weeks ago you would have likely soiled yourself if faced by the end of my blade. But I ask you, if I am a traitor, a scoundrel, and a fallen knight for saving the lives of innocent children, whose only crime was to share blood with a Rebel, then what good is our victory? At what cost do we declare this war over? At what cost are we in the King's service supposed to rest easy at night? Once every child to bear the name Talleth, or that of any family who supported their Rebellion, is dead?"

The interrogator laughed cruelly from his hiding place in the blackness.

"Aye. Every child and more, if that is what the King commands. And if High Lord Talleth had succeeded, it would be the King we now serve who would die... and his children, and the children of all his allies. I dare say your own family would lose a sapling or two from their tree, if the rebel Lords had triumphed."

Another strike. Another sudden swoop in from the side, a flash of metal, and twin grunts of effort as Delainy jinked out of the way of his captor's knife. Again, the interrogator did not pause for even a moment in the wake of his assault, melting back into the shadows with ease as Delainy called out after him.

"You're a monster. The King may just be afraid, and angry, and counselled by others who are afraid and angry... but you, you enjoy all this, don't you? The bloodshed? The thought of women and children being sliced apart in the name of power."

Laughter. Louder and louder. More grating and infuriating with every passing second, rang out all around Delainy as his eyes scanned the darkness for the slightest sign of movement.

"Oh come now, don't presume to judge me. It doesn't have to be in the name of power. There are many wonderful, acceptable reasons for killing man, woman and child alike. Power is but one. For instance, duty. It is my duty to kill you. A lost cause. A traitor so consumed by his madness, he believes it to be truth. Just as it was your duty to kill the Talleth children, not your fellow knights as they simply attempted to do their duty, honouring their monarch's command. We are, after all, serving at the King's pleasure. While you... You remain lowest of the low. Just as you said. A traitor. A scoundrel. If you wish to see the true monster in this cell, look not for me in the darkness, but seek yourself in the reflection of my blade, before I dirty it with your bloo—"

Before the interrogator could finish his thought, Delainy surged forward; throwing his body into the darkness, and grunting in satisfaction as he tackled the hidden figure head on. He had been in the room long enough now, and kept his blade-wielding cellmate talking for long enough to figure out the acoustics of the room. To understand where each echo was coming from, and trace it back to the source. Delainy pinned the interrogator against the nearest wall, their faces pressing close together. Close enough for the mutt to finally see his aggressor; a lithe, short haired dog with slick, greasy looking dark hair. He didn't recognise the figure personally, but the family resemblance was uncanny.

"You... you're..."

The interrogator didn't respond. He was too busy trying to fight the grip of both Delainy's hands around his own, slowly turning his knife around, towards his own quivering torso.

"You're a Talleth. You're the traitor who made our victory possible. The one who gave the rebel army the false reports of our movements to the south. The one who showed us how to break the Oaken halls defences with so little loss on our side."

With a whine of dismay as the blade began to cut through his leather jerkin and brush against his oh so short, grey fur, the interrogator began to cry out as he struggled more and more wildly.

"A-aah! And with your death, I would have proven myself loyal. I would have escaped the fate of my foolish cousin, and earned a place.

Your place, as a Knight of the realm. Kill... kill him! Kill him, n-now. Before he. Before I... o-oh. Oh."

The greyhound's eyes widened as he felt his own blade pierce his skin. It slid right in between two of his ribs, and with a quick downward pivot of the handle, sliced cleanly up through his pulmonary artery.

He coughed, a thin mist of blood spraying out over Delainy's face, and ceased struggling as the life drained from his eyes.

Delainy held him there, pinning the last living Talleth, the true traitor of this long and bloody civil war, up against the dungeon wall, his eyes closed and his breathing ragged as he fought not to gag on the coppery stench of blood rising from his victim's chest.

He listened, carefully filtering out his own heavy breathing, and sighed softly as he heard shuffling in the darkness.

"How many more of you are there? How many of you were watching... Waiting to see which of the loose ends would be left to tie up?"

No-one answered.

"Tell the King... tell him, t-that in my last moments, I... I served him with honour. I killed a true traitor, so that he would not have to dishonour himself by granting such a dishonest, disloyal scoundrel continued service in his ranks."

Delainy stepped back from the wall. He stood up straight, allowing the interrogator, knife still buried in his chest, to slump down to the floor like a sack of hay.

"Tell him I forgive him. And that I'll pray the gods show him more mercy than he did to me."

The blade that pierced Delainy from behind was freshly forged, and the knight who wielded it talented enough to hit his mark first time.

Darkheart. Scoundrel. Traitor. The former Sir Delainy Marrall. In a split second, the dog was none of these things any longer. He was at peace. His struggles at an end.

He was gone, and the world would carry on without him.
One fewer scoundrel. One fewer hero.
Gone. Though at what cost?

The world itself is a character in this science-fiction noir tale, and when Constable Handlin sets out to investigate the murder of a lemur woman, he finds himself exploring the darkness in all their lives.

A City With No Children

James Stegall

"Constable, I wish to report a murder."

All the noise in the busy precinct fled from those words. Constable Handlin set his stub pencil down on the report he was writing and looked at the rat-breed in front of him: a man with wide, pink ears on either side of his pinched face. He wore the black robes of a Receptor of the Guidance Church.

"A murder, Honesty?" Handlin asked, bear-breed nostrils flaring. A murder was common enough; a report from a Receptor was unusual.

The small gray head nodded.

"Please," Handlin said, offering the chair in front of his battered desk.

The Receptor folded his long, thin tail over his lap as he sat. This close, Handlin could see the thin gold filaments in his ears, one of the finely attenuated tools the Receptors used to judge truth. Handlin's broad back tingled as he thought of the Receptors he had known as a child in the Rows. It was the smaller breeds that seemed to enjoy judging a bear-breed a liar, and applying the whip.

Handlin flipped to an empty page in his notebook with a long foreclaw. He licked the tip of his pencil. "Your name please, Honesty."

The Receptor raised his chin as he spoke. "Arnharlin Manvailo, Fourth Tier of the Guidance Church."

Handlin acknowledged the title with a curt nod. The lowest tier for a Receptor, but a high station for a small neighborhood.

Manvailo described a visitor in his confessional at approximately midday (just one watch ago if Handlin had heard the bells correctly), a newly bred with a nervous voice, tapping repeatedly at the confessional window as he spoke. He said he had entered an apartment through an open window in order to rob it, and instead discovered a woman in the midst of a natural birth. He heard her cries and came upon her heaving in the bed, blood between her legs and the child a breech birth.

"Breech birth, Honesty?" Handlin asked.

"An old Earth word. It means a turning of the child so that it is stopped in the birthing process."

Handlin nodded.

"Yet more proof of the Guiders' Wisdom," the Receptor said. "Those who thwart the Plan are punished."

Handlin's face flattened but he said nothing. "Where was this apartment, Honesty?" he asked.

The Receptor shook his head. "I know not. The young man spoke with a South Commerce accent, I would reckon. And he smelled of the tar from that section."

"He said he climbed to the open window?"

"Yes."

"Did he say from the roof or the street?"

"He mentioned the fire ladder."

When Handlin finished taking the report, he took down the Receptor's own address. As the constable closed his notebook, the rat-breed stood carefully and raised a thin hand in blessing, first finger extended toward the ceiling.

"We are what we were made to be," he said. "Despite our humanity. Good day to you, Constable."

"And you, Honesty."

Handlin watched the crowd in the lobby split as the Receptor walked slowly yet assuredly through them.

#

The one open window in a long neighborhood block piled with snow was not difficult to locate. Handlin stood in the doorway with the landlord's head at his elbow. The other man was dog-breed but of some smaller stock, his face short and untrusting. His conical ears thrust forward as he sniffed the air.

"Her name's Allonia Diferrous," the landlord said.

"She lives here alone?"

"Far as I know. Some others come around sometimes. Lemur-breed, I think."

"You couldn't tell?"

He made a sour face and Handlin saw his hackles rise. "They all look the same to me."

"What did they smell like?"

The landlord shrugged.

"Allonia?" Handlin called, knowing there would be no answer. He stepped into the apartment, noting details. Thin curtains but neatly sewn. A side table with an earthen wash basin and pitcher. Through a short hallway, Handlin could see the kitchen. The opposite door was slightly ajar. He eased it open with an extended claw, and looked into the room.

"It must be good to be as big as you, and not afraid to go anywhere," the landlord said.

Handlin glanced at him but didn't answer.

The room was dim, and the air had the tang of blood mixed with chill moisture from the snow. The woman lay on the bed as described, arms open and eyes staring at the ceiling. Her long tail hung limp over the side of the bed.

"I'm not going in there," the landlord said, his nostrils twitching.

"Send someone to the station for me. Tell them I need the Coroner."

With the landlord gone, Handlin stood in the doorway and studied the room intently for several moments. Then he put a hand on the doorjamb and lowered his head. He saw the dead nearly every day; but the sight of her caught him deeply in his chest, making his breaths shallow. For most, sterility was a fact of life. For those few who discovered they were fertile, who went against the Church and the Guider's' Plan, this was the typical outcome.

She couldn't have been here alone, he thought. Someone had been here who loved her, who panicked. Someone else may have intervened. He breathed slowly to calm his mind, pushing away the scene he imagined.

The sheets were stained in waves of successively lighter scarlet, from the end of the bed to the darkest blood beneath the baby's protruding leg. He could see immediately that though the baby was breeched, her hips were too small. There was no way she could have delivered without surgery, and no doctor would ever assist with a natural birth under threat of the Guidance Church.

Handlin collected details to use later in his report as he looked around the room, breathing deeply, smelling, tasting, forcing himself to absorb detail.

Moving to the side of the bed, he saw a thick red line through the short hairs on her neck. He noted that she hadn't been strangled with bare hands. It had been something thick enough to leave a wide mark, yet not rough enough to leave rope burns or cut her skin.

Handlin sat in one of the small straight-backed chairs beside the bed, sighing deeply, and took out his notebook and pencil. He looked at her face: early thirties, covered in a light pale fur. She had yellow-ringed eyes with black irises. She was a different breed from him but he still saw her beauty. Her eyes raised away to a distant sight, maybe the Ship itself.

Only women's clothing in the closet. No attachments, then. His eyes fell on a painter's box. He knelt to open it and produced a sheaf of mock window advertisements, and under that a collection of wiped-clean paint bottles and well-maintained brushes. This was how she paid her rent.

He went from the bedroom to the bathroom with its wooden tub and small mirror. More evidence of a lone existence. In the kitchen he found a loaf of bread, recently sharpened knives, place settings for three. On the wall above the small kitchen table was a pencil drawing of Allonia, an older woman, and a younger man, all Lemur-breed with dark faces and spade-shaped ears. Handlin took it off the wall and studied it. Their resemblance went beyond breed, which seemed an odd artistic license. Carefully, he slid the paper from its frame, folded it once, and tucked it inside his blue jacket.

When the cat-breed Coroner surmised cause of death as traumatic loss of lifesblood and not strangulation, Handlin growled.

"Certainly strangulation was a contributing factor," the cat-breed said. "But she was dying before that started."

"But the cause of death was strangulation," Handlin said.

"I just stated."

"What killed her?" Handlin demanded.

The cat-breed's pointed ears twitched. He averted his eyes and turned to his bag to put away his materials. "The report will say strangulation," he conceded.

"When did the baby die?" Handlin asked.

"The boy?" The Coroner snorted bitterly. "After. Perfect example of what happens when we thwart the Plan. The innocent suffer."

On the street, Handlin buttoned his jacket against the blowing snow. He didn't need the jacket except as someplace to pin his badge, but lack of clothing made him look even more barbaric than people already assumed. He flexed his shoulders and arms as he walked, restless with strength.

The muddy streets were frozen, crunching underfoot, and the plank sidewalks slippery where traffic thawed them. Smoke stacks from the tar refineries leaked black smoke into the overcast sky. The air was acrid in his nose.

His gaze went to the smoke-stained storefronts alongside, flicking up and down the people inside, the people walking out, hugging themselves against the cold, sniffing the air. For the first time he noticed the painted lines in the frosted windows, ornate lettering of prices and goods, scrolls of musical notes, ordinary items like butter and chicken made elegant by the artist's lines.

He began entering stores, sharing the drawing. Many verified the identity of Allonia but no one knew the other two. Leaving a butchers shop, a gathering of people at an alley entrance drew Handlin's attention. As he crossed the street, words lifted above the hissing wind.

"They watch us from up there," a street preacher's voice accused. Handlin recognized the voice of an orator called Francis Tervanla.

"Five hundred years," the high-pitched voice enunciated bitterly. "They did not fail. They made no mistake when they landed us here alone. They wait for us to make something of this place. We are not their children but their slaves."

The crowd murmured over the word "slaves."

Though Handlin could see over most of the heads blocking the end of the alley, Tervanla was squirrel-breed and stood well below the shoulders circling him. His vehemence defied his size. His voice was seductive, drawing them all closer. Handlin felt the energy building in the crowd, heads nodding, tails twitching, teeth bared.

"We are tools to be discarded," the preacher grated. "Childless! Unable to procreate. We are not the ideal hybrid of Old Earth life the Guidance Church urges you believe. They are the liars! We die scratching away in Landing City, pounded by the Iron Sea."

"The sea-breed," someone wailed. Handlin couldn't locate the source. "Why did the sea-breed leave us?"

"Why not?" Tervanla scoffed. His disembodied voice seemed to move among the crowd. "Wouldn't you, given the chance? The Guidance will allow no more sea-breed. They can have no one else breaking free. Scrape at your rocks, slaves. Die childless, clutching one another in old age." His voice rose as he sing-songed: "Born of the Bulb and bred in the Rows," which brought on more grumbling. "You were made imperfect, and they watch and gloat from the Day Star."

Handlin felt the roar build in his chest, a roar of impotence that disguised itself in action, in enforcing laws because someone must... And then he was blasting his voice into the crowd. He ordered them to disperse. He stated the laws against sedition, his voice booming like a hammer. The crowd disintegrated and revealed a hobbled squirrel-breed with an orange face, two stained teeth curving from his upper lip. His hands cupped a small pile of coins.

"You incite sedition," Handlin said. "Cease or face adjudication." He loomed above the squirrel like a wall.

The squirrel-breed's nose twitched. He tilted his head to watch the last backs fleeing the alley. From between his coat-tails, his own tail twitched and flicked, its fur shiny against the smoke-stained walls. When they were alone, he said, "Your badge is dirty, Constable. You should get back to polishing it." He opened a leather purse at his waist and dumped the coins inside.

Handlin grunted. He reached inside his jacket and pulled out the drawing. He opened it carefully to shield the paper from snow.

"I'm looking for the older woman and the man, Tervanla. Do you know them?"

As Handlin held out the drawing, he realized that Allonia had made it herself. The lines were similar to the advertisements in her case, thick and assured. An economy of strokes. He glanced up as Tervanla took the page carefully from his hand.

"I know the women," he said finally. "The man is unknown to me."

"The girl is dead earlier today. Childbirth."

The small man crumpled slightly, his shoulders clenching inward. "She was a lovely girl, Allonia."

"You knew her well?"

He looked up, his brown eyes meeting Handlin's. "Enough. Not many lemur-breed to begin with, and even fewer talented like her."

"Who is the other woman?"

"Fonia Eyfander."

"Where can I find her?"

"Cooperside, on the third street."

Handlin nodded his thanks. As he took the drawing back, he found himself staring at it again, at the lines of the young woman's face. She would have had to hide herself away once she started showing, as lithe as she was. He thought of the neatness in her apartment, the paint jars wiped clean.

"You see the resemblance?" Tervanla asked.

"Of the breed, yes."

"Not just the breed."

Handlin did not look at the orator but knew he couldn't hide the suspicion from his face.

"Aye," Tervanla said. "We're all born o' the Bulb under the hand of the Guidance Church. No mother, no father, only brother and sister." He touched the edge of the paper with a short, thin claw. "But what if the Guidance Church knew more about the secrets of the Birthing Bulbs than commoners like you or me? What if they could choose who was birthed, and not the Guider's Plan? What if more of the Day Star's secrets made the Landing than we rabble know?"

When Handlin didn't answer, Tervanla continued, "Why do you think there have been changes after all these five hundred years? Why pregnancies now, and only certain breeds?"

"Don't waste your street rabble on me," Handlin growled.

"Fonia Eyfander is a Second Tier Receptor of the Guidance Church," Tervanla said.

The constable looked at him, narrowing his eyes. "Not according to this drawing, she's not."

The squirrel-breed shrugged. "You tell me why a girl would draw someone as she wished she was. But that's what she is. And what's the connection here aside from breed? Seems plain to me." The squirrel raised an eyebrow and whistled a wisp of shanty. "You'll most likely find her in the Third Street Sanctuary if not at home."

Handlin put the paper back inside his jacket. "Aye. Be well, Tervanla."

"And you, Constable." He grinned around his curved teeth. "Can't get any worse, can it?" He tapped his purse so it jangled. "At least until I think of something worse."

Handlin had not stopped frowning since the accusation about the birthing bulbs. "Do you believe even half of what you preach?" he said.

Tervanla gave a scoundrel's laugh. "Never attribute malice to pure incompetence. Why would our Makers be any less fallible than we? They made us after all." He paused. "That sounds like a fine idea for an oratory."

"Speaking of that," Handlin said. He opened his hand, claws extended like fan blades.

"Thought you forgot," the squirrel said, and he dug in his purse before reaching up to roll a large gold coin into Handlin's palm.

The Third Street House of the Guidance was made of long Ironwood planks, originally sky-blue but worn dull by the relentless sea wind. A faded white star shone above the tall doors.

Handlin pushed open one of the heavy doors and entered the dim, open-floored sanctuary. Hard pews filled the room in two columns, and he thought immediately of the Rows, and the hours he had spent sitting, kneeling, rising, eyes raised to the milk-colored glass star above the dais, sole source of outside light.

The walls were covered in the typical images of the Landing, but as he looked closer he realized these had been painted by the familiar hand. Here Allonia had chosen not only lines, but colors of lovely fading softness that recognized the rough Ironwood canvas. The first panel of the Ship leaving Earth reached from floor to the angle of the ceiling, and the Earth was a warm suffusion of blue ocean and green land masses, lonely in the mass of black surrounding it. Forced perspective made the Ship tiny against the horizon of its Mother Earth.

Two more panels showed the Journey, imagined planets, suns, stars, nebula. The fourth panel showed Home. The final panels were of the Ship in orbit, sending down its first and only lander to the surface, to the spot near the equator that would become Landing City, caught between a vast continent and a greater ocean. In the last panel, Allonia painted the Ship in the gray sky, now blinding white as the Day Star, gleaming down on the black orbs of the Bulbs. Men and women of the Guidance Church, many different breeds, drew out newborns and held them up to the light of the Star.

Handlin studied this panel closely, drawn by a woman who had chosen the risk of a forbidden natural birth.

The opposite side of the sanctuary was covered in images of breeds battling the stubborn Ironwood forests, scratching mines into the rock cliffs, the first small houses and then the gradual development of industry into great sailing ships cresting waves. These panels were older, the artist more stolid. Handlin noted several places where portions had been painted over, perhaps removing evidence of the sky and sea-breeds.

The Confessionals stood at the far end of the Sanctuary, away from the dais. Handlin waited in front of the one available door and studied the panels again in turn. When the door finally opened, a round rabbit-breed glanced up at him and blanched, his face going slack. The constable waved him away and stepped through the door, pulling it closed behind him. He sat on the worn wooden bench, and placed a gold coin in the receptacle beneath the grate.

It was overly warm in the closet-sized room, and the air reeked of pine. His nostrils flared as he separated smells in the cubicle. Details for his report: sweat, musk, alcohol. Muffled sounds reached him from the street outside, where the barrelworks was in full labor. Hammers banged metal, saws chewed wood, barrels rolling across the frozen mud street. People shouting, singing, laughing. There was life in Landing City, despite Tervanla's curated pessimism.

He heard the curtain move aside in the opposite cubicle, revealing light through the grate. He saw the Receptor's shadow.

Handlin cleared his throat. "Hear me, Honesty," he said, following a script he had learned with all the other children in the Rows. "I come before you to share my truth and receive the Guiders' wisdom. I am but one of many."

"We are what we were made to be," the Receptor answered, a deep female voice. "Despite our humanity. Share your truth with me, so I may hear."

Handlin made his voice low and urgent, but also slow, careful. "Honesty, my mate and I have made a terrible mistake. We hoped to share a child. She carried to term but now lies bleeding in our bed. I know not how to help her and dare not call a doctor."

Silence followed his statement.

"Honesty," he pressed.

"You must ease her suffering," the Receptor said finally.

"How?" he demanded. "Is there some medicine?"

"There is no medicine. You must—" She paused, then said, "end her suffering."

Handlin released a long breath.

"What about the child?" he said.

She began to answer and then her voice caught. He heard fingers scrabbling at the door in the opposite cubicle. She was running.

Handlin leaped to his feet and shoved his own door open. It slammed against the wall as he turned to find the Receptor half through the entry to her cubicle. Her black robe had caught in the door; from beneath its folds, her tail gripped a long knife. Her blunt face rose to his, the yellow-black eyes blazing. For a flash he saw Allonia Diferrous, and he nearly drew back, forgetting the knife.

Then the Receptor saw his blue coat and badge, and she collapsed. The knife clattered on the wooden floor as her tail dropped.

He stood over her as she sobbed, her hands working the material of her black robe. The gold filaments in her ears were dull in the afternoon light.

"Fonia Eyfander?" he said.

She nodded, and pressed her face against the threshold.

Handlin took a deep breath and drew himself to his full height. "By the power vested in me by the Council of the City of Landing, I, Constable Handlin Kronvelus, arrest you under suspicion of the deaths of Allonia Diferrous and her child, an infant boy."

A crowd had gathered at the Confessional entrance. Fonia's gaze went from Handlin to the faces in the door. She pulled her black lips back in a grimace.

"You did not lie," she hissed, her eyes going wide and then incredulous. "You told me the truth."

Handlin pulled her upright. He knotted the restriction band around her wrists and tail and sat her back inside the booth, where she glared at him with piercing yellow-black eyes.

When he showed her the drawing, she blinked, and then downcast her eyes.

"Who is this man?" Handlin said, pointing.

"Her lover," the Receptor said finally. "The dreamer who convinced her and then came to me when she was dying by his doing."

"His name?"

Her dark lips worked. "He belongs to the Guidance Church."

Handlin stared at her. "I will find this man whether you tell me his name or not."

The Receptor turned her face away.

Handlin growled deep in his throat as his claws began to ache, and he felt the anger in his shoulders and arms. A ferret-breed approaching the confessionals shrank behind a pew as he swung one arm and tore the side of the booth open, revealing more of the cowering Receptor bound inside.

"Call the Street Watch," he yelled at the cowering man in the Sanctuary. "Tell them I need the wagon."

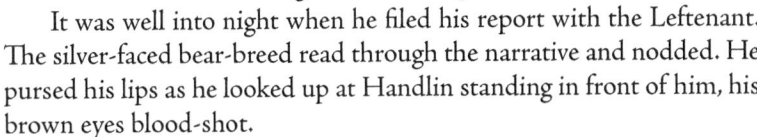

It was well into night when he filed his report with the Leftenant. The silver-faced bear-breed read through the narrative and nodded. He pursed his lips as he looked up at Handlin standing in front of him, his brown eyes blood-shot.

"She's already been released to the Church," he said.

"I guessed as much."

"You're making few friends with this."

Handlin nodded. He reached inside his jacket and took out the drawing. Unfolding it, he laid it on the desk. "I should have included this as evidence," he said.

"Aye," the Leftenant acknowledged. They were silent for several minutes as he looked at the drawing. Eventually he said, looking up at Handlin, "There is more here. Why do you think a Receptor reported the death at all?"

Handlin chewed his lip. "Aye," he said. "There is more here."

The Leftenant growled deep in his throat, a soft sound that indicated a constable's general frustration. He collected the report and drawing and placed them in a folio. "Always the way of it." He nodded to Handlin. "Be well, Constable. Dismissed."

"Thank you, sir."

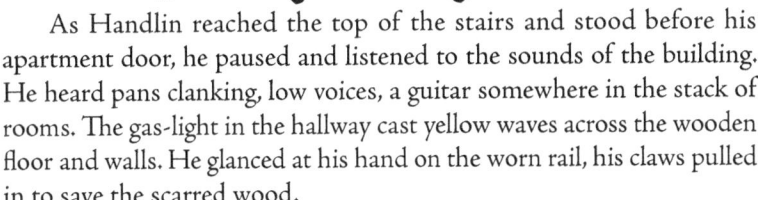

As Handlin reached the top of the stairs and stood before his apartment door, he paused and listened to the sounds of the building. He heard pans clanking, low voices, a guitar somewhere in the stack of rooms. The gas-light in the hallway cast yellow waves across the wooden floor and walls. He glanced at his hand on the worn rail, his claws pulled in to save the scarred wood.

He fitted his key in the lock and pulled the door open. Inside the small sitting room, he saw the fireplace with a coal glowing in its mouth, and beside that, Sarall sat in the rocking chair with a piece of wood in her hands, turning it beneath her carving knife. She looked up at the sound of him entering and smiled.

Handlin closed the door and crossed the room. "Don't rise," he said.

She laid her tools aside and brushed away the sweet-smelling wood chips as he fell to his knees in front of her and pressed his face into her belly.

As she knew he liked, she pulled up her shirt, revealing the soft fur on her stomach, and he pressed his ear against her body, clutching at her, listening for the second heartbeat inside.

Matthew is a bird in love, but he's not the one sitting in the catbird seat.

PERCH

Sarah Doebereiner

Matthew glided through the sky. A current of air caressed his red and green feathers. He dipped below the horizon of buildings. The structures cornered the wind until any hope of an updraft floated away. Matthew glided as best as he could to the ground. His clawed feet tapped as he fumbled to a stop. The shock sent reverberating pain up his muscular legs. He folded his arms, allowing the longest feathers to nestle against his sides. Deep green flyaways jutted up. Matthew sighed.

Flying was better than taking the subway. Most birdmen lived in open spaces and flew wherever they wanted to go. Bird taxis had the least profitable margin in the transportation sector. They were practically non-existent this far into the city. His feathers popped out of their sculpting. He paused in an alcove along the side of the building. Before preening, he poked his head out into the open.

A family of lemurs was hopping down the street, oblivious to his presence. Beyond them, he noted a few high school ground-squirrels chattering a greeting in front of a coffee shop. Matthew inhaled deeply. He had never been to a multi-species restaurant before. He didn't dislike the notion of it, it was more that not all multi-species joints could accommodate birdmen. Matthew poked at a watch on his ankle. He had some time before Clarice arrived. He wasn't sure which would be worse: to get caught looking so shabby, or to be primping when she came around the corner like a bad stereotype.

A thin leather strap wrapped around his waist. It was mostly obscured by his plumage. When he puffed up, the darkness of the binding

175

stuck out against his radiant colors. The strap had horizontal pockets just large enough to slide personal items in. He withdrew a printout of Clarice's picture from one of the pockets.

Clarice was a shy girl. The two had been dating for four months. Even if they hadn't, Matthew could have seen that trait just by glancing at her. Clarice was pale for a cat. If not for her pastel blue eyes, Matthew might have said she was albino. Her back curled when she slouched; which would have been fine, except that she always slouched. That slump in her spine shortened her. Matthew was average height for a birdman, about five feet tall. If Clarice straightened up, she'd have been taller than him. In the photo, her ears pinned low on her head. In all the time he had known her, those light, wispy ears never stood completely erect.

Matthew paced. It took conscious effort not to bob his head a bit as he moved. The motion was comforting. His eyes followed the path of a dogwoman walking hand in hand with a lizard. The woman held a puppy in her arms. A crest of very fine scales ran over its face and down its back. Matthew tried not to stare.

Hybrids were a gamble. They could be exotic—stunning even. Something unique and mysterious made them stand out in a crowd. Then, sometimes it went the other way, and you ended up with a gangly pup with splotches of scales sloughing off when he scratched.

Matthew didn't want kids. Clarice told him fairly early on that she didn't either. It was better that way for crossbreed couples. The nightmare of genetic mutation and hospitalized splicing wasn't something he could deal with. A kitten with wings could be movie star, but a bird with fur who couldn't fly, or a kitten with backwards knees would get stuck in menial labor somewhere far out of sight of the public. Matthew grimaced.

The family entered the restaurant. He was glad he had called ahead. He reserved the highest perch in the place. Matthew turned. He rolled the edge of his beak over his midsection. A rough spot in the pocket of his belt scraped against the flap of skin over his eye. He smiled gently at the thought of the pearl ring nestled inside. They wouldn't even notice the baby doglizard from a position in the rafters.

"Matt," Clarice sounded quietly. Matthew jumped. He beat his wings in surprise. The motion forced air towards the ground. Clarice's skirt fluttered up in the breeze. Stealth was one of the only things he disliked about Clarice. She was always sneaking up on him.

"Good evening," he said. The words sputtered out of his beak. Clarice's skirt was petal pink. Her blouse had ruffles over it that looked like feathers when she breathed. Matthew smiled. He extended a wing towards her. She folded her body underneath it and rubbed the side of her face against his cheek. Thick whiskers tickled his chin. Even then her ears slumped atop her head. They walked awkwardly to the door. His wing stuck out too much to enter the building interlaced. Clarice detached herself from him and scooted under the awning. Matthew followed close behind her.

The interior of the restaurant was dimly lit. Framed canvas paintings littered the walls. The main seating area was set up in a circular pattern. Tables were different heights—different shapes. Matthew gaped. His nostrils flared. Even with his weak nose, the swirl of smells overpowered his senses. The center of the room sunk into a pit. Above, perches and rock outcroppings protruded from the walls.

Clarice purred their name to the orderly. The blob of a man ran a tentacle through the black book. A frown spread across his face.

"I'm sorry," he spoke. "I see here that you reserved the crow's nest, but we've had a last minute VIP who has that space reserved indefinitely. We have plenty of other fine perches tonight."

"Ok," Clarice nodded her head. Matthew pressed past her. He fluffed his feathers.

"No, I reserved it. Make them move," Matthew demanded. He shifted his weight forwards. Clarice twisted her body to one side so that she could slide behind him.

"I can't," the man's voice was firm.

"I see how it is. So you don't like our kind of couple?" Matthew accentuated the word 'our'. His insinuation was plain.

"Sir, this establishment prides itself on being open and welcoming to all, regardless of appearance," the man spoke. The spiel came off as rehearsed. He had obviously had this conversation before.

"Really, Matt, it doesn't matter where we sit," Clarice commented. Her eyes drifted around the room. Seated patrons hadn't noticed the scene unfolding. Employees were monitoring the situation intently. Matthew wondered how often they gave away the finest table to the mystery guest.

"It does matter," Matthew affirmed. He brushed against her with the back of his wing. The other perches were too close to adjacent areas. They would get butted up against a space full of braying mountain goats, or cackling vultures. None of that would do for a proposal. Clarice batted at his arm. She tried to pull him backwards from the pedestal.

"We could sit somewhere else," she suggested. He refused to take his eyes off of the greeter long enough to check his watch. It was nearly seven o'clock. If they stormed out, the nicer restaurants would be full. Even if they weren't, he couldn't be sure they had seating that would suit both a cat and a bird. Clarice had her heart set on this place. The pair were an odd combination of extremes.

Matthew flattened his feathers. He stepped closer to the man. In a swift motion, he withdrew cash from his belt and laid it on the book. The man scooted it back at him. He shook his head. Anger welled up in Matthew's chest. His face grew hot. The waiter's eyebrows creased. His face sagged in on itself. The man's wide eyes looked legitimately sorrowful. Somewhere behind those eyes, Matthew caught a hint of fear. It took some of the steam out of his aggression.

"It's not a matter of cost or influence. No one would dare ask him to move. He just shows up a few times a week. Everyone has to drop everything." The man leaned close. "It's Andre Fatelli."

A small squeak burst from Clarice's lips. Matthew glanced back at her. She had taken a small step away from them, and clasped a paw over her face to catch the noise. Matthew opened his wings to her. Clarice stepped into his embrace. His feathers draped almost to the floor. It obscured her body almost entirely from view.

Matthew gazed up into the rafters. His sense of smell might be on the low end of mediocre, but his eyes were sharp and clear. Even at this distance, he could make out the form of a large cat. The cat's legs draped over the perch in the crow's nest. A bush of fur encircled his neck. A plate of meat was set out before him. Matthew frowned. He didn't know who Fatteli was, but it was illegal to poach human flesh. The whole restaurant would get shut down for it. Matthew's romantic ambitions moved to the back of his thoughts. The lionman lazily opened his eye. The slit of a pupil was almost entirely swallowed up by the pool of yellow surrounding it.

"Let's just sit, Matt," Clarice suggested again.

"Y-yea," Matt answered her after a long moment.

"Is there a problem?" The deep, resonating voice of Andre Fatteli boomed down from the rafters. The restaurant went quiet as he stood. He made his way down on all fours rather than standing upright. Even when he hit the floorboards he kept that stance. Clarice's claws scraped against Matthew's back. She kneaded his shoulder blade.

"Who is this guy?" Matthew asked

"Mafia," she whispered before the lion was close enough to hear. Fatteli strolled through the main dining area. Guests averted their eyes to him. They pretended that he wasn't even there. If he was so infamous, Matthew wondered why he'd never heard of him. Maybe it was a cat thing.

The blades of the lion's shoulders shifted as he walked. His body was long and lean. The thickness of his arms could probably snap Matthew in half with one swat. Matthew shuttled Clarice behind him. Her tail twitched back and forth in a sharp jerking motion. At the last moment, Fatelli reared into a standing position. He narrowed his eyes at Matthew.

"I've never seen a parrot in person before," he commented. The tip of his tongue flipped out of his mouth and rolled along his jowls. He looked up and down Matthew's body. Red across his head and shoulders seemed to particularly fascinate him.

"There aren't many this far north," Matthew answered. He took a deep breath in and forced the words out of his mouth with fervor to keep the syllables from shaking.

"That's right, that's right," the lion responded. He let out a long boisterous laugh that showed off a mouth of shimmering teeth. Scattered bits of meat caught in the largest crevasses and made his breath reek. "Parrots like warmer climates. I can relate to that."

"I suppose so," Matthew answered.

"So, what's the problem?" Fatteli asked. He towered over Matthew. His eyes remained focused forwards. He confronted only what was confronting him. Fatteli's size was impressive, but Matthew couldn't help but wonder how his intellect compared. Clarice seemed to avoid his detection entirely. Matthew pressed his weight backwards only to find a void in the place she had been.

"No problem, here," Matthew answered. He smiled his most genuine smile. He even squinted his eyes so that the grin appeared more genuine.

"Hmmm, that's strange," Fatteli started. "I could have sworn I heard raised voices down here. Then, there is you," he continued. He gestured to Matthew's body with a single curled claw, before shooting a sideways glance at the waiter. The man's tentacles coiled around themselves until he looked like a ball of knot work.

"Have you ever been in love?" Matthew asked. The question caught Fatteli off guard. There was no room for romance, children, or friendship in his line of work. All those ties that bind were a noose that could wrap around your neck.

"Hmm," Fatteli mused.

"I am waiting on my girl. I'm going to ask her to marry me," Matthew admitted. Clarice's weight shifted. Matthew barely caught the noise. It was hard to place her. They had been dating long enough that he could estimate her position just inside the door. He hoped she was waiting for a momentary distraction for her chance to escape. She hovered in the entryway.

"Lovebirds, huh?" Fatteli swatted Matthew on the shoulder. The weight of his paw nearly knocked Matthew to the floor. "I'll bet you had high hopes." He glanced towards the crow's nest. Matthew bobbed his head up and down affirmatively. The lion's claws were almost as thick as his beak.

"I always sit in the highest place. Not because it's most prominent, mind you, but because I don't want anyone sneaking up on me," Fatteli confided.

"Not lovebirds actually, she is a cat," Matthew answered without thinking.

"What?" Fatelli asked. The smile dropped off his face. He moved closer. The intensity of his stare made Matthew uncomfortable. Matthew drifted his eyes around the room to avoid Fatteli's eyes.

"I—" Mathew stared.

"Cats don't love birds," Fatteli interrupted. He glanced over Matthews's slender body. His ears folded backwards. The only time he broke eye contact was for a moment to scan the crowd. Matthew wasn't sure how to answer. He had backed himself into a verbal corner.

"I don't deserve her; she is in a whole different class," Matthew worded his response carefully. If Fatteli was a cat supremacist, then the strategy might buy some time. Time for what, he wasn't exactly sure. Business in the restaurant went on as though nothing was happening. No one would help them.

"It's not that. Your people serve a logical and necessary purpose. I've never had bad dealings with birds. That doesn't change the fact that a cat would never fall in love with a bird," Fatteli explained. Matthew threw a glance over his shoulder. Clarice no longer stood in the doorway, but the door hadn't opened or closed.

"Why not?" Matthew's voice broke around the words. He had spent a long time pondering that issue before he decided to ask Clarice to marry him. He had never known a bird and cat relationship to work out positively. Hearing someone else say it blew a wave of defensive anger across his mind.

180

"It's hard to explain. The hollow bones, the slight frame. You specifically?" Fatteli tipped his head to one side to better study Matthew. "You stick out too much. It's impossible not to notice you. You caught my eye from way up…" Fatteli trailed off. The muscles in his shoulders tensed. He bent his knees so that he was crouching lower to the ground. The stance put his head even with Matthew's chest.

"Are you ok?" Matthew asked.

"Who picked this joint, you or her?" Fatteli demanded. His teeth grated together. His tail twitched. He drew his limbs tightly to his body.

"Her. What's wrong with you?" Matthew stared at Fatteli. The greeter squid retreated to the safety of the kitchen. There was a wide berth between them and anyone else. Fatteli looked ridiculous doubled over in front of Matthew.

"How long have you known her? Do you go to your place or hers? What does she look like?" Fatteli rambled. He turned his back to Matthew. Matthew grinned. Rationally, he knew Fatteli would be angry if he laughed. He tried to pin the sound in his chest. He pinched his beak shut. *Four months, my place, a white shadow.*

"Take a look for yourself," the voice of Clarice wafted up from directly behind Matthew. Her body was cloaked behind his feathers. Her ears stood straight and tall. They angled forwards to listen to the sound of Matthew's racing heartbeat.

"Please, we don't want any trouble," Matthew said. He puffed up to more completely hide Clarice from view. It would have been better if she had fled. Jumping in to the situation wouldn't help him.

"Maybe you don't, parrot," Fatteli commented. He swivelled to face the couple. His eyes were dark and cold. He was ready for a fight. Clarice pressed her body against Matthew's back.

"Huh?" Matthew floundered in his confusion.

"Nice ploy. The parrot is so distracting I didn't even notice you," Fatteli commended her.

"I'm not here for conversation, I just didn't want to shoot you in the back," Clarice spoke. Matthew lost the last few words. A sound like cracking thunder consumed the space around them. Fatteli fell to the floor at his feet. Matthew looked down at his body. The red of his feathers usually stopped at the neck. The color seeped down from his chest and past his waist. Clarice shot thru him in order to hit Fatteli in the head. She didn't have to. There was no reason to do it that way. He fluttered to the floor.

Matthew expected to be trampled by the stream of frightened patrons rushing out of the building. Someone screamed once; no one moved. He searched the lobby for Clarice. She was gone as quickly as she had appeared, leaving only a gently swinging door in her wake.

Sarah Doebereiner

Cops and robbers; cats and dogs. Gunner the Rottweiler and his partner, Fred the bloodhound, are going to catch that cat thief for sure this time.

The Cat Thief

Laura "Munchkin" Lewis

"Come back here you damn street rat!"

The Rottweiler rolled his eyes as he silently prayed for a more creative partner. Calling a cat a rat was about as creative as calling a horse an ass. Gunner nearly slammed into the loping bloodhound as they skidded on a corner and into an alley, but they somehow managed to keep from breaking stride. He growled softly as they were led into the maze of backroads once more and barked, "Keep that nose of yours on target, Fred! We can't lose 'er again!"

"No chance no way Gunner! I got her scent but good this time, and there's the ol' Rabbit Wall just down a ways! We can cut her off at the pass!" The bloodhound charged forward, large ears flapping in the wind. The felid led them down a few turns when Gunner's blood suddenly ran cold. Wait, did Fred just say the Rabbit Wall? He tried to run through a mental map of the town as they continued to give chase, blunt claws clicking against the cobblestone. Another left, down three blocks, a right—the Rottie's paw shot out and grabbed Fred by the nape. His partner let out a sharp yelp and a rolling muted bark of protest, but a few shakes got him to shut his trap and listen.

"You got fleas in your brain or something? They tore down that termite-infested pile of ash a few weeks back and built in a new fence, complete with traps! Best we go down the other route and scoop 'er up when she's hangin' by a leg. Let her be the one to trigger the trouble."

Fred's dark eyes lit up as a long "Ooooh!" slid from the folds that made up his muzzle. His tail began whacking at Gunner's leg, who dropped him with a sneer.

"C'mon. Sooner we cuff 'er, sooner we can get somethin' t'eat. Sick of these damned cat burglars."

They doubled back and Gunner led his partner down a few turns that would land them a fair distance from the traps. He couldn't remember what all the Diggers had listed they were putting in, but it should be a good show either way. When they turned the last corner though, the cat had just tossed her sack over the top of the fence before making a leap at the twenty foot wooden barricade. Her fingers sank in between a couple of the slats and she scrambled upward, tail tucked close. Gunner cursed as Fred blubbered, "But... But what happened to the traps? Were you—"

The glare from Gunner made Fred snap his mouth shut with an audible click of his teeth. The Rottie growled and shoved Fred to the left path. "Go cut 'er off! I'll follow." Before his partner could object, Gunner was already racing down the alley, careful to stick to one side. He didn't have time to wonder after the traps, or if he might set them off, or what might happen if he did. If he was lucky, the blasted rabbits simply hadn't had time to set the traps yet, what with their business going better than ever. It looked like someone was looking out for him. When nothing seemed triggered by the time he was a couple of paces away, Gunner threw himself at the wooden slats, reaching as far and as high as he could. The entire fence trembled and shook as his claws struggled for purchase. He seemed to hang there for a full heartbeat, scraping desperately at the hardwood before his body fell to the ground with a thump.

He looked up to see that the feline had managed to use small paws and smaller digits to hang on even through the shaking, damn her! She straddled the top and took a moment to flick her thumb from under her chin in a derogatory gesture, tail snapping teasingly behind her. Gunner's upper lip curled back as he growled, and he slammed his body against the fence once more. The feline's fur fluffed out, but she managed to hold on tight. Maybe if he kept it up, Fred would be on the other side before she could get down.

He threw his body into the planks again and again, giving no time for the thief to find her center, or so he had hoped. On the third slam, she snubbed him with a different gesture, this time with a very particular digit, and jumped down the other side. Gunner let out a series of barks in frustration, striking his fist against the planks. Damn the felid, and damn his partner for being so useless! He finally tore himself away from the fence, flexing his sore paw as he began to stalk the twisting curving alleys. Maybe he could find a way past the barricade they didn't already know about. It was nearing dark by the time he found the bloodhound.

"Tell me you found her trail."

"I—I'm sorry Gunner. I got her as far as Esser's Place, near where the Bakers used to run business. Followed her right down into the slums a ways, but the stench there is something fierce! I tried, Gunner, I really tried, but I was starting to tear up from the smell! There was no telling where her scent was in all those layers of sewage and rot and-and-and death!"

Gunner sighed and shook his head. He should have expected as much. It was the same strategy the tramp had been using all month. He flexed his paw with a small growl. One of these days they were going to outsmart her, and when they did, she'd be sorry she was ever born.

"Is your sniffer at least workin' good enough to get us outta this gods-forsaken area?"

The bloodhound's folds seemed to double in volume as his frown deepened. "Yeah, that shouldn't be a problem. But, I mean, well, it's just—"

"What the hell you babblin''bout now?"

Fred shifted from foot to foot as his skinny tail curled in closer. "I mean, I don't get it though. Why would she steal those things? Even the meat's a lot more than one cat can eat."

Gunner shook his head and scowled. "Y'know how expensive that stuff is these days. She's probably gonna sell whatever she doesn't eat in some back alley somewhere."

"But... I mean, what about the dress? And the soap? She's never stolen anything like that before! How can you explain all that?"

"How the blood should I know! People've been crazy since the collapse a couple years ago. Maybe she's gonna try her luck on the streets. I dunno and I don't care. It's her head or our jobs." The Rottie sighed and rubbed the back of his neck. "Maybe we can try pickin' up her trail in the mornin' if it doesn't rain. Colder temp'ature should be easier on your nose, right?"

Fred nodded, though his frown lingered and his tail stayed still. He didn't seem at all excited anymore. Hopefully it was because he didn't want to lose his family's only source of income, and not because he was going soft on Gunner. The Rottie shook his head before the thought could take root and motioned his partner to him. "Now c'mon. If I don't get home in time to pick up Bella, th' missus is gonna have a fit."

"Little Bella's big date is tonight? Your daughter sure is growin' up!"

He stood a little taller, his shoulders a little more square, his chest a little more puffed. "Yeah, she sure is." He shook himself, though the pride still lingered in his eyes. "C'mon, leggo."

Tabitha listened to her kittens eat as she worked at the wash basin, her tail flicking to the rhythm of their voices as they chatted about their day between bites. There was plenty of food for her family, and should be plenty of links left over to drop off at the Baker's place after they were done as a thank you for tutoring her kittens. She worked a piece of the cloth against the washboard, relieved that her only dress still fit even if it was rather dirty from neglect. Once she managed to get it clean, it would work well for her interview tomorrow.

Her ears perked at the sound of her oldest daughter entering their make-shift shack, and she glanced up at the dress spread over their blankets with a grin. It was going to be perfect for the girl's first date tonight. Who was it with? A canid named Bella, described by her oldest as strong, sweet, and gentle. The squeal of delight from her daughter upon seeing the dress was music to her ears. Maybe things were looking up, after all.

Laura "Munchkin" Lewis

For want of a sandwich, the belly rumbled. For want of a full belly, the cougar snarled. Epic battles can be fought in office buildings, between the cubicles.

Food, Feuds, and Fake Flora

Ocean Tigrox

MONDAY

"It was a..." Sandra trailed off as she consulted the stack of papers on her desk. Finding the yellow complaint form and tugging it free from the pile, the tawny cougar adjusted her thick-rimmed glasses and read it aloud. "A roasted red pepper and provolone chicken sandwich with chipotle mayo on sourdough bread."

"As far as I know, I'm allergic to mayonnaise." The silver lupine turned his head away, swallowing his breath mint and wiping away a small drop of creamy, reddish-white sauce from his grey muzzle.

"Look, Jim." The feline took off her glasses and placed them beside the potted fake fern on her laminate desk. She sighed, sagging her shoulders as she clasped her paws together. "I'm not accusing you here. There've always been lunch thefts from time to time in this office. We're required to investigate each complaint." Sandra stood and turned to stare out the office window. She grumbled, "I'm sure the owner of that sandwich is terribly hungry right now. I would—That is to say, we all would like to know who took it."

"Well, I'm sorry to say that I don't know who took that tantalizing meal. But I've heard the deli across the street makes a mean smoked meat sandwich."

Sandra spun around and slammed her fists on the desk, shaking the fern's leaves and rattling the office supplies. "Well maybe that deli never prepares your sandwich right, or doesn't realize that some of us don't like to have their bread drowning in mustard!"

The middle aged cougar bit her lip and closed her eyes. Standing up straight, she took a deep breath and squeezed the bridge of her shortened muzzle. "Sorry, sorry. I apologize for that outburst. Let's just...move on." Sandra sat back down and wheeled herself back under the desk.

"Of course, Sandra. No apology needed." Jim nodded, picking out some crumbs from under his claws.

The cougar opened one of the desk drawers and picked through the files contained within. "I have a favour to ask. As you may have heard, management has hired a new employee to overlook our processes and update them so we can be a more efficient team."

Sandra withdrew a file and pulled out a stapled set of sheets, reading them over. "Yes, here we go, a mister Harold O'Connor. He should be waiting out in the lobby. Could you please show him around the office? His desk and cubicle are next to yours."

"I'll make sure he's given a warm Fake Ferns and Flora welcome." The wolf smiled and rose from his seat.

"Also." Sandra raised a finger. "It's too late today, but you're welcome to take him to lunch and charge it on the company card."

"Certainly, I'll take him to the deli." Jim flashed a toothy grin.

The wolf left before Sandra's grumbling about mustard could drag him back into another talk about improper office etiquette. He closed the HR manager's door behind him, preventing any of her outrage from slipping out into the office.

It was mid-afternoon and most of the other staff huddled away quietly in their individual cubicles. Next to each of their mailboxes sat a personal fake plant, each handpicked by Gene, the company owner, for them upon hire.

Jim slipped through the open area, past the small jungle of silk ficus trees and artificial palms, and through double doors into the lobby. Atop the front desk counter sat a pot of plastic yellow daffodils, the perfect pick for a bright and cheery receptionist. The vixen behind the counter waved at Jim.

"Hi Megan." The wolf flashed her a bright, white smile. "Sandra sent me for Harold."

"Of course, he's over there." The fox gestured with a paw to the large, chestnut-brown bear sitting quietly. Harold sat like a lump, his large belly pushing at the bounds of his white shirt, the buttons strained at the seams. His paws gripped a worn briefcase.

Jim stepped over to introduce himself. *Another basic, boring bear.* The wolf smoothed his grey pin-striped suit and offered a paw. "Harold O'Connor, right? I'm Jim Grossman, head of marketing and sales. Welcome to Fake Ferns and Flora!"

"Hello!" The bear shook the wolf's hand and rose from his seat. "Happy to be here."

Jim grinned. "Have you met anyone yet?"

"Not personally. I was hired over the phone so this is my first time in the office."

"Let me show you around then." Jim held the lobby door open so Harold could step into the office.

Jim started pointing out various associates. "Over there is Andrew, he's in charge of distribution. We've got Yelena next to him, she's lead design. They look busy right now, but I'm sure they'll introduce themselves at the ceremony."

"Ceremony?" Harold blinked.

"Yes, little tradition Gene likes to have when a new member joins the team." The wolf patted the bear on the shoulder. "You'll see."

Jim pointed to a cubicle on their left, near the entrance. Organized stacks of papers and reports occupied most of the tidy desk. A few other items fought for space: a business card holder, digital clock, and a single framed photograph of two wolves. The most colourful item was a vibrant trio of silk snapdragons: indigo, crimson, and pink. Gene's reasoning was that much like a real dragon, the sales team must be witty, cunning and fierce!

"Here's my desk." Jim's tail wagged as he showed it off. "If you have any questions or concerns, you can usually find me here. But you won't have to go far because..." The wolf took a few steps over and motioned to the empty cubicle beside his. "This is your desk."

"Ah, excellent!" Harold's ear flicked as he stepped forward to place his briefcase on the desk.

"Watch out!" A voice squeaked out from the cubicle. The bear's eyes widened as he stepped back and a yellow and grey figure crawled out from under the desk, stood up and waved.

"Hi there," the scrawny coyote greeted them. The hemp bracelets on his wrists, made of woven fair-trade fabrics and beads, clashed with his half tucked in yellow dress shirt and crooked, stained tie. "I'm just finishing setting up your desktop."

Harold nodded.

"This is Danny, our IT guy." Jim cut in, shooing Danny back to work. "Go away now please."

The office hummed with keyboard clacking and ringing desk phones as Jim guided Harold around, pointing out more associates. Eventually they came to the corner of the office where two doors stood.

"On the left you'll find Sandra." The wolf's ears flattened as he lowered his voice, hoping the cougar on the other side wouldn't hear. "I'd introduce you, but she's not feeling too friendly."

Harold nodded slowly, a look of confusion on his brow.

Pointing to the other door, Jim continued, "And on the right is Gene, our founder and boss. He'll introduce himself to you at the ceremony so let's continue the tour."

The wolf directed them around the corner into a large lunchroom. Along one wall stood a marble counter, various cabinets and a stainless steel fridge. Spread around the room were tables and booths, each with a pot of fake green tea plants, specially made because Gene heard green tea was good for digestion.

"Here's my favourite place, the kitchen!" Jim's tail swished behind him. "Employees can keep their lunches safe in the fridge." His sly eyes looked the ursine up and down. A bear with a belly like Harold's must be eating well. What delicious delights might he bring for lunch? "Feel free to store your food in there, anytime."

Harold smiled. "Good to know, I'm sure I'll take advantage of that."

The two continued through the kitchen to another corner of the office. Shelves of electronics and cords covered the walls with a single desk separating them from the hallway.

"If your computer isn't working or you need some equipment, Danny'll help you out here."

Atop the coyote's desk sat three polyester bamboo shoots. The skills of the IT department were regarded by Gene as a form of techno-wizardry. So when it came to picking a plant for Danny, he chose bamboo because he knew electronics came from Japan. Plus he'd heard bamboo was lucky.

Ushering Harold along, Jim showed off the various other office amenities: meeting rooms, bathrooms, printers, and with the supply room ending the tour. Jim pushed open one of the frosted glass doors to reveal the lobby.

Inside, all the employees from the floor gathered around a table in the middle. A pile of napkins, forks and Styrofoam plates sat on the table next to a plastic container of assorted cupcakes. A badger stepped forward from the crowd and cleared his throat.

"It's always my pleasure to welcome a new member to the Fake Ferns and Flora family. I've brought Harold on board to go over our processes and see what we can do to improve our efficiency. By streamlining how we conduct our business, I know we can go from number three to number two in the fake plant business!"

A few people politely clapped.

The badger stepped up to the bear. "Now Harold, I'm not sure if anyone informed you, but here at triple-F we take pride in our products. We all should feel connected to the fabulous plants we produce. So for each employee, I pick out a plant to represent them. You may not see mine often as it's in my office, but I have a single stemmed rose. A diamond with petals, it is the perfection of the floral world. The flower that all other flowers wish to be, a beacon of greatness to all, just as I am a model to all my employees.

"I'm sure you're wondering what I've picked out for you, so here it is." Gene revealed a plastic, groomed bonsai tree. "Only a plant dedicated to such precision and the smallest detail could be given to the one who will be optimizing the way we do business and work together." The badger handed the pot to the bear and shook his free hand. "Just remember our motto: Our plants are plastic, but our quality is real!"

"Thank you very much." Harold smiled shyly. "It will be a pleasant treat to work with you all."

TUESDAY

Jim's belly rumbled with discontent. He glanced at his desk clock to see the numbers 11:43 staring back. Almost time for lunch. What delicacies would be available today?

As Jim saved the document he was working on and stood up from his desk, he remembered Sandra nagging him to take Harold out for lunch. Sadly, this meant eating at the deli across the street. The wolf shuddered and put the thought behind him, instead turning and peering over the cubicle wall at his bruin co-worker. Harold sat happily chewing and working away, not noticing the silver furred muzzle poking over the wall.

"Hey Harold." The wolf sniffed the air, scents of sugary sweetness tickling his nose. "It's about lunch time, you wanna grab a bite to eat? Company's paying."

"Oh thanks, but no thanks. I've already eaten." Harold waved a sticky paw.

Jim's eyes narrowed, picking out smudges of yellow and blue colouring in Harold's fur. The bear had eaten the leftover cupcakes from yesterday's ceremony. The wolf cursed under his breath. *Damn, I was hoping to have those for an afternoon snack.* "I should have invited you yesterday. My bad. How about tomorrow?"

"Sounds like a plan." Harold sucked each individual finger clean.

Jim cringed at the sticky mess of coloured splotches on Harold's keyboard. He slowly lowered himself back down from the wall and flopped back into his chair, ears splayed.

The bear probably just assumed the left over cupcakes were for anyone. They were bought for his welcoming party after all. Jim grumbled about his loss while pulling a sandwich out of his bag. *At least I forgot about taking him out to lunch and packed my own,* he thought.

"Hey, Jim!"

The wolf looked up to see Danny smiling over him. The coyote munched on dried fruit slices and offered Jim a few from the plastic bag in his hand. "Want some dehydrated apple chips? I made them myself. They're great! Healthy, gluten-free, full of—"

"Go away, Danny," Jim mumbled into his sandwich.

WEDNESDAY

The pressure of the middle of the week dragged on Jim. At least on Wednesdays Sandra brought the best food.

Last week was a red wine beef brisket with cheese and bacon scalloped potatoes. Jim licked his lips, remembering the flavour. The week before that was a lovely chicken parmesan with a spicy chorizo carbonara on the side. The combination of spices and herbs still danced on Jim's tongue. He wasn't sure if the cougar was attending cooking classes on Tuesday night's or dating a young gourmet chef, but he wasn't complaining at the leftovers she brought for lunch.

The 11:50 alarm on his clock told him that it was time to make his way to the kitchen.

"Crap," Jim muttered to himself. *I told Harold we'd do lunch today. Oh well, after Monday's meeting with cranky ol' Sandra, giving her a day to cool off isn't so bad.* Still, it meant eating at the deli across the street. The wolf's fur bristled. *At least it's free.*

Taking a few steps out of his cubicle, he rounded the wall with a cheerful, "Hey Harold! You hungry?" Jim's trademark toothy grin drooped as his nose picked up the scent of paprika and chilies.

"Jim!" Harold exclaimed through a mouthful. He paused to swallow before continuing. "I'm sorry, I forgot about our plans. I guess I got so hungry that I decided on another early lunch."

"I must say, your lunch smells delicious. What are you eating?" The wolf licked his lips looking over the bear's shoulder.

"Oh this? Just one of grandma's old recipes. Simple pork and beans. Too bad I can't make it like she used to."

Harold took another fork full. Digging his utensil into the microwave container, he stirred up the rice and refried beans. The pink plastic container overflowed with corn, pico de gallo, beans and rice. On top of it all rested shredded chorizo pork in a lovely mole glaze topped with melted queso fresco.

"I didn't realize your grandmother was...Spanish? Mexican?" Jim leaned in closer, sniffing at the combination of spices and chocolate. He eyed the side of the container, making out the worn away letters on the side - *Sandra Perkins.*

"Ah, well..." Harold's eyes danced between the food and the wolf. "She—she married into the family."

The bear stared at Jim, chewing loudly, each bite raising the hackles on the wolf's fur. The sickening sloppy eater in front of him caused Jim's tail to twitch with each bite.

Jim's eyes narrowed in on Harold. "I should let you get back to work. Enjoy your lunch."

Harold gave a smug grin, turning back to shovel another mouthful, bits of rice and salsa falling on his keyboard.

Jim trudged off, grumbling to himself. Maybe there'd be something left in the fridge to salvage. As long as the only thing in there wasn't Danny's. A shudder rippled down the fur on Jim's back. *Stupid soy vegan fair-trade gluten-free dirt mush stuff.*

Turning the corner, a thought crept into his mind. He rapped on the door to HR. Jim's ears perked at the agitated sigh that followed before Sandra invited him inside.

"Good day, Sandra," Jim greeted her as he closed the door behind him. "I would like to make a complaint. I believe Harold is eating your lunch. In fact, I saw him just now. Fork in hand, devouring what looked like a microwavable container sporting your name on the side. If you look right now, you can catch him in the act."

A chuckle rumbled in the cougar's chest. "Oh, Jim. Jim, Jim, Jimmy, Jimbo, Jim. Well done." Sandra clapped her paws a few times. "You've out done yourself. After all these years, to think you'd stoop this low."

The wolf's jaw dropped. Ears splayed, he sputtered out, "S-s-stoop?"

Sandra leaned forward, resting her elbows on the desk. "Do you honestly take me for a putz? Do you really think I don't know where the missing lunches have gone? That I don't know the mysterious bandit who continues to take them?"

"It could be anyone." Jim loosened his tie and glanced around the room, avoiding eye contact.

"Just because I haven't been able to prove it, doesn't mean I never figured it out. Sure, Gene has a mini fridge so he never has to deal with you." Sandra scrunched up her face and lowered her voice to a mocking tone. "Now, now, Sandra, it's just lunch. Our employees work hard. We all need to pitch in and help out wherever we can, even if that means sharing a sandwich now and then."

Jim slipped a claw under his collar.

"And now, you think you can just waltz in here, accusing the new hire of being the lunch thief?" Sandra's breathing deepened; her extended claws dug into the laminate covering of the desk. The fake fern trembled. "I'm already wise to your tricks, Grossman!" The cougar leaned over her desk, ears flat and fangs bared. "You march out of here right now before I make you run to the deli across the street and order me a new lunch."

Jim gulped and nodded.

Well that was an unexpected failure. Being forced to eat at the deli across the street was just the mustard on the cake for this horrible day.

The slimy sauerkraut and sharp mustard stuck with Jim for the rest of the day. No matter how long he gargled with water or tossed back cups of coffee, the disgusting taste of stale bread and limp deli meat would not leave his palette. Only once work ended could the lupine dash home and brush away the never-ending aftertaste of the deli across the street. After a rigorous dosage of mouthwash and questioning why there was only one restaurant within walking distance to the office, the sour notes finally faded away and Jim's fur started to settle into place.

Frustrated from having to suffer through the last half of the work day, Jim decided it would be a 'Me-Time' evening. A quick call to his choice pizzeria, two frosty lagers from the fridge, sweatpants, and a quick pick through his DVD collection was what this night needed.

"I am Hosea, destroyer of men." Jim imitated the gunslinging actor on screen, sloshing his bottle of beer as he pretended to shoot at all the bar patrons with the action hero. 'Muchachos' had always been one of his best-loved classic Western films, watching the young anti-hero from Mexico rise to infamy in a blaze of bullets.

The doorbell barely managed to make a sound over the blaring fire fight on Jim's home theatre system. The lupine's ears still perked and picked it up, sending the slightly tipsy wolf dashing to the door, tail wagging behind him. A quick exchange of money and Jim's favourite double double deluxe pizza was in his paws: double the meat, double the cheese, double the sauce and all the fixings, also doubled.

The scent of the meat trio, salami, ham, and pepperoni mixed with the melted mozzarella and marble cheese blend, all in combination with peppers, onions, mushrooms and olives galore. Jim's muzzle dripped with saliva before he could sink his teeth into the first piece. The thick slices of warm pizza brought a happy sigh to the wolf. Each piece packed with so much meat and toppings that it only took a few pieces before his belly was sated, easily leaving leftovers for lunch. Even Sandra's leftovers couldn't beat the best pizza ever to touch his tongue.

Jim cracked open another beer and stretched out on his couch. *I needed this. Tonight was a good night.*

THURSDAY

The lupine had a bounce in his step the next morning. Giving Megan a cheerful smile and a hello, he entered the office. Jim waved to Yelena and asked how her cubs were doing. After a brisk walk to drop off his leftover pizza in the office fridge, he returned to his desk with a fresh cup of hazelnut coffee. Setting the mug down next to his colourful snap-dragons, Jim went straight to work.

Jim's morning slipped by in a flash. Only his alarm clock with its usual 11:50 buzzer broke him out of his work daze. Leaning back in his chair with an accomplished sigh, he smiled. *Lunch sounds great about now.*

Rolling his chair away from his desk, Jim stood and stretched. He yawned and took in the scents of the office. The usual smell of dust, recycled air, coffee, paper and his regular co-workers' deodorant slipped through his nose. The lupine grinned at the absence of any smells of food and walked past Harold's cubicle. His ears fell when he found only an empty seat.

The wolf rushed to the kitchen, throwing open the stainless steel refrigerator. His eyes darted around the empty shelves. Only one item sat alone in the barren fridge—Danny's see-through container with tofurkey curry on brown whole grain rice and home-made plain yogurt.

No. He shook his head. *No, no, no. Where did it all go?*

The sound of lips smacking perked the wolf's ears. Jim closed the fridge door and turned slowly. A scent of grease and bread directed his gaze over to one of the booths. His tail swayed lazily as he approached the table.

A chestnut-brown hulk of fur turned to see him and smiled. "Oh, hi Jim!"

"Harold." Jim growled through his teeth.

"How's your day going?" The bear talked with his mouth full, smacking his gums as he ate. Tomato sauce drizzled down Harold's cheek. In front of him sat empty and discarded lunch containers.

"I was hoping some lunch would help get me through the day." Jim ground his molars, glaring at the noisy eater.

Harold finished his food, tossing the left over pizza crust into a container with the others. After letting out a small, obnoxious burp, he nudged the container closer to Jim. "Would you like some leftover bread sticks? I just had a delicious Italian feast."

Jim's eye twitched as he wrapped his hands around the container, claws digging into the plastic sides. He tried to reply but a low rumble from his chest was all the sound he could muster.

"I did save some room for dessert though." Harold pushed the potted green tea plant out of the way and pulled a bright purple container closer. Popping off the top, Harold took a handful of the homemade sugar cookies with buttercream frosting from within and crammed them into his mouth. "Grandma makes such tasty treats," he said through a muffled muzzle.

"That's—those are Yelena's!" Jim gasped, releasing his grip on the food container and letting it fall to the floor with a clatter, spilling discarded pizza crusts across the tile. "She—her cubs—they baked those. They make them every Wednesday night so she can deliver them to Gran-Gran in the home when she visits each Thursday after work! Even I wouldn't stoop so low as to steal Gran-Gran's cookies. They're all she has left to get her through the terrible meals of stewed prunes and mushy peas they serve each week."

"Are they?" Harold paused for a moment, glancing down at the last two remaining cookies with their pink and blue pastel frosting. "Are you sure? These taste just like the ones my grandma makes. Let me check." A wicked grin slid up Harold's muzzle as he took the remaining cookies in his paws and stacked them on top of each other. Opening wide, he shoved the baked treats into his cheeks and chewed.

Jim watched in horror, frozen as the bear half-chewed his food and struggled to swallow the cookies whole. A streak of pain crossed the bear's face before he relaxed and sighed. Harold leaned back and patted his round belly. "You know, you might be right. I don't know if those were my cookies. I may have grabbed the wrong container by mistake. My deepest apologies to Yelena."

Jim slammed his fists on the table. "You can't keep doing this!"

"Oh?" Harold's ears flicked, he gestured with a meaty paw for the wolf to sit across from him. "And why not?"

Jim's ears fell flat as he looked around the room to make sure they were alone. He slid into the seat across from the bear. "You've already eaten everything in the fridge today. Well, everything edible. Once everyone comes in here for lunch and sees you sitting here with all those empty containers, they'll have your head."

Harold leaned forward, showing off another toothy smile with bits of spinach and peppers stuck between his teeth. "Word around the office is that the lunch bandit is none other than our prized sales manager, Jim Grossman. They're not angry at the new friendly process manager who's been hired to make their jobs easier. No, they're ready to tear apart the one who's been here the whole time, taking their delicious meals and forcing them to suffer on the sorry excuse for food that is the deli across the street."

A low grumble stirred in Jim's throat, his tail thumping against the booth seat. "Fine, you want to know why? You can't keep this up. If everyone's lunch continues to go missing and eaten, they'll no longer bring food. They'll keep it in their desks, safe and secure. Once that happens, no one wins. Neither me nor you."

"The way I look at it, if I remove the one who's been stealing food, then all those lunches he was going to eat will now be mine."

The wolf's ears perked. "You—you wouldn't dare."

"It's already begun. Have a good lunch, Jim." The bear strolled out of the kitchen.

Jim's eye twitched. His shoulders rose and fell as he huffed. *That pompous, wretched ursine. If he thinks—*

"Jim!" A screech snapped the wolf out of his train of thought. He looked up to see Yelena standing horrified over him. The lioness clutched her face in shock at the empty containers scattered about the table. "How—how could you? Gran-Gran's cookies..." Tears fell down the lioness's cheeks as she picked up the empty purple container. Turning it upside down, she watched a few loose crumbs trickle out.

"No!" The wolf's hands shot up. "I love Gran-Gran. I'd never eat her cookies."

"What's going on here?" The other associates were already filing into the lunch room for their break. Noticing the scene at the booth, they came over to investigate, only to find themselves also victims.

"Hey, that was my lunch!"

"Wow, Jim, this is a new low!"

"You know, we've been putting up with this for a while, but this is ridiculous."

Jim's head zipped between angry co-workers, each one staring him down with disapproval and disgust. The lupine slid out of the booth and pushed past them, dashing out into the hallway, yelling, "It wasn't me! I didn't do it!"

The mob chased after him, hungry for revenge and calling him out for crimes against their leftovers. The kitchen emptied faster than it filled, the lunch containers left alone on the table.

Danny walked in and looked around, wondering where everyone was. With a shrug, he walked over to the fridge, opened it, and pulled out his container. "Yes! Lunchtime!"

Jim sulked the whole trip home. His day had gone from great to horrible in a matter of minutes thanks to that conniving bear. Not only did everyone at the office accuse him wrongfully, they glared at him for the rest of the afternoon. Even after forcing him to buy them all sandwiches from across the street. Sure the food was terrible, but they could at least have been grateful for his generosity.

Cellphone tucked between his head and shoulder, Jim ordered another of his favourite pizzas while searching the fridge for any beer. Finding none, the defeated lupine grabbed a couple of cans of cola and flopped onto his couch, waiting for the delivery boy.

"No good, dirty-handed, scoundrel, scum bear." Jim muttered to himself between sips of his soda. He brooded as he slid a classic spaghetti Western into his media player.

The on-screen sheriff displayed his shiny badge with pride. He called out to the bandits causing a ruckus in the street, "You think you can come into my town and cause trouble?"

Jim's eye's narrowed at the screen, his tail wagging slow. "Yeah, you think you can come into my office and cause trouble, Harold?"

The two characters stared each other down. The villain pulled away his coat, revealing a shiny six-shooter strapped to his side. "I think it's too late for that, Sheriff."

Jim watched intently, replaying the scene from lunch in his head. Harold challenging his rule over the kitchen.

The camera zoomed in on the short badger with the sheriff's badge. He snarled, "This town ain't big enough for the both of us."

"This office ain't big enough for the both of us." The wolf repeated, picturing the bear standing in front of him, mocking him with that dumb grin. Jim spat at Harold's feet. The wad of spit hit his carpet with a splat.

The duo on screen dared each other to move, eyes never straying. The sun watched from up high as furry digits dangled beside firearms. The town chapel began to chime the hour with a solemn bell toll, each strike of the bell rising the tension higher and higher.

The clock struck again and again: nine, ten, eleven. On the twelfth and final chime, the desperado and the sheriff drew with lightning speed, firing off shots, and rolling for cover.

"That's it!" Jim sprang up, his cola spilling and mixing with his spent saliva.

When the pizza boy arrived, Jim asked, "Hey, kid, how would you like to make a big tip?"

FRIDAY

The entire office glared every time they passed Jim's empty cubicle, unsure if they were happy the lunch bandit didn't show today or angry since they wanted to ream him out more. The clock was ticking closer to the noon hour.

Megan sat by her desk, silk daffodils beside her looking the same as always. When the door to reception opened, Megan cheerfully called out, "Good morning and welcome to Fa—"

The vixen stopped mid-sentence, looking up at the wolf who just entered. "Jim?"

"Hi Megan," Jim waved at her from behind a pair of large aviator shades. The wolf stood in the middle of the lobby, a plastic rifle slung over his shoulder.

A quick rummage through the office supply closet and the wolf added to his arsenal a pair of staplers, hooked to his belt, and a set of packing tape dispensers peeking out of his pockets.

Jim stepped into the office and looked around. Everyone turned, the lupine scent filling the room and twitching their noses.

The door at the end of the room swung open and Sandra stepped out. "Jim! Where have you been? And what are you doing?"

"Jim?" The wolf sneered. His voice changed to a fake Mexican accent. "There is no Jim. I am *Hosea, destroyer of bears.*"

Before the cougar could offer a rebuttal, the lumbering head of a brown bear rose up over Harold's cubicle wall. The ursine pulled out his own pair of black tinted aviators and slid them over his eyes. "I knew you would come."

"Then you're prepared to die." Jim slid the action on the toy rifle back, the weapon making a resounding click as the elastic inside primed the foam dart in its chamber.

Harold stepped out from his cubicle, brandishing a pair of plastic squeaky revolvers, primed and ready to fire their own pair of foam darts.

"Wait, what?" Jim's voice snapped back to normal. He pushed his shades down his muzzle so he could glance at the fake weapons in the bear's paws. "You... actually have been carrying around a pair of toy guns this entire time?"

Harold shrugged. "You'd be surprised how often this happens to me."

The wolf blinked and then shrugged, pushing his shades back up. "Then it's come to this."

The two stood tall, unwavering. Jim's desk clock blinked from 11:49 to 11:50, setting off the alarm and crying out a series of buzzing.

One. Two. Three. As the buzzes continued, the two co-workers glared at each other.

Four. Five. Six. The rest of the office watched with a hush.

Seven. Eight. Nine. Twitchy fingers slid against bright coloured triggers.

Ten. Eleven. Twelve. The wolf squeezed his trigger; the bear's grip tightened. Both gunfighters fired.

Foam darts whistled through the air. Harold ducked behind a fake birch to dodge one; Jim rolled into his cubicle as another two flew by.

"You'll never make it!" Jim shouted. Popping up to fire another dart. "The people will know the truth about your deeds today!"

Harold dived into a nearby cubicle and away from the neon orange flying foam, toppling over the birch in the process. He then jumped up and fired two shots over the cubicle wall. "The truth will only hurt you as well!"

"Justice is cruel but must be served," grunted Jim.

"What are you two doing?" screamed Sandra. The cougar ran to the office beside hers, banging on the door. "This is ridiculous! I'm getting Gene."

Jim fired another dart but the bear was too entrenched behind cover to get a good shot. Setting his rifle aside, he pulled out the tape dispensers. He let two long strips of packing tape reel out before cutting them off. Taking the strips, he rolled them into their own individual tape balls, sticky side out.

The wolf's ear twitched at any sound as he peered over his cubicle wall. The snap of another shot sent Jim ducking. He glanced up to see a yellow foam dart arc over the wall and stick to his computer screen with a satisfying thwak. Now was his chance. He peeked over the wall and let his tape balls fly. The volley spun through the air and disappeared into Harold's hideout-cubicle.

A cry of pain cut through the air. "Gah, No!"

Harold rolled out from his desk into the main office, his arm flailing, trying to shake off the two tape balls stuck to his fur. The window of attack wide open, Jim leaped from the cover of his desk and fired another dart. The whistling orange streak pierced the air and struck Harold's shoulder. The bear wailed at the hit and fired in retaliation.

"What is going on here?" A voice boomed behind them.

The duo twisted around to see Gene staring in disbelief, Sandra smugly standing behind him, arms crossed and tail swinging back and forth.

"It's... uh—uh." Jim stammered, looking for an answer.

"Uh—A team building exercise." Harold picked up where the wolf left off.

The badger blinked. "Oh!" His ears perked, and he smiled. "Great work you two. I'm glad you have your priorities straight. Continue." Gene turned and headed back to his office.

"Wait! What?" Sandra screeched.

Silence swept over the room as the bear and wolf glanced around, their co-workers urging them to finish the fight.

"You can take my lunch when you pry it from my cold, dead hands." Jim dropped his rifle and whisked his arms up from his sides, snagging the staplers in his paws. Pointing them at the ursine, he squeezed them one after the other, strafing the bear and firing staple after staple into his thick brown coat.

"Argh!" Harold cried out in agony. He swatted at the incoming barrage of metal fasteners but was unable to stop their attack. "Okay, okay! You got me." The bear dropped his plastic guns and clutched at his chest.

"I want the truth." Jim nudged the bear with a stapler. "Tell our audience what you did yesterday. Loud and clear."

Harold grimaced. Only when Jim fired off another barrage of thin silver pieces did he conceded. "Alright, stop! I did it! I ate everyone's lunches."

A gasp echoed amongst the crowd.

"Even... Gran-Gran's cookies."

Yelena let out a wail, mourning the memory of the sugary, handmade treats.

Harold sneered at Jim. "But my confession doesn't make up for the months, years even, of stolen lunches before I arrived. Defeating me does nothing." The bear erupted into maniacal laughter that turned into coughing until he collapsed on the floor, feigning death.

Jim nodded, turning to face his officemates. "He's right. I've wronged you all. I've taken your precious food without asking. It was shameful of me. I don't deserve to be your sales manager. All I can do is ask for forgiveness." He tossed the staplers to the side, kneeling before them with his head bowed.

The lobby doors opened and Megan poked her head through. She blinked confused at the sorry sight of the office, scattered foam darts everywhere. "Jim? Zippy's Pizzeria is here. They said you paid extra to have them deliver all the way out here?"

206

"And offer a pizza party for everyone!" shouted Jim.

His co-workers burst out in a cheer.

"I can't believe all of you!" Sandra's screeching voice returned, leaving Gene's office. "Jim steals our lunches for months, has a ridiculous, disruptive, childish play fight in the middle of the office, and then you forget it all just because he buys you all pizza?"

The office workers looked at one another then back to the cougar. Andrew stepped forward, replying, "At least it makes a dull job entertaining?"

Sandra tugged her ears and twitched. "That's it! I quit!" She threw her hands in the air. Tail lashing behind her, she stomped past the group and out of the room.

The door to Gene's office opened and the badger poked his head out. "What's all the yelling out here?"

"Sandra quit." Jim answered.

"I'm going to miss eating her lunches," sighed Harold.

"I know, right?" Jim nodded in agreement.

"Oh, well, she was just a fern anyways." The boss stepped out from his office. "I heard something about a pizza party? Sounds like a great way to end a team-building exercise."

"Wait, she's a fern?" The wolf tilted his head.

"That's the plant I picked for her." Gene waved a paw in the air. "They're boring, simple, and easy to replace."

Danny peaked his head around the corner into the room. "Hey, there's a pizza party going on? Any vegan options?"

Jim glared at the coyote. "Get lost, Danny."

To change his heart, Mr. Carmelke Sr. has to change everything else about himself first.

I HOLD MY FATHER'S PAWS

David D. Levine

The receptionist had feathers where her eyebrows should have been. They were blue, green, and black, iridescent as a peacock's, and they trembled gently in the silent breath of the air conditioner. "Did you have a question, sir?"

"No," Jason replied, and raised his magazine, but after reading the same paragraph three times without remembering a word he set it down again. "Actually, yes. Um, I wanted to ask you... ah... are you... transitioning?" The word landed on the soft tailored-grass carpet of the waiting room, and Jason wished he could pick it up again, stuff it into his pocket, and leave. Just leave, and never come back.

"Oh, you mean the eyebrows? No, sir, that's just fashion. I enjoy being human." She smiled gently at him. "You haven't been in San Francisco very long, have you?"

"No, I just got in this morning."

"Feathers are very popular here. In fact, we're having a special this month. Would you like a brochure?"

"No! Uh, I mean, no thank you." He looked down and saw that the magazine had crumpled in his hands. Awkwardly he tried to smooth it out, then gave up and slipped it back in the pile on the coffee table. They were all recent issues, and the coffee table looked like real wood. He tested it with a dirty thumbnail; real wood, all right. Then, appalled at his own action, he shifted the pile of magazines to cover the tiny scratch.

"Sir?"

Jason started at the receptionist's voice, sending magazines skidding across the table. "What?"

"Would you mind if I gave you a little friendly advice?"

"Uh, I... no. Please." She was probably going to tell him that his fly was open, or that ties were required in this office. Her own tie matched the wall covering, a luxurious print of maroon and gold. Jason doubted the collar of his faded work shirt would even button around his thick neck.

"You might not want to ask any of our patients if they are transitioning."

"Is it impolite?" He wanted to crawl under the table and die.

"No, sir." She smiled again, with genuine humor this time. "It's just that some of them will talk your ear off, given the slightest show of interest."

"I... thank you."

A chime sounded—a rich little sound that blended unobtrusively with the waiting room's classical music—and the receptionist stared into space for a moment. "I'll let him know," she said to the air, then turned her attention to Jason. "Mr. Carmelke is out of surgery."

"Thank you." It was so strange to hear that uncommon name applied to someone else. He hadn't met another Carmelke in over twenty years.

Half an hour later the waiting room door opened onto a corridor with a smooth, shiny floor and meticulous off white walls. Despite the art—original, no doubt—and the continuing classical music, a slight smell of disinfectant reminded Jason where he was. A young man in a nurse's uniform led Jason to a door marked with the name Dr. Lawrence Steig.

"Hello, Mr. Carmelke," said the man behind the desk. "I'm Dr. Steig." The doctor was lean, shorter than Jason, with brown eyes and a trim salt and pepper beard. His hand, like his voice, was firm and a little rough; his tie was knotted with surgical precision. "Please do sit down."

Jason perched on the edge of the chair, not wanting to surrender to its lushness. Not wanting to be comfortable. "How is my father?"

"The operation went well, and he'll be conscious soon. But I'd like to talk with you first. I believe there are some... family issues."

"What makes you say that?"

The doctor stared at his personal organizer as he repeatedly snapped it open and shut. It was gold. "I've been working with your father for almost two years, Mr. Carmelke. The doctor patient relationship in this type of work is, necessarily, quite intimate. I feel I've gotten to know him quite well." He raised his eyes to Jason's. "He's never mentioned you."

"I'm not surprised." Jason heard the edge of bitterness in his own voice.

"It's not unusual for patients of mine to be disowned by their families."

Jason's hard, brief laugh startled both of them. "This has nothing to do with his... transition, Dr. Steig. My father left my mother and me when I was nine. I haven't spoken to him since. Not once."

"I'm sorry, Mr. Carmelke." He seemed sincere; Jason wondered if it were just professional bedside manner. The doctor opened his mouth to speak, then closed it and stared off into a corner for a moment. "This might not be the best time for a family reunion," he said finally. "His condition may be a little... startling."

"I didn't come all the way from Cleveland just to turn around and go home. I want to talk with my father. While I still can. And this is my last chance, right?"

"The final operation is scheduled for five weeks from now. It can be postponed, of course. But all the papers have been signed." The doctor placed his hands flat on the desk. "You're not going to be able to talk him out of it."

"Just let me see him."

"I will... if he wants to see you."

Jason didn't have anything to say to that.

Jason's father was lying on his side, facing away from the door, as Jason entered. The smell of disinfectant was stronger here, and a battery of instruments bleeped quietly.

He was bald, with just a fringe of gray hair around the back of his head. The scalp was smooth and pink and shiny, and very round—matching Jason's own round head, too big for the standard hardhats at his work site. "Big Jase" was what it said on his own personal helmet, black marker on safety yellow plastic.

But though his father's head was large and round, the shoulders that moved with his breathing were too narrow, and his chest dropped rapidly away to hips that were narrower still. The legs were invisible, drawn up in front of his body. Jason swallowed as he moved around to the other side of the bed.

His father's round face was tan, looking more "rugged" than "wrinkled." Deep lines ran from his nose to the corners of his mouth, and the eyebrows above his closed eyes were gray and very bushy. It was both an older and a younger face than what he had imagined, trying to add twenty years to a memory twenty years old.

Jason's gaze traveled down, past his father's freshly shaved chin, to the thick ruff of gray white fur on his neck. Then further, to the gray furred legs that lay on the bed in front of him and the paws that crossed, relaxed, at the ankles, with neatly trimmed nails and clean, unscuffed pads.

His father's body resembled a wolf's, or a mastiff's, broad and strong and laced with muscle and sinew. But it was wrong, somehow. His chest, narrow though it was, was still wider than any normal dog's, and the fur looked fake—too clean, too fine, too regular. Jason knew from his reading on the plane that it was engineered from his father's own body hair, and was only an approximation of a dog's natural coat with its layers of different types of hair.

He was a magnificent animal. He was a pathetic freak. He was a marvel of biotechnology. He was an arrogant icon of self indulgence.

He was a dog.

He was Jason's father.

"Dad? It's Jason." Some part of him wanted to pet the furry shoulder, but he kept his hands to himself.

His father's eyes flickered open, then drifted closed again. "Yeah. Doctor told me." His voice was a little slurred. "What the hell'r you doing here?"

"I ran into Aunt Brittany at O'Hare. I didn't recognize her, but she knew me right away. She told me all about... you. I came straight here." *It's my father*, he'd told his boss on the phone. *He's in the hospital. I have to see him before it's too late.* Letting him draw the wrong conclusion, but not too far from the truth.

His father's nose wrinkled in distaste. "Never could trust her."

"Dad... why?"

He opened his eyes again. They were the same hard blue as Jason's, and they were beginning to focus properly. "Because I can. Because the Consti... tution gives me the right to do whatever the hell I want with my body and my money. Because I want to be pampered for the rest of my life." He closed his eyes and crossed his paws on the bridge of his nose. "Because I don't want to make any more damn decisions. Now get out."

Jason's mouth flapped open and closed like a fish. "But Dad..."

"Mr. Carmelke?" Jason looked up, and his father rolled his head around, to see where Dr. Steig stood by the door. Jason had no idea how long he had been there. "Excuse me, I meant Jason." Jason's father put his paws over his face again. "Mr. Carmelke, I think you should leave your father alone for a while. He's still feeling the effects of the anesthetic. He may be more... open to discussion, in the morning."

"Doubt it," came the voice from under the crossed paws.

Jason's hand reached out—to stroke the forehead, to ruffle the fur, he wasn't sure which—but then it pulled back. "See you tomorrow, Dad."

There was no response.

As soon as the door closed behind him, Jason leaned heavily against the wall, then slid down to a sitting position. His eyes stung and he rubbed at them.

"I'm sorry." Jason opened his eyes at the voice. Dr. Steig was squatting in front of him, holding a clipboard in his hands. "He's not usually like this."

"I've never understood him," Jason said, shaking his head. "Not since he left. We had a good life. He wasn't drinking or anything. There weren't any money problems—not then, anyway. Mom loved him. I loved him. But he said 'there's nothing here for me,' and he walked out of our lives."

"You mentioned money. Is that what this is about? You know he's given most of it to charity already. What remains is just enough to pay for the craniofacial procedure, and a trust fund that will cover his few needs after that."

"It's not the money. It was never the money. He even offered to pay alimony and child support, but Mom turned it down. It wasn't the most practical decision, but she really didn't want anything to do with him. I think it was one of those things where a broken love turns into a terrible hate."

"Does your mother know you're here?"

"She died eight years ago. Leukemia. He didn't even come to the funeral."

"I'm sorry," the doctor said again. He sat down, let his clipboard clatter to the shiny floor next to him. They sat together in silence for a time. "Let me talk with him tonight, Mr. Carmelke, and we'll see how things go in the morning. All right?"

Jason thought for a moment, then bobbed his head. "All right."

They helped each other up.

Jason's father jogged into the doctor's office the next morning, his lithe new body bobbing with a smooth four legged gait, and hopped easily up onto a carpeted platform that brought his head to the same level as Jason and the doctor. But he refused to meet Jason's eyes. Jason himself sat in the doctor's leather guest chair, fully seated this time, but still not fully comfortable.

"Noah," Dr. Steig said to Jason's father, "I know this is hard for you. But I want you to understand that it is even harder for your son."

"He shouldn't have come here," he said, still not looking at Jason.

"Dad... how could I not? You're the only family I have left in the world, I didn't even know if you were dead or alive, and now... this! I had to come. Even if I can't change your mind, I... I just want to talk."

"Talk, then!" His face turned to Jason at last, but his blue eyes were hard, his mouth set. "I might even listen." He lowered his head to his paws, which rested on the carpeted surface in front of him.

Jason felt the little muscles in his legs tensing to rise. He could stand up, walk out... be free of this awkwardness and pain. Go back to his lonely little house and try to forget all about his father.

But he knew how well that had worked the last time.

"I told them you were dead," he said. "My friends at school. The new school, after we moved to Cleveland. I don't know why. Lots of their parents were divorced. They would have understood. But somehow pretending you were dead made it easier."

His dad closed his eyes hard; deep furrows appeared in the corners of his eyes and between his brows. "Can't say I blame you," he said at last.

"No matter how many people I lied to, I still knew you were out there somewhere. I wondered what you were doing. Whether you missed me. Where did you go?"

"Buffalo."

Jason waited until he was sure no more details were forthcoming. "Is that where you've been all this time?"

"No, I was only there for a few months. Then Syracuse. Miami for a while. I didn't settle down for a long time. But I've been in the Bay

Area for the last eleven years." He raised his head. "Selling configuration management software for Romatek. It's really exciting stuff."

Jason didn't care about his father's job, but he sensed an opening. "Tell me about it."

They talked for half an hour about configuration management and source control and stock options—things that Jason didn't understand and didn't want to understand. But they were talking. His dad even managed to make the topic seem interesting. A wry smirk came to Jason's lips when he realized he was getting a sales presentation from a dog. A dog with his father's head.

Jason and his father sat in the courtyard behind the clinic, under a red Japanese maple that sighed in the wind. The skyscrapers of San Francisco were visible above the fence, which was painted with a colorful abstract mural. A few birds chirped, and the slight mineral sting of sea salt flavored the air, reminding Jason how far he was from home.

A phone with two large buttons was strapped to his father's left foreleg. He could push the buttons with his chin to summon urgent or less urgent assistance. He sat on the bench next to Jason with his legs drawn up beneath him, his head held high so as to look Jason as much in the eye as possible.

"I would have had to have something done with the knees one way or the other," he said. "They were just about shot, before. Arthritis. Now they're like new. I was taking laps this morning, before you showed up. Haven't been able to run like that in years. And being so close to the ground, it feels like a hundred miles an hour."

Jason translated that into kilometers and realized his dad wasn't speaking literally. "But what about... I dunno, restaurants? Museums? Movies?"

"After they do the head work I'll have different tastes, and I'll get nothing but the best. Museums—hell, I never went to museums before. And as far as movies, I'll just wait for them to come out on chip. Then I'll curl up with my handler and go to sleep in front of them."

"Of course, the movie will be in black and white to you."

"Heh."

Jason didn't mention—didn't want to think about—the other changes that the "head work" would make in his father's senses, and his brain. After the craniofacial procedure, his mind would be as much like a dog's as modern medicine could make it. He'd be happy, no question of that, but he wouldn't be Noah Carmelke any more.

Jason's dad seemed to recognize that his thoughts were drifting in an uncomfortable direction. "Tell me about your job," he said.

"I work for Bionergy," Jason replied. "I'm a civil engineer. We're refitting Cleveland's old natural gas system for biogas... that means a lot of tearing up streets and putting them back."

"Funny. I was a civil engineer for a while, before I hired on at Romatek."

"No shit?"

"No shit."

"I was following in your footsteps, and I didn't even know it."

"We thought you were going to be an artist. Your mom was so proud of those drawings of the barn, and the goats."

"Wow. I haven't done any sketching in years."

They stared at the mural, both remembering a refrigerator covered with drawings.

"You want me to draw you?"

Jason's father nodded slowly. "Yeah. Yeah, I'd like that."

Someone from the clinic managed to scare up a pad and some charcoal, and they settled down under the maple tree. Jason leaned against the fence and began to sketch, starting with the hindquarters. His father sat with his hind legs drawn up beneath him and his forelegs stretched straight out in front. "You look like the Sphinx," Jason said.

"Hmm."

"You can talk if you like, I'm not working on your mouth."

"I don't have anything to say."

Jason's charcoal paused on the page, then resumed its scratching. "Last night I read a paper I found in the restaurant. The Howl. You know it?" The full title was *HOWL: The Journal of the Bay Area Transpecies Community*. It was full of angry articles about local politicians he'd never heard of, and ads for services he couldn't understand or didn't want to think about.

"I've read it, yeah. Buncha flakes."

"I found out there are a lot of different reasons for people to change their species. Some of them feel they were born into the wrong body. Some are making a statement about humanity's impact on the planet. Some see it as a kind of performance art. I don't see any of those in you."

"I told you, I just want to be taken care of. It's a form of retirement."

The marks on the page were getting heavy and black. "I don't think that's it. Not really. I look at you and I see a man with ambition and drive. You wouldn't have gotten all those stock options if you were the type to retire at 58." The charcoal stick snapped between Jason's fingers, and he threw the pieces aside. "Damnit, Dad, how can you give up your humanity?"

Jason's dad jumped to his four feet. His stance was wide, defensive. "The O'Hartigan decision said I have the right to reshape my body and my mind in any way I wish. I think that includes the right to not answer questions about it." He stared for a moment, as though he were about to say something else, then pursed his lips and trotted off.

Jason was left with a half finished sketch of a sphinx with his father's face.

He sat in the clinic's waiting room for three hours the next day. Finally Dr. Steig came out and told him that he was sorry, but his father simply could not be convinced to see him.

Jason wandered the lunchtime crowds of San Francisco. The spring air was clear and crisp, and the people walked briskly. Here and there he saw feathers, fur, scales. The waiter who brought his sandwich was half snake, with slitted eyes and a forked tongue that flickered. Jason was so distracted he forgot to tip.

After lunch he came to the clinic's door and stopped. He stood in the hall for a long time, dithering, but when the elevator's ping announced the arrival of two women with identical Siamese cat faces he bolted shoving between them, ignoring their insulted yowls, hammering the Door Close button. As the elevator descended he gripped the handrails, pushed himself into the corner, tried to calm his breathing.

He landed in Cleveland at 12:30 that night.

The other hard hats at his work site gave him a nice card they had all signed. He accepted their sympathies but did not offer any details. One woman took him aside and asked how long his father had. "The doctor says five weeks."

Days passed. Sometimes he found himself sitting in the cab of a backhoe, staring at his hands, wondering how long he had been there.

He confided in nobody. He imagined the jokes: "Good thing it isn't your mother... Then you'd be a son of a bitch!" Antacids became his favorite snack.

The little house he'd bought with Maria, back when they thought they might be able to make it work, became oppressive. He ate all his meals in restaurants, in parts of town where he didn't know anyone. Once he found a copy of the local transpecies paper. It was a skinny little thing, bimonthly, with angry articles about local politicians and ads for services he wished he didn't know anything about.

Four weeks later, on a Monday evening, he got a call from San Francisco.

"Jason, it's me. Your dad. Don't hang up."

The handset was already halfway to the cradle as the last three words came out, but Jason paused and returned it to his ear. "Why not?"

"I want to talk."

"You could have done that while I was there."

"OK, I admit I was a little short with you. I'm sorry."

The plastic of the handset creaked in Jason's hand. He tried to consciously relax his grip. "I'm sorry too."

There was a long silence, the two of them breathing at each other across three thousand kilometers. It was Jason's father who broke it. "The operation is scheduled for Thursday at 8 AM. I... I'd like to see you one more time before then."

Jason covered his eyes with one hand, the fingers pressing hard against the bones of his brow. Finally he sighed and said "I don't think so. There's no point to it. We just make each other too crazy."

"Please. I know I haven't been the best father to you..."

"You haven't been any kind of father at all!"

Another silence. "You've got me there. But I'd really like to..."

"To what? To say goodbye? Again? No thanks!" And he slammed down the phone.

He sat there for a long while, feeling the knots crawl across his stomach, waiting for the phone to ring again.

It didn't.

That night he went out and got good and drunk. "My dad's turning into a dog," he slurred to the bartender, but all that got him was a cab home.

Tuesday morning he called in sick. He spent the day in bed, sometimes sleeping. He watched a soap opera; the characters' ludicrous problems seemed so small and manageable.

Tuesday night he did not sleep. He brought out a box of letters from his mother, read through them looking for clues. At the bottom of the box he found a picture himself at age eight, standing between his parents. It had been torn in half, the jagged line cutting between him and his father like a lightning bolt, and crudely taped together. He remembered rescuing the torn photo from his mother's wastebasket, taping it together, hiding it in a box of old CD ROMs. Staring at it late at night. Wondering why.

Wednesday morning he drove to the airport.

There was a strike at O'Hare and he was rerouted to Atlanta, where he ate a bad hamburger and floated on a tide of angry, frustrated people, thrashing to stay on top. Finally one gate agent found him a seat to LAX. From there he caught a red eye to San Francisco.

He arrived at the clinic at 5 AM. The door was locked, but there was a telephone number for after hours service. It was answered by a machine. He stomped through menus until he reached a bored human being, who knew nothing, but promised to get a message to Dr. Steig.

He paced the hall outside the clinic. He had nowhere else to go.

Fifteen minutes later an astonished Dr. Steig called back. "Your father is already in prep for surgery, but I'll tell the hospital to let you see him." He gave Jason the address. "I'm glad you came," he said before hanging up.

The taxi took Jason through dark, empty streets, puddles gleaming with reflected streetlight. Raindrops ran down the windows like sweat, like tears. Jason blinked as he stepped into the hard blue white light of the hospital's foyer. "I'm here to see Noah Carmelke," he said. "I'm expected."

The nurse gave him a paper mask to tie over his nose and mouth, and goggles for his eyes. "The prep area is sterile," she said as she helped him step into a paper coverall. Jason felt like he was going to a costume party.

And then the double doors slid open and he met the guest of honor.

His father lay on his side, shallow breaths raising and lowering his furry flanks. An oxygen mask was fastened to his face, like a muzzle. His eyes were at half mast, unfocused. "Jason," he breathed. "They said you were coming, but I didn't believe it." The sound of his voice echoed hollowly behind the clear plastic.

"Hello, Dad." His own voice was muffled by the paper mask.

"I'm glad you're here."

"Dad... I had to come. I need to understand you. If I don't understand you, I'll never understand myself." He hugged himself. His face felt swollen; his whole head was ready to implode from sadness and fatigue. "Why, Dad? Why did you leave us? Why didn't you come to Mom's funeral? And why are you throwing away your life now?"

The bald head on the furry neck moved gently, side to side, on the pillow. "Did you ever have a dog, Jason?"

"You know the answer, Dad. Mom was allergic."

"What about after you grew up?"

"I've been alone most of the time since then. I didn't think I could take proper care of a dog if I had to go to work every day."

"But a dog would have loved you."

Jason's eyes burned behind the goggles.

"I had a dog when I was a kid," his father continued. "Juno. A German Shepherd. She was a good dog... smart, and strong, and obedient. And every day when I came home from school she came bounding into the yard... so happy to see me. She would jump up and lick my face." He twisted his head around, forced his eyes open to look into Jason's. "I left your mother because I couldn't love her like that. I knew she loved me, but I thought she deserved better than me. And I didn't come to the funeral because I knew she wouldn't want me there. Not after I'd hurt her so much."

"What about me, Dad?"

"You're a man. A man like me. I figured you'd understand."

"I don't understand. I never did."

His father sighed heavily, a long doggy sigh. "I'm sorry."

"You're turning yourself into a dog so someone will love you?"

"No. I'm turning myself into a dog so I can love someone. I want to be free of my human mind, free of decisions."

"How can you love anyone if you aren't you any more?"

"I'll still be me. But I'll be able to be me, instead of thinking all the time about being me."

"Dad..."

The nurse came back. "I'm sorry, Mr. Carmelke, but I have to ask you to leave now."

"Dad, you can't just leave me like that!"

"Jason," his father said. "There's a clause in the contract that lets me specify a family member as my primary handler."

"I don't think I could..."

"Please, Jason. Son. It would mean so much to me. Let me come home with you."

Jason turned away. "And see you every day, and know what you used to be?"

"I'd sleep by your feet while you watch movies. I'd be so happy to see you when you came home. All you have to do is give the word, and I'll put my voiceprint on the contract right now."

Jason's throat was so tight that he couldn't speak. But he nodded.

The operation took eighteen hours. The recovery period lasted weeks. When the bandages came off, Jason's father's face was long and furry and had a wet nose. But his head was still very round, and his eyes were still blue.

Two deep wells of sincere, doggy love.

A gravedigger dog faces prejudice and robots.

PUPPY LOVE

George S. Walker

In the Ninth Ward of New New Orleans, the CEO of Atomitronics unleashed a flock of flamingobots. John LeChien, walking to work in the morning, heard them before he turned and saw them: a stiff-gaited pink horde clacking across the street and sidewalks.

He evaded the sharp beak of the first one and dropped to all fours to snap its plastic neck with his jaws. The beak of the second ripped his overalls to expose short blond fur. There were too many of them, rushing him from all directions. Tail between his legs, he dove between them and rolled, hearing the too-close thok-thok-thok of beaks striking the sidewalk.

Back on all fours, he loped into the street, bounding off the fan hood of a hovercar to leapfrog a pair of flamingobots. Solar bicyclists swerved to avoid him. Their horns bleated and curses filled the air. No time to turn and see if the riders were swearing at him or at the flamingobots for snarling their morning commute.

He spotted a shortcut at the next intersection, running beneath a house on stilts to head for the canal bridge. Already he was panting, tongue lolling from his mouth. There were more flamingobots ahead, marching to cut him off. He barely raced past them in time, up onto the bridge. Only then did he see that escape was cut off. At least ten pink bird-machines were on the bridge already, blocking traffic as effectively as if the drawbridge were open.

John leaped onto the parapet, took a long look at the dirty water below, and jumped.

It was a long fall. He stretched to his full length, hind legs pointed down, fingered forepaws up at the sky.

The impact with the water knocked the wind out of him. He fought his way desperately back to the surface and gasped for air. Dog paddling to keep his snout above the filthy water, he looked up.

The sky was raining pink. He lunged from side to side as flamingobots began striking the water around him. They sank like stones, and after a couple of minutes, there was no trace of the flock. John heard traffic returning to normal up on the bridge. A bicyclist had stopped to look down over the parapet. He waved. Still panting, John lifted a forepaw to wave back. He began paddling toward shore.

In the Atomitronics high-rise on Tulane Avenue, William dropped onto the therapist's leather couch and looked at his watch. "Let's get started. I've got meetings all day."

The psychiatrist picked up his electronic tablet. "Katherine from the Board of Directors just called."

William waved dismissively. "He got away again."

Dr. Von Krafft sighed. "Did you watch the anger management holo-vid I emailed you?"

"Doc, I don't have time for that. I'm a busy man." He looked at his watch again.

The psychiatrist stroked his beard thoughtfully. "Let's talk about your daughter again."

"Britney is the sweetest girl in the world. And she is not marrying a dog. End of discussion."

"He's a transgenic, William. He's not really a dog."

"If it walks like a dog and it barks like a dog..."

"Maybe we should talk about your mother."

"Why? Does she want to marry a dog, too?"

John was late for work at the cemetery.

"Well, look what the dog drug in," said Ebony. Since she was a canine transgenic, too, she could say that. "Pee-uuu." She wrinkled the black snout on her face. "You been swimming the canals?"

John nodded. "What's it matter? We're stuffin' tombs, not selling insurance."

"Henri hates the smell of wet dog."

"He only shows up for funerals. What's he got us doin' today?"

"A couple 366's here, then prep a mausoleum at Lafayette No. 2."

"Bag 'em up and move 'em back," said John. Nearly all the tombs in New New Orleans were above ground. A 366 meant a year and a day had elapsed, so they were to open a vault, gather up whatever remained of the body, bag it, and pack it into the far recesses of the vault. City cemeteries were too overcrowded to let everyone who died have a private room for eternity.

"You gonna tell me what you was doin' in a canal?"

"Britney's old man's after me again. No point calling the police, 'cause he's a CEO and I'm a gravedigger."

"You learned anything from this?"

"Yeah. The only thing worse than a psycho girlfriend is a girlfriend's psycho dad."

"No!" Ebony shook her long black ears. "The learnin' here is that Uptown girls are trouble."

John was in a good mood the next morning, as he left his apartment. He'd talked to Britney for over an hour last evening. He remembered the concern in her blue eyes, the pout of her little mouth as she said she was going to have a serious talk with Daddy. He unrolled the phone from his overalls and was still captivated by the video of Britney talking when the grappling pincers latched onto him.

The tiny things stuck in his fur and overalls. So many! Twenty? Fifty? A hundred? Their gossamer lines stretched from above. He looked up.

A small robot ornithopter bearing the Atomitronics cold fusion logo beat its black mylar wings, and the lines tightened. John's feet left the ground, and his phone blew away.

"Help!"

Some children on their way to school waved as the ornithopter carried him over their heads.

He was headed for Lake Pontchartrain, swinging from a web of thin lines: nearly invisible, but too tough to break. He began gnawing on a bunch of them, but they were thinner than dental floss. He was already too high up to jump. He watched the wings beating rhythmically against the blue sky.

"Put me down!" he barked.

It continued on its preset course above the houses. He wondered how far it could fly. He wondered how far he could swim. They were making good time, keeping up with solar bicyclists on the boulevard along the canal.

The grappling pincers weren't in his skin, and didn't hurt at all. He carefully pulled one loose, then another. He removed ten of them before he decided maybe it was a bad idea. Better to take his chances in the lake than fall who-knew-where.

Britney would cry her eyes out if he died. Her father would finally feel remorse then, a changed man. He'd probably splurge for a proper tomb for John, not a rack 'n stack wall crypt in a city cemetery. Maybe a big mausoleum, and Britney would stop by with flowers every day. She'd wear black. Not a trendy goth black, but the kind that—

They were almost to the Lakeshore Monorail. A mag-lev train was just floating into the station crowded with morning commuters. Beyond the monorail lay Lake Pontchartrain, its glistening surface stretching thirty miles to the north of New New Orleans. A long swim. John wished he'd kept a better grip on his phone.

The ornithopter banked to avoid a public housing complex on FEMA Debacle Drive. The flyer was coming in behind the train, very close to the platform. Some of the commuters boarding the train turned to look. John tugged on a group of lines and found he could swing a little, like beneath a parachute. He began building up rhythm, which the ornithopter flapped to correct for. The last of the commuters were boarding the train.

"The doors are now closing," said a disembodied voice.

John pulled hard on the lines, swinging in through the train doors. He spun around, grabbed the ceiling rail, and planted his feet firmly above the doors. The doors slid shut, and the train floated away from the station. Outside, the ornithopter beat its wings frantically, trying to keep up. But the lines embedded in the door yanked it into a spin. The flyer abruptly tumbled away behind the train. The lines were still stuck in the door.

John swung down onto the nearest bench and began plucking the grappling pincers out of his fur and clothing.

Seated next to him, a black man in a business suit whistled. "That is one sweet commute arrangement you've got, son."

"I understand your wife gardens," said Dr. Von Krafft. "Lots of people find that relaxes them."

"Doc, that's what illegal immigrants are for."

226

The psychiatrist leaned back in his chair. "William, have you thought about what kind of message you're sending your daughter?"

"Hey, I love sending messages. Some people send flowers. I send... other stuff."

Von Krafft sighed. "We need to talk about your daughter. Your wife emailed me and said Britney tried to talk to you last night about going transgenic."

"Her fixation, you mean? I told her, 'Not my daughter!'"

"She is of legal age, though."

William stared. "Am I the only sane one in this room?"

"You have unaddressed anger issues, William."

"And I'm addressing them!"

"Not that way," said Von Krafft. "You can't keep this up."

"You obviously haven't seen the size of our Atomitronics web catalog."

Ebony was in the wall vault, sweeping out dust and bone fragments. John was the bag man, collecting the mortal remains and throwing away pieces of casket.

"She wants to have it done, Ebony, become a transgenic."

"She don't know what she's in for." Ebony's voice sounded hollow in the vault.

"She's been around transgenics, me at least."

"We're both second generation, John, born this way." Ebony coughed from the dust. "The looks I get sometimes, I wouldn't wish on nobody."

"I'm who I am. You wish you wasn't one?"

"Ain't sayin' that. But your girl, she doin' it like a fashion statement. She ain't got no clue what it's like to be a bitch." She poked her head out and stretched out a forepaw. "Gimme the bag."

John handed it to her. "You don't know what I see, lookin' in her eyes."

"Lust," Ebony muttered, barely audible. "A psycho girlfriend would be safer. How many times Pycho Dad try to kill you now?"

"They're talking. He'll come around."

She stuck her head out, looked at him with her sad brown eyes. "This could be your vault," she said softly.

There was no attack on his way to work, and for the first day in weeks, John got to work before Ebony. In the maintenance shed, he clicked on the work orders that Henri had posted for them on *cemeteries. newneworleans.*

The first one was to dig a new grave in the Jewish section of the cemetery. Jews buried their dead in God's earth, even in lowland New New Orleans. Wooden coffin, wooden nails.

But John was sure the Jewish section in this cemetery had been filled for years. How could they dig a fresh grave? He clicked on the gravesite link. It was an empty plot after all. He made coffee while he waited for Ebony.

The shed door opened. Ebony was startled by the sight of him.

"I thought you was some blond ghost," she said. She lifted her muzzle, sniffing. "And you made coffee. You is a changed man, John."

"No. Early man. Britney musta' talked sense into her dad."

Ebony looked skeptical.

After coffee, they walked to the Jewish section, carrying their shovels. It was a nice day to dig, and he loved digging with Ebony. The grass was dry, but as soon as they dug deep, there would be mud. The Jewish section was secluded, sheltered from the traffic by a row of trees. By tradition, there were stones and pebbles on the graves here, and few flowers.

But when they got to the gravesite where they were supposed to dig, there was already a well-weathered Star of David headstone there: Mel Goldschmidt 1902-1965.

"Weird," said John. "How could the website be wrong?"

They were both standing on the grass on Mel's grave when John felt a rumble, like a heavy cargo hovercraft on the street.

Abruptly the grave collapsed beneath their feet. Ebony yelped, and they both fell in together. Dirt was churning, mixed with crumbled casket and bones. The screw-tip of an Atomitronics boring mole appeared.

For a moment, John balanced on a rotten board, like a surfboard. He grabbed Ebony by the shoulders. Using all his strength, he hurled her up and out of the grave.

Something locked onto his left hind leg, then his right: grapplers for pulling pipes and cables through tunnels. The mole reversed, sucking John deep into the muddy hole. He gasped for one last breath of air and closed his eyes, feeling mud flow over his fur and overalls. He struggled with his forearms, trying to pull himself back to the surface, to no avail. He lost all sense of direction, hearing the deep growl of the mole, feeling the mud churning past him.

His last thoughts would be of Britney, her sweet face, her dimpled cheeks, her blonde hair blowing in the breeze, the sound of her giggling laughter—

Abruptly the pressure of the mud fell away, and John was dragged across hard concrete.

He blinked his mud-covered eyelids open to daylight and heard a couple loud clangs. The mole abruptly stopped. The grapplers, which had been locked onto his legs, went into loose, twitching spasms.

John pulled his hind legs free and sat up. He was in the middle of the cemetery drainage ditch. The mole had been trying to traverse the gap to the other side. He turned and saw Ebony on her hind legs, panting and holding her shovel like a club.

On the dorsal side of the mole, its metal-shielded controller box was flattened where Ebony had brained it with her shovel. The screw-tip at the head of the mole was still turning.

John shook, scattering mud from his fur and clothes.

"You O.K.?" asked Ebony.

"Yeah," he said. He kicked the mole. "The things we do for love."

Ebony muttered, "Yeah, the things we do for love." She looked at the collapsed Jewish graves and toppled headstones. "Henri's gonna have a conniption fit when he sees what Psycho Dad did."

William sat on the edge of the psychiatrist's couch, his hands balled into fists.

"You seem tense," said Dr. Von Krafft. "Sometimes when my patients are tense, I find it helps if they demonstrate their feelings with Sammy, here." He handed William a stuffed bear with soft brown fur and large, soulful eyes.

William studied the bear for a moment, then pinned it down against the couch and punched it. He savored the moment, then punched it again. Then he picked it up and beat it against the ornate wood carving that edged the cushioned headrest.

"You son of a bitch!" he exclaimed, pounding the bear over and over against the wood.

"William..." Dr. Von Krafft reached out a hand.

The bear's head came loose, and stuffing scattered over the couch. William stopped, panting, and stared at the mangled bear.

"Do you feel better now?" asked the psychiatrist.

William put his hand in the bear, feeling through the stuffing. "Where the hell are the servo motors?"

"How long's it gonna take?" asked Ebony.

"Two months," said John. "A long time without seeing Britney." He wondered if he'd find himself howling at the moon before her procedure was over.

"She show you pictures of what she gonna look like when it's done?" John shook his head. "She wants it to be a surprise. But it don't matter if they're Chihuahua genes or St. Bernard's. She'll still be Britney."

"Yeah, she still gonna be Britney." Ebony sighed. "Come on. We got bones to bag."

Two months later, Britney called John's cell, saying she was on her way to the cemetery. John coaxed Ebony into coming with him to the front gate, and they waited in silence. John shivered with anticipation. Ebony was just staring at the ground.

Britney's red Ferrari hovercar glided to a stop outside the gate. John remembered rides in her car with the top down, the air whipping through his fur, his ears. But the top was closed now, and there were two people inside. It settled to the ground, and the passenger door folded like an accordion and slid beneath the car.

Someone about Britney's size, wearing fancy clothes like hers, stepped out onto the cracked driveway. Her fur was pure white, like a West Highland White Terrier's. But there was something wrong with her face. Her muzzle wasn't long enough, the brow was wrong, and her pointed ears were too short. She smiled, revealing small sharp teeth.

Involuntarily, John felt his hackles rise.

"Isn't this fur just to die for?" said Britney's voice.

John looked at her beautiful blue eyes and saw vertical pupils. In horror, he realized that somehow, Britney had gotten feline genes. How could the doctors have screwed up? Could it be reversed? Adding genes was one thing, but deleting them?

"Britney, what...? Maybe your father can pay to..."

Then he noticed that the man sitting at the wheel of the Ferrari was a feline transgenic wearing mirrorshades.

"Sorry I can't stay," said Britney. "I just wanted you to see the new me!" She spun around like a fashion model, and he saw she had a long tail. Not like a lion, but cuter, like a kitten.

"Cher John," she said. "We had such good times, and I'm never going to forget you."

She came close and patted his shoulder. It wasn't really a caress, and he saw her own fur bristling in response. When she exhaled, it was almost like a hiss, and her little nose wrinkled.

"Um, yeah, it's been great," he said. "Good times." He couldn't think what else to say.

Britney waved at him and Ebony and walked back to her car. She got in, and the door of the Ferrari unfolded and sealed. The hovercar floated back away from the gate.

At that moment, John saw a small machine nestled against the curb. An Atomitronics HunterTracker 2000. The coloring blended with the curb like a chameleon. Its head swiveled to stare at John with beady robot eyes, and he froze.

Abruptly it spun around and scampered after the hovercar.

"Cher John?" said Ebony, standing beside him. "That what she calls you?"

John nodded numbly.

Ebony made a sound like stifling a laugh. She leaned close and licked his ear. "I hear you might have an opening for a psycho bitch."

John watched the Ferrari round a corner and disappear.

He turned and licked her nose. "Maybe."

As W0lf chases the ghost trail of a fox anima deeper and deeper into cyberspace, he risks losing his connection to himself.

OMEGA

Garrett Marco

Names are an outdated concept when considering consciousness through anima, virtual avatars, but nicknames gather like sad men at cheap bars. And the whole Net had turned into something like a cheap bar even before I came around.

W0lf. Hunter. 0mega.

Cheesy stuff. Old-school thoughts about what it means to have this kind of anima. The birds flying over the hub call it out like a chant, like I can score some points for the whole team. I'm a local hero in this hub, and a no-good hacker. My successes are their successes. My failures, however, are my own. And I suppose it's on account of my penchant for finding myself in plenty of bad situations. And when you're in a bad situation with me, well, that just increases the chances of survival for one of us.

So I sling down slum alleys and peel off curls of that positron mind melter app they got running through the Bottom Lane. That's where the good stuff is. The illegal, unethical software capable of turning your brainpan into a bedpan—drugs in software form. EE polices it, but tracking Hub-side transfers has always been out of their purview. They may have built the Net's virtual matrix, but they couldn't control it.

And when there's too much stress on a particular line, a ripple of loss connections can dump users out of their interfaces. I'm looking into a recent incident; twelve users got caught in a line's crash and got dumped into the Garden, EE's safety net for users straying too far from the more stable regions. A harsh crash like that messes a user up, and that's even with the Garden waiting.

A smart user wouldn't chase after something like this. But there were reports of something strange just before the line crashed. A glowing anima in the shape of a fox. A Spirit.

Full digital converts are ranging upward of five-hundred thousand. That's all it takes to live as a permanent anima.

Rare kind of thing to do to yourself. Not many permanent anima around. And that's exactly why I'm walking into this particular dive, looking to chat up a turtle with square glasses and a silly tie like he's supposed to be my accountant. His tag reads IO, but it could just as well be 10.

I take a seat across from him at a high table. Our meeting place isn't anything strange. A café. A speakeasy. Chatting patrons using the space to socialize, to disappear from the dreary and into the dreamy. It helps to learn, if one is attached enough to their anima. Whole classes are taught like that now. Wish I'd had the chance. But stealing my first EE-SIM went well enough. Exposure at a young age.

That's how you get them.

"You're not very punctual," he says.

"Tell me what you saw," I say. If he's concerned about time, then I won't waste his. "What did the anima look like?"

He stirs a drink—he's that type to take things seriously. "I don't recall."

"No visual," I say, confirming. I don't like the guy. He's afraid. It's clear all around us, and it's the type of thing you learn how to control in the first months of serious Net-use. That's why we're meeting in a place like this—fear permeates the line. Everyone's on watch. "What happened after the anima blew the line out?"

"Everything went dead, of course. Our animas got shifted to the Garden. Then we sat tight until some EE techs fixed the line."

Ten anima had been in that line when it went out, maybe due to a spirit's presence. They'd spent twelve hours in a virtual holding tank while their data was re-secured. A scary feeling, like floating in space without a lifeline. Oblivion might swallow you up and no one would ever know.

I'm there as a shadow—an empty shell, an image, an avatar of an avatar. No risk of anything like that happening to my consciousness. I'm sitting across from this turtle in my Hunter anima—normal enough, just another anthro like the rest. A wolf. Keeps my senses sharp. Ninety-five percent sync. Top out of the ninetieth percentile, and you'll start changing biologically—that's the rumor. Let me squash that for you right now.

But even my shadow's nose, behind two protective barriers, could pick up the stink of the whole place.

I hear ninety-nine percent sync, though... But I've never met a real spirit. I don't know what it would be like, and that's why I'm scared. Because there's another way to go full-digital, or at least there's a rumor. High enough sync ratio, and that's it. Your consciousness flees into the vast vacuum of the Net. The Final Transfer.

I've been working on a contingency plan—Omega, my latest anima project. The goal is to have it mimic consciousness, a virtual mind to fill the vacuum and assist in processing. Everything's done, but having data from a real spirit would ease my worries of possible miscalculations on my end.

"All the others reported similar experiences," I say. I access a list of those ten and some notes I've already assembled. "You got hit hardest of them all." A savings account emptied. An investment portfolio sold then re-sold then blocked and hidden behind China's Dead Line. Maybe the spirit needed funds for some reason. Hire out some processors. Buy some virtual real estate.

IO stirs his drink until a funnel appears in the meaningless liquid. He's a coder with skills beyond my own. He runs an independent firm. Former EE employee, of course—all reputable virtual-coders got their start with EE. Even I did some independent work before I started doing things for the Net itself. That's how I ended up a virtual addict.

"I was lucky, really," he says. "I had the most to lose. They didn't get everything."

"Hmm." I make a note of it. Real truth to him. I read it off his anima like an exit sign on the highway. It's a route. That's how it works here. Thought-patterns are just roads to be mapped. "Two of the others described the anima in question as a fox. Female. Does that not match with what you saw?"

IO shakes his head. "It could have been a lot of things."

Two out of ten isn't enough of a lead to drive me. I need more, but I think this guy is about empty. "I'm glad you weren't hurt too bad by it, and you're certain there are no residuals from the transfer to the Garden?" It isn't uncommon for some static to form in the neural pathways after a harsh transfer like that.

Turtle-man gulps. "I hope not." And finally he brings his drink to his lips and downs the entire thing. He'd packed his coffee with cream and sugar. He probably likes mixed drinks, too. "The whole thing unnerved me. I felt attacked."

"You were," I say.

He nods and almost smiles. "I know about you. A real hero of the hub." He says it with enough of a hitch that it comes off as knowing. And there's a lot to know. I'm not a hero, just a user who makes good on promises, no matter who I make them to. "I'll share whatever information I come across, and if you need anything from me... don't hesitate."

I stand, as if to say I'm done, but I won't be walking out. "A pleasure, IO. If you think of anything else, contact me right away."

IO looks at his lap, already dismissing our time together. EE had put out a gag-order on the story, on the harsh transfer, and the ten who'd gone away weren't to talk to anyone outside the family about anything. But I dug deep in the right circles and pressed the right people. Information flows like wine, intoxicating gossip to poison our ears. And so I search through this virtual veil at my suspect on the other side—a spirit lurking about my hometown hub.

My sync ratio has been on the climb for a while now. I'll pass certain thresholds in a few weeks. Natural apotheosis is only theoretical. I need to find this spirit and get some answers.

I kill the shadow and return to my nearby proxy. Much more comfortable looking through W0lf's lupine eyes. Hunter is my first anima and still wears the trappings of humanity, an extra skin stretched across something real. It wears clothes and an almost cartoonish anthropomorphism. In making W0lf, I ripped away that veil and blew away the smoke. Four paws on the line connection, keen ears and a long snout. All processes moved to a compartmentalized, virtual system—my favorite anima excels at speed and sense.

Lagros is the next name on my list. She's always at her shop in the outskirts of the hub. A real shaker—not so much a mover. I point my nose in that direction and plug into the nearest transfer line.

Lines make up the Net's circulatory system. They take you from one hub to another. It's also where consciousness meets interface. A fragile spot.

Soft transfers run like a shock from head to crotch. I can only imagine what a harsh transfer must feel like. Never experienced one myself, but the stories are rough. Wipes out active code and messes with your emotional-mental state.

In an instant, I'm at the hub's outer wall—a barrier to keep out malware and worse. Nothing too bad out there these days, certainly nothing to deserve the size and power of the wall. It's mostly broken-down code. But I don't need to cross that threshold today. Just need to sneak down a dusty stairway and under a few dark arches to reach her shop.

Lagros isn't a pusher, but she's not a pimp. She's a supplier, a networker; she has what you need, they say. Whoever they are, they know something about what everyone wants, because certainly Lagros has it. And she's an old friend, to my eternal fortune.

The shop's full on account of the early-evening rush. These simpler folk are looking for a quick fix or fuck for a few bucks before turning in for the night, returning to reality in good time. Normies who spend more of their lives awake in meatspace than on the Net. Not exactly a dying breed, but maybe on the endangered species watch list.

I weave through the crowd. Stinks like nerves in here, like anticipation. A pornographer. That's what Lagros is. And her shop smells like electric sex.

Some cat's watching the back door. Baggy clothes. Hoodie pulled over his orange head. There's a spike on him somewhere, a nasty bit of software that'll cut clean your connection to the line. Harsh transfer is the best result of that scenario. He's already giving me a mean eye.

"I'm expected," I say. Lagros is one of my biggest fans, a real proponent of my good deeds. Made me run for her without knowing it. Made me track down users owing her money. I already said I'm not a hero. We're not on the best terms anymore, but she owes me.

I don't know who this cat is, but he knows who I am. He stands, opens the door for me, and then closes it after I step through. A blue-lit hallway stretches like a corkscrew before me. As I move forward, a ping in the back of my mind alerts me to a few well-placed barriers and other protective elements. It's not meant as a threat, just as a caution sign: we're not responsible for what happens when you walk off the trail.

I pass several locked doors on my twisted journey and finally come to the boss' back room.

No one can stay mad at a cat for long. At least, that's what they say. But on this count, I'm not willing to give it to them. Heat forks up my haunches when I see her—that plump, black cat sitting on a bed like some storybook queen. Has she really come to this? Excess, indeed.

I feel like pinching my nose. There's virtual food everywhere, and that stuff already smells like static without having the overwhelming perfume stagnant in the virtual space. Not like I need my sense of smell at the moment.

"Lagros," I say, shifting my anima into something more presentable—back to Hunter. Slacks, a jacket, loose tie, mangy hair, and lots of code dedicated to enhancing my social interactions. Hunter makes it easier to deal with people, even when I feel like setting the Net on fire.

I'm already lighting up that positron app just to distort the line enough to show her I don't care. Nothing pisses her off more than dealing with me while I'm in an altered state. I lose out on some of my senses, but I gain a better hold of my temper—and relieve myself of the worst of the smell.

"Hunter," she drawls, making fun of me. Always does that. "You came to see about my misfortune, to ask if there's anything you can do to help?"

I roll the positron around an outstretched paw. It ripples my outline, cutting away bits of visual code. Feels like the bubbling of carbonation on your tongue. "Want it?"

She puts up a black paw, claws out for show, but her ears are up and her eyes wide. "No, sir. I see what it does to young cats with good ideas."

"Because you push it on them." When I said she wasn't a pusher, I was maybe going easy. "And I am here about the great misfortune of the Net being without Her Majesty's presence for all of a few hours."

"Twelve hours," she says, taking a long time about it. "Twelve hours of insufferable nothingness. And that wasn't the worst part."

I pull up my notes again. "One emptied account. One slagged bit of virtual real estate. One fried server."

"Two servers."

"One. I've already done the research. No sense trying to score an additional ride off EE's blunder. They'll pay out to keep you quiet anyway. Bet they already have."

Lagros crosses her arms. We've been alone this whole time, but I'd have thought there would be a guard or two. "It hardly covered what I lost, let alone the emotional torment."

"I'll let you deal with EE on that one. With me, we work in whole-truths." I don't like the workaround. "Any thoughts you want to share?" She's one of the two who had a visual on the anima, but I want her to come to it naturally.

"I want to know why you're looking into things."

"That's not really relevant."

She perks up. "Oh?" She's onto me. "A personal stake, because I know you're done helping me out."

"Yeah," I say in a snarl, "on accounts previously ignored."

"Say you recover my property," she says, scratching at her chin. "Maybe a reconciliation could be in order."

"I do you a favor, and then you do what you should have already done?"

That sounds about right for the kinds of deals Lagros usually runs. The top-down, fuck-the-little-guy sort of deal.

"Exactly," she says with a laugh. I want nothing more than to rip her anima's throat out. But for now, I've got to smile nice. "If you know so much about servers, maybe you already know I got a good look at the Spirit."

It made sense that only two of them had seen it. A permanent anima bleeds excess information like a body expels heat. A virtual consciousness weaves information into a web, a network of synapses that still fails to truly match the complexities of our central nervous system—at least in theory. Only the most astute of anima could pierce that veil of ambient energy.

"A fox, right?" I asked, growing weary of her company. She's already pissed me off, and I'm ready to leave. I dig a hole straight down to the line and wire myself a direct-exit while we speak. I want out of there right away.

She nods. "Bushy thing. Quite the vixen. Glided through the hub like a phantom."

"There's a reason they call them Spirits."

"You don't sound like you believe me."

"You're echoing what Sly already told me."

Lagros' ears perk up. "Already? You work fast."

I don't have time to play stupid games with stupid cats. "Listen, Lagros. I'm helping you out, aren't I? Why don't you stop it with the bait and move past your trolling. I want answers."

Her whiskers bristle at that. "All I know, promise." She pouts. "You don't have to be such a big jerk all the time, Hunter."

I let out a huff. She has a point. "You push me on purpose. What do you want from me?"

"A little sympathy for an old friend. Now how about you follow the trail and talk to the others."

I shake my head. "You're the last one. The trail's dead. The line's cut. If you don't give me something, it's back to hoping."

Lagros doesn't like to give up information she thinks she could otherwise sell, so she's probably thinking of how much she might ask for it, or if she can buy my goodwill with such a deal.

More than anything, though, Lagros always surprises me.

"If it's the Spirit you want, then you'll have to look further ahead than the tip of your snout. There isn't a trail, because ghosts don't leave trails."

She's pissing me off again. I snarl and drop the positron. Then I plug into the next line, phasing this anima out of the hub and into the Net proper. Let Lagros make whatever she wants out of my hurried exit.

I feel obvious, overt. I can shout and moan about it, or I can move forward. But there's not much of a forward in the Net when you're just packets of information floating free. Maybe this is what being a Spirit is like; you float and drift and whirl and twirl across a million lines to billions of people. Is anima manifestation even necessary?

Streams of data zoom by, and my perception slows enough that I can see it happening at a normal pace. I've become more of a hacker. It's easy when you can pluck the packets out of the air. But that's why full-digitals are illegal. It's a security risk. Maybe EE has a few Spirits working with them—that's the rumor. Maybe this Spirit I'm chasing is one of theirs. Or a renegade. But the thefts are such an obvious focus. They could be a distraction.

I normally keep most anything that's trying to contact me to a backup node that sorts through the junk and alerts me to anything that needs my attention immediately. I have it set up so I hardly ever get an alert anymore. But this message passes right through my gates and pops into my general HUD:

EE out for you
For us
-S

That's Sly's card. Something has changed. I went to Sly first, as he was the other one who'd seen the Spirit. He hadn't had anything to say, but he'd been interested in looking into things. A hacker got hacked, and that never sits. Now he's taking the risk of cracking through my defenses. Something's turning.

He'll be waiting. I shift into W0lf and tap into a fast line deep into the hub again. Lagros will forgive me for dropping on the conversation so suddenly. She's kind like that. And she's right. I should work on that whole not-being-a-jerk thing.

Sly's like me; he practically lives on the Net and spends the majority of his hours in-anima. But he works from a base—a virtual mainframe with processing power way beyond my portable stuff. So he needs an office.

I drop in like I'm welcomed company. I was earlier today, so I don't see why I wouldn't be now.

A fizz of packet loss permeates the office. Sly's mustelid scent is everywhere, and I don't hear anything except a clicking sound. There are lines of desks—he has it looking like a real-world office, floor-to-ceiling windows and water coolers. His setup sits in the middle of the room, a buzzing hydra of monitors and snaking cords, flickering displays of scrolling feeds. It's all for show, but it's got that cyber-retro feel that gets some people going.

Cast blue by the monitors' glow is Sly's skinny weasel anima, spiked to hell and bleeding information. A spike can be made to partially sever the link between anima and the physical brain. Left to bleed like this, he'll die.

The clicking darts along the wall behind me.

I turn toward the exit line as someone passes out of the office. They're running, and I haven't bothered to set a tether to the line yet. No time for anything but a rushed transfer. If a smooth transfer is a bridge, and a harsh transfer is a fall into a gully, a rushed transfer is a motorcycle jump across the gully.

But Sly's a goner if I don't help. Hell, I owe him more than he owes me. It takes some time, but I kill the spike and twist his connection into something like a data-suture. After mopping up what information I can, I set about restoring where it can be done.

It takes special skills to stick someone like that. Normally, a spike just kicks you over to the refuge of the Garden in a harsh transfer, where you're protected until you can safely transfer back.

First a single alert pops. The line's being monitored. Next I get three pings—incoming EE crew. If Sly was warning me about EE, then he probably isn't any better off with them. He's most likely unconscious on the other end, so he won't mind if I take over his anima for a moment.

This is a trick I've picked up recently. A side-effect of the increased sync ratio. I shudder out of the hub before jumping into another user's connection to the line. My anima registers as floating free, but my mind is set squarely alongside whoever I choose. Mostly I've only used it as a test, to see what's possible. But when someone's sleeping with an open connection, you can start to interfere in interesting ways.

I sit his body up and go to work on his virtual consoles, first activating barriers and false gates for my EE guests. I want to run a test of my sync ratio, but I don't have time. There's pain in my shoulder, in my back where the spike hit this anima. I'm sweating and panting, and this weasel body of his is running my mind faster than I'm used to. I'm skipping over information, making mistakes.

Two barriers down. One gate destroyed. I raise a false attack spike as a diversion for putting up another gate. Meanwhile, I'm transferring Sly's virtual console to a secure server. Just as the new gate goes up, they're through the other. But I have the console. Now I just need to secure escape.

I can't pop Sly's anima out of the hub in the same way I did mine, so it's got to be through the line. And that means I have to wait for the EE crew to clear the last gate before trying to dive past them and hope Sly's speed hasn't been too affected by his data-loss.

I have my path to the line set just as the final gate falls and three EE monitors burst into the office. They're here to wipe the line clean, and already superficial code is being eaten away all around us. But they don't make a move for me or Sly. These guys are just software running on protocol. A coincidence. But that means EE could be involved. Sly might be a ruthless hacker deserving of the treatment, but he's too good to have been caught out like this.

Since they're not looking for us, I slip past them with ease, shooting down the line and popping out in the central terminal. I immediately disconnect Sly from his SIM-card for the smoothest transfer possible while unconscious, and I open my eyes back in W0lf to an unexpected void.

My heart—my real heart—clenches and I almost hit my emergency stop before I realize I still have some control. My HUD flickers to life, and it only takes me a moment to realize there's no other visual data to process. I'm sitting in front of a live feed, and a blinking white line starts leaving a trail of letters and words.

FOOLISH TO LEAVE YOUR ANIMA UNATTENDED

My HUD flickers again and reads back some bogus data. Whoever's in charge of this display has me locked out of my own software, and I can either induce a harsh transfer outside the hub or suffer whatever torture awaits.

YOU'RE FOLLOWING ME
I SUGGEST YOU STOP
"Fine," I say, finding my voice. "You have me. Now what?"
AS I SAID
CEASE FOLLOWING ME
"I don't even know who you are." There's nothing to pick up with any
sense other than sight, and obviously this experience is being manufac-
tured especially for me. Does my anima still float helpless in the Net, or
have they taken my ethereal form somewhere else?

The white bar blinks in the rhythm of a heartbeat. I can't even detect
the line here. I might be outside the Net altogether, the connection to
my body severed.

It's freak-out time, and I pull the plug—my emergency stop.

Everything goes deep-quiet. It's darker than nothing. Slowly, my
senses come back. Vision is last, remaining fuzzy even as I slip off my
visor and shakily stand to get ahold of myself.

The hallway from my living room to the restroom stretches impos-
sibly, and, as I stare, it twists into the same corkscrew shape as Lagros'
labyrinthine sanctum. There's that clicking again. A dark shadow glides
along the ceiling, and before me now stands a presence, dark and towering
like a monolith.

My breath catches, and I heave before sucking in urgent lungfuls
of air. There's grit in my face, in my mouth, and it's far too hot. I'm
face-down in a desert of broken architecture and leaking code. A veritable
minefield for any anima—anything could cause rapid destabilization in a
place like this, outside the hub's outer walls. That's where I am; there'd be
no Garden for me—unless what I saw for a moment there had been it.
My first harsh transfer, and since it'd been in the open Net, I get bounced
around until I end up... wherever. And now I'm here, no line back, and
only a virtual path to trek until I can find a proper access point.

My body aches as I take what feel like physical steps. I can't fully
disconnect out here, not so soon. I need a smooth transfer or else I could
fry my hardware. Or my mind.

I try bringing up my HUD just in case, but my software is corrupted
beyond repair out here.

A harsh transfer and journey through what most certainly was the
Garden leaves me thinking things through. I've fallen too hard already
just because I'm hopeful for an answer. The display before I transferred
must have been the Spirit I'm chasing. But if it really has any kind of

243

malicious intent, it would have done me in right there. It only tried to scare me. I'll put it in a category of its own.

No use trying to go after that lead; like Lagros said, ghosts don't leave trails.

Then what kind of path am I walking? The remnants of old content have been scattered across this wasteland. I know there are scavengers out here, seekers of intact code and thought-forgotten information. Funny how things never change too much.

I didn't get a good look at the user who fled Sly's. That's my lead. Probably the one I'm really chasing. So why does he double-back and hit Sly again? The poor guy already had his servers raided during the harsh transfer. Probably the same reason I'll be a target now: he dug up something unkind about EE.

Scandal is nothing new for them. But it's hard to do anything about it. They've practically set up the Net as a sovereign nation.

Being tired while connected isn't healthy. Falling asleep can be dangerous because a virtual dream quite often changes into a real nightmare. Not recommended. But I'm coming down from that positron brain melter, and my brain sure feels all melty. It's been an unreasonable amount of time since I've slept or eaten.

I can't even check my sync ratio. What if it's already gone past the threshold? What if my corporeal body has already died and I'm a Spirit myself? The torture of not knowing isn't a kind way to suffer.

And then my second harsh transfer cuts me clean of consciousness. No wasteland. No Garden. No blank screen. Nothing.

I wake at my desk again. Slipping off the visor is more difficult than I expect it to be, like peeling off a bandage from around my eyes. I slap myself. Still alive. No fuzz from an interface. Just a headache. Setting the visor down, I can't help but think I'm never going back there. If I do, I might never make it back here.

A warm shower feels good against my skin. Dinner fills me despite being an instant meal. I take the time to clean up a bit. Go through my fridge and toss out old food. Take out the trash. Cycle the air filters. All my actions are necessary upkeep, but they feel so unnecessary in this moment. I go so far as to wash my bedding before the headache subsides, and I get the itch for higher stimulation.

My apartment is so empty. A window. A door. Neither open. So how do I get out?

This really might be my last time connecting. I don't have the time to write a note or anything. I'm not sure what I would say if I did.

I slide the visor back on. A spark of adrenaline hits the back of my brain, sending a controlling share of my consciousness across the Net and landing me in W0lf. Relief spreads like water to deep roots. I'm back in the open Net. My HUD's still busted, but I have some options open to me.

First I ring up Sly, but it seems like he's still out. There's too much to do; I can't wait for him. So I go about clearing up my damaged software on W0lf. The second harsh transfer wiped most of my main cache, so I reset everything then load some month-old backups that'll have to serve until I have more than a few hours.

My sync ratio is hovering above the threshold now—ninety-nine percent. I can't believe it's gotten this high and I have to focus it through outdated software. I must be reading it wrong, because I don't feel different. A bit distant, if anything.

I glide by Sly's old place, just to see if there's anything left. The whole section of line is blocked. A couple monitors are in the area, but as W0lf, there's no chance of them catching a whiff of me, up-to-date software or not.

I'm only in long enough to do a quick scan of the area, and then I dive into the line again, heading along the outer Hub.

Easy enough—only three users active in that particular line at the time I arrived: me, Sly, and a user named Tix. That must be the user who spiked Sly.

Running a search on Tix will take time I could be using to fix what the harsh transfers broke. So I go back to Lagros, flashing a more diplomatic grin to the hooded cat guard this time around. But he says Lagros isn't around. I end up dropping my request off with him, and then I head to the outer wall at a slow pace.

I'm good at avoiding trouble, but I'm not so great at making it. I'm not trying to dig into sensitive information or anything covert; I want to catch this user and force the truth out of them. Defensive won't do. Time for a more appropriate anima.

0mega isn't what I consider complete. It mixes the interactive strength of Hunter with the line-speed of W0lf. Beyond a mix of skills, it better utilizes my growing sync ratio to allow for faster processing—my ability to defend myself as 0mega will go far beyond W0lf or Hunter's capabilities, the offensive possibilities will be in my own understanding of another user's defenses. It's a bet on my ability to sniff out intent.

I put some extra pieces in place, though, and my intent is to look to the future. Lagros is wrong about me. I know the world doesn't end at the tip of my perception; it doesn't end at all.

I have the sync ratio necessary to run Omega at this point, but I lost a lot of its code during the harsh transfers. My backups are a month behind, which means Omega is a month behind. It's a sensitive anima, a porcelain wolf-mask—I have to use custom code. I can't crunch that much work out in the time I want it done by. I'll need help.

I contact IO, and we agree to meet at the outer edge of the hub. The turtle and I stand together on the wall and look over the wastes. He sticks his head out of his shell as the whistle of cyber wind rushes past—a phenomenon caused by sudden shifts in nearby line traffic. It feels like the air gets sucked from your lungs, but in a good way.

Maybe I just need more of this and less brain melting.

"One of my secrets to quick coding is a bit of software I created," IO says, motioning to the wastes. "It's a self-coder that uses strings of existing code to form solutions to relatively simple problems."

"Sounds like you need a lot of processing power for that kind of work. I don't want to inconvenience your operation."

"Money isn't my concern here," he says.

IO uses the discarded code of the waste as a resource. Time is his real commodity, so we don't waste it and head straight past the threshold, into the scrapheap. There, IO puts his processes to work gobbling up old code and filling in the blanks between the Omega code I already have. Watching it all work makes my programming skills look like the junk he's turning into gleaming gold. Better take notes.

We do in hours what once took me a month. And maybe we get a bit further still. When it's all there, I activate Omega in front of IO.

He takes a step back, shrinking into his shell. "This is..." I don't often see the kind of fear in an anima's eyes as I see in IO's. I imagine his hand hovering over his console's power-cord, like he's ready to suffer a harsh transfer rather than face the anima before him.

Omega takes the shape of W0lf but has skin as smooth as glass—dark and gleaming, circuits of indigo for eyes. The only sharp edges are my ears and teeth. Weightless, I feel like I can drop through the line like a ghost and sniff out anyone, anywhere. I'm both separate and one with the Net around me.

I smile. This is what I've intended. This is what I imagine a Spirit to be: an ethereal representation of the power of a virtual consciousness.

I really don't know at this point if I'm dead or alive on the other side. I feel like sunlight. My arms have a reach I feel so readily, and my feet twitch, eager to take me to any far corner of the Net. I can shift into the ground or disappear forever into the endless sea of the outer Net.

IO adjusts his virtual attire then clears his throat like he's about to give me a quarterly report. "Did I just help digitize you?"

"My sync ratio has crossed the borderline, so at least that means I'm still sending out a chemical signal." If there were no signal, it'd mean I'm dead.

"Do you want me to call an ambulance?" IO asks with cruel pragmatism.

I estimate my body can sit unconscious for no longer than twenty-four hours. I'm risking soiling myself, but at least I won't die of dehydration.

"No," I say. "Unless you don't hear back from me by this time tomorrow. Then you can call the morgue. That'll save everyone some time."

He gives a half-smile. "I have a feeling that'll be the case no matter what happens."

I give him a wave goodbye then shift into the open Net for some alone time.

I think of all the hard things IO must go through in his life that are so different from my own troubles. I don't know why. It's just silly how strange this must be for him to witness, a person deciding to commit corporeal suicide for the sake of personal enlightenment.

I no longer want to know what I'd set out to know. The puzzle had never been the right one. It had never been a question of why, but a question of how and when and what next.

A direct link comes in from Lagros. It's not like her to use such an unsecure method of communication. "Hunter, my sweetness, I have that information for you-oo."

She's so condescending when she's pleased with herself. "I'll be there soon."

"No way, sweetness. You got a bad scent on you right now, and I don't want any monitors following you to me."

"We're talking on a direct line," I say. Besides, I already removed that scent the moment I activated 0mega. I doubt EE has the ability to ever track me down now.

"I know you've already locked it up tighter than necessary! The safest way is the way you make safest. You can tell them Lagros taught you that!"

She's right. I secured the link as soon as I noticed it. Now I secure a file she sends through the link.

"There's your information. On me, this time. I know you can figure this one out, sweetness!"

The link dies on her end.

Her file holds records of Tix's illegal digitization and an arrest warrant; there's also a bit about their many illicit activities, as viewed by EE. But if they have this info, they could have pinched Tix long ago. There's a list of locations I can look, as well as two possible informants.

Lagros' information is always so perfectly useless to me, but not because it isn't of quality. This might well have led me to the true perpetrator. But right now I'm hearing a familiar clicking coming up from behind me.

Omega's senses aren't needed here. Tix, if that's who this is, wants me to know what's about to happen. The Net around me swells with random chunks of information leaking behind the communication architecture.

I turn and bear all offensive software, ready to annihilate this anima before it can so much as give a threatening glare. But the world falls away, and my adversary is granted their glare. This anima is appropriately hideous to me: a walking roach, with scything arms that are likely modified spikes.

We've most certainly suffered another hard transfer, and this is the Garden. I don't feel it, though. Maybe it's Omega's protection.

I doubt Tix has similar inclinations.

"New anima," Tix says, voice cloaked behind a deep modulation. The Garden around us is flush with blooming hedges and detailed stonework. We're both so out of place here—a Kafkaesque roach and Big Bad from the fairytales. "Your sync ratio exceeds the physical threshold. Welcome to godhood."

If bugs can laugh, Tix laughs.

"If that's what I am," I say, trying desperately to launch any kind of attack on Tix's security while also keeping a calm presence. But Tix has a lot of his own software. While we talk, we wage a silent war for control of the Net around us. I scan for weak points as Tix sets up false entries and misleading barriers. I do the same in response to Tix's probes. Stalemate so far. "I've achieved it without purposeful digitization."

I create a redundant loop of code. My hope is to throw new information Tix's way to overload their ability to predict my actions—that's my true fear of Spirits, their ability to pierce all masks and reveal a truth beyond truth. I certainly can't pierce Tix's stoic expression.

"Purposeful digitization," Trix echoes. "Isn't that precisely what you've done?"

"I didn't seek this path."

"But you walked it. You prepared for it. And now you've come to its end."

"Yes, but..." They're right. If my body is dead, that is. Doesn't mean I can't dance around the possible truth. I sigh, trying to sound more angry than upset. "You're right. This is what I wanted, in a way. I just didn't know what I was doing."

"Some of us do, some of us don't."

"But nothing excuses slicing someone's connection like you did. The theft I can look past, but attempted murder is something I take issue with."

"A thief, yes, but I didn't spike your friend. An EE operative did. You caught me at a..." Tix lets out several clicks. "Anxious moment."

I'd felt the same when I realized my position back at Sly's: pinched, setup. If I'd been Tix, I'd have run, too. "That actually makes sense." The EE agent cut the connection, paralyzing Sly long enough for the monitors to sweep the area clean. It would have looked like he fell asleep while connected and gotten himself the harshest of disconnects.

"I'm no killer," Tix says. "I want to believe you aren't either."

No killer, but definitely a demon of coding might. Tix has more varied attack patterns than I expected possible. But 0mega lets me keep up and push some pressure of my own.

"I can't fight EE," I say. "Even now." There's sadness in my voice, and I hope what I'm feeling is a tear rolling down my physical face. "Would they go after Sly if he stayed off the Net for good?"

"You know the answer."

I lower my head. "I can probably help him out of the country."

Tix unleashes a defensive barrage of aggressive code. I blast it away, but behind it is an attack that shoots straight past my haggard defenses. I barely put up a new barrier in time to block it. Diversionary tactics.

Guess my effort makes Tix smile. "He went where he shouldn't have. I'm telling you now, a warning, to respect other Spirits as you would your closest ally and your worst enemy. EE, as a whole, is likewise to be treated."

"How long do I have to be a Spirit before I adopt such a shitty way of speaking and thinking?"

"Your humor..." More clicks. Their defenses aren't replacing as fast, their attacks weaker. But they're not slowing down. "It won't get you far."

I fake a laugh. "What about that fox anima? Something you use to hide your identity, to have fun with where no one can see?" Now I'm using a distraction. While Tix is busy being offended, I slip bad code into some of their own defensive systems.

Tix's antennae twitch, a reaction I can't read.

"And that blank screen setup," I say, pushing the question as I take advantage of Tix's waning defenses and my own anger. "I'd like to know how you pulled that off. If that falls in the lines of respect, that is?"

I break through Tix's last barrier of security. Slipping inside, I let loose a flood of false data to make it look like I'm readying to gut their systems. It's obvious on purpose, and Tix backs off. I would have too.

"I don't know what you mean," Tix says, voice buzzing with fluctuating distortions. "You are... dangerous, W0lf."

"Omega," I say. Another name, another mask, another life ahead of me to live.

We don't have to fight anymore, and that's fine with me. Tix, a Spirit like me, perhaps, flees. But Tix isn't the fox both Lagros and Sly claimed to have seen—not the Spirit who warned me away.

Three pings are closing in. EE monitors. I'm too revved up and kicking dirt about what EE did to Sly to just run.

So I wait.

The monitors tear into the Garden as intruders. The very nature of the Net is on my side, or at least it feels that way as I run self-destruct codes through two of them. The third I encase in a copy of IO's software I took for my own use. As I find out, the Garden is full of interesting flows of data, and there's plenty of random information to pull from, just like the code wastes.

I save a copy of the monitor then wipe its memory of the encounter. Then I assemble two clones out of the materials leftover from the slagged remains. I'll install some nasty stuff later, but for now all I do is encase a backdoor uplink. I'll get back on the trail, on what Sly had found out. I can't fight EE directly, but I can spread information—if I can find it.

I select a random user with a good health record and within my digital reach, which now seems to stretch across the country. I initiate a hard crash for them, filter their anima to my location, and then bleed my anima into the open Net.

This is the best outcome. I'll transfer some real money into that user's real bank account, and you can be sure it'll stick. I'll keep an eye on them just in case.

Just as I'm finishing, the Garden sucks me back in—or at least I get that same feeling in my chest, like someone's reaching in there and gripping my heart. I'm tired of being tugged around, god damnit. If I'm a Spirit now, and Spirits deserve respect, then I'm going to get mine.

I assemble another monitor—I don't know where the materials come from, but I send it at whatever's got ahold of me. It takes out a bunch of code before this force crushes it too then redoubles its effort, dragging me into the Garden in what turns out to be a soft transfer.

Instead of a white shell or the expansive gardens, I'm before the grand monitor and its blinking, white line.

APOLOGIES, 0MEGA

It knows my new name. Must have been listening to Tix and me. And it's apologizing. I almost feel honored.

APOLOGIES, 0MEGA

Epiphanies form out-of-context clues—a slow reveal until enough of the recognizable pattern is assembled for a chemical switch to trigger.

"You're an AI."

That makes the most sense. A natural entity to the Net has been predicted for a long time now, and after everything that happened with EE's first major virtual reality project, it's all but inevitable that we'd encounter sentient AI roaming the outer Net. This is what EE wanted to keep quiet.

The white bar blinks. My heart beats. No answer.

"I'd also like to apologize, but I also have a question or two. Can I promise you anything to answer them for me?"

AN APOLOGY TO ME?

"I feel like I might have given you the wrong idea. I'm curious. I'm sorry I scared you."

Again, no answer.

"So, will you answer my questions?" It doesn't answer. I go ahead and ask anyway. "You're the one causing the big line crashes. I'm guessing it's not intentional. But why is it happening?"

IT'S NOT INTENTIONAL

It probably doesn't know, in that case. Fine. "What do you want from me, from anyone?"

The Garden, or whatever realm we're in, collapses like a cardboard box before I get my answer. I'm in the open Net once more.

There's plenty of time before I need to disconnect, so I take my time heading back to the hub. I have more to think about now than I ever have before, and I have far more questions than I do answers. Not even a Spirit could enlighten me; it seems even what's maybe a true divine creature doesn't have anything but apologies.

I don't think I'll see Sly again. And I hope I don't run into Tix anytime soon.

Tix said EE had spiked Sly, but I think about it again, and I only detected the three of us in the line around that time. Maybe Tix works for EE. It isn't beyond EE's capability to erase that kind of information from the line, but I'm not going to take chances. Like Tix told me, treat a Spirit like they're your greatest ally and enemy.

I can't know what's waiting for me. I can attempt to disconnect and might just fail. My body could still be alive, just brain-dead. Perhaps disconnecting will pull the virtual consciousness with me. I can't begin to theorize what that would do to me.

At the terminal, I stand and wait, adopting W0lf's appearance like a mask over 0mega's form. A few anima stare, probably wondering what I'm up to, what good deed or underhanded deal I'm pursuing. I can't say I even know. At this point, I understand about as little as they do. Some days it's nice to be my friend, and others it's best to keep your distance. The latter seems more common recently. Depending on what waits for me on the other side of this final transfer, it might be getting a lot worse.

Garrett Marco

Today, Abner is a slim gray fox. But who was he yesterday? Who will he be tomorrow?

SKINNED

Kyell Gold

"I'm Abner," the slim grey fox said, extending a paw. "Such a pleasure to meet you."

In the virtual Oblique Club, furries gyrated together to a trance mix, paws and tails and ears sparkling amid the flashing lights. Around the outskirts of the dance floor, couples and trios chatted via messaging that allowed them to hear each other over the music. Currently the grey fox leaned against the wall next to a cacomistle in a tight bikini. "Nice to meet you, too. I'm Charrine."

"What kind of music do you—" Abner paused. "I'm so sorry. I have to go."

"Hey," the cacomistle said. "You came over to me!"

She was talking to empty space. "Hey!" she repeated.

He hated to leave, but there'd be other girls. And when the red light went on, he had at least ten minutes but no more than an hour before things got bad.

First thing he did was jump to another location in Furtopia, then deployed his cloning hack. You weren't supposed to be able to have your avatar in more than one place, so that would confuse them a bit. He ended up this time on the ridge overlooking the forest. Several couples cuddled on the grass nearby as the sun set.

He rerouted his access, first off. That would protect him in meatspace. Next he—

"Jim Gutmann?"

He spun around to see a tall white tiger in a sharp business suit. "I'd love to talk to you for a minute."

SKINNED

The grey fox vanished.

He was in a warehouse in a deserted part of Furtopia that people used occasionally for zombie games. Crates stamped with "FURR INC." rose around him in a dim grey half-light. His tail flicked from side to side, betraying his agitation, and he checked around every corner before leaning against a crate.

Shit, he had to find another identity. Normally he'd have one lined up, or two, or three, but his backups had been disappearing...

Wait. Goddamn it.

"Mister Gutmann, I really wish you'd stay in one place."

Enough with the grey fox. He was Johnathan, a silver husky who was going to be his next identity anyway. He wore a blue t-shirt and a casual collared shirt open over it, with digitigrade jeans under a fluffy tail. While Johnathan rested at the edge of a trail that led up a virtual mountain, he burned Abner into virtual ash. Then he re-routed his access through one of his backup accounts and a different server, one in Bangalore. The dappled green light through the leaves helped him breathe more easily, calmed the switching of his tail against the bush behind him. Birds sang and a breeze ruffled his fur.

He dug into the pouch at his side and pulled out a bag of jerky. Snapping off a piece, he chewed and closed his eyes. He'd just chill here for a bit, until...

Leaves rustled and footsteps approached. The white tiger rounded a corner of the trail. "That wasn't very considerate to Abner's owner," he said severely, to an empty patch of grass where a silver husky had just been sitting.

That was the plan, anyway. But when Johnathan opened his eyes, he saw leafy green, felt the cool mountain breeze, and stared up into two dark eyes in a white-striped muzzle. "Nor is it very considerate to walk out in the middle of a conversation," the tiger said.

"Abner's a dirtbag," Johnathan said. He tried a backdoor, but they'd gotten that too. Fine, then, if they wouldn't let him run away, he'd have to go for some other tricks.

"You're familiar with the Personal Right to Individual V-Skins And Cybernetic Interfaces to E-Space Act?"

"Sure, who isn't?" Keep talking. White tiger, suit, oh, he'd disguised his connection well, but Johnathan was better. There was the thread, there were the little info packets zipping back and forth.

"By our counts, you've violated that act sixteen times."

"Really? Do you have a list?" And there was the source. Johnathan pulled the data stream toward him, pinched it off, substituted one of his programs on the end.

The tiger barely flickered. "We're not interested in your past crimes unless you choose not to cooperate." He started removing his pants. "We want to—Mister Gutmann, what—" The tiger kicked his shoes and pants off, dropped his underwear, and then shrugged out of his jacket. "Stop this. We just want—" He ripped the shirt off and stood there nude. Then he began a jerky dance.

Johnathan laughed. "You want to take dancing lessons," he said.

"We want to recruit—I'm a little teapot, short and stout." The tiger's eyes bugged out as he sang the nursery rhyme. "Here is my handle."

"I don't want to work for you," Johnathan said. He let the song finish and then shook his head. "I mean, that's obscene, what you just did. In a public place, no less. Lucky there weren't any more people around. I think I should get rid of you."

He called up the burn program again. The tiger waited, unable to do anything else, and then was gone, scattered to the virtual winds. If the agent was smart, he'd bailed before the burn, otherwise he'd have a hell of a headache.

Johnathan went the way of Abner, just to be safe. Virgil, a slender anole, sat up in a small apartment, generic, one of thousands pre-made for newbies. They'd gotten closer that time than ever before, and that worried him. He didn't have any more backups to waste. If they were closing in on him this quickly, then—

"Mister Gutmann, it should be obvious by now that—"

No. No no no! He wrenched the headset off and kicked his office chair back so violently that it tipped over backwards on the loose wheel. He put his hand in a discarded bag of tortilla chips and stood up quickly. Okay. He had to burn Virgil, first of all. Standing at his desk, he barked out the commands, his voice rough. Talking was so cumbersome after you'd been in the v-world.

There was no acknowledgment. Why not? He repeated the commands and then realized he'd muted the speakers. When he flicked them on, the computer was just saying, "No such skin found," which meant that Virgil, like Johnathan and Abner, was good and gone.

His phone rang.

The sound was so unexpected that he just stood there wondering what the hell was going on. When it became clear that the sound was coming from his pocket, he pulled out the phone and stared at it. He had muted the phone, too, but certain emergency services could override it.

And they could override other things. As he watched, the phone answered itself, and the face of a balding man in a suit very like the one the white tiger had worn spoke to him. "Before you hang up, listen to our offer." He tried to hang up. "We've been following you for a while."

The phone hit the floor and he kicked a Matrix t-shirt over it. All right, assume fifteen minutes—or twenty? Ten? He had no idea how fast people could move in meatspace. His legs were sweaty and clumsy, his breath came in short gulps, and his room smelled of unshowered hair and filthy t-shirts and stale food.

"You've got to know you can't hide from us," came a muffled voice from under the shirt.

There was a plan for this, too. He grabbed the computer and headset and shoved them into a backpack. The phone kept talking, but he headed for the door as quietly as he could. Hopefully the shirt would muffle the microphone enough that they would think he was still there.

He should have some kind of recording of his voice to fool people. Or a speaker, another phone through which he could talk. The ideas flooded his head, keeping panic at bay as he wedged his way through the window at the end of the hall. God, he hated meatspace. Bad enough not having fur and a tail; actually moving from one location to another was a nightmare. But when you lived under the grid—not off it, never off it—you had to be prepared to do unpleasant things.

It was only a two foot drop from the window when he was hanging with his arms fully extended, but he managed to twist an ankle anyway. Great, Gutmann, he told himself, that oughta help you get away. Abner the fox would have landed lightly on the balls of his clawed feet, with his tail swaying for balance.

He didn't take the street, but hurried behind the house. None of the fences between these houses were in good repair any longer, but people still lived in the houses, so he'd have to be careful. Ethereal blue light glimmered through cracks and if you listened in between the growls of cars and motorbikes, you could hear the sounds of v-world games (some more adult than others) going on.

Meanwhile, he picked his way over broken glass and frayed wires, discarded electronics and broken bricks. He hadn't yet heard the cars pull up, but if they used electronic cars, they could glide up to houses like ghosts and be inside before anyone knew they were there.

The receiver in his ear had let out a stream of beeps as he passed houses with wireless; as he approached a less decrepit one, the beeps became a long whine. Strong signal here, and the Nex-90 on his wrist was already hacking through the password. He looked again to both sides, alert for motion as well as sound, but the night remained quiet.

Wireless was a sucky option, easier to be caught hacking, but he only needed it for five minutes. He pulled out the mini tablet and called up RideMe to see if anyone was cruising nearby and would be willing to pick up Randall March, respectable developer for XTerra Games.

Within four minutes, he had a ride reserved, and five minutes later he was in the passenger seat of a boxy sedan listening to a young woman chatter about her pregnancy cravings. "I just need to get close to Willow Hill," he said. "I can walk from there."

"XTerra," the woman said. "Must be exciting. What have you made?"

"Nothing most people see," he said. "But I'm my own boss."

"That must be amazing." She turned to give him a smile. "I'm not married or anything. I just wanted a family."

"Great," he said, and closed his eyes. "You gotta chase what you want because this world sure ain't gonna give it to you."

"I wish you could talk to my mom." She laughed, and went on about her family. That came with using RideMe; most of the time you got people who just wanted someone to talk to for a few minutes. Honestly, he didn't mind, although if they didn't have fur, he was a lot less interested.

She dropped him ten blocks from his first backup apartment, with a cheery wave and a click to Randall March's debit account. He circled the area twice but didn't see any suspiciously new vehicles lurking around, so he tapped the entry code to the building and then hurried up to the apartment.

He would have to set up a new backup place and probably, to be safe, a new RideMe account, and would have to get food deliveries to this apartment organized, but first things first. He pulled the computer and cables from the backpack and plugged them into the splice in the wall that ran to the main trunk, then put on his headset and booted up.

With a filter, he scanned several forums, people talking about their relationships and friends and enemies. His filter picked out negative-tone entries and aggregated them based on proper names that recurred. Some were female; more were male, and though occasionally he liked to cross-gender, mostly he stuck with the guys. There was never any shortage.

Tonight he found a guy named Ragnar, mentioned in six different entries. Real prize, this guy was: had stolen money from three different roommates, had pushed around a couple girlfriends, and was showing up in the filter now because he'd just had assault charges dismissed for lack of evidence. And he had a gorgeous lion skin.

The details were different, but the story never changed much. Just like Abner the grey fox, scumbag landlord; or Johnathan the husky, who'd get young guys to move in with him and then kick them out when he was tired of them; or Virgil the moocher, who'd exhausted the hospitality of several friends and then roasted them online when they suggested he might want to get a job. The cops would never punish these guys. It was up to a lone vigilante to hijack their skins, have a good time online, and then burn the skins when he was done.

It was a lonely life, but that suited Ragnar the lion. He just wanted to have fun and stay one step ahead of the feds. He skinned up and dropped into v-space to recover from the evening's ordeal.

A reporter tracks down an elusive hacker, but the story she gets from him is more than she bargained for.

Relics, Rabbits, and Tuscan Reds

Slip Wolf

I have a seat at the café and order a frizzante water, recorder hid under a napkin as I wait. The sun is getting lower over the *Piazza del Campo*, dragging the massive shadow of the *Torra del Mangia*, the tower of Siena's town hall, across the open court. The shadow of the great tower is like a sundial's hand ticking away the remains of the day.

Waiting is always the hard part.

A glass of Chianti would settle my nerves, which rarely need the help. I've been in hotter spots both literal and figurative in my years on the job, but never has finding the right place at the right time been so difficult or so worth the trouble.

I get a drop of water on my whiskers and shake it off. The heat is ebbing slightly; my brown pelt is still warm from the cloud-peeking sun. I look like any other female weasel out here on this square in a quaint little city in the heart of Tuscany, but it's doubtful he'd recognize me. The bylines on all the articles I've published have no photos, and my face is hard to turn up with a Google search. Soon though, I may be famous. And earning a serious payday, can't forget that part.

With all the difficulty putting his clues together, the encrypted coordinates to the bus-station down in Rome, and the coded graffiti on the shuttered shops in Bologna, I should be tired right now, but I'm giddy. A one hour window is all he's granting. His choice, his rules. It's all I'll need.

Four ways into the Campo, can't keep eyes on them all. People of all species, sizes, and ages move in and out with consistency. I don't have any description. I check to make sure my camera bag is still tucked between my feet. It's doubtful he'll let me take a photo, but I need my kit close.

A snap to my right flicks my ear. A neighboring table has a rabbit taking photos of the Torra, and I realize my contact may assume he's my photographer. For the fourth time, I start to worry. Can I ask this rabbit to put his camera away? There are several others with equipment, including a lion couple four tables over who are comparing shots while pointing to various features up and down the tower. Only this rabbit, though, is snapping away with abandon.

The time is now. I stand the three bread sticks up in a pyramid as requested. The camera snaps as it turns my way. I try not to growl. "Please don't photograph me. In fact, could you give that a rest?"

The rabbit, white-furred with a Trixies band shirt and two blue studs on his left ear, lowers the camera for a second and gives me a baleful blue eye. "I'm testing this out. Just got this DSLR. I don't mean to annoy you."

I frown, and my tail steals a quick lash, betraying how on edge I am. A minute overdue. I can't have gotten this wrong. "I'm not annoyed. I just... would rather not be photographed."

The camera slips low, and the rabbit's face gets long, ears like de-masted flags. "Not even if I can bring out that cute nose of yours?" He weakly tries to smile, blush bordering on a cringe as though uncertain if he's being lame.

Despite myself I have to resist a smile. I've been told I have a cute nose before. Many parts of my anatomy have been given stars, to be honest, but the nose was a favorite. "I think you'll remember this nose well enough without a photo, don't you?"

The rabbit sighs and shrugs, guilt rising on his face. "Well, I don't want to bother you because you're clearly waiting for somebody, but I can prove you photograph well." He fiddles with the switches on his camera, turns it around to hand it to me. I don't take it at first, looking around first to see if anybody had reacted to my bread-stick pyramid yet. Nothing. People wander out of the nearby enotecca with bottles of wine and peruse the souvenir stands for carved sculptures.

If he has photos of me...

I scan through a slideshow with the arrow button. There are shots of the tower, shots of the square, people milling about, and... me. A sunbeam falls across the water glass on my table as I stare into it, my fur almost gold against my brown t-shirt's collar, jeans creased as my feet self-consciously clutch the camera between them. Next shot is me again, wider angle, standing out against the throng of patio-diners. The final is from an extremely high angle, almost looking at the wisp of fur standing atop my head. I look up to the only obvious vantage point. He'd shot me from the tower.

Just like that he's sitting across from me. "Thanks for your diligence," he says with a toothy smile. "Good looks only gets a reporter so far, right?"

I sigh with relief. All that effort hadn't been in vain after all. So this is Updike, the King of Hearts. "Much to my dismay," I deadpan. "Hello, Updike."

"Nancy Spencer, reporter for the New England Herold. You've come a long way from exposing corruption in the Congo haven't you?"

He's read up on me. Excellent. "And you?" I push the napkin back so I have a place to rest my elbow and set his camera down. My elbow triggers the recorder. "How far have you come?"

Updike shrugs. "To be quite honest, I'm always from right where I happen to be."

"Man of the world?"

He cocks an ear as he nods to the waiter over my shoulder. The greyhound waiter is at my side, and Updike orders two glasses of Brunello before rolling his eyes left, looking for a creative lie. "It's helped me a lot to not be tied down."

"Not in your line of work, right?" I cross my legs. Clock's ticking. I'll need him talking if I'll get enough for a decent profile with what he gives me in this hour. After that...

He just nods.

"So how many aliases have you gone by? I know Updike is something you adopted rather than chose."

"Yeah there've been a few." He looks at his paws on the table. "I've forgotten most of them."

"Back when law enforcement was first after you, you were the King of Hearts."

That smile again, this time a little less earnest. "Generic title for a mediocre operator."

That gets me sitting up straight. The tables around us are absorbed in their own conversations, and neither of us can really be recognized, but I keep my voice down. "You call breaking into the FBI's secure servers mediocre?"

Updike takes a deep breath, his grin settling into something more neutral, the true emotions within those blue eyes guarded by a youthful sparkle as he sizes me up. "Everything is doable with patience, and a little confidence." The sparkle recedes. "But where did that get me, huh? The information I got for my employers at the time caused a lot of real grief. I didn't know that at the time, just counted my money."

Grief was one word for it. "So after that happened, is that when you... changed direction? Is that when you changed your alias again?"

Updike leans back in his chair, eyes darting to the crowds in the square. "Like I said, I changed aliases like underwear. Let's not stand on ceremony. The Yakuza calls me 'dead man.'" The smile returns as though it's a joke.

"I only ask because I want to know what identities to tie to your work."

"That's what you call it?"

"What should I call it?"

The wine arrives. Updike twirls a bread stick in his fingers, dipping it in olive oil and chewing on it before sipping his red. His eyes meet mine. "I'm not worried. If I'm found, it won't be poison, trust me."

Time to get to the heart of the matter. "Why? It isn't just the Japanese. The Tongs, the Mafia, two banana republics and, I suspect, a Russian cabinet minister all want you dead. You did work for them, then you stopped. So what is it? Why are you the most wanted person on Earth?"

"Banana Republic? What? Did I hack their Black Friday flyer and forget?"

Cute and infuriating aren't supposed to go this well together. That muzzle wears its grin so naturally, the fuzz under his jaw fluttering in the slight breeze. Smarmy bastard for somebody in as much trouble as he is. "You know what I mean," I mutter, restraining a laugh.

"I slept with the Yakuza bosses' paramour, then wooed a Mafia don's daughter. Or was it his son? What can I say, I like to make friends.

His blue eyes search mine for a reaction. I'm talking to somebody whose life is measured in hours, and here he is cracking jokes. "Come on," I say, keeping objective with effort.

His face falls in what seems like earnest hurt. "You don't think I can do that? Just 'cause I program computers doesn't mean I'm not good with people, Nancy." He looks away as he sips the wine. "I need a minute to get myself together after that put down. You really should try some of this."

"If I do, will you tell me what you did after running away from the mob?" I fold my hands and try to look calm and disaffected. My tail beats the brace bar of the patio chair I sit on, betraying my excitement. My tail is sometimes a problem in situations like this. Tension has to go somewhere.

He nods. He's having fun and delighted to show it as he takes another sip.

I raise my own glass and try the red. The Brunello is fruity, yet sharp, and washes my palate with spicy tartness that smooths out slowly. I sigh and make myself relax. If this is his game, I can play it and keep things together. It's not like we will be playing it for long.

"Yeah, After the FBI job, I found myself in high demand. But there were issues I had to deal with. As cool as the stunt was, as wonderful the notoriety, there were consequences. An embassy in a Far-East country was raided and somebody was killed. They had the codes to gain access. I provided those. That's the one use of my stolen info that I know of." His smile was gone now.

"Who was the employer?"

"Does it matter? I got somebody killed, clapping myself on the back for being a coding ninja and—" He took another rushed sip of the wine to disguise that he had to collect himself. "I couldn't do it anymore."

"So you ran off, and they're mad."

"They wouldn't be happy with me leaving, but that's not what got me on their bad side. No, they're mad because I took every job they offered."

I blink. "I don't follow, why would they—"

"And I didn't do them." Updike stares at the breadstick in his paw and takes another bite, munching slow. "That's how it started anyway."

"You took their contracts to hack computers for them... and didn't complete them?"

"Yup." When Updike finds his smile again, it's wry and slightly bitter. "They wanted to know where aid organizations hid their medical shipments, what the security details were like for bribe-resistant politicians, all kinds of really bad stuff. I accepted the contracts, took the money, sent messages to warn their targets somebody was going to ruin their day... and ran."

I sit back, the wine starting to sing in my veins. I take another sip without thinking as it all sinks in. "So you betrayed all those organizations at once."

"Nope, one after the other."

"But surely they put the word out."

"They did. I went underground, made some aliases and spoofed some IPs to get into all the criminal and evil-asshole networks I could. That done, I started taking on contracts for every hack, theft, and assassination being offered, posed as known players in the underworld, took advances to bank accounts I'd had set up for the retainers... and then I sent warnings to local authorities and ran for it."

I blink. This was getting to be too much. I'd known that Updike had been evading the U.S. feds for a long time, and some criminal enterprises had him on their open books, but the reasoning behind it had never been clear. Now that it all makes sense, it's just dizzying.

"So what did you do with the money?" I ask. Updike sips his wine and looks confused. "The money you stole from all these people for the jobs you didn't do. They have to be extremely pissed off, right? What did you do with all the retainers and down-payments? Did you give it all to charity or something?"

Updike looks upward as though trying to think. "Oh, uh... no. I spent it."

"Spent it! Spent it on what?"

"Besides transportation to keep moving? Hotels. Cars to get around. Game systems I like. Lots of booze." He sees my expression and raises his glass. "Hey, I need to unwind. Alcohol helps that a lot." He pauses to scratch the fur under his chin and shrugs. "So does sex. I pay well for that too."

I nearly choke on a mouthful of Brunello. "What?"

He looks at me like I'm crazy. "I'm a healthy male rabbit with needs like anybody else who can't have a steady girl or boyfriend cause they might get, you know, killed." He draws a blunt clawed finger across his white throat and then tugs on his shirt as though adjusting an invisible neck-tie. "I sleep with... professionals because I'm a responsible fugitive Nancy. Nobody knows who I am, nobody gets hurt." He leans forward with a smile that might or might not be genuinely lecherous. "There are some wonderful places to go just outside Rome, let me tell you."

"No, please don't. I can't believe this." My head swims as I try to figure out how much of this I can take seriously. "So what is this, all a game to you?"

Updike finishes the last of his wine and looks up to see where the waiter went. "Yes. My life has always been a game, Nancy, always. I just don't get played anymore by rich sociopaths with expensive suits and bloody knuckles. I'm the one with the chips on the table and the combo finishing move. You should really appreciate what I do, now that I'm a good guy." His eyes travel over my shoulder, and I turn for just a moment. Just people chattering, coming going. No eyes our way. I turn back to find Updike pushing his chair back. "I've got just one question for you; I feel you owe it to me for spilling my predicament to you and making you reporter of the year or month or whatever."

My gaze darts around to see what has drawn his attention. His expression is calm, almost amused, but he's suddenly in a hurry. I frown at him. "I don't even know how much of what you just told me was real."

"It's all real, Nancy. I lived a lie at first, back when I told myself I was a good person while doing pretty bad things, but I let it become something real. I decided I could do something better with my talents and went for it, made a difference that mattered to people under the gun. You know what that's like. When you exposed corruption in the Congo last year in that article, you demonstrated that exposing the bad things people do is important to you too." He stands up.

His praise would bring a blush to my ears under any other circumstances. Right now I'm too dialed up. "Where are you going? You promised me an hour."

"Yes I did. Read your napkin." He turns and hurries off into the evening crowd of the Pallazzo, ears fluttering as he sprints. He waves something silver in the air that I can't make out before he vanishes.

I swear, looking down to notice there are Euros down in front of me next to my napkin. I turn it over to read the message on it. "Museum in the Duomo's knave. Twenty minutes. Take a direct route and hurry."

I ponder this for a split second before I realize my recorder is gone.

The silver thing in Updike's paw. "Bastard," I mutter, grabbing my bag and hurrying across the Pallazo after him.

He hasn't headed west to the Basilica. He's hurried south to the Piazza Mercato where my car is parked. I see a commotion in the crowd ahead but realize I'm not going to catch him now. After a moment's indecision, I follow his directions and head west, the cobbles rising between the buildings out of the Palazzo. I pass shops with their ornate wine displays, spherical bottles of sweet grappa filled with crystal ships, souvenir books in multiple languages. Ursine, ungulate, and canine kids chatter in colorful Italian as they queue up outside the gelato shop. Countless flavors tickle my nose and tongue with hints of praline, chocolate, and espresso. It's a beautiful city here, preserved in its medieval aspects on the directives of Mussolini, whose fascism created many indirectly beautiful things in the wake of his horrors over sixty years ago.

I take the knowledge in stride. My line of work seems to always put me in direct contact with what's wrong with the world, even in places where things couldn't be more idyllic. If it weren't so exciting I don't know how I could deal with many of the disquieting things I've seen. I watch an otter lick mint chocolate off his own nose and envy the kid's innocence. Don't I deserve a break from war-torn Republics and their soul-rending terrors? I can only blame myself. This is the life I chose after all.

Winding past a pizzeria—mozzarella and herb scents drifting airily as one more seduction to slow me down—I come to the steps that rise to the back end of *Il Duomo*, the second largest domed cathedral in Italy after Brunelleschi's masterpiece in Florence. The walls arch several stories high, white and black marble in horizontal stripes. The museum Updike refers to lays just south of it, where a failed extension to the cathedral in the fourteenth century left a long outer wall joining it to the Duomo. Inside, architectural components of the cathedral are stored out of the elements, as well as some other surprises. I notice the metal detectors immediately and realize the contents of my camera bag will set it off. I find a pay locker at the entrance, insert it gingerly, and then settle the admittance fee with a relaxed badger watching an action movie on a tablet before moving in amongst the curios and curious.

Updike said twenty minutes, and I feel my heart thrum in my chest at the prospect of meeting him again, providing he hasn't given me the slip for good. The desire to run after him had been a strong one, even if catching him would have been nigh impossible in these late-day crowds. I realize that if my recorder would set-off the alarm, it might shortly be in one of these lockers where my kit is, if it isn't already.

Keeping my senses open stops me from getting too furious at myself. I had him there, right there, after months of sifting and searching. And I let him go. If he's gone... Taking my recorder was just an added shame, and I'm glad I have no other interviews on it.

I wonder if he'll realize that I've been seeking only him for the last two months and find that suspicious. No other stories, no interviews. No other work. For just a moment, I can feel those blue eyes looking through me, his face curving a sly smile around his regrets. How long did we have for all that work, ten minutes? Twenty? There's still so much story to be told, so much to learn. And then of course, my employer wants results.

As I quickly move from statue to stain-glass to transplanted frieze, I see some well-preserved period restoration work, but the only rabbit here is brown-furred and bent with age. Updike can't have disguised himself that quickly. I keep his slim-jawed, short-muzzled image in my mind, and it's a rather easy image to hold onto actually. He's much more attractive than what I'd imagine any computer hacker would look like, truth be told—yeah I've got an outdated imagination, sue me—and obviously takes care of himself. Honestly, it's the least I should expect from somebody who spends his life running from mobsters and media. Updike does a lot of running.

Also, there's that ego of his. Contrite or honestly sorry for his misdeeds, I kind of expected the overconfidence part. What does surprise me is the reasons behind everything he's into. I knew the honest facts regarding the fed's interest in him, but the criminal side of things was supposed to be a little different. Word was, Updike had just disappointed a few powerful people.

Yeah, and a couple disappointments can put every criminal organization and corrupt nation you can think of hard on someone's heels.

All the bad people, who of course don't go on record, say he's just a nuisance who needs to be made an example of and nothing more. This is what my digging has told me, and at the time, it seemed to add up. My mind has long worked fast enough to sniff out lies, and Occam's razor is warm to my touch right now.

I hear the breath behind me before the soft touch at my shoulder, and I resist the urge to turn around. "Sorry I'm late," Updike says jovially, pausing to catch his breath. "I was having a drink in an Internet cafe when my server went down on me."

I groan as I turn around, my tail brushing his knee as I do. He's close enough to touch now, so soon after I let him go. "You owe me more time," I say evenly.

"I owe you more than that." Updike's eyes dart around the room and then to the door. His chest rises and falls quick as though he is slightly out of breath. "I owe you an explanation."

The look in his eyes hides a little more than a few regrets. "What do you mean?"

"Not here. Let's go up a floor to the relics room. The stairs are the only way up there."

"Why does that mean anything?"

An eye on the entrance again. "I'll tell you when we're not here. There are cameras all over the place. That's a good thing."

I narrow my gaze at him as we move up the stairs. He leads the way, looking ahead, then past me. "I didn't think cameras would be good for somebody like you," I mutter.

Less than a minute later and one floor up, we stand in a room full of gilded ornate boxes and chalices behind glass. There is only one other person up here, a horse standing carefully back from one object that he blinks at in amazement. I turn myself and see one long box with a glass top. In it, on a velvet bed, lays a long white stick of wood. I blink as I realize the ends are too round and knobby for it to be wood. It's a mammal's femur. The next item, in an octagonal chalice, catches the room's weak light. On a stand of incense and herbs, a jawless cat skull regards me coolly.

"Relics of saints and bishops and holy men," Updike sniffs. "This is probably the most surveillance-filled room in the city right now, though I hope there's no sound recording." His long ears swivel as he looks from camera to camera, paws in his pockets, fluffy feet shuffling on the sound-reducing carpet.

"Aren't you worried about being seen?"

"The FBI doesn't know what I look like. And those who do aren't watching this feed, trust me. It's a place no assassin would try anything."

"So why are we finishing our interview in here?"

Updike looks at an arrangement of metacarpal bones built into a crafted replica of a golden paw. "It kind of fits. We both seek precious things to expose, and you've turned up a few bones in your time, haven't you?"

"You have no idea." It's true; I've been in rooms with some real monsters, getting their sides of things only to later find bones as real as the ones we're standing near, in places I'm not supposed to look. I don't want to waste time talking about my experiences, so I say no more.

Updike's smile weakens. He has the bearing of somebody trying to avoid something unpleasant. He scuffs a claw on his foot. "I think I do. Aw hell, there's no easy way to say this. Have you wondered yet why it's you?"

My whiskers twitch with my nose. The air is too dry in here. All I can smell is rabbit. Worried rabbit. "Why it's me?"

"Who I picked to interview me. Wolf Blitzen with CFN offered me a million dollars for a sit-down in an anonymous location. Turned him down. Al-Jazerra? Them too. You wouldn't guess what they offered."

I did wonder, but was certain as to why he had chosen me. "You've read my stuff. You know about my exposure of corruption in the Congo, and my exposé into police brutality in many countries." I can see a reluctance to answer in his eyes and strangely, though I've just met him, the hurt in those eyes puts a surprising pit in my stomach.

"Yes and no. I am here for your reporting, and the Congo corruption article was a factor, but not in the way you think. I'm here because of what I do, Nancy. I buy contracts to do bad things and don't do them." He beams crookedly. "I just did it again."

The room grows colder and tighter, the bones catching sickly light as his words sink in. "You mean—"

"Yeah. That wine I bought you on the Palazzo out there? That was bought with the advance on your contract. The one on your head, specifically. You have to admit it was some damn fine wine."

I've been in mortal danger before, me and my camera bag and my tenacity, shooting in places I'm not supposed to shoot, biting down on information, scandals, things in places I shouldn't be with people I shouldn't know. My life and profession have been dedicated to honing myself against fear so I'm not afraid right now. Hell, I'm not even surprised. If you read my article and understand exactly what befell those hyena and lion families whose ring of sins had been exposed, well, anybody reading that could imagine why they would want me dead.

"Dammit." I say it a little louder than intended, and the horse throws a glare in my direction before leaving the exhibit.

"Pretty much," Updike offers weakly. "Welcome to my world."

"What the hell am I supposed to do?" I wonder if all these cameras on us are helping or hindering us right now. Being totally alone with Updike, I realize that any move against him, or me, will be captured by dozens of lenses. "We can't stay here forever. Plus it's not like they're following me now, is it?"

I really don't like that wince. "I'm sorry, but I wasn't the only one to pick up that contract. I did some research on the other IP that accessed it, and let's just say there was somebody across the plaza whom I recognized. It was... him."

"Him?" My heart is pumping now. I'm anxious, but it's an anger now, not a fear. Go ahead and think that's stupid, but this tendency is one of the reasons I'm so good at my job.

"The coyote they call Sinjun Clairemont, lairs in Tennessee. Lots of kills in lots of places, mostly for the New York and other East-coast syndicates, very rarely works abroad unless the pay's really good. I posed as him online to secure a couple murder contracts and then warned his intended victims. Yeah, he's not too happy with me about that." Updike licks his lips to get them wet. "I saw him here today. There's no chance that's a coincidence."

Goddammit. A hired gun in Siena, and Updike manages to spot him. I haven't gambled on something like this. I have to get out of here. I have to get my camera bag from my locker and go.

And Updike, who I've come for—what to do about the rabbit who showed himself to this murderous coyote? I should just get what I've come for and get out, get him someplace without cameras where every word won't be heard, and finish this so I can collect my payday.

But I'm frozen in place, and not out of any fear for my own life.

For the first time ever, after relentlessly chasing dozens of people around the globe who don't want to be found, who don't want to see my determined muzzle and hear my insistent voice, I realize I'm having doubts about the whole thing.

It hits me all at once that this rabbit has literally been engineering all his moves in the last half hour in a bid to protect me. The stories in my file tell of harassment and intimidation and scrapes with politically corrupt people of power who hate what I do, but despite all this, despite threats enough to fill a whole journal, I've never had an assassin after me in any of those misadventures.

And I've never had someone who's just met me trying to protect me either.

It makes no sense. Updike knows that all I want from him is a story, that he is a meal-ticket to me, a claim to journalistic fame. And yet he's risking his life for me anyway, has been since he picked out my contract on line and arranged the clues to our hookup. He's been feeding me clues for days now, which means he's been trying to protect me for that long. And he hadn't even met me.

And all the people I've talked to about him, in desperate bids to scrape together his backstory, lied about him. They told me he was a coward, a cheat, a sexist pig—that last part still maybe true—and deserved a bullet far more than any breaking exposé. He'll slink away to the shadows as soon as you get close. Now go get him, little mustelid.

I should thank him, right here and now, but realizing how much I've been deceived pisses me off a little, and I don't want to show him. Why did this have to be so complicated?

274

In the space of these few seconds, Updike is figuring what else he should tell me. "I ran past him," he says, "and I introduced myself on the way by. Fortunately he was distracted enough when that happened for you to slip away. I'm a bigger fish, right?"

"You... you could have been killed," I mutter.

"Nope. I kept to the main streets and found the right alley. I know this city really well; it's one of the reasons I picked it to meet you. He can't do what he wants to do in public, or in a place like this where the cameras are everywhere. I know how to stay in sight as often as I can stay out of it." There's that self-satisfied smile again.

"So how do we keep doing that?"

"There's an exit up here, goes to the rooftops. I can get us to a safe place nearby until we can leave."

"I have to get my camera bag."

"Leave it. I'll buy you another camera."

My mind races as I realize what he's saying. "But my passport is in there, as is my wallet."

"What? Why would you—?"

"I didn't know I'd be fleeing this place, did I?"

"My camera is downstairs too. I'm willing to let it go."

"I have to get my passport. And I guess you don't need the contents of your bag to do your job. Speaking of which, is my recorder down there?"

"You're going to worry about that? With your life in danger?"

"You already know, Updike." I fold my arms. "That's when I'm at my best." Anxiety is starting to creep in, the reality of the situation catching up to where we are, but I keep it buried under a professional demeanor.

His shoulders slump. The rabbit is kind of cute when he's defeated, which is a disturbing thing to realize.

We make our way back down, a longing look at the upper floor roof exit drawing a sigh from the rabbit. I don't know what he had in store three stories up, but I guess it's better than what he fears awaits us elsewhere.

Out at security, we get our respective shoulder bags and trade looks that ask, What now? I walk over to him. "He has to be outside, right? If he's got a gun?"

"Or knives." Updike frowned. "Sorry, that's not helping. Here. Another for your collection." He hands me another scrawled napkin before gazing past me at the entrance to the bright outdoors. His expression hardens. "Don't turn around, look at me. Straight at me."

I freeze, ears flicking backwards. "What's—"

"Walk over to the security stand, and tell them you've lost your wallet. Stand as close to him as possible, and get his full attention. Do it right now."

I can tell from the way his voice drops, from his narrowing eyes, the way his legs part to widen his stance—the assassin is here.

Correction, 'his' assassin. "I'm the big money, my face in every hired gun's wallet. Lucky me," he observes with a dry chuckle as I step away, hurrying ten paces over to the security desk. I knock the counter for the agent's attention. The badger looks up from an exploding jeep on his tablet, ears rising in question as Updike hops the turn-style, bag setting off the security alarm, and hurries past a shocked terrier couple to the stairs.

A tan-furred coyote in a dark checked shirt and slacks leaps the turnstile. His grey flinted eyes turn briefly to meet mine, recognition dawning for one cold dispassionate second as he sees the security at my shoulder.

He's off through the crowd, my presence filed away for later. The badger security guard shouts Italian imperatives in hot pursuit of both of them.

I'm out the front door, pulse pounding, every shadow a phantom as I hurry around a corner, down the nearest alley and find cover, my bag dangling at my waist. The tools of my trade bounce against me as I settle my frayed nerves with clinical practice, honed in countless tight spots the world over, and truly process what just happened. Updike has led the assassin away, having gotten away from me for the second time.

And I let him go again.

I imagined I could do something good with my talents and went for it, made a difference that mattered to people under the gun. I haven't felt an ache like I'm now feeling in a very long time. It's a strange thing to feel guilt while doing what you're good at, after so many years. This is just another job. What the hell is wrong with me?

I open the napkin of the rabbit whose second act of sacrifice in my name could very well mean he's dead at this very moment. In it, under a cartoon scrawl of his own whiskered face and ears, is an address west of here, so close and yet so far in regards to Siena's winding streets. He has a safe-house right here. Was that genius or foolishness?

276

I realize that I have to get there fast, in case the assassin finishes Updike off.

There's that worry again. I frown as I double-time it.

I duck into a souvenir shop, buy clothes off the rack. I won't return to my hotel for the meager disposable things I've left there. I change in a public washroom and put on a University of Siena hoodie which I cover my head with before ducking outside. It's a hot ten minute jog to the address, up a flight of stairs that seem to have plenty of ins-and-outs and then into a tiny, almost dormitory-like apartment with a key under the matt where the napkin said it would be.

Other than the bathroom and kitchenette it appears to be just one room, less than three yards from door to window. There is a computer here, a laptop running some sort of script. I see an airline website come and go, and I leave the machine alone to do what it's doing. Next to it is an open bottle of wine, then another one that isn't. A takeout container with pizza crusts sits open next to it. Three bottles of high priced scotch are holding up an adult magazine like an improvised reading rack and across from this mess on the desk there's another fur-mag on the bed, open to a vixen lounging naked on a yacht's white-waxed deck. An unspooled yo-yo rests on the nightstand.

With only a few randomly-strewn props, it's the most stereotypical guy's apartment I've seen anywhere in the world. I feel I'm no closer to understanding this rabbit, or what any story about him can accurately say. I wonder if he knows he can't go on, that his clock is running out and that all the wrongs in the world he's righting are going to bite his tail off. I'm just sitting on that bed, watching his computer wander aimlessly through websites, doing whatever its doing, a shadow of Updike at play even though its master may be dead, and I don't have a thought in my head, not one, when the door-handle turns.

My hand has my camera bag unzipped as the door opens carefully, and I see a white foot step messily into view. Updike peers around the door, his fur matted by moisture as he slips into his own apartment and shuts the door behind him. "Losing that guy was a bitch," he says by way of conversation, all but wheezing. "Good thing I took a way up that hides dripping water well."

I remove my hand from the bag, zipping it shut over the camera there. I've wasted a chance to photograph his living environment. I don't care. I'm on my feet and moving over to him. I'm somehow not even surprised at myself when I give him a quick hug. It's brief; I'm not one to do that kind of thing, and I could almost laugh at myself. I gather his scent, and he stinks a bit.

He sees my nose wrinkle. "Yeah, the catacombs in Siena are all off-limits, but if you know where maps can be obtained..." He gives a long sigh. "Too bad our canine friend didn't have those maps. If he's lost down there, it could be awhile. He certainly won't smell his way out. Did you see what kind of gun he had?"

"No. Sorry."

His wet whiskers twitch. "Oh, well, it was an impressive looking gun. I bet it could have really messed me up. He was a scary guy. I'm serious."

I grin and laugh, pushing my camera bag away with a foot. It's not just so he won't drip on it. I just don't think I'm going to need anything in there. I don't want what I came for anymore. The realization of that is a strange thing, considering all I've done to find him.

"What's funny?" he asks.

"Besides you?" He reads my tone and seems pleased with himself. "Honestly, Updike, I came here to find you, catch you just like every other fed and crook in the world so I could get famous. That's literally all I had planned."

"Well, getting interviewed and maybe photographed is a lot less grueling than being shot, stuffed, and mounted if you want to know the truth," he snickers.

"You went out of your way to save me." I chuckle. "I don't know how I can even repay you."

He nods sagely, his paws around my shoulders as he whispers. "We could have sex."

"What?" I push him away. "No!"

His ears splay, blushing as he points. "Well, not smelling like this. I've got a shower right there."

I grit my teeth to keep from shouting. His charm is laid on thick, but as fun as he is he's got a long, long way to go. "Seriously, we could be dead right now!"

"That was the very line I was going to use." He says, grin parting his face like the dawn.

I can't help laughing out loud. It's the first time I've felt this light-hearted while this deep in mortal danger. It's a foreign emotion for me to feel in a situation like this.

I like it. With effort, I get serious. "Shouldn't we get out of here?"

He searches for the next words to implore with, sighs expansively. "I guess you're right." He looks at his scotch and wine collection. "Too bad I was getting settled here."

Silence passes for a few moments as we stand there and he drips. "Why did you do it? Why did you risk your life for me?"

He lets go for a moment, steps past me to his computer. There's a little trail of water from the door to where he's standing, shining on the cool floorboards. He watches it cycle through another website. "I told you; I've done bad things. Thing is, it's a bit more than just being sorry for what that FBI data was used for. I was lied to, Nancy. They told me they were going to break in and steal some papers or something. The news said the killing of that staffer was deliberate. They murdered somebody, with my help, and I was lied to. And for all I know, they did a lot worse I just haven't found out about yet. So I owe them. I owe every evil bastard in the world who tries to use people like me to do things nobody should ever have to live with." He turns and faces me, looking smug again in a way only he can pull off. "How am I doing so far?"

I swallow. I know everything going on behind those angry, guilty eyes. I can't explain why I feel it too. "Why not turn yourself into the feds? Get protection while you do what you do."

He uncorks a scotch, and the standing nudie mag falls to the desk as he takes a swig. "Because the rabbit does his best work while he's running, Nancy. There's no simpler answer.

It's like how you run after your stories, taking down bad people with your columns. You get hooked and you love it."

I had loved it, for a long time. But time had taken its toll. There are consequences to being as good as I am at chasing 'bad people.' Eventually, you get used for other things...

Updike registers the doubts I'm turning over, puts an arm around me. The touch is not invited but not unwelcome. "The Congo piece was a doozy. Take it as a compliment when I say that I know why they want you..." He trails off and looks out the window. "Anyway."

I nod shallowly. "I think I could make some changes, fix some wrongs of my own." I gaze out the window, over the roofs falling away into the distance.

"Wrongs of your own?" Updike splays his ears uncertainly. "What kind of wrongs does a reporter—"

The door to the apartment all but shatters as it's kicked in. The coyote's voice is rough but genteel, like an antebellum crop-sharer come to collect his cuttings. "Time to meet the devil, you code-cracking son-of-a-long-eared rodent."

His gun is in the air, but so is the wine bottle I've already thrown. End over end, it collides with his muzzle and shatters, dousing the already wet wolf in Tuscan red. I take long strides. Ferret-reflexes have me in fight-or-flight as I grab the thick barrel of the wounded wolf's submachine gun and yank him forward over the wet floor, sliding. He doesn't release the gun, and that's his mistake. A fist to the belly makes him grunt and he goes down over my ducking, waiting shoulder.

Updike falls back on his bed as the transfer of the wolf's weight completes, and the assassin's back meets the plate glass of Updike's apartment window, shatters it, and keeps going.

There's a short howl that rips the air through all three stories down to the alley's cobblestones. The crunch is sickening. The bounce and second landing sound worse.

We are both still for a moment, Updike staring at me with wild eyes from the bed. "You killed that guy."

A wave of nausea passes quickly. "Yes," is all I can say. I've killed a guy.

"How did you do that?"

I take a moment to catch my breath. "I learned a lot about rape prevention in judo class. I had a lot of opportunities to use it... on assignment."

"I'll say." Only already-spent adrenaline keeps him from shouting it. I have to get myself under control, my reflexes still at breakneck speed. I almost died just now, and the exhilaration of avoiding that is the most precious elixir ever.

But at what cost? I don't think of the broken coyote's body fifteen yards below. "We have to go, now," I tell him.

"Okay, my program bought six flights out of Italy. I'll decide which ones we're taking on the way."

"Train station's just north of here." I have enough of Siena's layout in my head to know that.

"I'll grab some supplies and meet you at my other safe-house in twenty minutes. Write it on something."

"You have another safe-house?"

"I always arrange for a few places." Despite his cool exterior, I can see the stress of the moment starting to crack at him. I'm actually going to run away with this guy. He's immature and fun, smart and yet self-aggrandizing. He kind of looks adorable when frightened.

I have no idea if I'm even interested in staying with this scoundrel beyond our flight today. The future is more uncertain than it's ever been, and it actually feels wonderful. Fleeing, I feel alive.

He resists looking out the broken window and takes me in his arms. He smells like the sweet desperation of each moment he lives in, and my eyebrows go up as he moves in for a kiss.

"Too fast, rabbit."

"Right. Sorry." He coughs. "I'll meet you; I promise." I can still feel the electricity off him as he hurries from the room, looking back longingly once, probably for the first time ever in his life.

He doesn't hear what I hear as the door shuts. He doesn't hear the groan from far below. Moments pass. I head down the stairs, silent as a ghost, my camera bag at my side, turning left rather than right so as to enter the alleyway. The assassin is there.

"Hello Sinjun," I say.

The coyote rolls on his side, wheezing, one paw holding his ribs together. Blood haloes the ground around him. I kick his gun away, far down the alley and the coyote looks after it before gazing at me, confusion muddled with pain. "You had that rabbit alone. When I came up. You beat me to him."

"Damn right I did."

"Then if you found him first why didn't you... Are you soft headed? You draw him out and then, what...?" There's blood on his lips. His tan face is shamefully pinkened by red wine. "Have you gone crazy?"

I watch him bleed. "No. No, quite the opposite." I feel my heart beat and my tail twitch and the cool air on my fur. And something else. I don't know what to call it, but a certainty settles down around me. "I've just come to a decision. I'm sick of this work. I need a change."

It hurts Sinjun to laugh but he does. I've heard from many he has quite the sense of humor. "You're going with him. Why? Why walk away from all this? You love the chase and you know it."

"Not anymore. I love that thrill, but I'm going after the wrong people. This one doesn't deserve my... attentions."

I don't know if the wink is a sly joke or if Sinjun's suffering from the onset of brain damage. "Please, you took the contract knowing he was a softie. You wanted to lure him in. Don't say it wasn't what you planned."

"Yes. I thought he'd take the money for my contract and try to run, but... He thinks you were here after me, not him."

"Why should that mean a damn thing? You were given a job. So was I."

I don't answer.

"He'll find out someday, sooner than later. He'll know you planted all those articles you wrote, faked those press credentials. He'll discover you put that hit out on yourself to draw him in for the bounty on him, and it'll all come crashing down. He'll learn what you really do for a living." Sinjun takes a pained breath. "He'll run again. So will you. And you'll both get caught."

"I'm betting otherwise," I answer calmly. Inside my heart is racing.

Sinjun sneers. "You don't walk out on a contract and live to brag about it. That doesn't happen." That last outburst hurts like hell, and he groans into silence, his muzzle settling against the cold cobblestones as he draws shallow breaths.

I let the weight of his words sink in, but I don't say a word, merely walk away. He won't shout for help, won't get a bystander involved. That isn't how things are done.

And I won't kill this 'yote. I can't. My choice can't start after him, stupid as that sounds. This decision has to count right now. Time to start making amends.

I turn a corner and descend several steps to arrive at the Fontebranda, Siena's oldest fountain under the Basilica. I take a moment by the recessed fountain, water dark under the travertine roof, and stop. This late in the day, there is nobody here, and as I gaze into the water's depths, I reach down to my bag. The carefully-forged press badge on top of my bag glints back in the moonlight. I remember what Updike said and make it my wish. "Please, let the lie become something real."

I'm still alone. The moment won't last. I reach into my bag, past my virtually worthless camera, and pull out the Heckler Koch forty-five pistol I've packed for this job. Its frame and suppressor tube gleam dully as I pull the magazine, clear the pipe, and drop the hollow-point ammo, chosen for taking down a fleeing rabbit, into the murky water. The copper-heads of ammunition shine like coins for my wish. I hear the muttering of late-night walkers approaching as I rise and slip the gun itself down a sewer drain's gap at the curb nearby. A cold flutter travels through me, a whole new life beckoning me with celebrations of each passing moment as I lift the lighter bag, bearing only a reporter's camera and recorder now, and head to the next destination to meet the rabbit I've caught.

Slip Wolf

Will a scoundrel grant the dearest wish of a pure heart?

SHADOWS OF HORSES

Phil Geusz

"Hey!" a booming voice roared out from over Scott Bohanson's left shoulder. "Do you belong back here?"

Scott spun on his heel, terrified. The circus was an intimidating place for someone like him. He'd been wandering around for the better part of an hour, lost amid the bizarre sights and sounds of the show's underbelly. Scott had attended many circuses over the years; in fact, he hadn't willingly missed a single performance. Somehow, however, he'd never thought much about what the day-to-day lives of the performers might be like. What being a gypsy truly meant, with all of life's essentials crammed into a trunk or two and living elbow to elbow with the most amazing variety of humanity to be found anywhere.

The narrow tent-lined alleyways were fascinating. Everything was larger than life; a thousand secrets normally hidden by makeup and darkness and brightly-colored silk stood starkly revealed under the midsummer sun's glaring eye. In front of one tent a group of midgets leapt in careful synchronization, while just beyond them an overweight middle-aged man in greasy coveralls cursed a complex-looking bit of machinery. The improvised streets weren't laid out in any sort of pattern, or at least not one that Scott could discern. Clowns lived next to barkers, riggers rubbed elbows with roustabouts, and everyone seemed to have one sort of freak or another as a neighbor.

"Hey!" the voice cried out again. The speaker was a barrel-chested giant of a man, probably not a performer but certainly someone who lifted heavy weights and carried large loads for a living. "What are you doing here? You're trespassing!"

"I... I..." Scott stuttered in reply. He didn't often speak to others, and when he did his voice was difficult to hear and his words overly apologetic. "I'm here on business."

"What kind of business?" the roustabout demanded.

"I... I've come to see your magician."

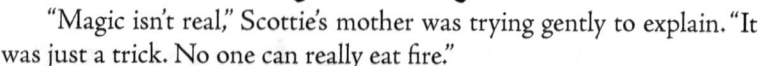

"Magic isn't real," Scottie's mother was trying gently to explain. "It was just a trick. No one can really eat fire."

"It was so magic!" five-year-old Scott insisted in reply. He was lying in bed, a worn stuffed pony clutched tightly to his breast. His father had declared repeatedly that it was time for Scottie to give up his baby-toy, but the boy screamed and cried every time it was taken away from him. "I saw it myself! The fire went right into his mouth, and he blew it out again. It was magic!"

The young woman sighed and rolled her eyes. "Scottie," she explained. "It was a trick. He had lighter fluid in his mouth, that's all. I keep trying to tell you that there's no such thing as magic in this world. There's no Santa Claus and no Tooth Fairy and no Easter Bunny, either. When are you going to listen?"

"There is too an Easter Bunny!" the boy countered. "Charlie's Mom says so! And Billy got a quarter from the Tooth Fairy!"

"All right, hon," Scottie's mother replied after a long, thoughtful silence. "Hush now, and go to sleep, You're still a tad young for this kind of thing, I suppose. There'll be plenty of time for science and reason later."

"There is a Santa Claus!" the boy repeated, gripping his pony so tightly his hands shook. "And the fire-eater was magic!"

"If you say so, dear," his mother replied wearily, kissing him lightly on the cheek. "I love you!"

"Hey, Shazam!" the roustabout declared when, after prolonged knocking, a bleary-eyed face appeared at the back door of the magician's trailer. "There's a rube here says he wants to see ya. Says that you invited him to come by after your late show last night. If you want, I can get rid of him."

The magician blinked slowly in the bright light. His eyes were bloodshot, Scott noticed, and his hair seemed much grayer when you looked at it up close. The young man winced as a sick-making wave of stink rolled out of the door from behind the magician. Unwashed clothes, cheap whiskey, cigarettes, all these aromas and more were well-represented. For a very long moment The Great Machimoro stood with his head hanging out the door, looking his would-be visitor up and down. Then he raised a cigarette to his lips, puffed on it thoughtfully and turned to the roustabout. "It's okay, Pete," he replied. "I remember him. Kind of."

Pete grunted unhappily. He'd been looking forward to ejecting the intruder, all the while lording it over the skinny little rube as so many had lorded over him for all of his life. But the kid had genuine business after all, it seemed, and that was that. "All right then, Shazam," the roustabout declared, offering a not-very-apologetic half-bow to Scott.

"Thank you for showing me the way," the young man answered.

"Don't mention it," Pete replied over his shoulder, his slow mind already on the next shipment of soda syrup or bulk popcorn or empty balloons or cotton candy powder that needed unloading. For him today would be one in an endless series of nearly identical days filled with hard labor and then capped with too much beer. Then he might buy a whore. Or sometimes he picked a barfight instead and pounded a rube or two into paste. Then the circus boss would bribe him out of jail, so that the whole cycle would begin anew. Thus the wheel of Pete's life would spin endlessly round until someday he met his end. Then there would be no more hard labor and no more beer and no more barfights, only a meaningless inscription on an otherwise featureless tombstone in a forgotten corner of a nameless cemetery.

"But why don't you want to play baseball?" Scott's father asked, genuinely puzzled. Every American boy loved to play baseball. Didn't they?

"It's... It's..." At age nine, Scottie's speech was already marked by long hesitations and annoying breaks in the flow of his logic. His father waited patiently, knowing from bitter experience that there was nothing to be gained by trying to hurry things along. Heaven knew that he'd made the attempt often enough.

"There's other boys there," Scott finally explained. "I don't like them. They don't like me. And they play too rough!"

Scottie's father pressed his lips together. It was long past time for his son to begin his journey towards manhood, for him to leave the house and explore the mysteries of frogs and snakes and squishy bugs. Past time for him to explore the universe beyond his mother's skirts instead of sitting around the house reading all of the time. Still, it was impossible for Scottie's father to look down into the angelic face of his only child and find fault, for despite all the boy's oddities and shortcomings he was doing his level best to be a good father. Baseball could wait another year, he decided. Some kids were late bloomers, that was all. "Okay," he agreed with a smile. "Next season maybe. So tell me, what have you been up to today?"

"Oh!" young Scottie cried out in ecstasy, practically dancing in joy. "I read such a wonderful book! It was about a horse that could fly, and a little girl who rode him all the way to the Moon!"

The great Machimoro sipped at his whiskey and listened patiently. "I've never fit in anywhere," Scott began, trying for the third time to say what was on his mind and failing utterly. "I've got no friends, my mother and father hate me..."

Suddenly there was a loud snore from the other side of the room. A man lay naked there under the cover of a single thin sheet. He rolled over onto Machimoro's side of the bed, snored again, and then fell back to sleep. A caged white rabbit, part of the performance of the night before, scurried fussily about his cage at the disturbance, then peered eagerly out through the bars and pricked up his ears, as if it too wished to hear what Scottie had to say. He was cute when he wriggled his nose, Scott thought. Very cute indeed.

"Come on, kid" Machimoro replied, his tone gentler than his words. "Spit it out and say what you've got to say. I've got a new act to rehearse."

Scottie licked his lips. Suddenly they were very dry. "Last night," he began again, "I watched you transform a woman into a tiger..."

"I don't believe it!" Scott's mother raged. Of the two parents, Dr. Sicklemann judged, she was having the greatest difficulty dealing with the bad news. "I simply do not believe it! My son is bright, intelligent..."

"And has failed the seventh grade," the doctor interjected. "Not only that, but he's about to fail it again." He paused for emphasis. "The situation is very serious, Mrs. Bohanson. This isn't the kind of recommendation I make lightly, believe me."

"It explains a lot of things," Scott's father allowed. He turned to face his wife. "I mean, our son has never exactly been the kind of kid they feature on the covers of those parenting magazines you read all the time."

"But the Special School District!" she hissed. "This man is saying that Scottie is retarded!"

"No," Doctor Sicklemann corrected her. "That's not a word that we use around here. But Scotty does have serious developmental problems. It's not his intelligence, though. His social skills are years behind those of his peers." The doctor paused, then looked the distraught parents directly in the eyes. "Did you know that he often tries to hug his classmates in greeting?"

Mrs. Bohanson blushed, while Mr. Bohanson looked down at the floor in shame. "Yes," he replied eventually. "I've seen him try to do that myself. I keep trying to break him of it, but..."

There was a long silence. "Scottie is not stupid," Dr. Sicklemann began again, this time making a conscious effort to emphasize the positive. "His basic reading and math skills are excellent. The main problem seems to be that he can't function in a normal school environment. Given special care and opportunities, most likely he'll do just fine."

Scottie's parents sat and looked at each other in silence for a moment. Finally Mrs. Bohanson lowered her eyes, then gingerly extended her hand. Mr. Bohanson accepted it in his own, smiled gently, and squeezed it for a moment. Then he turned back to Dr. Sicklemann. "Do what's best for our boy," he declared, forever abandoning all dreams of hot-rodding old cars and selling insurance with his son. "Do what's best, and we'll provide all the support that we can."

At the Special School, Scottie reacted well to the companion animal programs, if not to much else. The companion animal program featured horses.

"But you did change her!" Scott insisted for perhaps the fourth time, nearly loud enough to awaken the snoring man in The Great Machimoro's bed. "I saw it! I watched her eyes the whole time! It wasn't some cheap trick; I've seen a million of those."

"Kid..." the magician began. Then he sighed and poured himself another two finger's worth of cheap whiskey. "Look, that broad I supposedly changed; she lives three tents down and across the way. She's married to one of the animal trainers. I could take you to her, introduce you. Would that straighten you out?"

Scott shook his head firmly. "No," he declared. "It was real, and I know it. I want you to change me, too."

Inside his cage, the rabbit skittered about a little before once again thrusting his face against the bars, as if determined not to miss a single word. Machimoro paid the bunny no heed, however. "Shit!" he muttered under his breath. "It's too goddamned early in the day to be dealing with this sort of nonsense. Why do all the loons and nutcases have to come and visit me, of all people? Why?"

Scottie stood his ground. "Because you're real," he whispered. "You really can do it. And we nutcases can tell."

❧

"No, Connie," Mrs. Bohanson mumbled into her phone as she sipped at her gin and tonic. "It's not any better at all. He's sweet and innocent, but also so gullible! Scottie doesn't do anything but sit around and read books about magic and wizards and all that useless fantasy shit. Bob's tried so hard to get him to show an interest in college, or even just an ordinary sort of job. He yells at Scotty all the time, and I push too. But our son can't even make it through his first day without getting fired!" A lonely tear crept slowly down her cheek, leaving a damp, shiny trail. "He still collects stuffed horses, Connie! He's eighteen, and he collects stuffed animals. It's embarrassing to go to the store with him! I don't know if he's gay on top of everything else, or what."

There was a long pause as Connie mouthed well-meaning reassurances, then it was Mrs. Bohanson's turn again. "No, it's a lot worse than that. Scottie's never going to hold a job, or get married or have any kind of meaningful life. He spends all his time living in a sheltered little make-believe world, shutting out everything that he doesn't want to see. He'll never be normal. Not ever! Bob and I are going to have to support him and his damned stuffed animals until we're old and gray." A second tear joined the first. "Why couldn't we have had an ordinary child, Bob and I? What was so wrong with us, that we deserved this instead? Aren't we plain, regular, everyday folks?" Her face screwed up. "Why, damnit?" She pounded the table in frustration. "Why? Why? Why?" Then the tears, loosened by the gin, began to flow for real, so that presently Kathleen Bohanson was sprawled on the floor weeping her eyes out at the injustice of all.

In the next room Scottie sat reading a book, seemingly oblivious to his mother's pain and suffering. A closer examination, however, would've revealed tear-tracks on his cheeks as well, and a single salty damp spot on page two hundred and fourteen.

The book was about unicorns, and women who remained virgin forevermore.

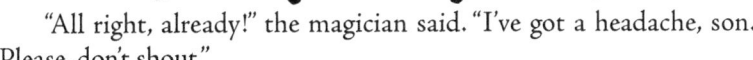

"All right, already!" the magician said. "I've got a headache, son. Please, don't shout."

Scottie almost never shouted. But he also didn't like being lied to, especially not about something so important. "Then you can do it," he growled.

Machimoro sighed and shook his head, then poured himself another shot of bourbon. "I'm tired of arguing with you, kid. So, okay. I won't claim that it's a trick any more. All right?"

Scottie's eyes slowly closed, then opened. "All right," he agreed. "I'm ready."

The magician rolled his eyes, then tossed off his drink in a single swallow. "Now hold on just a damned minute," he said. "Why on earth would you want to become a horse, anyway? What do you stand to gain?"

The young man shrugged. "Freedom," he said at last. "Peace. I... really can't explain."

"You'd find freedom as a horse?" Machimoro chuckled, more than a little drunk already even though it wasn't yet ten in the morning. "Horses aren't free, son. Not around this circus at least. We can't afford to feed useless mouths; every single one of our animals works and works hard. They go where they're told to go, when they're told to go there. They get slapped around and whipped and saddled and ridden, and there's nothing at all they can do about it."

"They're free," Scottie countered. "All of them. They can be whoever they want to be and no one cares. Nobody stares at them and laughs."

Machimoro snorted, his bloodshot eyes glittering in the half-light of the trailer. "They can't be half as stubborn as you are, that's for damned sure. Or else they'd get whomped right up the side of the head. Is that the life that you want, sonny?"

Scottie nodded and smiled. "Yes," he answered. "More than anything! I want for there to be rules I can understand. I want to be able to nuzzle and touch others without being called a pervert. I want to be gentle and tender and soft-hearted. I want to be able to be myself." He closed his eyes. "Most of all, I want to be accepted as I am. I want to be loved."

"Your parents love you," Machimoro replied gently, setting his glass down.

"No they don't," Scottie answered. "They used to. But not anymore."

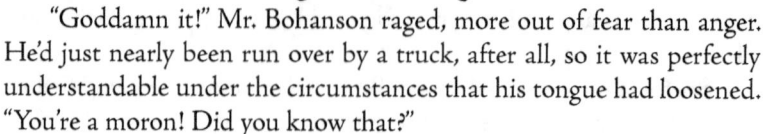

"Goddamn it!" Mr. Bohanson raged, more out of fear than anger. He'd just nearly been run over by a truck, after all, so it was perfectly understandable under the circumstances that his tongue had loosened. "You're a moron! Did you know that?"

Scottie sat behind the wheel of the car, trembling gently. He was twenty-four now, and trying his very hardest to learn how to drive. He wasn't doing too well.

"If I've told you once, I've told you a thousand times! You can't stop on an entrance ramp! Are you trying to get us both killed? You can't just stop halfway! Aren't you ever going to grow up? Can't you learn anything, you little freak?"

"I... I..."

"Oh, shut up!" Mr. Bohanson shouted, striking his massive fist on the dashboard in sheer frustration. He didn't want to be a bad father, but the near-miss had been very real and the driving lessons had dragged on weeks and months too long. No one's nerve lasts forever. His heart was still pounding and the adrenaline was still poisoning his system. "Just shut up!"

For a long time the pair sat silently in the car on the shoulder of the highway, an occasional horn blaring to remind them that Scottie had not pulled quite far enough over to the side. "All right," Scottie's father said finally. "Put the car in gear."

Still trembling, Scottie complied.

"Good. Pull us about three car lengths forward, and put the right-side wheels all the way over next to the grass."

Once more, Scottie tried his best to do as he was told. He swung much too far, however, and the car sank hub-deep in the mud. His father freed them up eventually, after much cursing and spinning of wheels, but it took many difficult, frustrating minutes. About halfway home Mr. Bohanson reached over and placed his hand on his son's shoulder. "I'm sorry," he whispered gently.

"I know," his son replied. "And I'm sorry too."

"Aren't we a sorry pair?" The older man laughed a little at the old joke, then turned to face his boy once more. "You ride a horse beautifully, son," he said. "So why can't you learn to drive?"

"I don't know," the young man replied lamely. There was a long silence, and then he spoke again. "I'm... This isn't going very well. I'm not getting any better, am I?"

"Sure you are!" his father lied. "You do better every time out! We'll try again next weekend."

But they didn't, of course. Not that weekend, nor any other.

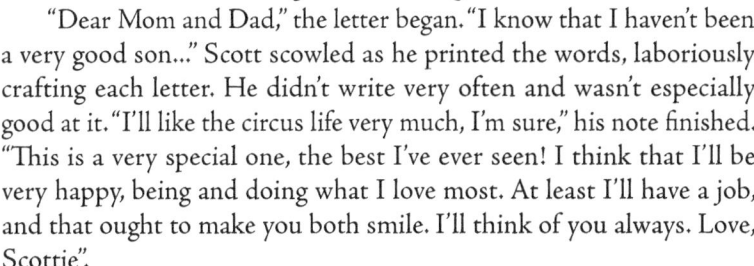

"I don't have a life," Scottie insisted. "So I've nothing at all to lose." The rabbit was gnawing at his wire prison now, not in a feverish attempt at escape but instead slowly and with deep pleasure, as if the little creature were reassuring itself that the bars were still really and truly there. He still seemed to be listening closely.

"Hmm," the magician replied. "It doesn't sound as if you do, really. Which is a special shame, you being so young and all."

"No one has a life," the young man replied. "I see more than people think. My parents don't have lives, neither did my teachers. You don't have a real life either, do you?"

"Heh!" Machimoro glanced over at his sleeping lover, who was snoring again from underneath his stained sheet. "I suppose not. Certainly nothing special."

"Then you do understand!" Scottie exclaimed. "You can do this for me, and you will!" He grinned, the seldom-seen expression lighting up his face like the sun. "I'll do tricks for you!" he exclaimed. "I promise! And I'll help you move things, and—"

"Whoa!" declared the magician. "Just hold your horses there, son." He turned to his rabbit. "He says he'll do tricks for me, Chester. Imagine that!"

The rabbit ceased gnawing, then performed an awkward backflip.

Machimoro grinned, then looked back at his guest. "Even if I could do this for you, son, and even if I thought that it might be the right thing for you, you still haven't answered one key question."

"What question is that?" Scottie asked, looking confused.

"What's in it for me?"

"Dear Mom and Dad," the letter began. "I know that I haven't been a very good son..." Scott scowled as he printed the words, laboriously crafting each letter. He didn't write very often and wasn't especially good at it. "I'll like the circus life very much, I'm sure," his note finished. "This is a very special one, the best I've ever seen! I think that I'll be very happy, being and doing what I love most. At least I'll have a job, and that ought to make you both smile. I'll think of you always. Love, Scottie".

Then Scott folded up the letter and placed in the center of his neatly made-up bed. He lived in the basement now, and often didn't see his parents for days at a time as they pursued their careers and socialized and swam gracefully through a world that Scottie couldn't quite fathom. The note looked lonely lying there alone in the center of the quilt, Scottie decided. He wanted his parents to be happy when they found it, not sad. So, he picked up his pencil once more and drew them a playful little picture in the blank space beneath his signature. Then he left the little basement room behind him and, with nothing but the clothes on his back, ran away to join the circus.

When Scott's parents found the note they decided to give their son a chance to grow up a little and be on his own for a while; after all, he was an adult now and knew the way home. Perhaps he needed to work in a place like a circus, they decided after much talk; maybe that was indeed the best career choice possible for someone unable to connect with the bigger, wider world. They'd give him a week, they resolved, before looking around and asking questions.

The young man was right. The note did indeed make his parents happy, though it made Mrs. Bohanson weep a little as well. On the bottom of the page was scrawled a child's rendition of a smiling cartoon horse.

The Great Machimoro, despite his heavy drinking and insatiable roaming from sex partner to sex partner, was one of the finest magicians on the circuit. Both performer and circus boss were fully aware of this, and as a result the prestidigitator was one of the most pampered and privileged figures in the entire troupe. Everyone nodded respectfully to Machimoro as he strode arrogantly down the mud lane towards the private little tent that was his and his alone from eight in the morning until two in the afternoon. It was there that he developed new tricks, there that he practiced and rehearsed his old ones until they shone with perfection, and there that he reigned as an absolute monarch with only his rabbit Chester for company.

The circus's assistant costumer, who used the tent to make repairs from two in the afternoon on, was rather a gossip. She spoke freely of the strange oils that she sometimes found smeared on the rude wooden workbench, and of the phallus-shaped magic wand that he'd once accidentally left behind. It'd been far too small to be used for sexual pleasure, she asserted over and over again, yet Machimoro was noticeably anxious until he had it safely back in his own possession. To this day, she avowed, the arthritis was cured in her right hand, the one with which she'd handled the ugly thing. The assistant costumer also often spoke of ghosts that she'd seen and of dreams which had come true, however, so no one really listened when she rambled on about obscene wands and miracle cures. Still, it was no wonder that, for all the esteem in which Machimoro was held, everyone stared a bit as he passed.

"Love, you said," Machimoro muttered once safely behind stout canvas, as he pulled various phials and potions out of his pockets. "You said that what was in it for me was love."

"Love," Scott agreed. "Unlimited, unrestricted, uncomplicated love. The purest love that there can ever be."

"Love is indeed the magic word," the magician agreed. "Not sex. I can get all of that I want, anywhere and anytime." He grinned at Chester, who'd been allowed free run of the workbench. Oddly, the rabbit didn't sniff at any of the little bottles or go running about knocking things over. Instead, he sat calm and still as he looked adoringly up into his owner's eyes. Machimoro replied by smiling and scratching the rabbit's ears fondly. "It's simple love that's truly precious. As so very few understand."

"Unreserved love," agreed Scottie. "That's all I have to offer anyone. I want to love and be loved more than anything else in the world. What else really matters, anyway? What else can matter?"

"Nothing," Machimoro agreed. "Though it took me many more years to figure it out than it did you."

"When I'm a horse," Scott continued, "I'll be able to love you with all of my heart. And I will! I'll love everyone who doesn't hurt and abuse me. I'll also love the sun and sky and the rain and the green, green grass; my heart will be filled with love! I'm not good enough as a person to be loved. But as a horse, I'll finally be right inside. People won't always be looking at me funny and expecting me to grasp things I'm just not able to. It'll be so wonderful!"

"You'll be full of the kind of love we lost when we became the lords of everything," Machimoto agreed. "Our species is poorer for the exchange. So many centuries it took me to learn this!" Absently he reached out and stroked Chester's fur again. The animal's eye's rolled in pleasure. Then he turned to face Scottie. "Did you know," he asked, "that I have to turn my tiger-lady back into herself every single night? That I have to suppress her memories of the change, or else she'd go insane?"

"Go insane?" Scottie blinked. "But she was so beautiful and so graceful! What an awful thing it is for her to have to change back. How closed her mind must be!"

"It's a terrible thing," Machimoro agreed, this time patting Scottie's head.

For a time the magician busied himself with his tools, dusting a little powder here and anointing Scottie there. Presently the younger man was stripped down to the skin, waiting patiently on hands and knees as Machimoro gestured with his odd little wand.

"What kind of horse?" Machimor asked presently, though his eyes and gaze remained very distant.

"What kind do you need?" the young man replied. "I'll be happy as anything, so long as I can love. That's what's important."

"A pony, then" the magician declared. "I could use a pony in my act, a white one to match Chester there. There are all sorts of tricks that I could perform with a white pony."

"I'll be so happy," Scottie answered back. "That's what I should have been all along, what I was meant to be. I've always known that. So very, very happy."

"Very happy," agreed the magician. "Not a want in the world, I swear it. Just like Chester here." The bunny nodded his head emphatically, and then Scotty felt a tremendous rushing of sweet pasture air, flavored with dandelions and sunshine and clean, cool healing love...

"He's so beautiful when he sleeps," Mrs. Bohanson whispered to her mate. She was twenty-five, and the baby had been home for three days.

Her husband didn't speak, though the squeeze he gave her hand was more eloquent than words.

"He's so beautiful," she repeated. "And so perfect! We're the luckiest people in the world, you and I." Still a bit sore from giving birth, Scottie's mother turned to face her husband, then rose up on her bare toes to kiss him. He swung his arms around her, and for a moment that might have stretched into eternity they stood so, locked in love and swaying ever so slightly to and fro. A gentle night's breeze blew in through the open window, making the tree limbs nod in time with the young lovers. Then the moon burst out from behind a cloud and shone gently through the mobile hung lovingly over young Scottie's crib.

Utterly unnoticed by anyone, perfect little shadows of horses danced joyously across the nursery wall.

Phil Geusz

There's been furry fiction as long as there have been fables. Here's a new fable.

Coyote's Voice

Altivo Overo

In the dawn of time, ever so long ago, after Mother Gaia sang the world into existence with all its oceans, lakes and rivers, mountains, plains and forests, she made the creatures to be her children and to live in her world. Since they were made from clay and dried in the sun, all were the same color. Though their forms varied, their shapes were vague like the mud from which they had come.

Gaia sat and pondered how to best improve her creations before breathing life into them. Her songs made the world itself beautiful, brightly colored, and filled with myriad plant life. The birds of the air and the animals of the earth and water needed to fit into that. At last she had an idea, and taking each individual creature into her hands again, she closed her eyes briefly and sang to them the gifts they would receive. Finally, she opened her eyes and breathed across them, giving them awareness and the breath of life. As this took place, the birds received their wings and bright feathers. The fish grew scales and fins, opening their mouths to suck in the water as Gaia released them into the oceans and lakes. The furry creatures of the earth were most complicated, and she took more time with each of them. Many received a special gift.

So it was that Fox received an amazing sense of smell that let him identify everything for miles around, and even things that were no longer present. Horse was given his hard hooves and the ability to run for miles without tiring. Bear huffed in surprise as his claws grew long and strong to let him climb trees and tear open nests or dig to find food. Wolf got a lush fur coat that could withstand the coldest winter. Rabbit got feet that could run like the wind and also dig a hiding place in an instant.

When at last she came to Coyote, Mother Gaia pondered him for a long time. Eventually she stroked him and sang. The dull yellow clay became a mixture of colors that could hide him whether he was in the desert or on a meadow, with fur that could keep him cooler in the desert sun yet warm him and keep him dry in a winter rain. She breathed on him, and Coyote was alive.

All the birds and animals had now received their form and their gifts. Gaia clapped her hands three times and sang again, summoning them to a meeting. When all of the air and earth dwellers sat around her, row upon row, she spoke to them.

"Beloved children, you are my family. That means you are all brothers and sisters too. I know I have made you so that you will sometimes quarrel and even kill each other, but always remember that I love every one of you. Think carefully before you turn your backs on one another, and always share as much as you can." The animals blinked and nodded. The birds chirped their assent. Gaia continued her speech.

"You have each received gifts according to your kind and nature, but I have one more thing to give to you. One by one, you will come to me and tell me your greatest wish. If it is in my power to grant it to you, I shall do so. Think carefully before you ask, because you will have only one chance. You and your children and your children's children shall live forever with the gift you select." Then Mother Gaia sat down on the grass, and summoned each of them to her, one by one, to let them whisper their wish to her. It took many days and nights before she had listened to each and granted every wish.

It was on the last day, in the afternoon, when Raven stepped up boldly and sat on Gaia's wrist to tell her his desire. She regarded him, waiting. His feathers were black and glittered in the sun. His bright eyes indicated a mind sharper than many of his winged cousins possessed, and like most of the birds, he had a talented singing voice that could be heard from afar. Gaia leaned toward him and he hissed something into her ear. She blinked at him and laughed.

"I never expected you to be vain," she told him. But she granted his wish just the same, with conditions attached. As she brushed her fingers over his wings and breast, the feathers turned to crimson red with black tips. "There you are. But remember, you may wear the bright colors only in the spring. By autumn you must put them away and appear black as you were at first. That is safer in the winter against the snow and the barren branches." Raven promised to do this, and bobbed his thanks before flying off into the trees.

Eventually, Fox had his turn. He settled comfortably into Mother Gaia's lap, wrapping his fluffy brown tail over his feet. His fur was brown you see, for camouflage in the forest shadows, but his eyes were bright as he murmured his wish to Gaia. She smiled fondly and stroked his head between the ears. "Granted, and may you have good use of it," was all she said. Fox dared to brush his pink tongue against the mother's fingers as a thank you, then whisked off into the dusk.

Coyote came last, and sat on his haunches in the grass, his yellow eyes regarding Gaia. She leaned toward him and he breathed something into her ear. As when she had given him his original form and gifts, Gaia stared at him thoughtfully. Finally she nodded her assent. "It seems a bit strange," she admitted, "but I agree that the world needs some laughter. Everyone cannot be serious all the time." She blew hard across Coyote's ears, so that they fluttered in the breeze she made and he shook his head and sneezed twice. "Use your sense of humor wisely," the mother advised him. "Not everything should be a joke, and not everyone will laugh."

Coyote bowed to Gaia, lowering his forelegs to the ground even as his tail wagged behind him. Then he sprang into the air with a shrill yip and ran off to the dry plains.

Gaia looked around. She saw that there were no other supplicants left and nodded to herself. "Time for a long nap," she sang, and laid herself among the grasses and spring flowers to rest. With the subtlety of a gentle breeze she faded into the ground and disappeared. The creatures of earth, air, and water went about the business of feeding themselves, making homes, and soon, multiplying their numbers.

The summer days fled by and the world began to develop a daily routine. Everyone was busy, and when the nights began to cool, they knew winter was coming. Even more had to be done to prepare for that.

Coyote, however, was a dreamer. The harsh desert climate of his chosen home would not change much even in winter, and he had time to ponder. Some would tell you that thinking is never a good thing, and that idle paws are sure to find mischief. Coyote would laugh at that. On a cool evening in September, he sat on a rocky outcropping to watch the sun set. As it happened, the sky that day was particularly clear but strong winds whipped dust into the air as it cooled. The fire and color of the sun's descent was magnificent.

Watching the sky turning from yellow to orange to red, Coyote felt an urge deep in his heart to sing a farewell to the descending sun. He drew breath and tried, but all he could produce was a shrill bark. "Perhaps I need to keep my mouth closed more tightly," he thought, and did that. This time a mournful whine was the only sound that escaped him. He tried several times, but just couldn't find a singing voice. Of course, he had never tried singing. Maybe it had to be learned, but he wasn't sure how to learn it.

As he lay on his bed of dry grasses that night, Coyote tried to think how he might learn to sing musically. Birds did that, he knew, but none of the furry animals had shown any inclination to song. Or at least, they hadn't while he was around to hear it. Before he slept he promised himself to ask among the birds for a teacher.

Coyote awoke at dawn to a chorus of chirp and twitter. Even in his desert, there were birds. The doves chortled softly as they flew against the brightening sky. The cactus wren sang his hoarse little tune again and again, even though the time for nesting was many weeks past. Coyote was not very impressed by the wren's singing, but approached him anyway.

It seemed the wren wasn't very excited to see Coyote, either. Flying to the top of a spike armored saguaro, the spotted bird perched among the sharp spines and made buzzing noises to show his contempt. Coyote was not about to be dissuaded in his quest, though. He padded around the base of the giant cactus and called up to the wren.

"I am not hunting," he cried. "I wish to learn to sing. Will you teach me?"

Cactus Wren peered down at Coyote before answering. "I am no great singer," the bird buzzed. "You should go to the Raven. He sings each evening in the mountains north of here." The wren nodded, and pointed his beak at the blue line of peaks against the northern horizon.

Coyote followed the bird's gaze, and nodded. "Perhaps you are right, my friend. I will go and hear Raven sing." Without even waiting to find some breakfast, he set out at a dog trot over the sand and tussocks, traveling ever northward.

For much of the day, it seemed that the blue mountains grew no closer. Made for the desert, Coyote did not give up. He paced himself, and took advantage of what water he could find. As the sun began to redden and sink on his left side, he heard the doves flying overhead, traveling in the same northward direction he was taking. He knew that there would be water and shade wherever they went for the night, so he kept his direction.

The slope of the ground became rougher, and the heat of the day fell off into a pleasant cool that refreshed Coyote's energies and gave him a second wind. When he could no longer see the mountains, though, he sought a resting place for the night. Between two rocks that still held the sun's warmth, partly hidden by a fragrant sage, he settled for a nap but kept his ears perked. Sleep without supper was no stranger to him, and he would be awake at the first light or at any suspicious sound. Or so he thought.

False dawn crept into the sky before he opened his eyes and yawned. His nose prickled with a scent he had not known for many months and it took him a moment to identify it. Fox! What would Fox be doing here in the desert? Coyote raised his head slowly and peered into the half light. Sure enough, Fox was sitting by another rock just a few yards away and watching him.

Seeing Coyote stir, Fox rose and stretched before coming closer by a pace or two. "Good morning, cousin," he began. "A dove told me you were coming this way, so I thought I'd seek you out. What brings you to the mountains?"

Coyote stepped from his sheltered spot, and let his tongue loll for a moment as he considered a response. "I come seeking Raven, as I wish to bargain with him," he answered. "Have you seen him recently?"

A bark of laughter escaped the Fox. "You too? Yes, he's quite close by, but I haven't been able to talk him into any kind of deal."

Coyote wondered at that. What could Fox be seeking from the Raven? Certainly not the same thing he was looking for. He knew the fox sang only hoarsely, but it served the purposes of his brown-furred cousin. "You were trying to trade something with Raven?" he asked.

Fox nodded. "I thought he might share his red color with me. Gaia forbade him to wear it in winter, so perhaps he would let me wear it then and return it to him in the spring. Think how handsome I could be to impress a mate. I'd give the red vest back to Raven in the spring, when he needs a mate himself."

"How very clever of you, cousin," Coyote answered. "You could protect and guard the vest for Raven so he wouldn't have to watch over its hiding place, and he'd have it back safely when he needed it. My request is simpler. I want him to give me singing lessons."

At this the Fox grinned. "What will you trade him? That's the sticking point I reached. He demands a payment and I have little to offer other than protection for his fine colored vest."

"I have considered that carefully," said Coyote. "And I'm willing to share my sense of humor with Raven."

The Fox narrowed his eyes and peered at his dusky relation. "Walk with me," he said. "We have things to discuss. And you must be in need of breakfast, no?"

Coyote stood and stretched again before they set out. Fox trotted quickly enough that Coyote was forced to pant a bit. He felt stiffened by his long run of the previous day, but after a mile or two he could lope along easily enough. The fox brought him to a stream of flowing water, with sour plums growing in the sand along the bank.

"Drink, cousin," said Fox. "The water is good, and the plums are sour but edible. Don't swallow too many of the pits, though."

Bending to drink, Coyote caught a movement out of the side of his eye and pounced like the desert lightning. The unfortunate mouse had no chance, for such is the way of Gaia. There are eaters and the eaten. The eaten must be wary and quick, or they will be dinner.

Fox nodded approval when Coyote turned to him, the fat mouse in his teeth. "You needn't offer to share," the fox told him. "I had breakfast already." Coyote wolfed down his meal whole, and drank from the stream before grinning toothily.

Rising again, the fox pointed at the mountains with his muzzle. "Raven should be quite near us at this hour," he said. And indeed, Coyote realized that they were standing in the foothills of the mountains, at the edge where the desert meets the greener lands. His ears perked at the sound of a faint bird song. Fox winked. "You hear him, I see."

Raven sang like a nightingale in those days, but unlike his cousin, he sang at morning to greet the new day. Fox and Coyote followed their ears and before long found the black one perched over a trickling spring where snow melt from the high mountains bubbled to the surface after trickling down through cracks in the rock. They sat a while and listened. Coyote thought his heart might burst with the desire to sing like that. Fox, however, appeared unmoved.

At last the raven ended his song and peered down at the two canids below. "Ah," he croaked, for his speaking voice was much as it is even today, "An admiring audience? Or have you come to ask a boon as well, dog of the desert?"

Coyote made a formal bow, lowering his ears in respect. "I have come, Raven, to ask for your teaching and advice," he said. "Can you teach me to sing?"

Raven stared at both of them for a while before answering. "I might be able to offer some instruction, yes. But I will require a fair exchange for that service."

Coyote nodded. "Gaia gave me a generous gift, a sense of humor and the ability to play marvelous tricks on the senses of others. I'm willing to share it with you, half and half, if you will only help me to sing. I know I cannot sound as magnificent as you do, but I would like to be able to honor the sun at evening and the moon in the night with my hymns."

"How can you share Gaia's gift?" the raven asked suspiciously. "Surely she gave it to you alone."

"Fox here will be witness to our bargain. Then I will show you what Gaia showed me." Coyote nodded to Fox, and moved nearer to Raven.

Unruffled, Raven sat and watched the coyote. "All right," he agreed. "I will give you lessons, the best I can do. I have no magic to change your voice, though. Show me Gaia's secret so that I can also play tricks, laugh, and make others laugh."

Fox nodded. "I witness this agreement," he said. "And I will bear that witness before Gaia should she question it."

Coyote raised his muzzle to the raven. "Come down then and stand where I can whisper to you. I promise not to harm you. After all, how could you fulfill your half of the bargain if I did so?"

After a brief hesitation, the raven spread his wings and glided down to stand on the ground within Coyote's reach. In his turn, the coyote leaned toward Raven and breathed on him, ruffling his feathers ever so lightly, and making a little whine in his throat.

The bird blinked, and flapped his wings once. He shook his head. "How did you learn that?" he asked. "I can feel your gift growing within me though. You really did something." Raven edged away from Coyote, but kept his eyes on him.

Neither of them noticed as Fox crept off through the underbrush, silent as a fox can be and that is indeed very quiet.

"Well?" Coyote asked after a few minutes. "What about your part?"

Raven ruffled his feathers a bit, then flew back up to the top of his rock, out of reach for any but another bird. "Show me what you can do," he commanded. "I must hear your voice before I can offer advice."

"Very well." Coyote raised his face to the sun, which now stood well above the horizon, and closed his eyes against the glare. He tried to sing, but as with his past attempts, all he could manage was a few barks and whines. He stopped and coughed. When he raised his eyes again to find the raven, the bird had already taken flight.

Circling over Coyote's head, Raven called down his derision. "That's hopeless. There is nothing I can do to help you with that." And with that insult, the bird rose into the sky and flew away, leaving the coyote alone and dejected.

At first he just felt hurt, but it didn't take long for Coyote to realize that he had been cheated. He had truly given half his sense of humor to Raven, and he could tell it was gone because he couldn't laugh at all at what had just happened. He looked around and realized that Fox had vanished too. With a sad little whimper, he laid down in the dust, shaded by the tall rock where the raven had perched, and covered his face with his paws. Unhappiness, a feeling quite unfamiliar to him, threatened to draw his very heart from his chest.

After a while, though, his nose warned him that Fox was returning. Coyote sat up and peeked around the sheltering rock. He couldn't believe what he saw.

Fox strutted proudly into view, his lush coat flaming red in the sunlight. He sat down a few yards from the rock, and groomed himself with his tongue as Coyote watched. Finally he could hold his peace no longer and took a step forward. "Cousin," he asked, "What have you done to your fur?"

The fox stood and danced in a circle, showing Coyote how he looked from all sides. His white chest ruff and belly fur were unchanged, and the tips of his ears and nose remained dark brown as well. His legs were dark brown as before, but only from the paws to knee or elbow. The rest of his coat was a lustrous red, almost as bright as the crimson of the setting sun. "Can you not guess?" he asked.

Coyote realized that his wits were not completely dulled yet. "You have stolen Raven's red vest," he accused. "How do you expect to get away with that?"

"Possession makes it mine, does it not?" the fox replied. "How can the stupid bird take it back? It was easy to find it hidden in the bushes under his nest. Thank you for distracting him."

"Well, he cheated me," Coyote growled, shaking his head. "I truly gave him a large portion of my trickster's sense, and then he told me he could teach me nothing." The coyote scuffed the ground with his back paws, ears lowered.

Fox raised an eyebrow. "Where did he go then? I did not see him at all."

Coyote pointed with his muzzle in the direction the raven had taken. "He flew off high in that direction. Is that the way to his home?"

The fox nodded. "Gone to check on the hiding place. Come quickly then, he'll be looking for me and will want to gloat over you."

The two canids took off at a steady pace, heading back toward the spot where they had met. At first they seemed to be making good time, but no more than half the way to their goal, they heard an angry shriek from the air over their heads. Raven dived at Fox, screaming "Thief! Thief!" before he began to tug at the red fur over the fox's shoulders and peck at his ears.

Fox looked about desperately for a place to shelter, and quickly scrabbled into a spot under two rocks that leaned drunkenly against each other. He didn't quite fit into the space, and his tail was left hanging out.

The angry raven was not to be put off so easily. He flew at the tail and grabbed it in his beak, biting down hard. Fox yelped in pain, but the crevice he had chosen was so narrow that he could not turn and fight. He had to back out carefully. As he did so, Raven gave a triumphant cry and flew into the air, with half of Fox's luxurious tail hanging from his beak. The bird flew back toward the mountains without saying anything.

Fox was now the one left to sit dejected in the dust, licking at his injured tail and whimpering. Coyote shook his head. "Justice finds us all, sooner or later," he remarked.

The fox didn't laugh. He grimaced in pain before declaring "Well, Raven won't be getting his vest back come spring, that's for sure."

"Nor I my ability to make light of everything, I fear. So far I'm not inclined to laugh at all. I feel empty instead. I'd advise you to find some cool water to soak that in, cousin. It should take away at least some of the sting."

Looking back at his ruined tail, Fox sighed. "I suppose you're right. Red fur is flashy, but with only half a tail I'm no better looking than I was before. Travel safely on your way home, cousin. I found the raven for you, but little good it did either of us." With that, the fox set off for his own den at a slow lope.

Coyote watched the fox fade into the distance before turning his own paws toward home. As he trotted southward, he tried to formulate a plan to get his clever abilities back from Raven, but could see no way to do it. After all, Raven would see through any trick he tried now because his own mind could work in the same way. And without Raven's cooperation, there was no way for him to take back his talents by force. There was no physical object linked to the gift, the way Raven's removable vest of scarlet had been made.

Reaching the edge of the desert just as the sun set in the west, Coyote sat down to admire the shifting colors and shadows and enjoy the creeping coolness of the approaching night. When the reds and purples flared just before the sun vanished, his heart ached. He still wanted to sing. The only sound he could make was a sad whine of disappointment, so he crawled under a sage bush to sleep.

Tired, the coyote slept well until just before dawn when he dreamed of Raven taunting him and chuckling just above his reach. Light touched his eyelids and he opened them as light began to overspread the sky and drown the stars. He realized he was still hearing the chuckling.

It was just Cactus Wren, though. As Coyote stretched and yawned, the bird paused in his buzzing song. "Did you find Raven? Did he help you?" the wren asked.

Coyote shook his head. "I found him and he agreed to teach me in return for a share of my gift of wit. After I transferred the gift to him, he said he couldn't teach me because my voice was not good enough."

Cactus Wren clucked loudly. "Even Raven knows that he must treat you more fairly than that. I think you had best appeal to Gaia. You did nothing wrong and she will rule in your favor."

"Nothing wrong? I gave away half of her fine gift to me, the one that I had asked her for. That may not have been wrong in any sense, but it was foolish. Very foolish of me." Coyote sank down onto the ground again and covered his eyes in shame.

The wren fluttered past his ears, ruffling the fur. "Foolish is not wrong, puppy," he buzzed. "Ask the Lady to forgive and help you."

Coyote peeked from beneath his paws, but Cactus Wren had left. At first he thought he had gotten into this mess by taking a bird's advice, but in the end he decided that the worst Gaia might do is refuse to help him. Without looking for breakfast, he set out for the place where the gifts were passed out in hopes of finding the Lady there.

It was the best part of a day's travel to the south, and Coyote arrived footsore and still fasting. He sat on the little knoll where Gaia passed out her final gifts, and sighed. The sun was setting, but it was veiled with clouds and the display didn't inspire him. Without even bothering to look for cover, he laid himself down on the ground and was immediately asleep.

When he felt the sun on his eyelids and a chill autumn breeze over his ears, Coyote kept his eyes closed. He didn't feel ready to face another day, but a soft voice spoke to him. It said "Wake up, child. Do not try to hide."

Coyote opened his eyes, and found Gaia squatting in front of him and looking right into them. "Ah, there," she told him and stroked his ruff. "It isn't as bad as you think. Tell me what happened." So he sat beside her and told the whole story, ending with how sorry he was to have lost part of her magical gift.

Gaia laughed, a bright and gentle sound. "You could have done far worse, my little one," she said. "In fact, some have. And I will see them now. Just stay still and don't be afraid." With that, the Lady stood up and clapped her hands once. A cloud covered the sun, and thunder rumbled. Coyote felt the earth shake a little. To his surprise, he realized that both Raven and Fox stood blinking before her. He was even more surprised when he realized that both were cowering and unable to look at Gaia.

"I see," the Lady announced in firm tones, "that some of my children did not listen to my advice in those first days." She looked first at Raven. "What do you have to say for yourself, black bird?"

Raven winced at her voice and stared at the ground. "Fox stole your gift from me," he croaked.

"Indeed. But what did you steal from Coyote? And what did I tell all of you about sharing and treating each other well?" Raven stood silent and trembling, staring at the ground.

Then Gaia turned her gaze on Fox. "I see," she said, "that I was perhaps too generous with you. It was a good gift that you asked for, and I never thought you would misuse it so. What do you have to say for yourself?"

Fox opened only one eye. "Raven bit my tail off," he whined.

"Indeed again. But what did you steal from Raven? Both of you are thieves. Coyote at least tried to make an honest trade, but the two of you have embarrassed yourselves and me as well. What judgement do you think is appropriate? And don't expect to escape punishment either."

Raven looked up into the Lady's eyes at last. "Fox tried to make a bargain with me," he admitted. "It would have been a fair one, but I refused. Let him keep the vest. I deserve to remain black."

Fox opened both his eyes and looked straight at Gaia. "No, let Raven have his vest back," he said. "I shouldn't have deceived him and stolen it."

Gaia watched them, pondering the situation for several minutes. If either had been able to sweat, they surely would have done so before she rendered her verdict.

"Fox first," she announced. "You are guilty of envy and theft, but I am guilty of giving you too much cleverness, making it easy for you to commit this crime. You shall have your tail back, but the tip of it will now be white to signify that you are a known thief. Your children and your children's children shall wear that mark until the end of time." Fox nodded sorrowfully at this.

"Now Raven," Gaia continued. "You are guilty above all, of pride. But you were also deceitful with Coyote, because you knew you couldn't teach him to sing or give him a voice to sing with. Yet you took his gift, willingly offered, knowing you could return nothing. As you say, you deserve to remain black, and so you shall do, and your children, and your children's children. I cannot take back what Coyote gave you, for it was his to give. But I can take back what I gave you, and so I shall do. I grant your singing voice to Coyote in return for what he gave you.

"Furthermore, since the beautiful red vest should not go to waste, Fox shall keep it. But in payment, I award part of the gift I gave him to Coyote in recompense for his lost wit." She held out a hand to Fox. "Come here."

Reluctantly, the now red devil obeyed. Gaia touched his tail lightly, and it was renewed just as she had promised, with a brilliant white fluff at the end that would betray him even in dim light. Smiling but with a sad look in her eyes, she stroked his head again, and it seemed to Coyote that some of the spark in his cousin's eyes dimmed a little. "Go now," the Lady told him. "To the end of your days, others will hunt you and despise you. Your scent will betray you, and the colors you coveted will show you up when you would rather hide. Even so, you still have more wits about you than my other children, and you and your family will fare well enough." Obediently, the fox ran off toward his home, tail flashing in the sunlight.

"Raven now," Gaia commanded. She held out her right hand, and the bird flapped his wings once and settled on her wrist. She touched his throat and he blinked as he felt his voice shrink and vanish. "Blackguard you are and shall be, and your children through all time," she told him, shaking her head. "I had better hopes for you. All you have lost is your voice and your vanity. Use Coyote's gift to appreciate how much worse it might have gone with you. Fly now." Raven took flight and flew away north as fast as he could go.

Gaia turned to Coyote and smiled. "Shy Coyote, come to me." Coyote obeyed, but tucked his tail under in embarrassment. He sat before her, but did not meet her gaze even when she rubbed his head and patted his throat and chest. "You will be able to sing to the sun and moon now," she promised. "Not as musically as the birds perhaps, but it will sound good to you and to your children, and I think the moon at least will hear and approve. You have rubbed shoulders with two scoundrels and their scent has touched you. Some will always call you a thief and a deceiver as well, but you can rise above that. Remember that no matter how lowly you feel or how badly you are treated, I love you still. You did well, and acted in good faith, so you are rewarded with what you asked and more. Do as well with it as you can."

Coyote looked up into Gaia's face then, and felt the warmth of her approval and love. A shimmer of light, and she was gone. He turned toward home with sore feet and an empty belly, but his heart was full.

People see what they expect to see. In this story,
you should expect to see a scoundrel.

Prof Fox

Mark Patrick Lynch

"The fox went out on a chilly night,
he prayed for the moon to give him light."
—Traditional folk song

When people saw the "Prof" on Danny Foxx's business card, they nearly always leaped to an assumption he did nothing to discourage and thought it was an abbreviation of "Professor".

Clothes made the man, and his tweed suit played to people's assumptions, reinforcing what they thought they already knew. As they fastened on the inscribed "Prof" Danny would study their expressions. They'd be thinking: here stood some horrible bore they needed to extract themselves from—and quickly, before he indulged himself in the finer points of one of his inscrutable Big Thought papers. Some way to spend a party that would be, they'd worry.

"Prof"—short for "Professor." Well, what else could it be?

But that was the thing. Though the "Prof" was indeed an abbreviation, it didn't make a diminutive out of "Professor". This "Prof" was short for "Professional."

Danny was a professional fox.

"It's an easy mistake to make," Danny would say with utmost sincerity to the few people he confided in—as he did now to the girl in the clinging party dress, a measure of wolfish grin to his lips.

She shook her head.

"I can't believe I got that wrong. But it's obvious when you say so." She shrugged after laughter to hide any embarrassment, which dipped her dress, which revealed more cleavage, which charged Danny's animal self. "I mean, you must think I'm some dipsy airhead not to notice! A fox. A professional fox. How could I miss that?"

"Oh, you'd be surprised how many people don't notice, Amanda."

Danny remembers her name from earlier. He stored it away when a friend called her across the room. It's a trick he's learned from his cub days: never let anything go. Amanda's a popular girl; everyone here at this party he's crashed knows her. He watches her now with perfectly polite fox charm. She's still holding his card, hasn't returned it as so many others have done before moving on, assuming him a dusty professor of paper dryness and autumn knowledge. If she keeps his card, with the cut of her dress, Danny doesn't know where she'll put it.

"After all," he says smoothly, eyes moving between her face and the curve of her body, "here I am, a fox in men's clothing, right in the middle of the room. No one's concerned about it. But if they knew I was here, I'd say a good number would be mounting horses and calling for their hounds. Sound the bugle and all that. Tally ho."

Too true at a gathering like this. Four-by-fours and top range saloons parked outside the sprawl of the farm buildings: Land Cruisers and Jaguars, the odd Japanese equivalent. The people here were mostly investors in property and land, with the occasional old banger outside failing to disguise heavy loans against the inheritance. Ever the wily old fox, Danny had scented money at a mile's distance. Couldn't help but be drawn here.

"So," Amanda says, "a professional."

"Quite."

"And uh..." she's not walking away, Danny's pleased to note "How come you do that, then? The fox thing?"

"Born like this, I suppose."

Danny's not teasing. It's perfectly true. He was born a fox, remembers the burrow, the fox hide, nips from his older siblings in the litter—scampering through long grass in the first quarter of the moon, the lessons his mother taught him, hearing her encouragement as he made spirals in the fields, faster and faster. Learning how to be a fox.

"It runs in the family," Danny says. "My father was a fox too."

Ah, Amanda laughing. Danny can smell the wine on her breath, the hint of the toothpaste she used before coming out this evening, thinking she'd obscured her true scent in perfumed mists. She's not eaten since the middle of the day, a ploughman's lunch, which must make her light-headed on the wine in her half empty glass.

"And I bet your mum was a fox too, right?"

"Actually, no," Danny says. "She was a schoolteacher. Taught infants and juniors."

"Stop it."

"It's true. My father kidnapped her one night, stole her away and wooed her. A fox has a surfeit of charms, all his to deploy. We're rather accomplished thieves too, you know. A heart unguarded, that's as easy as an open chicken coup."

"So your mother. She was a… a person?"

"Human. A woman."

"But that means you're only half fox? I suppose that's why you're standing on two legs."

"Oh, I'm pure fox. No doubting my qualifications. Seriously. I've inherited all my father's traits. His eye for beauty too."

She's looking at the card once more, hasn't really heard that last, or has decided not to acknowledge it if she has. Danny watches her nod lightly. The points of her lips twitch upwards as she delineates the swirl of brushwood colour on the textured card. It's a fox depicted in scalloped strokes; not a flame, not a symbol of long-solved Greek mathematics. A fox. Like magic.

"I still can't believe I thought you were some sort of professor. I mean, you're a fox—even if you're wearing tweed!"

"Country living rubs off. It's all young farmer and landed gentry types around here. If you're stealing eggs then it's good to look like the sort you're stealing from. People see what they're expecting to see, they rarely take a second look. It's the truth of these things. Everyone's guilty of it."

"So I was seeing what I expected to, not looking properly? Because you're a fox and the clothes hide that."

"You wouldn't want me walking around naked. That'd be embarrassing."

Danny smiles, a wide one, not concerned about the animal he's exposing of himself. He wants her to look, wants her to see this in him. He tilts his fine, hairy muzzle, bringing it back up so she can't miss his snaggled but otherwise clean and busy little teeth. His fox eyes fix her with the adventure of the moon and for a moment she holds his gaze, before sliding her attention to his fine red pelt. He swishes the proud

315

brush tail protruding from above his behind, where a carefully tailored slit in his country set apparel allows for such a venting. The white flash at the tip of the brush is hard to miss as it turns, a little stirring of fox magic.

She doesn't blush, as he half hoped she might. But maybe that's to be expected. She has, after all, for whatever reason, sought him out.

"So why're you here tonight, Mister Foxx?"

"Danny. Please."

"So why're you here tonight, Danny?"

"Thievery. I saw the lights from across the field, and I never care to miss a party."

"You've been to others?"

"Countless. And made my thefts, I should probably warn you."

"Consider me warned."

"What about you? Why're you here?"

"My father's idea, actually. This isn't really my scene."

"No?"

"I thought I'd given this up a long time ago, but I keep getting drawn back to it. Maybe you can't escape your inheritance, after all. I used to think there was a choice, what you can take, what you can leave. Staying and following your parents' example's the easiest. But I decided to leave. Maybe because I never was all that a traditional girl. But you get called back..." She sighs, dissatisfied. "So. Care to steal anything tonight, Danny?"

"I'm thinking about it," Danny says.

She slides his card under her dress, flat against her breast, nudging the rise of a nipple that's very much in evidence beneath the clingy silk. "For later," she says. "So I know where to find any thief that might be about."

"You have a card with your number on?" Danny asks. "In case I come across anything that was stolen. So I could be sure to return it, I mean. Naturally."

"Actually, I do. Outside, in my car. Why not come with me, we can exchange in private."

"All kinds of wild animals outside," Danny says, thinking how his father stole a schoolteacher and wooed her on fox trails by moonlight. There's a moon tonight, though a shallow one. Quarter moons are good for stealing all kinds of things. Hearts of girls in party dresses most certainly among them.

316

"You wouldn't let anything happen to me, though. Would you, Mister Foxx?"

"Protect you from the spirits of the night. It's a fox's honour he should do such a thing—though slyly, of course. Step beside you all the way."

"You must promise me that."

"Oh but I do."

They leave the party room, Danny's heart beating with excitement at the exquisite prospect of thievery and stolen hearts.

The music softens in the hallway, past the painted rural scenes on the walls. Coats hang from a banister beside the cloakroom. Amanda flips light switches. The front door's old and sturdy, the lock ratchets open, and they descend the stairs to the cars. It's noticeably colder out here. Danny's eyes are good in the dark, but a halogen security lamp springs on and has him squinting as they pass the gathered vehicles in which the partygoers have arrived. There are a couple of old Fords freshly added to the gathering, but mostly it's the country four-by-four and top range saloon he passed when he arrived.

"I'm away past the back," Amanda says, leading him on to darkness.

Danny follows, trying to blink away orbs the security light has left on the back of his eyes. They round the outbuildings, where Danny can smell cattle and chicken. He cannot see a car nearby, despite his night-vision slowly returning, and he wonders if Amanda's heart doesn't need stealing but will instead be gifted to him tonight. The thought sends a delicious shiver through his fur, all the way to the tip of his brush.

Walking beside her as he promised, he lids his eyes and breathes the scent of the moon-charmed night in anticipation of his thievery, enjoying the warmth dancing in his loins. He is lost in the glee of anticipation.

And feels the agonising bite of the trap close around his ankle with a terrible snap.

Danny barks his pain, tearing around in anguish as much as he can, suddenly restricted, free no more.

Oh but it bites deep, bites terribly. Metal teeth have sprung quickly, snapping the bone without question. Searing pain overwhelms him, will not relent. Trapped. Oh my God, trapped. A hand to his leg, but he can't unfasten the springs of the trap—he hasn't the leverage. He's fox now, all fox, whimpering and caught, trapped and out of luck.

He turns to Amanda, his captive heart for the night, but she's not there. He looks around frantic—help, he needs help. Then he sees her through narrowed eyes, standing out of his reach, the party dress girl haloed by the empty sizzle of halogen lamps clicking on around the courtyard.

"I'm sorry, Danny," she says. "You were such a good fox, too."

"What?" he barks through his pain.

It takes a moment for him to understand that Amanda has led him here purposefully, masked her reason with charm of her own. "You're a professional, Danny. But I'm very good at my job too. It's why my father called me here tonight, expecting you. A farm girl learns a lot, you know, about catching wily old foxes like you." She does a twirl in the clinging dress and high heels, bumps out her hip. "Clothes, weren't you telling me? They're so good at letting people see what they expect to see, disguising the truth." She waits a second before delivering her killer line. "Well, you wouldn't want a poor little farm girl walking around naked, would you?"

Danny groans at how stupid he's been, feels his instinct for escape gnawing at him, ready to devour him. Survival, at whatever the cost. Danny Foxx being a fox.

Amanda turns her back on him, fades like a ghost behind the bright lights; he hears her unlatch the door and walk inside the barn and he knows he has to make any escape now. There follows the appalling sound of a gun barrel being breached, cartridges loaded. And then her swift and purposeful steps back toward the door and out into the courtyard to the trap.

But now it's Amanda's turn to gasp. Amanda in clinging silk and the sizzle of halogen, mouth hanging open. "What?"

Because there's no fox in the trap. Not a whole one, anyway. Amanda ticks across the cobbles, taps her party shoe against the remains of Danny's loafer and the lower leg of his trousers. They're filled with the fur-covered flesh and the bone he's chewed through and left behind, a professional fox overcoming one of the hazards of the job. She stands there in wonder, then sees the trail he's dragged behind him. Blood flowing from the stump of his leg, and so much of it.

"Oh no you don't. Not tonight, Mister Foxx," she says. "No escape tonight."

Amanda hoists the up-and-over shotgun to her shoulder, cocks the hammer, and follows the trail around the stone barn, ready to draw a bead on movement. Farm girl in a party dress, munitioned up. She's wary as she goes, checking shadows. Hadn't Danny said there were wild animals out here? There is now, one at least.

She's armed, but she's not silly. She takes her time, careful along the trail he's laid beyond the outbuildings. Which is what Danny wanted and too late she realises this.

"No," she whispers as the streaks of blood lead further away from the farm and she finds herself on the edge of open fields beneath the smoky sly night, drawn after him by her own lust and an eager finger on the trigger.

When she understands this is a trail put down for her to follow, she hauls the shotgun around and runs as fast as her impractical shoes allow. Back to the lights of the outbuildings, knowing she's already too late, that she's been outfoxed, but hoping it's not true all the same.

She checks on the chicken coup, where all the eggs are gone, and she stands in the violence of feathers and carcasses, the chickens torn to pieces for fun. She sees a card hanging from a nail on the wall. A card with a flourish like a mathematical symbol: a fox, just to let her know, in case there was ever any doubt.

Amanda stands at the door to the chicken coup breathing heavily, lowers the shotgun, way too late. He's gone, somewhere out there in the laughing night under the smiling quarter moon, pockets loaded with the spoils of his thievery, heart perhaps a little bruised, injured but fleet enough to make his escape.

But she knows she shouldn't be surprised.

Danny's a professional. And he told her from the start.

Life is made up of stories; stories are how we deal with life. This story shows how a storyteller deals with a scoundrel.

WOLVES AND FOXES

Amy Fontaine

His sister came home one night practically glowing.

"You would not believe who I just met!"

The fabulist put his pencil down, setting aside his notebook. Turning towards her, he raised an eyebrow.

"Who? The President?"

"No!" She gushed over to his desk in the corner, beaming. "I met the most handsome... civilized... foxy man I've ever known, just walking down the street!"

He returned to his writing, a frown on his face.

"If he was foxy in any way, I wouldn't trust him. Foxes are always up to something."

Standing beside his chair, she looked at him. He seemed so pensive, sitting there at his desk. Laughing, she gave him a one-armed hug.

"Oh, brother! You're always so superstitious!"

He shook his head.

"I know what I'm talking about. Haven't you ever read any works by Jean de la Fontaine?"

She giggled. "Of course not, silly! Those stories of yours are totally beyond me."

She floated over to the closet to hang her coat.

"He said we should go to the club tomorrow at ten. He needs a lift, but I told him it would be no trouble." She gazed at her brother curiously. "Would you like to come? You've been so sullen over losing Anne lately; maybe it's time you met someone new."

He hunched over his notebook, engrossing himself in his work.

"I'm not interested in that kind of place."

She stared for a second, dismayed. Then, returning to her ecstatic, dreamy state, she pranced down the hallway toward her room.

"Whatever," she called. "Have fun with your storybooks."

He furrowed his brow, still writing. "Just don't wreck the car."

She came home the following night with a scream and a scowl. She punched the door open, storming in with a frustrated howl. She threw her jacket on the floor, fuming.

He looked up from his desk in the corner. "What happened?"

She glared in his direction. "I don't even want to talk about it. That bastard!"

She stomped toward her room. Changing her mind, she came rushing back. She glowered down at him.

"I'll tell you what happened," she growled. "After I gave that creep a ride to the club—I had to pay his admission too—he was flirting with all the other girls in the place! He kept coming back to me asking for money to buy drinks, and I was furious but I gave it to him anyway—I couldn't resist his damn pretty face, and I thought if I was generous he might be generous in return. But he sure wasn't generous to me! He didn't hang out with me the whole time!"

Trembling with rage, she paced around the room.

"And then, to top it off, I was driving him home—he was texting the whole time on his stupid fancy Blackberry—and he suddenly asked me to change directions—to not go to his house—and I asked where we were going now and he said his girlfriend's place. His girlfriend's place!"

She stopped in her tracks, snarling to herself. He imagined that, were she a wild animal, the hackles on her back would be raised.

"He said he was single!" she yelled. "I knew I shouldn't have believed it!"

Her brother looked at her curiously. "What did you do?"

She grinned viciously.

"Well, I thought of murdering him, but instead I just ditched him on the sidewalk." She snorted. "Let him find his own way home!"

Picking up her jacket, she hung it in the closet. Grumbling to herself, she marched towards her room.

"Who needs a twerp like that, anyway? I'm above people like him."

The fabulist heard his sister's door slam shut. He sat in silence for a while, lost in thought. At last, he picked up his pencil and opened his notebook.

Once upon a time, a wolf and a fox were traveling down a forest path. The wolf was heading north and the fox was going south. Eventually, of course, they ran into each other. This is the conversation that ensued.

"Hello, Ms. Wolf," said the fox. "Your fur looks particularly splendid today."

He bowed to her large, gray form, his fine red muzzle nearly touching the earth. Lifting her paw, he kissed it softly.

The wolf's heart was all aflutter. Never had such a dashing creature complimented her in such a way!

"Thank you, Mr. Fox," said the wolf.

Rising to his full height, the fox began stroking the wolf.

"Yes, what fine fur you have," he crooned. "Oh, what I wouldn't give to ride upon such a luxurious coat—even for a little while! But such good fortune shines upon me only in dreams."

The wolf's blood was aflame. Never had such a dashing creature touched her in such a way!

The wolf smiled alluringly down at the fox.

"You may ride for a while, if you wish," said the wolf.

The fox, in his suave way, looked taken aback.

"Really? Oh, but I couldn't! What polite gentleman would trouble such a fine lady with his silly needs?"

The wolf's head spun. Never had such a dashing creature called her a fine lady!

"Oh, it's no trouble, Mr. Fox," she murmured.

The fox put his face close to the wolf's. Before she knew it, she was staring deeply into his dazzling eyes.

"Really, Ms. Wolf? Really, truly? I would love a ride; my little paws are ever so sore. My destination is rather out of the way I'm afraid, and I would hate to inconvenience such a lovely creature as yourself, but... traveling with you for even a few moments would make my heart sing."

The wolf's pulse raced. Never had such a dashing creature come so close to her!

"Certainly, Mr. Fox," breathed the wolf.

Smiling widely, flashing perfect ivory teeth, the fox hopped onto the wolf's back.

"Thank you kindly," grinned the fox. He pulled her fur, steering her to face the direction from which she had come. "It's just a few miles that way, straight ahead. Thank you ever so much."

With the fox affixed to her back, the wolf began to trot southward along the dusty path. Gossipy little birds peeked out at the pair from the trees.

"Is that Ms. Wolf?" asked the sparrow.

"With Mr. Fox?" gasped the robin.

"She's in for trouble!" cackled the crow.

"She should know better," moaned the loon.

The wolf continued down the path. This was the way she had come, but the going was tougher now. The fox's weight pressed down on her. Meanwhile, he sat on her back like a king and picked blackberries. The fox could not normally reach the best berries, but his new position atop the wolf helped him gather them with ease. She heard his pleased smacking sounds; as she trudged on, doing all the work, he was snacking and enjoying himself. She thought, for a moment, of shaking the fox off her back and walking away. But then she remembered his dazzling eyes and his pleading tone, and the gentle way he kissed her paw. She decided to hang on a little longer.

"So..." the wolf began. The fox was still smacking his lips, but once he heard her speak he fell silent. He was a civilized fox; he could stop eating when a lady wanted to talk.

"So," said the wolf, "is there a Mrs. Fox?"

The fox caressed her neck. She was pleased at first, but then she shivered with disgust; his paws were sticky with blackberry juice, and he was using her as a towel. Still, she chose to bear it; after all, it wasn't every day that such a dashing creature wanted to wipe his paws on her neck.

"Alas," the fox said dramatically, "I am not married."

The wolf stopped dead for an instant. Then she quickly kept walking.

"I see," she said, attempting to imitate his suave manner. Then she crashed into a tree.

With a yelp, she stumbled backwards. From her back, the fox laughed lightly, unperturbed and unharmed. He seemed to know what his mount had been thinking about when she crashed. His laughter was so appealing—but why did he have to be so cocky, so sure of his power over her?

Growling under her breath, the wolf kept walking.

The wolf reached the barren desert she had passed through earlier. The path was worn, laden with cracks and potholes. The sun tore down upon her like a merciless bird of prey, adding to the heat in her heavy coat. She strained every muscle, forcing herself to push forward. It had been hard the first time, but her new passenger made it almost unbearable.

From somewhere out of sight came the sounds of satisfied smacking. Evidently, the fox had stored some blackberries from the forest in her fur. Now he was eating them and sipping their cool juices. She might be dying, but he was just fine.

She tried to convince herself that his good health was a comfort to her, but it wasn't.

"How... much... farther?" she panted.

The fox blinked, looking around at the desert. His ears twitched.

"Actually, my dear, you've gone too far. Turn back, please."

She might have eaten him then, but he asked so nicely.

The two traveled back to the forest. The fox, meanwhile, never offered the wolf a single blackberry.

The shade of the trees provided the wolf some relief, but she still felt like collapsing. She needed water. But the fox cooed in his soothing voice, "Just a bit farther, my pet. Just a bit farther."

They reached the place where they had first met. She knew because the same stump sat on the right side of the road.

"Turn left here," said the fox.

The wolf shook like a volcano about to erupt.

"When we were here before," grumbled the wolf, "you said your stop was straight ahead."

"I know," said the fox, "but I changed my mind."

Too tired to argue, the wolf turned left, leaving the path.

She tramped through brambles and thorn bushes. Every step was a battle with the underbrush. Branches scratched her sides, slashing her lovely coat. The fox remained untouched, pristine atop his lupine steed.

"That's it, my dear," purred the fox. "Keep going. Follow the scent of fox."

The wolf sniffed the air. "Fox?" she asked.

From his spot on her back, the fox beamed. A faraway look entered his eyes.

"Yes," said the fox. "The scent of my lover."

The wolf exploded. Bucking the fox off her back with a roar, she seized him in her paws. She glowered down at his trembling, whimpering form, squeezing him tightly.

"You said," she snarled, "that you are not married!"

Although he was wincing painfully at her strong grip, the fox managed a shadow of his cocky smile.

"Yes," he said, "I am not married. There is no Mrs. Fox." Her snarling, contorted muzzle was inches from his fine nose. His voice rose to a high, squeaky pitch.

"There is, however, a Ms. Fox. I... have a... a girlfriend."

The wolf rumbled like thunder, pushing him down against the forest floor. Twigs snapped beneath the combined pressure of the fox's body and the wolf's paws.

"You are a liar," she snarled, "and a cheat! You are all theatrics and no substance. I helped you because that's what wolves do. We are loyal creatures; we look after others! But you don't care about anyone but yourself. You just used me to get your ride and your precious blackberries... Because the truth is you're powerless on your own!"

She smiled cruelly down at him. He was tiny beneath her paws. His body quivered, but she only pressed harder, increasing the pressure with every word she spoke.

"Beneath your dazzling eyes and your fine red coat, beneath your suave chit-chat and your civilized ways, beneath your clever actions and your romantic air... Beneath you there is nothing at all!"

Pressed against a bed of broken twigs, the fox gazed tragically up at his tormenter.

"It's true," he coughed. "Foxes are flatterers. We have wandering minds and inconstant hearts." Sadly, he touched his heart with his paw. "I am sorry, Ms. Wolf. You deserve a better man."

At a former time, the wolf would have been moved by this display. Now, however, she knew better. She debated whether to pop him in her mouth and chew him up, to tear him to pieces in her paws... or to go to his home where his mate waited and destroy their den.

Instead she left him there, lying amidst the dirt and twigs. He was motionless as a lady's scarf. Tears dripped from his dim, ordinary eyes, leaking into his plain, mud-caked fur.

She left him there and headed north. She hoped to find a river soon.

Wolves can cavort with fine foxes in fun,
But in the end, when the day is done,
The handsome prince may prove a rake,
And the heart that trusted the flatterer, break.

After drinking her fill at the river, the wolf scratched this poem in the dirt on the bank with a claw. Then, in a burst of inspiration, she started writing a story about a man and his sister.

*Quarnates push furry to the limit—fuzzy veloci-
raptors with feathery tails and crests. Mohawk is a
Quarnate, but she's undercover, disguised as a lizard-
like Larsivian. Only, she's not the scoundrel.*

Unexpected Bouquets

Ellen Saunders

Seven body lengths down the lightless ventilation shaft, my left foot's claws slipped off an algae-coated bolt. My knee slammed into the slimy wall. The boots I'd slung around my neck rammed into my breasts and tried to shove me into thin air. I hung from clawtips, arms shaking, scrabbling with both feet for some rusty crack or bolt hole. Sweat ran through my fur beneath the lizard suit. Second Planet's gravity sucked on me, hungering for a lethally swift descent.

Breaking into Lanctin's smuggling lair through his ventilation shaft might not have been my most brilliant plan. I should have known the motherless egg would be too cheap to pay for proper rootweavers; he'd lined the shaft with salvaged and stolen sewage pipe.

At least my allergies protected me somewhat from the reek. It was spring in Sakatos City, nearly Clutch Mother Day. Second Planet isn't known for its foliage—they import most of their bouquet-flowers—but the swamplands flora makes up for its lack of beauty via scent and sex. Pollen irritates my entire under-ocular ridge, inflating my cheeks the full length of my snout, squeezing my eyes into slitted crescents. Since Quarnate cheek pouches involuntarily swell with anger or adrenaline, I looked like I was spoiling for a fight from early bloom to berry set.

It was a reasonable enough expression for dealing with Lanctin. The scuzzy jerk had ratted me out to Customs twice.

I kicked a foothold through a rusty section of pipe. Once I got both feet in a semi-solid spot, I rested my quivering arms.

I can toss a drunk Spacer out of Torrie's bar with one hand while bouncing his buddies across the room without breaking a sweat. But I am two-thirds heavier than the average human, and we Quarnates aren't built for climbing. Our predecessors were more the leap-and-shred kind of predator. Our tails are made for maintaining balance mid-jump, our feathery crests primarily for inconvenient displays of arrogant ego. Tom Green, the Spacer pilot who'd found me stowed away in his cargo all those years ago called us "muscle-bound dinosaur fashionistas." I snorted. I liked and missed the Greens. They were okay for humans, but like all Spacers, they could be such speciesists.

I shook out my arms as I glanced at the grating far above. My young Larsivian helper, Jacklor, had actually followed instructions for once and taken off. I didn't want him getting hurt if my plan sank.

I'd bruised my toes punching through the rusted metal. I wriggled them as I reached for new handholds. The support under my right foot crumpled. My face and chest smeared against the wall as I plunged sideways. My boots fell. Greasy algae clung to my snout, filling my lungs with the reek of ripe sewage. My breakfast lurched upward, but I was too busy to vomit.

I caught something semi-solid with two claws. A few heart-stopping scrabbles later, I had all twenty-four clawtips firmly holding me against the moist wall. I took a slow breath, trying to filter out as much reek as possible, and wiped my snout on my sleeve.

I lifted my ears and flicked them around. The morning wind whistled above. Water dripped all around me. All else was quiet. I hadn't made enough noise to wake Lanctin or any of the low-lifes he hired.

I also hadn't heard the boots land. I shrugged. I might die down here, but at least I should be able to see and breathe.

I flattened my ears against the back of my head and continued down. My lizard suit, an old work uniform that covered me head-to-toe and made me look vaguely Larsivian, covered my feathery tail and swaddled my crest against my back, but algae and oily condensation and Goddess knows what else soaked through the human-made fabric to the short curls that cushioned my knees and forearms. Assuming I survived this job, I'd need to burn the suit and take a deodorizing shower, maybe even shave—going furless like a Spacer.

My not-so-sainted grandmother would have perished at the thought.

I chuckled. Speciesism was such a bizarre thing. My grandmother's cohort believed Quarnates were the apex of all the Goddess had created, and our class, the Apiques, the apex of all Quarnates. And yet my client, Old Mother Syluss, would estivate in shame if she knew her clan had hired a Quarnate, or any immigrant, to recover her prized heirloom. I had to admit I looked forward to holding that gorgeous amber necklace, something not even the Syluss' snooty friends would get to do.

I smiled, and my cheeks blocked my eyes entirely. I hoped I wasn't allergic to algae too.

Then again, Old Mother Syluss had probably already gone catatonic at the vision of her granddaughter Glorsiv on Lanctin's arm. I grinned. The dysfunction of the wealthy Larsivian clan was far more entertaining than the pipe I was descending.

The Syluss clan, who'd hired Mohawk's Problem Solving Service (me) sight unseen, were Old Family Larsivians; bipedal lizards with a loose hold on their scythe-like tails and a death-grip on their wealth. Old Mother Syluss had upper-case-p Plans for Glorsiv, her eldest grand-daughter, that had involved an arranged marriage. She had tried to keep Glorsiv at home under her clan's watchful eyes after Glorsiv's friends scattered across the galaxy seeking adventure and educations.

Glorsiv had shown her true Syluss heritage in rare fashion. She took up with the skiffiest smuggler she could find—Lanctin, naturally. The grotesque dalliance served her purpose perfectly, although Lanctin managed to steal her family's most cherished jewels in the process. As I skulked deeper into her former boyfriend's lair, Glorsiv was enroute to the expensive Galactic University she'd chosen.

I'd gotten a map of Lanctin's lair from Glorsiv herself. She'd treated me as a dumb courier, and I acted the part. I suspected she'd engineered the theft as a backup plan.

I could relate. I'd been born to an exalted clan. But that was then, and my rent was due now. The only other grue-making opportunities lately were public bounties I had no hope of collecting. I wasn't about to waste my time on the manhunt for Attila the Space Pirate. For one, he was said to be ruthless and brilliant, and for two, how do you collect a bounty on a cipher? So far none of his victims had survived to identify him.

My immigrant status meant the other reward was also a waste of time. The Florist's Association had put together a big bounty (by Larsivian measure) on the perpetrator of the Blooming Heist. The thief had taken every flower imported for the Clutch Mother celebrations right off the port dock, then offended every Larsivian living and dead by demanding ransom. Ransom! I chuckled.

Grue flowed toward Larsivians, not away from them. The fact that it had to be a native job had green blood boiling. The Sakatos arm of the Sleepers, the galaxy-wide policing authority, had been slapping their tails in frustration, often across the bodies of unlucky suspects. Jacklor had been badly bruised by one of them. I was still peeved about that.

No, I liked solving people's problems, even for the Syluss clan. No competition, a quiet if death-defying climb, and most importantly, a chance to mess with Lanctin. Just the thought of getting back at that pip-spit warmed me up inside.

One foot squished onto a flat surface. I'd reached the bottom. I stood and indulged in a glorious stretch, then brushed off sweat and bits of rust, orienting myself. I found my boots half-imbedded in a pile of algae. I crammed my sore toes into my boots.

I crouched in a corner. The vent shaft that slanted further down into the hill in front of me was dimly lit with squares of light leaking up from the rooms below. It was narrow, but the walls were properly root-woven and the floor was reinforced terracrete. The tunnel to my left, damper and dark, took a shallower slope across what I knew was the face of the hillside. Some distance down it turned a corner into the hillside, from which came a bit of glow. That would be the corridor to Lanctin's office.

I crawled two steps down the dark shaft before a low, deep thrumming ahead of me made the fur on my arms rise. I backed up. I did not want to meet a poisonous caretoad down here. One touch and I'd never care about anything again.

I quickly crawled down the lit tunnel. I'd have to get into one of the rooms through the vents and cross to the corridor to get to Lanctin's office.

The tunnel ended in a muddy wall. I backed up and leaned an eye to the last vent. White and yellow and violet splotches slowly resolved into piles of flowers. I exhaled slowly.

Lanctin? Responsible for the Blooming Heist? Maybe I'd underestimated the little skink.

I yanked the grate up and listened. All I could hear was the thrumming of the caretoad. It was getting louder.

I shoved through the vent hole head-first, intending to curl around and clamber across the ceiling. I'd forgotten my shoulders and arms were coated with slime. Or maybe I moved too fast, being more concerned about the toad than I wanted to admit. So I fell.

I rolled mid-air, catching glimpses of arches peeking above the flowers at opposite ends of the room. Then I plowed into a suffocating floral sea. I closed my inner eyelids. Sticky softness slowed my fall. I rolled up on all fours. I couldn't see anything but flowers. The multi-color hues in every direction and the random stems were disorienting. I wasn't sure which direction to go. I swam through colorful poison in a straight line, hoping I was headed for the right door. Tacky petals and burred stems grabbed at me. I had to constantly pull things off my suit. At least when I hit the wall I was moving slowly enough to only bruise my snout.

I groped along the moist soil until I found the arch. The door was locked and my pocket was empty. My picks were either in the shaft above or somewhere in the blossoms behind me. I dug my claws into the seeping soil to climb the wall. Handfuls of mud pulled away. I exhaled, frustrated, beginning to feel like a useless debutante myself. I turned and started back across the sticky morass. I had almost reached the spot where I'd fallen in when I heard a Larsivian snarl somewhere ahead of me.

"After my treasure, are you?" Lanctin's hiss was muffled, but I'd know that skink's loathsome voice anywhere. "I'll slice you up and then I'll eat that tail of yours."

Fiery Asteroids. How did he know I was here? I could see my death clearly. Descended from bottom-dwelling amphibians, the Larsivian would have no trouble squirming though a sea of flowers. Lanctin would writhe his way across the floor until he touched me. Then he'd dice me with that bony blade that ran the length of his tail. Most males kept their ridges razor sharp. Smugglers liked to top theirs with various poisons. If I was lucky, he'd toss my pieces into a garbage pit. Or eat me.

His thrashing tail sounded creepier for coming through all the pretty colors, and more menacing because I couldn't see him—couldn't see much of anything at this point—and had no idea where the door was.

Maybe the wall would be drier and I could climb it. I pushed sideways, timing my moves to what I could hear of his swearing. Four steps aside, I bumped into a heavy crate.

"There you are," Lanctin said. The thrashing sounds sped up.

I stepped up on the crate. Groping sideways, I found another—there was an entire stack. I couldn't imagine what Lanctin was doing with legal, Customs-stamped crates, but I was grateful for his sudden lawful spree. I kept climbing. My head crested the petals. Vision, blurry though it was, was sweet. I located Lanctin by a wave in the room's bloomy sea.

He and his sharp tail scythed closer. "You think flowers are tasty, do you?"

Tasty? If my tail had been free, I would have slapped myself with it. He thought he had flower-eating vermin. I found a blob of algae on my back and hurled it. It hit the back wall with a satisfying splat. Gouts of blossoms spouted into the air as Lanctin changed direction.

I fought the urge to sneeze as he worked himself into a frenzy at the back wall, sending waves of poison pollen into the air. *He has no idea how effective he's being at killing his intruder,* I thought. If those florists actually paid a ransom, though, it would be Lanctin who'd be dead. Those blooms were going to be pulverized.

"Bitter bugs," Lanctin muttered. Petals churned in his wake as he moved toward the back door. I heard a rattle, then the flowers moved as the door opened and closed. Almost immediately I heard water running.

Only a Larsivian would lock an indoor bathroom. Only Lanctin would block the route to his own bathroom with fragile stolen goods.

The wall the crates were stacked against was dry enough to hold me. I dug in deep and labored across to the door he'd come in. The pressure in my cheeks started to affect my balance. The second time I slipped I just waded sideways to the door.

Except for some scattered petals, the lair's corridor was empty. It was a straight run with a single door at the far end where Glorsiv said Lanctin's office would be.

I calculated the risks. Lanctin was cheap. He would have had to pay his minions extra to piss off every mother on the planet. So he wouldn't pay for guards, especially when nobody was going to suspect him of pulling off this job.

Which meant I could have swum through the front entrance in the first place.

That thought irritated me enough that I made the dash to Lanctin's office nearly blind. I stumbled inside. I could make out ceiling-hung cabinets and a huge central desk. I almost missed the little Spacer in the chair near the door. The human strained against the leather binding him into his chair, eyes white with fear.

I could imagine what I looked like, algae smeared over my nose and lizard suit, petals clinging to my upright ears, cheeks at killing-rage stage.

"Lanctin double-cross you, too?" he asked.

I gave him points, he regained his composure quickly. But he looked a little familiar. I didn't need one of Torrie's customers recognizing me.

"I get what's mine." I squeezed past the desk and yanked open the cabinets. I dug behind the liquor bottles, where Glorsiv had said Lanctin might hide the bag. Nothing. My hopes sank. That meant I had to trust a debutante's memory for a safe combination.

"I can give you far more than he can," the Spacer said.

"You're not my type," I said. I found the safe in the back of the lower drawer. I tapped in the combination Glorsiv had given me. Nothing happened.

"You want the safe combination? I can do that."

I tried her combination again, then backwards, then scrambled. Then I grabbed a miniscythe from Lanctin's top drawer, rolled over the desk, and sliced the bonds on the human's legs. I stepped back, waiting.

He frowned, apparently thinking I'd be more trusting. I recognized him then; Ali Poiyde, a cook on the Green crew who'd found me as a stowaway.

"Snap up," I said. "We've only got his bathroom break."

He gave me a combination. As I rolled back over and tapped it in, he said, "Is there somebody back home who wants to know where you are? I could get them a message."

"Everybody who cares about me lives on this planet," I said. Which was almost true. There were people who wanted me dead back home, but I wasn't stupid enough to tell him that.

The safe popped open. Squatted behind the desk, I allowed myself to slump in relief. Then I yanked out frog skulls, bronze knuckles, a blaster and finally a leather bag tied with a black cord. I shoved the blaster into my pocket and pulled out the bag. The leather was worn and looked a lot like Larsivian skin. I didn't want to think about that too long.

I untied it as I stood and dumped the bulky contents into my right hand. Amber beads encasing small leggy things climbed away from a golden yellow orb that filled my palm.

Filling the orb was a perfectly preserved arachnid poised to strike.

I might have made an involuntary noise or two. The burning desire to fling it across the room fought with the irrational fear that breaking it would free the massive spider. The orb vibrated on my palm, looking more alive with every bounce. Finally, the small voice in my head screaming that this necklace was worth more grue than my life drowned out the other screams, and I shoved the horrid thing back into the bag.

Gorgeous, they said. I should have taken into account Larsivian tastes.

The Spacer gasped for air, practically suffocating with laughter.

I tied the bag's mouth twice, then tied the laces to my belt and stuck the bag in a pocket, which I snapped shut. I rolled back over the desk, trying to regain some dignity, and sliced Ali's remaining bonds.

"Stay away from creeps like Lanctin," I said. "He's bad news. You in town with Tom?"

He stood, rubbing his wrists. "Still sneaking into places you shouldn't?"

Asteroids. He'd not only recognized me, it was clear Ali wasn't just a cook anymore. I pulled the blaster from my pocket and motioned to the door. "After you."

He took a long look at the blaster, then my face, before he turned and went into the corridor.

Lanctin waited for us in the hallway. "Going somewhere, Attila?"

Attila? My brain scrambled for a survival plan. "Attila? Lanctin, Lanctin." I laughed. "He really buried your snout in it, didn't he? This guy's a cook."

"Can't afford any rumors, little Quarnate," the Spacer said, with a confidence that froze my barely-moving breath. "Kill her, Lanctin."

Space Pirate he might be, but he clearly hadn't worked with Larsivians much. I gathered all the indignance I could muster on Lanctin's behalf and blurted, "Ali! You don't give a smuggler orders in his own lair. Especially not one who just pulled off the heist of the century!"

"That's right." Lanctin puffed up, his two-hundred-canine grin glinting.

"You little two-bit mudball," the Spacer snarled. "You'd never have even considered a job like this. Hell, I had to talk you into the ransom! This was my plan, every step of the way!"

Lanctin snapped his teeth together and lashed his tail against the wall.

"Arrogant, isn't he?" I said. Then pushed the Larsivian detonator. "You know he offered me more than half the haul to cut you out of the deal, right?"

"WHAT?" Lanctin lunged at the Spacer, catching him by the throat and slamming him into the wall. "You miserable thieving tailless flat-faced..."

The invectives continued as I galloped down the muddy corridor and dove into the front entrance pool. I surfaced in the creek next to a brand-new ambi-terrain rig. It wasn't garish, so it had to be Ali's. I climbed aboard, turned it on and roared down the swamplands to Sakatos City.

The rushing air helped my sinuses. As I dodged vehicles and other obstacles, squinting over my swollen cheeks, I sorted my options. If Ali survived the confrontation with Lanctin, and actually was the space pirate, I was in deep muck.

I could report them both, but I'd never see a cent of the reward. There would be innumerable reasons given, but I'm Quarnate, and that's that.

So back in Sakatos City, I went looking for Jacklor. I found the lizardling a block from my office.

"Mohawk?" Jacklor backed up, webbed palms out. "I did everything just like you said, I swear!"

It took a while to convince him my allergies were worse. Finally I got close enough to whisper Ali's alias and his real name into his leather-flap ear, and "Lanctin's lair is full of flowers." Jacklor leapt away like a flying kite, all elbows and knees and toothy grin. Somebody needed to feed that boy.

I tossed the suit into the incinerator tube and took three showers, but I didn't feel better until I handed the bag with its horrid contents to Torrie. Glorsiv's clan surprised us both by paying me right away. I hustled the grue to my landlord before I could retail therapy myself out of a place to live. Back in my office-apartment, I slumped on my lumpy couch and sniffed. My fur still smelled funny. I turned on the vid and skipped through Larsivian soap operas until I found the news.

Lanctin's arrest for the Bloomin' Heist was the lead item, including Jacklor's interview at the Florists' press conference announcing the reward. The street kid carried himself pretty well. *He's a good eggling; he deserves some good luck,* I thought. Then one of the reporters from the Old Larsivian Standard stood. Looking down his long snout at Jacklor, he pointedly asked the spokeswoman if it was wise to give so much grue to a "shiftless unemployed street lizardling".

"Hey, I contribute, and I got a job," Jacklor said. He leaned back on his leathery tail and said, with pride, "I work part-time for Mohawk's Problem-Solving Service."

My vision got a little blurry. Must've been my allergies.

The fact that Attila had been involved in the heist was the second item. He had escaped. My gut clenched until Ali's picture flashed on screen, listed as a "Spacer of Interest." I took a deep breath of relief. I wasn't the only person in the galaxy who knew who he was.

The news anchor, a jet-jade Larsivian well-known for her no-nonsense delivery, ended the newscast with a rare smile. "All over Sakatos, mothers have renamed the smuggler Lanctin, calling him 'Clutch Day Stinkweed.' But Attila the Space Pirate, called many unrepeatable names in many languages, also gained a new nickname today. The pirate has been demoted to 'Lanctin's Blooming Skink.'"

I giggled all the way through my fourth shower.

Ellen Saunders

Things are wrapping up; it's time to go home. But the otteroid aliens of The Victory of Dobleth *can't get anyone to sign their clearance papers.*

CLEARANCE PAPERS

Fred Patten

The docks were unusually quiet.

Normally this area of the spaceport was almost deafening with the clamor of cargo ships loading and unloading cargo; the shouting and hissing of crewmen—human and otherwise—as they hauled their bulky loads into and out of gaping holds onto the grav-floats to shift them to the dockside areas where they would either be inspected and approved as incoming raw materials or finished goods for this capital city, or elsewhere on the busiest world of what was grandiosely called by humans "the New Empire"; or as outgoing cargo meant for one of the myriad worlds of known space. Until today, the noise level was a known annoyance that the multi-species spacers were used to, and barely noticed. But today, the area was quiet. Everyone had gone somewhere else.

Almost everyone.

"Put 'em over here!" the non-human *ch'rr'pt* called to four of the port's AI-controlled labor units in Dock 8-GH, one of the smaller of the commercial areas of the huge spaceport. The *ch'rr'pt*, who resembled a bipedal, human-sized Earth mammal similar to a North American sea otter or a Southeast Asian binturong, spoke in his own language since the spaceport's mechanical staff was programmed to understand all interstellar languages. *Akkk'rrchk*, the first mate of the *ch'rr'pt* merchant trader whose name translated as *Victory of Dobleth*, was supervising as the final cargo was loaded and lashed down on board. He nodded approvingly as it was secured to his satisfaction, and scribbled an acceptance on the human supervisor's electronic manifest. The latter flashed a grin as he prepared to leave with his labor units.

"That's it," the dock supervisor said in human speech. "I was afraid you were gonna take so long that I'd be late for the festivities," he said. "Have a safe voyage home."

Victory of Dobleth was one of the smaller and older of the cargo ships that plied interstellar space. It was a *ch'rr'pt* ship, owned and crewed by one of the merchant clans of that shaggy and bearded non-human species. Despite their fiercely piratical look, dressed in little more than a vest and harness to hold pockets, writing implements, and the other small necessities of civilization, the captain, officers, and small crew were all peaceful merchants—well, the officers and crew, anyway. Captain *Brr'ttcheerpt*, better known as "Bucky" to his human trading partners despite his annoyance, was notably short-tempered. But on this trip, everything had gone smoothly despite the humans' increasing distraction as their big celebration approached. Bucky was in a good mood.

Akkk'rrchk, in the cargo hold, spoke into a paw-held communicator. "Just finishing loading, Captain!"

In the control room, Captain *Brr'ttcheerpt* (whom we will call Bucky to avoid having to write *Brr'ttcheerpt* all the time) grunted an acknowledgement. "Thank the Gods! Whoever heard of a whole planet closing down for a holiday? Get ready to break dock as soon as you're finished."

A few moments later, *Akkk'rrchk* joined him in the control room and handed over an electronic tablet with what was still called their latest "paperwork." Bucky connected their comscreen to the Port Master's office, commenting, "These humans aren't bad, but thank the Gods we don't run into a celebration like this every time we come here. I'll be glad to get back to *ch'rr'pt* space!"

However the Port Master's office, where a secretary usually answered promptly, showed only a "Closed For The Holiday" notice on the comscreen. Bucky frowned and continued to hold down the "connect" button. Eventually the lone bureaucrat left to man the Port Master's office came on the comscreen.

"Sorry. We're closed for the big celebrations."

"I'm Captain *Brr'ttcheerpt* of the *Victory of Dobleth* at Dock 8-GH. We've just finished loading, and we're ready to leave from your New Empire to return to *ch'rr'pt* space."

The human frowned. "I thought that all the ships that were scheduled to land or leave here during the next week had already done so. Unfortunately, we've just closed for the special occasion, and we won't open again until next week. You'll just have to wait until then."

Bucky went from placid to choleric in an instant. "What do you mean, next week!? I don't give a damn for your human holiday; we're ready to leave right now!"

The human shrugged patronizingly. "Really, this is a historic occasion! The uniting of the two greatest human space empires! Anyhow, only the Port Master or someone higher can sign your clearance papers, and he's already gone. We'll see you next week!" With that, the comscreen went blank.

Bucky stared unbelievingly at the screen for a moment, then tried to reconnect to the Port Master's office. The screen stayed blank. Bucky punched furiously at the connect button for a few moments, then screamed and pounded on the whole control panel before getting up to stalk around the control room. *Akkk'rrchk*, who was used to Bucky's outbursts, stood quietly aside, idly grooming his fur. Bucky, whose tantrums were short-lived, turned to him saying, "Historic occasion be damned! We're not going to lose a week just sitting here! I'll go up there and stomp around until someone signs our clearance papers just to get rid of us!"

For thousands of years, ever since their never-forgotten civil war had split the human space empire into two independent realms, there had been abortive attempts at reconciliation; some almost succeeding, others degenerating into new feuding. At last, despite a few unreconstructed warmongers, it looked as though the peacemakers would win. The emperors of both human space nations had agreed to merge. The largely symbolic climax of the merger would be the wedding of the New Empire's young royal heir—that Emperor's grand-nephew—with the Old Empire's young princess; popularly believed to be a genuine love affair rather than just an arranged marriage. The humans of both space empires were wildly enthusiastic, and in the two capital cities, all businesses were closing for a weeklong festival.

Akkk'rrchk assumed that he would be assigned to watch over the Dobleth while Bucky was gone, but "I'll" turned out to mean "we're." Bucky pressed the ship's intercom. "*Rru'gg?* Get up here, to the control room. *Akkk'rrchk* and I are going out, and you're in charge until we get back!"

The intercom gave out a piercing whistle and chirp that meant, "WOW! Yessir!"

The young *Rru'gg*, the Dobleth's most junior crewman and the youngest of Bucky's clan out of puberty, arrived at a lope, beaming eagerly. *Akkk'rrchk* glanced disapprovingly at his gaudy lavender vest and electric blue harness. The *ch'rr'pt* youth had "gone human." The otteroids had adopted many human customs and devices since the two spacegoing cultures had met, but with their thick, dark brown pelts, the *ch'rr'pt* had no use for human clothing. That had not kept some of them from going overboard on what the humans called "fashions." Their traditional utilitarian vests and harnesses had been as brown as their fur. Since meeting humans, many *ch'rr'pt*—the younger ones in particular—had taken to offsetting their fur with embroidered and brightly-colored (clashing, if possible) vests and harnesses, some with flashing lights. *Akkk'rrchk* thanked his Gods that the brief fad for styled fur had not lasted long.

It turned out that *Rru'gg* had exaggerated notions of how much authority he would have while Bucky and *Akkk'rrchk* were gone. The Dobleth's crew were already familiar with his attempts at initiative.

"Do you want me to—"

"No."

"Well, I can—"

"No."

"Um. How about if I—"

"NO! Just keep watch and don't touch anything. The humans have closed their Port Master's office for the next week, so we shouldn't get any calls, but if we do, just answer that we're out and take a message for our return."

The two *ch'rr'pt*—Bucky with his first mate trailing along—went to get their papers signed. Frustratingly, it seemed that the Port Master's flunky knew what he was talking about. By now, the dock area was completely deserted. All the humans from the most influential to the lowest peon had left for the better areas of the city where the festival was in full swing. The capital's main square was filled with celebrants dancing exuberantly around the clock, awhirl flashing with glittery body-lights during the nighttime hours.

Finally, Bucky and *Akkk'rrchk* found a drunkard and his bottle sleeping it off in one of the spaceport's loading areas. The two *ch'rr'pt* exchanged dubious looks, then Bucky kicked him awake.

"Yaaahh!" The drunk was momentarily terrified at being awakened by two furry, ferocious-looking, human-sized, pseudo-otters looming over him.

Akkk'rrchk left the talking to the more fluent Captain Bucky.

"Hey, you!" Captain Bucky said in heavily-accented human. "Where can we find somebody in authority around here?"

"Uhh... the Port Master's office, I guess?"

The drunkard waved in the direction of a public information screen. Unfortunately, it just unhelpfully told them to contact the "always open" Port Master's office.

The whole city was not celebrating. In the New Empire's imperial palace, the elderly Emperor paced nervously as the time to leave for the big wedding approached. The long-desired reuniting of the two empires was popular with the people, but a few diehards among the nobility of both nations had opposed it for as long as they could.

Some wanted the Old Empire and the New Empire to remain separate interstellar nations. Others approved a merger, but not as equals. They wanted their own nation's aristocracy—and themselves—to be the upper-class of the reunited empire.

It had taken decades of negotiations, but finally everything had been agreed upon to almost everyone's satisfaction. There was still loud political griping from reactionaries among the out-of-office minority. The New Empire's monarch just hoped that all would go as planned.

"It would be nice if my grand-nephew were older, but he's shown that he can handle the responsibility," the Emperor mused. "They say that the Old Empire's Princess is an intelligent girl, too."

A couple of hours later, the two *ch'rr'pt* had not exactly given up, but they were taking a break in a bar that was still open on the fringe of the festival—fortunately, alcohol was popular with both species. Bucky and Akkk'rrchk were discussing what to try next when they were surprised by a fancily-dressed, slightly tipsy human joining their conversation in fluent *ch'rr'pt.*

"You sound like you've got a problem that can't wait until the end of the festival."

Bucky was in no mood for friendly chit-chat. "You look like you're some kind of aristocrat. Are you authorized to sign a spaceship's clearance papers?"

"Alas, no. I'm not even from here. I'm a cookie-pusher, a member of the Terrestrial delegation to the New Empire. I am, frankly, slumming."

Bucky tuned him out.

"However, I do think that I can help you."

Bucky tuned him back in again.

"Anybody high-ranking enough to sign those papers will be in the palace by now for the wedding ceremony, which is in just a couple of hours," the human told Bucky. "I have to get back to the Terrestrial delegation there. I can get you past the guards with me. You can wait at the back of the crowd until the ceremony is over, and then grab some big shot as they're leaving and have him or her sign your papers."

The vast throne room was already packed when they arrived, with diplomats and both empires' aristocracies, waiting to watch the ceremonial wedding of state of the barely-adolescent New Empire's Prince to the Old Empire's Princess that would unite the two interstellar nations. But the crowd also contained those who were not happy about it, and had not given up loudly protesting the union in their political rants—plus others who were quietly planning to turn the festivities to their own advantage.

The lushly-dressed Baron of Happy Valley—he hated that saccharine name, but the title had been in his family for generations, and it did make it easier for him to pose as a benevolent philanthropist—smiled thinly as Duval, his henchman, forced his way through the crowd toward him. Duval, sweating, nodded toward a large ornate bust of some long-forgotten nobleman, positioned toward the rear of the throne room near where one of the higher-ranking dignitaries had chosen to be with his supporters rather than where his rank entitled him to be.

The Baron was displeased by Duval's nervousness, but the henchman was well-known as his closest retainer, and any other aide might be noticed and raise awkward questions. The Baron planned to discreetly get rid of Duval as soon as he could.

Duval whispered what the Baron already knew: "The bomb isn't in the bust, sir, it is the bust! It's a copy, made of explosive plastic!"

The Baron grinned inwardly with satisfaction. The explosion would be blamed on the extremists who opposed any union, and the Baron was well-known to favor it. He really did; he just wanted to be in charge of it. Duval continued to stage-whisper what they both knew: "After the Duke is killed, you'll be the next logical choice for appointment as the Prince's guardian, sir. Then you can make sure that the Emperor has a fatal accident while his heir is still young enough to need a regent, which will be you."

The Baron frowned at this reminder of his supposed "friend."

The Duke of Brightwater was one of the New Empire's leading liberals; a staunch supporter of the faction that believed in the amicable merger of the two nations. The Baron had posed as one of his non-political social allies, all the while secretly supporting the Duke's enemies. He was the real leader of those who denigrated the Duke as "the Duke of Bilgewater," portraying him as that ancient fictional scoundrel and con-man, clearly untrustworthy. Yet it had not worked. The Duke of Brightwater was too famous for his honesty and his provable good deeds to be a convincing target for slander. Well, after tonight the Baron would not have to worry about the Duke. He would tearfully take up the martyred Duke's mantle.

The two *ch'rr'pt* and the Terrestrial delegate arrived shortly before the imperial wedding was due to start. The huge throne room's main entrance was flanked by ceremonial but alert royal guards, but the Terrestrial delegate's diplomatic ID enabled the three to enter past them. They paused before mixing into the crowd.

"Well, this is where we part," their benefactor told the two otteroids. "I have to join the other Terry diplomats. You can make your way to the rear of the room and look for a likely official while you wait until the wedding is over, then get them to sign your papers before leaving."

Akkk'rrchk looked slightly confused by the change of tenses, but Bucky was used to the vagaries of the human language. He gruffly thanked the Terry "cookie-pusher"; then he and *Akkk'rrchk* squeezed their way through the mostly-human crowd to the rear of the throne room, causing a few raised eyebrows as some human guests wondered how the two *ch'rr'pt* had gotten invitations.

Akkk'rrchk supposed that the brightly garbed aristocrats were examples of the pinnacle of the human "fashions" that the "gone human" *ch'rr'pt* hoped to emulate. He shuddered, imagining himself with his thick fur also smothered in unnecessary and sweltering clothing.

They found a good spot to watch the wedding and scan the crowd, except their view was mostly filled with a big, imposing bust in poor taste. After finding the bust in their way, whichever way they turned, Bucky told *Akkk'rrchk*, "Let's move this aside." The two otteroids manhandled it into a corner, incidentally away from the group of humans nearby.

The Baron and Duval stiffened in alarm. The Baron called over a palace functionary and angrily asked, "Who are those aliens? Get them out of here, and put that bust back where it belongs!"

"Yes, sir!" To hear is to obey, was the functionary's motto. He went with a couple of guards to escort Bucky and *Akkk'rrchk* out of the throne room.

Bucky, who was quietly fuming at what he considered wasted time, exploded noisily. The Baron watched from a distance as the otteroid's body language made it clear that the two *ch'rr'pt* were not going to leave peacefully.

The functionary, hoping to keep everything quiet, tried to pass the buck. "It's the Baron's order! You'll have to talk to him about it!" he said, pointing toward the nobleman and his nervous assistant.

The real scoundrel, also hoping to deflect attention, tried to brazen it out. He strode majestically towards the group around the two *ch'rr'pt*, dragging Duval with him. "What are you two doing here?" he hissed. "I'm sure that no non-humans were invited to this event—even non-human nobility, which you clearly aren't!"

"I'm Captain *Brr'ttcheerpt* of the *Victory of Dobleth* at the spaceport—" Bucky started to explain at as little length as he could. The Baron listened impatiently, then cut him off.

"I don't care! That's not our concern! Even if you were invited in by one of the Terrestrial delegates, he had no authority to bring you into the throne room! You have to leave NOW!"

Bucky did what he always did when he lost his temper. He began shouting, which of course drew attention, and pounding on the nearest thing—which in this case was the explosive bust. At that point, the increasingly-nervous Duval, who did not really understand explosives, totally panicked.

"NO!" he shouted. "YOU'LL BLOW US ALL UP!" He turned and began to frantically push his way through the crowd, which began to stir with alarm.

The Baron tried to bluster the situation back under his control, but it was too late. The guards were confused, but their standard orders covered this. In case of what even looked like a suspicious event, grab everybody involved and wait for Higher Authority to sort it out.

In this case, no waiting was necessary. Duval was babbling the details of the plot to anyone who would listen. The nearby humans backed away hastily from the bust, the guards dragging the Baron, Duval, and the two otteroids with them.

Bucky, who did understand explosives, shook himself free of the human guards. "It's all right!" he said exasperatedly. "It's a safety explosive! It needs a detonator to be dangerous!"

Even so the humans, guests and guards alike, showed signs of imminent panicking.

"Oh, for the Gods' sake!" Bucky muttered, then called aloud, "Here, *Akkk'rrchik*, you help me!" The other *ch'rr'pt* didn't know much more about explosives than anyone else, but he trusted his captain.

Bucky realized that, as long as the Baron was willing to stand next to the bust, it was not likely to go off. Even so, the two lost no time in turning the bust onto its side and looking for the explosive timer hidden in it.

"I hope you know what you're talking about, Cap'n," the first mate said quietly in *ch'rr'pt* as they found something out of place.

Bucky did not answer, but pulled out the object. "Here," he said in human, thrusting the detonator into a startled guard's hands. "Make yourself useful. Take this thing out of here!"

The guard did so, as quickly as he could, hurling it into an ornamental fountain.

Explanations were made, although the Baron's furious glowering at Duval and the sight of Duval in hysterics made them largely unnecessary. The Duke, who had been quietly watching, thanked Bucky and *Akkk'rrchk* for foiling the Baron's plot to play the liberal and conservative factions against each other.

Bucky protested impatiently, "I'm not interested in human politics! I just want to get our damned clearance papers signed and get back to *ch'rr'pt* space."

The young Prince stepped forward. "After what you've done today, let me sign your papers!"

Bucky bent down, and the Prince solemnly signed the electronic document.

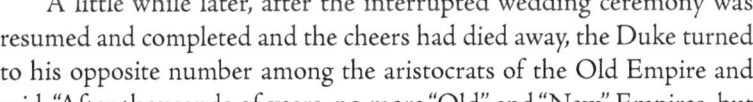

A little while later, after the interrupted wedding ceremony was resumed and completed and the cheers had died away, the Duke turned to his opposite number among the aristocrats of the Old Empire and said, "After thousands of years, no more "Old" and "New" Empires, but a single United Empire once again!" They drank to it.

Bucky and *Akkk'rrchk* were not there to hear him. *Victory of Dobleth* was just lifting from human space to return to its *ch'rr'pt* homeland.

Life itself is a scoundrel. Things go wrong with no rhyme or reason. But when they do, find hope in the fact that even a Very Little Bear can be Very Brave.

Edward Bear and the Very Long Walk

Ken Scholes

He was a bear, and his name was Edward, and he lay twitching in the corner of a room that smelled of death.

He didn't exactly know what Death smelled like, but he knew that's what he smelled. Because Something Very Bad had happened here. He just couldn't remember what.

A small boy in short pants flickered over him, smiling. "Hello Bear. It's about time you woke up."

Edward sniffed and stirred. "Hello. Are you...?"

"No. I'm not. I am the Funplay Holographic Nursery Brain."

"Oh." Edward stood. "It's just that you look like, I mean I thought you might be, well, you know..."

"No. I'm not."

Edward reached out a paw to touch the boy's arm. It passed through. "Oh. I see."

"Do you know what's happened to the children?"

Edward swallowed. Suddenly, he wanted to cry. "Yes. They're... sleeping?" He hoped and hoped and hoped and hoped, grimacing as he did. He looked around.

Makeshift beds lined the room. Small hands gripped blankets, small eyes stared at the ceiling.

"No." The boy frowned. "They've died."

"Because of Something Very Bad?"

"Yes. And I need you to be a Very Brave Bear. Can you do that?"

Edward nodded once, twice, three times, and blinked.

"Good. I need you to leave the Nursery and find Someone. Tell them about the children."

Edward heard a squeaking sound and knew he made it. He felt a Tremendous Fear growing in him. "Why can't you go? I can't leave the Nursery... I've never left the Nursery alone." The boy hissed and his image warbled, then came back into focus. "Yes you can. You must. I can't leave... I'm not real. You must go, Bear. But first you have to open the door."

Edward shuffled out of the corner. The room was stifling, heavy with rottenness and a buzzing dance of flies. He tried to remember the last time he'd played with the children, but couldn't. He squinted, trying to conjure up any memories of the Something Very Bad.

He faintly remembered his birthday, waking up surrounded by laughter, in the midst of the Nursery. And distorted tales from the children about traveling Very Far to Find a New Home. They had such bright and shining faces, and they were all so smart. Whenever he couldn't understand what they told him, they called him "Silly Old Bear" and "Bear of Little Brain."

He also carried vague recollections of the grown-ups, pausing in the Nursery door or sitting with their children. They were even smarter than the children. And they never talked to the toys.

He was a bear, and his name was Edward, and he was a toy. He remembered being told this on his birthday when he woke up after a Very Long Sleep. It was as if he'd gone to sleep in his comfortable house in the Wood (under the name of Sanders) and woke up here. He had hoped for cakes and cream and possibly honey and candles to blow out when he first opened his eyes. Instead, he led the children in a song and then a dance.

A few weeks later there was no one left to play with.

Edward simply went to sleep.

"Over here, Bear," the boy said. The boy stood by the door, pointing to a flat button in the wall. "Push this." With a static pop, the boy disappeared.

Edward's fur paws whispered over the vinyl floor. He reached the door and stretched as tall as he could. The button was an arm's length out of reach. "Bother."

He looked over each shoulder, spotting an oblong plastic box. He waddled to it, picked it up easily, and lay it against the door. "This

should work quite nicely," he said to no one in particular. He climbed
and stretched and reached. "Bother."

Edward hopped down and began pacing the narrow aisle between
beds, trying hard not to notice the white, stretched skin and puffy, staring
eyes. Pillows, he thought.

Moving from bed to bed, holding his breath and squeezing his eyes
shut at each, he carefully wriggled four pillows free. He placed them
against the door and scrambled up, striking the flat button just as he
tumbled to the floor.

Nothing happened.

"Drat and Bother. Chris—I mean, Holo-what's-it Nurserious
Brain?"

No answer.

"Are you there? Hallo?"

Silence.

Edward sat, head in his paws, and thought. And thought. And
thought. Then, he sighed.

His stomach growled, even though he knew he didn't need to eat
exactly. He could go long periods of time without food. Still, mouths
were for eating and bellies for filling and a bit of something would be
nice. But not in this room. So how to leave? That was his Question of the
Moment. And he had to find Someone and tell them about the children.

The hairs in his ears tickled to a faint sound above. He sniffed.

"Air," he said, leaping to his feet. "Air... But from where?" A grill set
high in the wall grinned down at him when he looked up.

Edward paced the floor, thought of a song that went nicely with his
Difficult Situation, hummed it through a few times and then thought
of A Plan.

The grill was too high to reach.

There was no one to ask for help.

He would try the button again.

With a whisper and a groan (and a thud as he fell down) the door
hushed open—just a bit. Squeezing through, his gurgling stomach
protesting the pressure, he padded into the hall to find Someone.

Edward heard the crying long before he saw the girl. She sat in a
large room wrapped in fading stars, holding her head in her hands.

"Hello?"

The girl looked up and sniffed. She stared at him.

"I mean... er... I hope I'm not interrupting." Edward entered the room. "I really wouldn't want to bother you but I seem to be very lost and you seem to be very sad."

She stood and flickered as she moved.

"I'm looking for a grown-up." Edward used his most confidential and important tone.

The girl started crying again. "They're all gone," she said through her tears.

"Oh." Edward shifted uncomfortably from left to right.

"I killed them all," the girl whispered. Her eyes widened. "All of them."

Edward backed up a step. "Oh. Well. In that case perhaps it would be best if I were—"

The girl suddenly began to stretch upward, her legs, arms and torso extending themselves like taffy, her hair spilling down around her shoulders like milk. Her eyes grew faraway pale and her skin pulled then sagged.

"It was an accident," the old woman said. "A terrible accident." And she pointed at a console as the stars disappeared. She flickered again.

Edward followed the line of her finger to a dangling cord.

The children called them their "Jack-in-the-necks"—a small hole that helped them know things when they plugged wires into it. Edward himself had a "Jack-in-the-belly" so he could play with other toys.

"Plug in," she said.

Edward plugged in and suddenly found his head full to the point of bursting, as if hands tugged at his ears and snout, pushing and pulling at once. "Oh," he said and sat heavily on the floor.

Her name, Edward knew, was the *Nancy Bell*; she was a starship, the first of five to hastily leave a dying home. Earth. A place he couldn't remember well but now understood was once green and blue and full of life. The old woman who had been a little girl was a manifestation of the ship's brain and she was dying, trickling away with the moments.

After nearly a century of travel she'd reached her goal and awakened her cargo—three hundred men, women and children. But there was a flaw... A minute tear in her program that gradually became a gaping hole. Critical EM shields had malfunctioned, the comm-array burned off in an unforeseen asteroid belt, air-tanks ruptured. It was all she could do to launch her comm-sat.

The *Nancy Bell* crash-landed on an otherwise quiet Tuesday, using the southern hemisphere's tepid ocean to break her fall. She dragged herself onto the wooded beach to die, a massive diseased whale of charred metal. The virus awaited and systematically executed the survivors.

"We worked so hard."

Edward looked up from the floor at the sound of her voice. *Nancy Bell* still stood in the center of the room, staring at nothing.

"We did?"

"Yes. For a vaccine."

"Oh." Another burst of data, white light collapsing his field of vision. He saw blood cells and antibodies in a kaleidoscope, twisting and turning on themselves.

"We found it," he heard her somewhere outside of himself. "But it was too late."

Yes, he realized. The grown-ups had programmed the necessary information into the ship, dying before the *Nancy Bell* had gotten results. The formula, the cure, lay in so many sparks of electricity in a dying ship's mind. Life for four other vessels, en route and unsuspecting.

"You must help me save them."

"Me?" Edward's voice was more a squeak than anything else and having been somewhat unsure of it, he repeated himself. "Me?"

"You're all that's left." She changed again, shrinking into a boy in short-pants that immediately filled his heart with hope. "You are going to go on a very long walk to climb a very tall mountain."

"I am?"

"Yes. I need you to be a Very Brave Bear. Can you do that?"

Edward thought for a moment. "Y-yes."

Another blast and the room spun; he closed his eyes. He saw the communications satellite turning in slow orbit, dish tilted toward a green-blue haze, thirsty like a sponge for water. He saw the muted ship, unable to answer the repeated blip of questions. And he saw the portable transmitter lying in the great ship's belly and the red hover-wagon near the airlock. Then geography swept at him, over him, like a rushing beast.

He knew his minuscule toy brain, designed for telling stories, singing and playing with the children, couldn't contain the flood of information. He knew he'd begin forgetting Everything as soon as he unplugged.

He also knew the ship didn't have the strength to tell him again.

But he would remember the most important parts: The wagon. The pack. The walk. The mountain. And the Big Green Button.

Edward Bear unplugged and stood up. The boy smiled at him, then flickered and began to fade.

"Silly old bear," he said. "I know you can do it."

Edward Bear left the ship on a quiet Friday, his muzzle still wet with something quite like (but not) condensed milk and his paws still sticky with something quite like (but again not) honey. His send-off party, launching his great Expotition, had been a smashing success. There had been plenty to eat for Everyone—which was especially important, him being the only Someone in attendance.

He stepped through the yawning hatchway giving the wagon a tug. It buzzed noisily behind him and he looked back. It bobbed up against the lip of the door. With the slightest lift it cleared and floated easily. Edward couldn't remember exactly what the Something strapped to the wagon did—already most of what the Nancy Bell told him had leaked away. But he knew it was Important and that he had to take it up the mountain.

And press the Green Button. He mustn't forget that.

Bear trudged across the sand, head turning side to side, nose working the wind. The air was heavy, a thick salt smell. A breeze cut across the massive ship, whipping up the sand and bending the brush that grew behind a line of driftwood. A golden sun in a blue sky. Behind him, he could hear waves rushing the beach with tiny, deep-down-inside roars followed by satisfactory sighs. When he reached the driftwood he climbed onto a log and watched the ocean for a while. He'd heard the boy in short-pants talk about the ocean a long time ago. It was bigger than Anything.

Nancy Bell lay half-submerged. Scattered around her lay the remnants of camp. Canopies, stacked boxes, a line of clothes dry now for weeks that no one would wear. Toys nearly buried by the shifting sand, toys that no one would play with ever again.

Edward sniffed back a tear. He looked the other way now, back to the forest. Trees stretched thin and tall, reaching for the sky, blossoming like green balloons. Beyond them, purple hills rolled up and over like a rumpled quilt and, looming behind the hills, a mound of stone, white and enticing as vanilla ice cream. His mountain. He climbed down from the log and followed the line of wood until he came to a trail that disappeared into the forest. Dragging his red wagon, he waved goodbye to the ship.

The woodland swallowed him and at first it reminded him of Home. Only none of his friends seemed to be about. He'd always loved the Wood, and this one was not so different. Certainly the ferns were larger and the berries had an unfamiliar gray hue. Some of the trees stood straight and thin and very, very tall with branches that swept out and down covered with small dark needles. But the branches began too far up for convenient honey-gathering climbs.

Once, about two hours into his walk, Edward heard a buzzing louder than his wagon and his heart jumped. He spun round and round, finally seeing the bearer of glad tidings. The biggest bee he had ever seen zipped past his nose.

"Bees mean honey," he said out loud. His stomach rumbled its agreement.

At four hours he came across a small hole. He poked his head inside, shouted "Hallo," and then thought better of it and moved on. Once, forever ago it seemed, he'd found himself stuck in a hole very much like it.

At six hours into his Very Long Walk, Edward Bear decided that this forest wasn't anything at all like Home. The sun disappeared somewhere behind him, leaving the wood painted in charcoal shadow.

At six-and-one-half hours into his Very Long Walk, the noises started up and the light gave out altogether and Edward decided that it was actually the Wrong Sort of forest for Small Animals Entirely On Their Own.

He parked his wagon and hid in the hollow between two large stones. Edward tried to sleep but didn't for a long while. Unfamiliar sounds and smells troubled him. At last, he slept fitfully.

In the morning, he met the Parrotishes.

They were standing around his wagon, poking it with long sticks. Thin and tall, like the trees, they hooted as he crawled out from his makeshift bed. There were five of them, all wearing bits of skin around their waists. Their brown, bark-like skin blended with the forest and their wide black eyes shone like pools of oil. The tallest wore a vine around his forehead hung with feathers, leaves and twigs.

"Hello," Bear said in a quiet sort of voice. He felt a little afraid.

They jumped, looked at him, and backed away slowly.

He jumped, too, and wondered if he could edge himself back into his bed and start over again after having a bit more sleep and a bit less company.

They studied him carefully and suddenly self-conscious, Edward patted himself down, raising a small cloud of dust. "I'm a bit of a mess. I'm on an Expotition, you know."

The four shorter Parrotishes looked at what seemed to be their leader. It stepped forward.

Edward saw no time like the present to make introductions. "Good morning. I'm Edward Bear. Pleased to meet you." He moved closer and stuck out his paw.

The leader sprung back, hooting and whistling. The followers hooted and whistled, too. Then, clearing it's voice, the leader shuffled cautiously closer to Edward and stuck out its own three-fingered hand. "Good morning," it said. "I'm Edward Bear. Pleased to meet you."

Edward blinked, dropped his paw. "You are?"

A pause. "You are?"

"I am. Who are you?"

"I am. Who are you?"

"I'm Edward Bear." Edward shifted uncomfortably.

"I'm Edward Bear." The leader imitated his shift. Then, the others behind him did the same.

"I'm Edward Bear," four voices said.

Edward nodded enthusiastically. Just like parrots, he realized. And so he called them Parrotishes.

They were still nodding enthusiastically when he grabbed up the handle of his floating wagon and continued down the trail.

The Parrotishes shadowed him through the forest for three days, always disappearing at dusk, always reappearing at dawn. They moved apart and silent, occasionally whistling or hooting or proclaiming themselves to be Edward Bear.

On the third day, he made up a Song for Bears on Very Long Walks. He called it "Edward Bear and the Very Long Walk" and found himself suddenly part of a choir. Around the forest, thin and reedy voices parroted back his words. He tried to conduct them but gave up in the end; they wouldn't sing their bits properly and no harmony could be found. He began to whistle instead.

On the fourth day he found a beehive that no one seemed to care much for. He declared a holiday and helped himself. If honey could be sweeter and stickier, this honey was. The Parrotishes watched from a distance, imitating his "Oh My's" along with the wet smacking noises.

As he walked, the terrain changed. The trail gave out but so did the choked foliage. The trees began to thin and long purple blades of grass took over. At the forest's end, a bright blanket of rolling prairie met his eyes. Looming over him, the brilliant mountain shone against an azure sky.

Leaving the forest meant leaving its shade. For half a day Edward moved across the prairie, feeling the heat through his fur. The wagon whispered along behind him, occasionally sputtering over a rock or hissing reluctance as he tugged uphill, cresting rolls and ridges. He paused several times to look for his troupe of emaciated echoes, but they were nowhere to be seen, as if owned by the shadows of the wood. Overhead, large birds zipped between spherical clouds, riding a wind he couldn't feel. As the sun set, the air chilled and the sky became a painting gently fading into gray. He spent his first night in the open, curled into a tight ball on a bed of grass.

The next morning, he took a few steps toward the mountain before he realized his wagon was gone.

At first, he looked about frantically, his head moving quickly, his nose sniffing the air as if he might catch the scent. Nothing.

For a few hours, he sat down and cried. He had failed. His Expotition had ended.

The sky choked with clouds that suddenly cut loose and water sliced the air around him, soaking him completely and turning the prairie into purple sponge. Lifting his snout to the darkened sky, Edward howled.

A howl answered him and he looked up into the black eyes of a single Parrotish. "I'm Edward Bear," the Parrotish said, and motioned for him to follow.

Belligerently, Edward trudged behind the Parrotish. The rain let up as they entered the forest at a point someplace other than where he left it the day before. Once, the Parrotish broke out into "Edward Bear and the Very Long Walk," but Edward didn't feel like singing. An anger settled over him, mixed with sadness. His thoughts kept wandering back to the children's hollow eyes, fixed on nothing ever again, shining for No One. He couldn't remember how many other children were coming, or when, or even how, but he knew their eyes would be empty, too, now that he'd lost his wagon.

A hoot and whistle stopped his little brain. He looked up to see that his guide had joined the four others, the leader among them. It held a length of wood in its slender fingers and it pointed to a round, dark mouth in the side of a low hill. His guide prodded him and Edward turned.

The Parrotish pantomimed dragging something and then pointed to the hole. "I'm Edward Bear," it said. The others chimed in eager but low voices.

Edward moved toward the hole. Some dreadful stench that smelled very much like Death leaked out of it. He felt afraid and his hackles rose. "Oh. In there?"

"Oh. In there?" they echoed.

"Uh. Well." He shifted. "Oh bother."

They echoed him, then backed away and motioned at the hole. He looked back and forth, between them and the dark opening. Then, he made what he believed was a Very Brave Decision. "Well, then," he said in as cheerful a voice as he could, "let's just go and have a look." He marched to the hole and paused as the leader touched his shoulder. When he turned, the leader thrust the stick into his paws.

It was a spear, he realized.

The dirt walls gave off a damp smell that mingled with the odor from deeper within. As his eyes adjusted to the dark, Edward saw that the tunnel stretched gradually down. His ears picked up various sounds: water dripping, gentle snoring, soft whimpering and an electric buzz that he at first mistook for bees. Clutching his spear as best he could, sharpened point thrust before him, he made his way downward until the tunnel widened into a larger den. He felt something like wet wood shifting beneath his feet and as he moved them the smell grew worse.

In the center of the room, near two mounds of breathing hair, his wagon hummed while lights flickered off and on along the pack it supported. In the far corner, thin, small figures cowered.

Edward tip-toed toward the wagon, listening carefully to each snore. He shifted the spear to one paw and stretched the other toward the wagon's handle. He could leave quietly, he knew, without waking them. And he should, so he could climb the mountain. To Save the Children, he told himself.

The softest hoot and whistle came to him from the shivering forms across the den. He looked at the wagon, then to the mounds of hair, then to the corner. He picked his way past them and went to the three small Parrotishes huddled together. They were children. Their hands were tied and as he turned the first around to bite at the tough vines one of the mounds snorted and barked. Edward put down his spear and went to work, tooth and claw, finally severing the bonds. The free Parrotish began untying its neighbor while Edward went to the last. Quietly, he led them out of the cave.

Outside, the five Grown Up Parrotishes surrounded the children, clutching them as well as Edward in tight embraces while they whistled their pleasure. When they turned to leave the clearing, beckoning him to follow, Edward hesitated. "Uh...Excuse me please?"

They stopped. "Uh...Excuse me please?" the leader said.

"Let me just fetch my wagon." He turned back to the cave. He plunged back into the darkness, spear held loosely. Softly padding to the wagon, he lifted its handle and tugged. A growl rose up behind him and he spun around, dropping the handle with a clang.

"Uh. Terribly sorry to have awakened you. I think I'll just slip out now. Please, go back to sleep."

The hair mound became a creature nearly twice his size, short back legs supporting a massive torso and long arms. A horn slowly sprouted from the head and saliva splattered the floor from a wide, tooth-lined mouth. The other stirred now, as well, and Edward tried another approach.

"This," he said with a squeak, "Is just a dream you're having. It will be over soon enough so—"

The first beast sprang, tumbling Edward to the ground. He rolled himself into a ball as best he could.

Edward knew he should run but his paws closed over the spear. He couldn't leave without the wagon. He managed what he thought was a fierce growl and leaped to his feet. The creature barked loudly, scooping up a large, heavy-looking stick. Swinging the club, the monster charged and Edward thrust the spear forward with all his strength, feeling it hesitate against skin before breaking through the beast's shoulder. It shrieked in pain, dropped the club, and lashed out with a long arm.

Hidden talons tore into the side of Edward's face, dropping him to the floor. He kept his tentative hold on the spear and dragged it down with him, opening a larger gash in the beast. Out of the corner of his eye, Edward saw its companion watching the fight for an opportunity to jump in.

The wounded creature pounced, fastening its mouth on the top of Edward's head while its talons raked his torso and belly. The spear broke beneath the weight with a loud snap.

Edward heard a low murmur that crescendoed to a loud shriek. He knew, in a distant way, it was himself. His paws scrambled over the stinking, matted hair as he tried to roll over and away. Fire flashed its way deep into each wound and bits of fur and toy-gel stung his eyes. His paw closed over the sharpened end of his broken spear and, in a panic, he gripped it and thrust it upward into the soft throat of his adversary.

It howled, talons working fiercely, mouth opening and closing on Edward's head. Then it went limp.

Edward struggled free, rose shakily to his feet, and roared. The other beast slammed into him before he could turn to face it. He went down hard. He vaguely heard angry hoots and whistles racing down the tunnel before cotton filled his ears. He vaguely saw five forms burst into the den, rocks clutched tight in small fists. When the lights stopped flashing in his head, a muddled darkness descended.

He awoke to sunlight and pleasant smells and eight faces staring down at him. He tried to sit up but gentle hands pushed him down.

"I'm a bit of a mess," the Parrotish leader said, mouth working carefully around the words. "I'm on an Expotition, you know." It sounded hollow and far away.

Edward noticed that one of his ears, stained yellow with crusty toy-gel, now decorated the leader's headband. He also noticed the lacerations on its arms and chest. The others crowded around him, too, and he could see they fared no better. Two of them held horns that dripped blood. Another held a steaming handful of something that looked like mud. It began dabbing the mud on Edward's head.

Turning his head slowly, he took in his surroundings. He lay in the clearing outside the cave. Nearby, the red wagon hummed and bobbed on air. An owl swooped down and perched at his feet.

"Oh, it's you." Edward tried to smile but couldn't find the strength.

"You'd better hurry," the owl said. "You haven't much Time."

Edward nodded.

"Oh, it's you," the Parrotish leader said.

Edward slept.

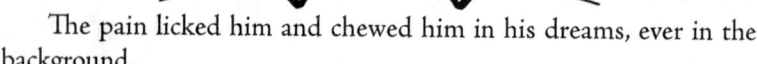

The pain licked him and chewed him in his dreams, ever in the background.

Large metal whales swam across the night while children slept safe inside. A pig and a bear went round and round a bush. A spinning top moved in slow motion around a blue-green marble. A bear and a rabbit sat down for cakes and milk. Eyes stared empty at the ceiling, hands clutched blankets.

"Tell them about the children." The boy became an old woman who became an empty balloon discarded in the sand.

He awakened to movement. Somehow they'd tied him to a bed of ferns on top of the pack and he rode the wagon as they took turns pulling.

"Hello?" They stopped and looked down at him. His head pounded and his arm felt like jelly as he raised his paw. The mountain could be seen looming above the tree-line, squatting in its purple nest. "There. I need to go there."

The Parrotishes paused, huddled, and a lively debate ensued. Edward tried to make up dialogue to go with their gibberish but gave up. It hurt too much to think.

After a few minutes, they turned and broke from the cover of the forest. Edward lay back and closed his eyes.

Time rushed like a brook over pebbles, daylight fading into dusk, dusk giving way to dark and dark becoming dawn. The Parrotishes only stopped to force water or honey into his mouth. He spat most of it onto his chest, unable to hold it down. At one point, one of the children gave him a doll made from the purple prairie grass. It looked something like a bear, and he clutched it with his good arm as best he could.

Gradually, it grew cold, but even when Edward saw his breath he still felt like he was on fire. A cold bit of mud to roll in would be quite nice, he thought.

As they climbed, he saw a pig throwing snowballs at a baby kangaroo. They both paused to wave at him; he waved back. Later, a tiger bounced over and kept pace with him long enough to ask how he felt. The tiger bounced away before he could say "Terrible, thanks."

At some point, two of the Parrotishes came around to his feet and pushed the wagon while two pulled. The three children and one of the others, Edward realized, weren't with them any longer. In the fog of his fever they had left the Expotition and he hadn't noticed.

Tirelessly, they pushed on. With one last shove and yank, the wagon skipped across the slightly rounded summit and came to a halt. Edward began tugging at the vines that held him in place and the Parrotish leader helped untie him, but when Edward tried to stand he wobbled. They crowded in to steady him and he sat heavily in the loose-packed snow. "Bother," he said.

His right arm didn't work and neither did his left leg. And the missing ear had bobbed in front of him every time the Parrotish leader leaned over to check on him during the journey.

From where he sat, he waved to the pack and then pointed to the highest point of the summit. They unstrapped it and carried it over, propping it up in the snow. When he tried to stand again, they caught him up beneath the arms and carried him to it.

His left paw lingered over the green button. He felt he should say Something Quite Clever. He closed his eyes and sighed. "For the children."

The chorus rang out around him: "For the children."

Then he pushed the button and sagged back against his friends.

He was a bear, and his name was Edward, and he lay against a snow-clad rock watching the ocean swallow the sun far away. A pink flash of fading light on metal caught his eye below where the gray water met the white beach. He tried to make up a song about the Nancy Bell but couldn't. His friends, the Parrotishes, stood aloof and talked in low tones. They had tried a half dozen times to load him into the empty wagon. He'd waved them off and finally had snapped at one them, growling as he did.

He finally felt cool, but weariness soaked him through like bread in condensed milk.

"Hello, Bear!" The boy sat down beside him.

"Oh. Are you here now?"

"No. Neither are they." The boy waved to a line of animals that stood at a respectable distance. Tears ran down the pig's face.

"Well then. I'm afraid I don't quite—I mean, if you're not here now, then exactly who is talking to me right now?"

"No one. You're talking to yourself." Edward thought about this. "I see," he said, but didn't really see at all. He tried to twist his head back to the pack. With his good ear he could hear it twittering and bleeping into the sky. "Did I finish the Expotition?"

The boy smiled. "You did. You're a Very Brave Bear."

He sighed, the words making him quite comfortably warm. "Well," he said in a satisfied sort of voice, "I suppose I am Somewhat of a Somebody now." He coughed violently.

"Yes you are. You're a Hero, Bear." The boy packed a snow ball and sent it flying out over the rim of the mountain. "Someday Everyone Who Is Anyone will know all about Edward Bear and how he saved the children. Someday there'll be statues of you and stories and—"

"—And pomes and songs?"

He laughed. "And poems and songs."

Edward smiled. "I especially like songs about honey."

There was an uncomfortable silence before the boy spoke again. "Do you understand what's happening to you?"

Edward couldn't help it; the sob escaped him before he could grab it and hold it in. "I-I'm broken."

"Yes."

"That's why all of you are here now but Not Here."

"Yes. We're a part of your sub-brain. For Comfort and for Calm in Times of Great Distress."

He waited, watching as the last sliver of sun fell into the sea. He felt a tear slip out. "Am I dying?"

The boy nodded twice slowly.

"And there's Nothing To Do for it?"

"I'm sorry, Bear."

Edward heard the sound of crunching snow and turned his head. The Parrotish leader squatted next to him. It untied the decorated headband and then re-tied it around Edward's head. "I'm Edward Bear." The leader then handed him the purple doll.

Edward took it and nodded. The leader turned and re-joined the group. Tugging the wagon, they trudged away, disappearing downward.

"So this is the End of Me?" He felt something heavy squeezing inside him and he choked back another sob.

The boy nodded. "It is. For this you, anyway."

"But I was Brave?"

"Yes. Very."

"And a Hero?"

"A Hero, yes."

He smiled and closed his eyes. "I'm very tired."

"Then go to sleep."

"I will but..." He peeked at the boy.

"But what?"

"Will you stay with me and hold my hand and tell me about Someday again, only very slowly, until I fall asleep?"

The boy looked at him and Edward saw that his eyes sparkled with love and tears. "Silly old bear, of course I will."

As the boy talked quietly about statues and stories and poems, the familiar sound of a song drifted up to Edward Bear from somewhere down below.

ABOUT THE AUTHORS

Pete Butler and his wife Jasmine live in Pittsburgh, PA, where they toil ceaselessly in the region's infamous intertube foundries. Working alongside teeming hordes of other faceless minions, their sweat, tears, and blood ensure that the modern global economy is never deprived of the nourishing flow of cat videos, pictures of cats, and wacky cat anecdotes without which it would surely starve. Pete posts sporadically on his blog blairhippo.com, and even more sporadically on twitter as @BlairHippo.

Sarah Doebereiner is a short story author, novelist, and poet. She graduated from Wright State University with her BA in Creative Writing in 2010. Sarah has work appearing in anthologies by Knightwatch Press and Amoeba Ink in late 2015 as well as the upcoming release of her F/F romance novella by Black Opal Books. She lives in central Ohio with her husband and two small children. For more information visit sarahadoebereiner.com.

As a wildlife biologist, **Amy Fontaine** has observed the behavior of many strange creatures, including fishers, wolves, honey bees, and other wildlife biologists. Such creatures figure prominently in her fiction and poetry, along with shapeshifters, unicorns, dragons, and the weird beast from your dream last night.

Amy's writings have appeared in various publications in northern California, where she recently graduated from Humboldt State University.

In addition to writing and conducting wildlife research, Amy likes wandering wild places, playing guitar, and drawing. She enjoys seeing the world, not only as it is, but as it could be.

Phil Geusz is the author of more than twenty-five novels and novellas, many of them furry, as well as numerous columns, short stories and articles published in various furry venues. He began writing in a serious way in 1997, and soon after became active in the fandom. Today Phil is retired from his "day job," but still writing as eagerly and joyously as ever. He takes pride in the fact that his work—both furry and not—spans multiple genres, including action-adventure, literary fiction, fantasy, horror, science fiction and even political fiction. His books have sold in the tens of thousands.

A multiple award-winning screenwriter, **Kevin M. Glover** is perhaps best-known as the producer of the cult classic movies *Dinosaur Valley Girls* and *Venus Flytrap*. As a writer, his biggest successes to date are the scripts for the LGBT vampire rom-com, *Love Bites* and the horror thriller *Sisterhood of the Shewolf*, (which he co-wrote). Kevin's first two short prose stories, the campy sci-fi tale "Space Bimbos" and the Nazi horror action yarn "Inglorious Zombies" were both published in anthologies in 2014. "CSI: Translyvania" is his third short. He also wrote a series of scary parody comic book stories that will be published later this year in *Fractured Scary Tales, Volume One*. Kevin resides in Hollywood, CA and can be reached through his website: ScreamWriter4Hire.com.

Kyell Gold is a California writer who is best known for his gay furry fiction, although he has also included historical, supernatural, mystery, science fiction, fantasy, and sports elements in his writing. He has won a dozen Ursa Major Awards and two Rainbow Awards for his novels and short stories. With his husband Kit Silver, he often attends furry, SF, and comic conventions around North America and occasionally abroad. You can find more about him and his work at www.kyellgold.com.

Alice "Huskyteer" Dryden's stories and poems have been published in *Heat, Allasso, ROAR*, and *Apex Magazine*, amongst others. She divides her leisure time between writing and motorcycling, and is never happier than when taking just the right line through a corner—unless it's when writing just the right line in a story.
She has owned and loved many, many gerbils, whose cheerful idiocy and dangerous curiosity inspired "Gerbil 07".
She can be found at huskyteer.co.uk, or as @Huskyteer on Twitter.

Blake Hutchins lives in the green hills of western Oregon with his daughters and two highly opinionated cats. He has worked as a firefighter, creative writer, teacher, public defender, and software industry executive. Though not paid to practice longsword, ukulele, or yoga, he pursues those activities anyway. Published works include "The Sword from the Sea," in *Writers of the Future Vol. 22*, a modest number of short stories, a novel, an online graphic novel, and a number of videogames, including *Night at the Museum 2, Starsiege,* and *Starsiege: Tribes.* He is a member of the Wordos writing group in Eugene.

Jeeves the Roo has been active within the furry fandom for almost a decade, and still greatly enjoys producing a wide variety of content in his stories for all to enjoy. When not writing he makes his living as a chef, and seeks to excel in his passion for both food and fiction. He lives in Dundee, Scotland, and can almost always be found in the company of other local furs at meets, board game nights and coffee gatherings.

David D. Levine is the author of the novel *Arabella of Mars* (Tor 2016) and over fifty SF and fantasy stories. His story "Tk'Tk'Tk" won the Hugo, and he has been shortlisted for awards including the Hugo, Nebula, Campbell, and Sturgeon. His stories have appeared in *Asimov's, Analog, F&SF,* multiple Year's Best anthologies, and his award-winning collection *Space Magic.*

Laura "Munchkin" Lewis is the author of "Tech Flesh" from the *Furtual Horizons* anthology and an as yet unnamed short from the upcoming *Will of the Alpha: Volume 3* anthology. A geek of all trades, dungeon master of none, she knows a little about most things and a whole lot of nothing. Her hobbies include driving her husband crazy, poking at Eurogames, and cave exploring—the latter only as often as it doesn't harm the cave bats. A munchkin cat in sona and a dwarf in truth, this writer has learned to embrace all of life's 'shortcomings'.

Your fearless editor, **Mary E. Lowd**, is a science-fiction and furry author in Oregon. She's had more than fifty short stories published, as well as several novels through FurPlanet. This collection is her first foray into the world of editing.

Mark Patrick Lynch lives and writes in the UK. His short fiction, mainstream and genre, has appeared in print anthologies and journals ranging from *Alfred Hitchcock's Mystery Magazine* to *Zahir.* His book, *Hour of the Black Wolf,* is published by Robert Hale Ltd. An e-book original novella, *What I Wouldn't Give,* is available for e-readers. You can find him online at markpatricklynch.blogspot.com and @markplynch on Twitter.

Garrett Marco is a writer and editor living in Portland, Oregon. When not freelance editing and writing speculative stories, he edits for Soul Mate Publishing and Legion Publishing. Sometimes he even finds time to do things that don't involve writing and editing!

Lyn McConchie began writing professionally in 1990 since which time she has seen 32 of her books published and almost 300 stories, appearing in 9 countries and 4 languages. She lives on her small farm in New Zealand where she breeds coloured sheep, and has free-range hens and geese. She shares her farmhouse with her Ocicat Thunder and 7469 books by other authors. Lyn says that the main character in her story in this anthology was real and the story is in memory of Brownie who died at almost eleven in 2014.

Marshall L. Moseley has been a computer-industry marketing professional, and a software developer, for thirty years. During that time he's maintained a parallel career as a writer, penning three books on technology, writing columns for *CADalyst Magazine*, and serving as Technical Editor for *PROFILES* magazine. His original screenplay, "Wildcard", placed in the top three in the 2004 season of Project Greenlight, and was optioned by director Wes Craven through Dimension Films. Marshall is a longtime-member of the Oregon-based writers' critique group, the Wordos, and currently lives in Eugene, Oregon.

Joe McCauley, known in the furry community as **mwalimu**, got a late start as a writer. In high school he was a straight-A student in math and science but got Cs in English. Many years later he got hooked on *The Lion King* and began writing fan fiction. Though his interest in that film faded, his interest in crafting stories did not. He's been a writer on and off for more than fifteen years, and his efforts to date include two conbook stories and a novel-length SabrinaVerse fan story. mwalimu is on staff for two furry conventions and has admin privileges on Wikifur and a few other websites. He lives in Central Illinois where he loves to sample craft beer (and occasionally brew his own), watch trains pass, and listen to all kinds of music.

Altivo Overo was born in a barn when dinosaurs still walked the earth. He got to where he is today by eating his vegetables and not listening to neigh-sayers. A professional librarian in real life, he and his husband live on a tiny farm in Illinois, where they are kept by three horses, some ducks, and several discerning dogs and cats.

Fred Patten joined the Los Angeles Science Fantasy Society in 1960 while in college. He began writing for fanzines in 1961, and has written over a thousand reviews of anthropomorphic literature since 1962. He has written two books and edited seven anthologies of furry fiction. He founded the Ursa Major Awards in 2001. He is a member of the Furry Writers' Guild and the Furry Hall of Fame. He writes a weekly column on animation for Jerry Beck's Cartoon Research.

A stroke in 2005 has left him bedridden, from which he carries on his fanac via a MacBook Pro laptop.

Rechan is a mad scientist. One of his projects is mind control via subliminal messages in stories. Have you noticed any changes after reading his story? No? Back to the drawing board. In addition to his love of fantasy—urban and high—he writes horror and erotica. His stories can be found in *Abandoned Places, Heat,* and *Will of the Alpha*.

Ellen Saunders is staff, referee and lap-bed for four opinionated, quirky cats. They live with her and her partner in the Willamette Valley, where Ellen writes science fiction, furry, fantasy, space opera, suspense and anything else that makes her prick up her ears. When not paying obeisance to felines or writing, Ellen sings, gardens, cooks, and occasionally dons garb Victorian or medieval. Past iterations of self have been a massage therapist, bumbling traveler, newspaper reporter, university public relations staff, and a writer for a nutrition education program. "Unexpected Bouquets" is her first short story sale.

Ken Scholes is the award-winning, critically-acclaimed author of four novels and over forty short stories. Ken's eclectic background includes time spent as a label gun repairman, a sailor who never sailed, a soldier who commanded a desk, a preacher (he got better), a nonprofit executive, a musician and a government procurement analyst. He has a degree in History from Western Washington University.

Ken is a native of the Pacific Northwest and makes his home in Saint Helens, Oregon, where he lives with his wife and twin daughters. You can learn more about Ken by visiting www.kenscholes.com.

Slip Wolf has been running from the law for about three years now, planting invasive, subversive and annoying ideas into anthology in-boxes everywhere. Only past co-operation with grammar-enforcement agents have kept him from a well-deserved life behind bars. He has done jobs for Sofawolf's *Heat*, Issues 11 and 12, Rabbit Valley's *Trick or Treat 2* anthology and FurPlanet's *FANG 6*. He has pending jobs with other crews coming up, but won't divulge those for fear of another contract on his tail. If you see him, entice him with book sales and alert local authorities.

James Stegall is a chicken wrangler, Corgi companion, and black cat scratching post living in Oregon. A graduate of the University of Oregon, and now a veteran, he made friends in a lot of places he would like to re-visit under better circumstances. Drop him a line at james.stegall.org or @stegall.

Andrew S. Taylor was born in Bedford, Massachusetts in 1973. He wandered for many years, working as manual laborer, a bookstore cashier, an office temp, and a Broadway ticket-seller. Inexplicably, he is now a lawyer in New York City. In the meantime he has published over 30 stories covering a wide range of genres, and numerous essays and book reviews. "Two Crows" was written in rural Japan, shortly after the author observed two crows on wires having a conversation about the moon. It's just the sort of thing that happens there.

Ocean Tigrox is a writer hailing from the Western prairies of Canada with dual citizenship in both Alberta and Saskatchewan. Never far from his headphones, he's often found shaking his stripes to his love of electronic music. Along with writing, Ocean also enjoys motorcycling, travel, and games of all varieties. He is the lead cat herder, editor, and co-host of the furry writing podcast *Fangs and Fonts*. You can find more of his published works in *PULP! Two-Pawed Tales of Adventure* and *The Furry Future*. To read his random ramblings, follow him on Twitter: @TigroxTales.

George Walker is an inventor working for Acme Corporation in Portland, Oregon. He has sold stories to *Abyss & Apex*, *Andromeda Spaceways Inflight Magazine*, *Every Day Fiction*, *Ideomancer*, *Electric Spec*, *Perihelion SF*, *The Colored Lens*, *Bastion*, *Plasma Frequency*, *Bards and*

Sages, Stupefying Stories, The Third Science Fiction Megapack, Mothership: Tales from Afrofuturism & Beyond, and elsewhere.

He confesses to having watched too many Road Runner cartoons at an impressionable age. Links to some of his stories can be found at https://sites.google.com/site/georgeswalker/

Eric M. Witchey has made a living as a freelance writer and communication consultant for over 24 years. In addition to many contracted and ghost non-fiction titles, he has sold more than 90 stories, including 4 novels. His stories have appeared in nine genres and on five continents. He has received awards or recognition from New Century Writers, Writers of the Future, Writer's Digest, The Eric Hoffer Prose Award Program, Short Story America, the Irish Aeon Awards, and other organizations. His How-to articles have appeared in *The Writer Magazine, Writer's Digest Magazine,* and other print and online magazines. When not teaching or writing, he spends his time fly fishing or restoring antique model locomotives.